And now

"You're going _____ ___ly scorekeeper said. "You are going to find Amy Cameron a husband to replace the one who betrayed her with you."

That didn't sound too bad.

"Not just any husband," Stan continued, "but the best possible husband, a man who will give her joy enough to make up for the happiness you and David stole from her."

I began to hope. The job sounded right up my alley, and certainly it was better than shoveling brimstone with a pitchfork.

"I can do that with one hand tied behind my back," I assured Stan. "But just how are you going to explain my coming back to life?"

"Don't worry, Lydia. That is not a problem."

His smile should have warned me, but I suppose I was still a bit dim from dying. So I was unpleasantly surprised when I didn't awaken in a nice, clean, comfortable hospital to be hailed as one of those people who have near-death experiences and live to write books about them. Instead, when I opened my eyes I found myself in an alley—the very same alley, in fact, where I'd met my unfortunate end.

The moments that followed were the most confusing and terrifying that I've ever experienced. I reeled, gagged, drooled, and stumbled, not understanding the nightmarish feelings that tortured me, until I saw my reflection in a puddle of rain. What looked back at me had a black nose and big ears.

I was no longer Lydia Keane.

I was a pudgy, flea-bitten, funny-looking dog.

FINDING MR. RIGHT

Emily Carmichael

BANTAM BOOKS

New York Toronto London Sydney Auckland

FINDING MR. RIGHT

A Bantam Book / February 1999

IBSN 0-553-57874-X

Published simultaneously in the United States and Canada

Bantam Books are published by Bantam Books, a division of Random
House, Inc. Its trademark, consisting of the words "Bantam Books"
and the portrayal of a rooster, is Registered in U.S. Patent and
Trademark Office and in other countries. Marca Registrada. Bantam
Books, 1540 Broadway, New York, New York 10036.

PRINTED IN THE UNITED STATES OF AMERICA

OPM   10 9 8 7 6 5 4 3

THIS BOOK IS DEDICATED TO

ALL THE LITTLE ANGELS IN DOG SUITS

WHO BRING LOVE AND LAUGHTER INTO PEOPLE'S LIVES

—INCLUDING MINE

PROLOGUE

*W*HAT *HAPPENED IN* the alley that night in Denver was not my fault. No way, no how, am I going to let anyone pin that disaster on me.

True, I did meet David Cameron in the restaurant bar, but that wasn't my idea. David called my apartment and practically begged to see me. He knew the Wynkoop Brewing Company was my favorite restaurant. He knew I wouldn't be able to resist an offer of dining and barhopping on a Friday night—and then a roll between the silk sheets of my king-sized brass bed. David was a talented lover; I have to give him credit for that. He was a jerk in some ways, but in bed he had the magic touch. It's a real crime he got killed that night behind the Wynkoop.

My own death was an even greater crime, to my way of thinking. Not that anyone has given me an ounce of sympathy about it. But I suffered in that alley. I suffered a lot. Imagine, if you will, coming out of your favorite restaurant on the arm of your currently favorite man. You're looking forward to a bit of dancing at a great club up the street, and then, pow! Everything falls apart. Some lowlife is breaking the window of your car—actually, it was David's minivan, but that's beside the point. And your man, instead of hustling you back inside where it's safe, puffs up in macho fury and takes after the crook like some hotshot hero in a police show.

That's exactly what happened. David chased the burglar into the pitch-black alley behind the Wynkoop, and I, like a fool, followed. I called David to come back, but all I heard in reply were grunts and thunks, and then a string of curses as a flashlight beam snapped onto David, who lay in a crumpled heap at the base of a big Dumpster. His head was a bloody mess, and so was the corner of the Dumpster. I shrieked. Not very brave or sensible, I'll admit, but what do you expect? The beam of light swung in my direction, blinding me, and I ran.

Footsteps pounded behind me, and that's where it all ended, just about. I barely remember the painful wrench as the crook yanked me from behind by the chin. My guess is he was trying for my mouth, which I admit was being very loud, and missed his aim. I slipped. My head twisted, and poof, everything faded to black. I didn't even get to see the scumbag who ruined my evening—not to mention my life.

But you can see that absolutely none of this was my fault. I was clearly just an innocent bystander.

Of course, there are varying degrees of innocence. I will admit to one or two mistakes. That's only fair. David was Amy Cameron's husband, and Amy was my best friend. She and I went to grade school together. High school, too. I made the pom-pom squad; Amy made the girl's softball team. I'll let you guess which of us got the most dates. Amy wasn't jealous, though, even when I had the football quarterback—and the star running back and tight end—all begging to go out with me.

Those were good days. Pep rallies at Littleton High. Football games with the whole stadium watching my pom-poms. Hanging out in the cafeteria and rating the boys at nearby tables while we ate our pigs-in-a-blanket and downed our lukewarm milk. At least that's what I did to get my mind off the taste of cafeteria food. Amy didn't have much of an eye for the guys. She was a bit dense when it came to what was important in life. If Littleton High had voted on such things, Amy would have been named the girl least likely to ever get a date. She wasn't ugly, mind you. More like awkward, tongue-tied with boys, shy—an all around champion wallflower if I've ever seen one.

My friendship with Amy lasted through college and beyond. We were sorority sisters at CU in Boulder. She didn't make it into the sorority our freshman year, but once I was initiated, I made sure that she got a bid the following year. I did a lot of nice things like that for Amy. We were friends, after all, and good friends are hard to come by. She did nice things for me too. If it hadn't been for Amy, I never would have passed Biology 101. Amy was a wiz in school.

She wasn't a wiz at the important stuff, though. I don't think she ever caught on that I was sleeping with David, at least not while I was alive. When my body was found with David's in that alley, she probably got a glimmer of the truth, however. He'd told her he was going to a sales meeting at his car dealership, and she would have known for sure that I didn't have anything to do with BMW sales.

Oh, well. David was a self-centered prick, and Amy's better off without him if you ask me. Not that David's wanderings from home and hearth were my fault. They weren't entirely David's fault either, to be perfectly fair about it. Amy wasn't exactly a model wife. She was into dogs—dog shows, dog classes, dog this, dog that. The smelly little creatures were always underfoot in her house, and David used to complain that the animals got more attention than he did. So it wasn't as though he didn't have reason to go out looking for a little female company.

Still, I wouldn't have hurt Amy's feelings for the world. If not for that little incident behind the Wynkoop, my affair with David would have petered out soon enough. I've never yet met a guy who could hold my interest for longer than six months. Two husbands and a pantload of lovers can attest to that.

But I digress. The point of all this is that none of what happened was my fault. I, Lydia Keane, was definitely not the villain of this story. Unfortunately, as I discovered when the grim reaper so prematurely overtook me, there were some who disagreed. Take it from one who knows: Dull as the idea seems, there is some advantage in life to paying less attention to the here and now and more attention to the hereafter.

Technically, I don't think heaven is where I landed when I died. For sure the place wasn't my idea of paradise. I don't remember much about it, to tell the truth. I was a bit groggy when I first became aware of my surroundings—having one's neck snapped does that to a person. Then, once I began to feel more myself, my attention was all on Stanley. Stanley was the person—or being, or whatever he is—who seemed convinced that what happened with David left me with something to atone for. My affair with David wasn't the only thing that stuck in his craw. He made that perfectly clear. But sleeping with my best friend's hubby was the big ticket item.

Stanley isn't God, or if he is, the pope, Michelangelo, and all those TV and radio preachers are going to be mighty disappointed. He wasn't the guy with the pitchfork either. He looks a bit like my old high school principal, Mr. Collins— short, scrawny, middle-aged, with a bad haircut and a pinched look on his face. And like Mr. Collins, Stanley didn't seem all that pleased to see me.

"Where am I?" I asked.

It was a reasonable question, I thought, but Stanley's expression became even more pinched, if possible.

"You, Lydia Keane, are in a great deal of trouble."

"Tell me something I don't know." I rubbed my throat where that fellow in the alley had grabbed me. Strangely enough, the skin didn't even feel bruised.

"You are dead," Stanley stated unsympathetically.

That bald statement came as a bit of a shock. Not that I didn't suspect the truth. I can put two and two together as well as the next person. Still, he could have been more tactful.

I looked around. "David, too?"

"David also."

"I figured. He didn't look too good with his head all caved in after falling against that Dumpster."

"Don't worry about David. He is being taken care of. It's you we're here to discuss."

"I'd guess from the look on your face that I'm not on the most-favored list up here."

My dynamite smile had worked on virtually every man I'd ever met, but it didn't soften old Stan one iota. I practiced that smile in front of my bedroom mirror for days when I was in high school. It didn't seem fair that it would fail me in the final crunch.

"No, Lydia, you're not exactly on our A list. We could spend half of eternity discussing your shortcomings."

The fellow's holier-than-thou attitude was annoying. It was totally unjustified as well. I mean, really! Was I some Middle Eastern dictator who ate babies for lunch? Was I a Nazi, laughing at the miserable prisoners in some concentration camp? Was I the lowlife in Denver who had just robbed David's car, not to mention slaughtered the two innocent people who tried to stop him? Where was that guy? I ask you. He was probably home enjoying a beer and watching The Tonight Show, while I had to sit there in that nothing place and listen to that miserable excuse of a heavenly scorekeeper nitpick me to death.

There's no such thing as justice in the world, or in the afterworld either. Take it from one who knows.

I interrupted Stanley's recitation of transgressions. "Just wait a minute, you . . . whoever you are!"

"You may call me Stanley."

"Okay, Stan, I—"

"Stanley," he corrected from beneath a raised brow.

"Stan . . ." I drew the name out and smiled wickedly. "Why don't we cut to the chase here. Just hand me my pitchfork, or whatever, and save us both some time."

"Pitchfork?" Brows furrowed over his eyes before the light dawned. "Oh. Pitchfork. Very funny. No, Lydia. That's not the way we work. Those old folk tales of punishment for wrongdoing are colorful but sadly inaccurate."

I might mention here that Stanley has no sense of humor, or at least not a very nice one.

"My purpose is certainly not anything so petty as reprisal," he continued solemnly. *"We like to think of the afterlife in a more positive vein. I'm going to grant you the opportunity to discover some truths that you've failed to learn so far. To that end, you're to make amends for the wrong you've done."*

"Which wrong?"

"The most recent one."

"You mean dating Amy's husband?"

"We call it adultery."

"Well, what about David? It takes two to tango, you know." There's no way I was accepting the entire blame for this.

"David will be busy elsewhere, learning lessons of his own."

The further this progressed, the less I liked it. Stan had a smirk on his face, it seemed to me. Since that first interview, I've learned the fellow does have some redeeming qualities, but right at that moment he was at his most officious.

"You're going back to Earth, Lydia. Not for your own enjoyment, but with a specific mission. You are going to find Amy Cameron a husband to replace the one who betrayed her with you."

That didn't sound too bad.

"Not just any husband," Stan continued, *"but the best possible husband, a man who will give her joy enough to make up for the happiness you and David stole from her."*

I began to hope. The job sounded right up my alley, and certainly it was better than shoveling brimstone with a pitchfork. No one knew men better than Lydia Keane. No one was more adept at casting out the lure and reeling the poor suckers in. It shouldn't be too much trouble to take one off the hook and toss him Amy's way. A good one, of course. A really good one. After all, Amy was my very best friend.

"I can do that with one hand tied behind my back," I

assured Stan. "But just how are you going to explain me coming back to life?"

"Don't worry, Lydia. That is not a problem. Just concentrate on your mission." He smiled like a cat who has a mouse dangling by its tail. "You'll be hearing from me from time to time. I'll expect a complete progress report when we next meet."

His smile should have warned me, but I suppose I was still a bit dim from dying. So I was unpleasantly surprised when I didn't waken in a nice, clean, comfortable hospital to be hailed as one of those people who have near-death experiences and live to write books about floating around and seeing some weird light. No indeed. Instead of the clean smell of antiseptic, my nose was assaulted—and I do mean assaulted—by the odor of motor oil and garbage. I'd never smelled anything so rank! And the noise was deafening, a pounding clamor that rattled my very brain.

When I opened my eyes, I found myself in an alley, the very same alley, in fact, where I'd met my unfortunate end. It was nighttime, and the street was quiet. The thundering I heard was rain. The drops pounded the pavement with the roar of at least a dozen waterfalls.

The sensory overload should have given me a hint of the terrible trick Stan had played, but I was so concerned with trying to get up and out of that damned alley that I wasn't paying attention to much of anything else. My legs and arms were strangely uncoordinated, and the simple task of rising from the dirty pavement was daunting.

The moments that followed were the most confusing and terrifying that I've ever experienced. Being murdered had been bad, but at least that had happened fast. This went on for what seemed an eternity. I reeled, gagged, drooled, and stumbled, not understanding the nightmarish and strange feelings that tortured me until I saw my reflection in a puddle of rain that was lit by the streetlight at the alley's mouth. What looked *back at me had a black nose and big ears. Ridiculous, short legs—four of them—supported a sausagelike furry body.*

I was no longer Lydia Keane. Neither was I an angel, a cupid, a cherub, or any of the other fanciful forms that rotten, conniving, mean-spirited Stanley might have chosen for me.

I was a pudgy, flea-bitten, funny-looking dog.

ONE

IN SPITE OF free love, complicated joint tax returns, and the outrageous expense of wedding gowns, weddings still took place in Colorado with comforting frequency. And a damn good thing they did, Amy Cameron told herself as she watched the newlyweds march down the aisle. If not for weddings and dog shows, she would be very hard put to make the monthly mortgage payment on her new house.

With a slight twitch of a smile, she resisted the temptation to make comparisons between today's glowing bride and the Old English sheepdog she had photographed as one of the winners at the dog show last weekend in Greeley. The hairdo was similar, but the Old English sheepdog obviously had a better sense of style. Amy hoped the bride hadn't paid some hairdresser big bucks to create that coiffure.

"Hold it right there," she told the couple.

Bride and groom obediently stopped. Amy raised her camera, zoomed in for a close-up, then zoomed out for a more inclusive shot. Despite the Old English hair, the bride looked sweet, ecstatic, and nervous at the same time. The groom looked as though his tuxedo was binding him somewhere he didn't want to be bound, but when he looked down at his new wife, his expression relaxed into a smile.

"Okay." Amy backed away. "See you up front." She glanced up to the church balcony to make sure her assistant was catching the whole procession on video. The bride wanted both video and stills. Amy had chosen to do the camera work and leave the filming to Tony Greene, her part-time help. When the entire wedding party had passed and the audience began to file out, she motioned Tony down to the church lobby to film the meetings, greetings, and milling confusion of friends and relatives while she set up for formal pictures at the front of the sanctuary.

"Ain't love grand," she murmured to herself, as she positioned lights and reflector screens. She wondered if the twenty-three-year-old groom and his nineteen-year-old bride had a clue about what lay ahead of them. Probably not, and that was no doubt a good thing. Amy certainly wished them well. She wished them better luck than she had had.

"Amy, Amy! You are doing such a beautiful job!" The mother of the bride bustled up the aisle, swathed in a teal chiffon confection that echoed the bridesmaids' colors. "Mark and Kathy are going to be so happy with these pictures. And the video, of course. It seems like one can't do anything these days without preserving it all on video."

"Mrs. Adams, you're glowing almost as much as the bride."

"Oh my, yes! A wedding is as much for the mother of the bride as for the bride, you know. It's hard to believe my little girl has grown up."

"I'm just about ready here. I know Mark and Kathy want to get this picture taking finished so they can go to the reception."

"Yes, but it'll be a few minutes, dear. Kathy had to

visit the ladies' room, and it'll take her awhile . . . with the dress, and all."

Amy smiled. "It is a very big dress."

"Beautiful, isn't it? Cost us three thousand dollars, but I told Roger: 'Give her the dress she loves. The cost doesn't matter. Our Kathy is only going to marry once, God willing.'" Her face instantly fell. "Oh, Amy! I'm sorry. That was very insensitive of me, wasn't it? This must be hard on you, dear, what with everything that's happened. I don't know what to say."

"It's all right, Mrs. Adams. It doesn't bother me. Really. I'm doing very well with the whole thing."

"And isn't that sensible of you? You're so brave, and eventually you'll find someone else. Just keep the faith. There will be another wedding for you. And a happily ever after."

Amy managed to smile.

"I'll just go see what's keeping Kathy," Mrs. Adams said. "We only have the church until three, after all." She hurried off, plainly eager to be gone.

Tony sauntered up. His raised brow indicated he'd overheard. "Keep the faith, baby!"

"Oh, shut up," Amy said mildly. "Watch out or she'll be pairing me up with you."

"I wouldn't object," Tony replied. "My wife might get funny about it, though."

"You think?" Amy gave him a smile. "Sometimes I want to move to another state, where no one knows what happened with poor David and Lydia and no one gets tongue-tied around me because they don't know what to say. Everyone I meet seems to think I should be tottering around wearing sackcloth and ashes."

"Don't. Sackcloth would look very bad on you. As a fashion statement, it would be a complete failure."

"Great! My choice is between maudlin commiseration or irreverence. Will you quit slacking about and set up the video camera? We don't want to keep the wedding party here all day."

Amy's amused smile took the sting from her words. Tony threw her a smart military salute and went to collect his equipment.

It took a good hour to finish the posed photos of the wedding party in the church, and most of the remaining afternoon and evening to capture the reception on film. The new Mr. and Mrs. Mark McCoy really knew how to party, and Amy's job was to preserve all the partying—along with the excitement, eagerness, and sentimentality—so the couple could look back someday and remember how happily they had begun. Not that she assumed they wouldn't continue in that happiness. She wasn't bitter or cynical, Amy told herself repeatedly throughout the evening. Just because her own marriage had ended badly didn't mean every marriage was doomed. Not every husband was David Cameron. Not every lifelong friend was Lydia Keane. Not every wife was naive enough, stupid enough, blind enough, to miss the signs that her marriage was on the rocks.

Toward the end of the evening, Amy found herself alone at a corner table, one eye contemplating the cake and champagne in front of her, the other keeping track of Tony, who was filming the best man reciting a toast to the bride and groom. The best man was long-winded, as befit the occasion, and joked about how the happy couple had met, how they'd courted, and what a fine future awaited them. As she lifted her flute of champagne with the rest of the well-wishers, Amy admitted it: She *was* bitter; she *was* cynical.

Amy missed her husband, and she missed her good friend. She was horrified at the senseless violence that had overtaken them. But sometimes anger at them both—and at herself—almost overshadowed the horror. Anger—black and bitter, chilling as winter and caustic as acid. Sometimes her head swam with it, her mouth grew sour with it, her heart raced in double time with it. Up until a few months ago, she had not known the meaning of such anger or grief. It had been a parting gift from David and Lydia, and, God forgive her, Amy hoped that wherever the two of them were, they were forced to pause a moment and feel her pain before they went on to their final reward.

MORNING CAME TOO early the next day. Bright Colorado sunshine speared through the bedroom curtains of Amy's Niwot home, but instead of driving the champagne muzziness from her brain, it seemed to arrow into her head like a hot poker. As if that weren't enough to wake her, an eager kiss from one of her bed partners brought her mercilessly from the refuge of slumber.

"Yeccch! Your breath is terrible! Go brush your teeth or something, will you?"

Drover's foxlike face regarded her quizzically. A comment rumbled in his chest and finally emerged as a sharp bark.

"No! Ouch!" Amy clapped her hands over her ears and grimaced.

Egged on by her response, Drover twisted over on his back, short little legs paddling the air, liquid brown eyes pleading for a tummy scratch.

"No! Get your own breakfast."

Amy glanced at her second bedmate. Molly lay at the foot of the bed in matronly dignity. Big triangular ears erect, the Divine Miss M gazed at Drover in unmistakable contempt. With her short forelegs tucked neatly beneath her, she looked very much like a brown pudgy sausage. Behind her tailless, furry butt, her rear legs lay flat out in the characteristic corgi frog kick. The pose robbed her dignity somewhat, but her expression made up for it.

"Can't you do something with him?" Amy asked Molly.

Molly's expression conveyed without doubt that Drover and his antics were Amy's problem. Molly would be perfectly content in a one-dog household.

"Just go out to the dog run, both of you, and let me sleep for another three hours."

Both dogs stayed where they were. Drover aah-roooed from his upside-down pose, and Molly's almost invisible tail stump twitched. Amy groaned and buried her face in the pillow.

There had been a time, almost a decade ago at the sorority house at CU, when Amy had been renowned for her capacity to hold liquor. Beer, wine, champagne, rum—nothing got to her. That time was well past. She was out of practice and had no desire to go back into training. From now on, the order of the day when photographing any wedding or reception would be complete teetotaling. Amy repeated that promise to any merciful deity who might ease her headache in return for an oath of abstinence.

A sharp tap on her bedroom door felt like hammer blows on her already pounding head.

"Amy? Are you in there?" asked a feminine voice.

"Yes," Amy groaned.

"Are you alone?"

"Of course I'm alone, Selma. What did you expect?"

The door opened and Selma Marshall appeared, ponytailed and smiling puckishly. "One never knows. You didn't get home until after two A.M." At the ripe age of twenty-five, Selma still looked sixteen, complete with girlish dimples and the ever-present light of mischief in her eyes. "I hoped maybe you had a good time," she hinted broadly. "You know, a *good* time."

"Yeah. Right. You're keeping track of what time I get home these days?"

"When one lives over the landlady's garage, it's hard not to notice what time the landlady puts her car away for the night. How'd the wedding go?"

Amy sighed. "It was a wedding. The bride and groom are officially preserved on film for all posterity. And I made a bundle appropriate to having to work on Labor Day weekend."

"Good!" Selma invited herself to a seat on Amy's bed. Drover hastily righted himself and scrambled out of the way, casting her an indignant look as he did so. "Sorry, kid." Selma scratched between his ears in apology. "Then, since you just made this bundle of boodle, you won't mind if my rent is just a teensy bit more late than it already is?"

"Ow! You're making the bed bounce. Don't!"

"Sorry. It wasn't me. Drover had to scratch."

"I told you before, Selma. You don't have to pay rent."

"But I'm going to! Really. I'm going to pay my own way, Amy. It's just that right now the divorce lawyer's costing me big bucks, and Gary's making everything ten times more difficult than it should be, and . . . Well, you know how it is."

"Not really, but I probably would have, if David hadn't gotten himself killed first."

"Oh . . . geez! I didn't mean it that way. Now I've gone and ruined your whole morning."

"No, you haven't." Amy covered her eyes with one hand. "A whopping hangover is ruining my morning. You don't know any miracle cures, do you?"

"How about a nice, warm shower, then strong coffee along with a healthy breakfast?"

"Uk!"

"It'll be good for you. Trust me! You take a shower, and I'll fix breakfast. You'll feel better."

"Take the dogs with you."

"Shall I feed them?"

"If you don't, they'll eat their way through the pantry door to the dog food. Feed 'em."

At the mention of food, both dogs bounded off the bed and danced around Selma's feet as she headed out the door.

"Oh yeah. Before I forget." Selma stuck her head back into the room. "The TLC Animal Shelter called yesterday. A stray corgi was turned over to them five days ago, and no one's claimed it. They wanted to know if Corgi Rescue will take it."

Amy sighed. "I suppose they'll be closed until Tuesday."

"The guy said someone would be at the shelter between ten and three today if you want to drop by."

"Yeah. Okay. That's as good an excuse as any to get out of bed."

Selma grinned and struck a heroic pose. "Amy Cameron to the rescue!"

THE TLC ANIMAL SHELTER in Longmont looked fairly deserted when Amy pulled her minivan into the empty parking lot. One scruffy-looking pickup truck was parked behind the Dumpster in back of the building. Amy assumed it belonged to the kennel help who was unlucky enough to draw duty on a holiday weekend.

A colorful Welcome! sign with a border of cavorting kittens and puppies greeted her at the front door, along with arrows directing her to the side for receiving, the front for adoptions. The double glass doors in front were tightly locked.

Amy made her way around the main brick building, through a maze of empty outdoor kennel runs, to a long, low wooden frame building that noticeably lacked the polished patina of the public area. The door needed paint, and the glass panes in the upper part of the door needed the enthusiastic application of a bit of ammonia.

Like all private shelters, TLC depended upon donations, which meant that money was always in short supply. Maintenance that wasn't absolutely necessary to pass state inspections and impact the animals' welfare often got the short end of the budget. As animal shelters went, TLC was a good one. They housed their animals in clean runs and cages, provided necessary veterinary care, and diligently tried to find their charges suitable placements. Unlike some shelters, they cooperated actively with the local breed rescue groups—dog clubs that took in homeless dogs of a specific breed, neutered or spayed them, and found them good homes. As an active volunteer in Corgi Rescue, Amy had made trips to TLC more than once to collect some poor corgi who had been picked up as a stray or surrendered to the shelter by owners for some reason or other.

Amy peered through the dirty windowpanes of the door. Lights were on inside. Selma had said someone would be there until three, and the hour was only two. The door was locked, so she knocked loudly.

A full minute passed before a face peered out at her through the dirty panes. When the door swung open, Amy was momentarily taken aback by the size of the man who looked down at her. She had been expecting Martin, a scrawny, cheerful teenager who always seemed to get stuck with holiday duty. But this was not Martin, not scrawny, nor short, nor afflicted with acne as was the unfortunate kennel help. In fact, the man who greeted her was over six feet, quite broad in a well-proportioned sort of way, tanned, with a stalwart square jaw and hazel eyes that smiled at her from beneath thick, intriguingly arched brows. The whole was crowned by rumpled, rusty brown waves that were sorely in need of a trim. The guy's face would never land him on the cover of *GQ*, but it was a nice face, a pleasant face that looked as though it often creased with laughter.

"Hello?" he inquired.

"Uh . . . hi." Amy felt her face flush. Only because she was surprised not to see Martin, she told herself. "I . . . where's Martin?"

"Fishing, I think. I'm sort of covering for him."

"Oh."

"We're closed, you know."

"Oh, I know. I'm Amy Cameron. With Corgi Rescue. I got a call that you have a Pembroke Welsh corgi here at the shelter and I could pick it up today."

"Oh sure. Amy. I remember you. Come on in."

Amy frowned as she followed him through a tiny anteroom into an area that was a combination grooming, storage, and exam room. There *was* something familiar about this guy. "You remember me?"

"I think we met for five whole minutes three years ago . . . downtown Denver at the Boston Half Shell. You were sitting at a table with your husband. I was with a friend of yours who stopped by your table to talk for a few minutes."

"Lydia," she recalled.

"That's right. Lydia Keane."

"You were Lydia's date." An unwanted chill entered Amy's voice. "Small world."

"I'm not sure date is the right word. I think our relationship began and ended on that evening that we saw you."

"Lydia had a lot of relationships like that."

When a good friend betrays you, especially in such an intimate way, the betrayal hurts. That one act poisons all the good memories, all the shared good times. For the rest of her life, Amy's heart would cringe at the sound of Lydia's name. If this man had been one of Lydia's boyfriends, one of the many, many good-time guys she hung out with, then Amy didn't want anything to do with him . . . other than to collect one small stray dog and leave as quickly as possible.

"I heard what happened," the man said more somberly. "I'm sorry. It doesn't seem to be quite enough to say, really, but . . . I am sorry."

Amy nodded. Everybody knew what happened, thanks to a slow news day. Both the *Rocky Mountain News* and the *Denver Post* had run the story on the front page, complete with gruesome pictures and lurid speculations about the prominent car dealer/city councilman found dead with a beautiful woman in a Denver alley. No one else knew quite what to say, either, but this fellow looked as though he actually expected some response.

"I'd rather not talk about it, really."

"Sure. I can understand that."

"It happened six months ago. I've dealt with it. A person has to get on with life, you know."

"That's right. Smart attitude." He sounded unconvinced but had the good sense not to press the point. "I'm Jeff Berenger, by the way."

"You work here full time?" Amy asked. He didn't look like the sort of fellow who would hire on at minimum wage to scoop poop and and hose down kennel runs, even though his cuffs and collar were a bit frayed and his jeans were worn through at the knee.

"I'm not exactly employed. I volunteer a couple of hours a week. Martin wanted to go up to Barr Lake with a buddy, and I didn't have any weekend plans, so I told him I'd come in."

"Oh."

"Worthy cause, you know."

She didn't react to his smile. "Can you sign out that stray corgi to me?"

"Sure. No problem."

"Are you sure she's a corgi?"

"She's a corgi, all right. I'll go get her."

A few moments later, he returned with a reddish brown tubular dog in his arms. A splash of white on the neck and chest, along with white socks on the feet, were the only markings. Short little legs scrambled for purchase on the exam table when he put the stray down; an almost indiscernible tail stump was tucked firmly into a plump little butt; and big, triangular ears twitched back and forth in agitation.

Amy sighed. "Female, I see. Is she spayed?"

"Four days ago. She's recovering very nicely."

"Who brought her in?"

"An older couple picked her up as a stray in Denver and took her home. They decided they didn't want her, and I can't say I blame them. She's a cranky little girl."

"Why do you think the females are called bitches?"

Jeff smiled crookedly. "If I comment on that one, it'll get me into a world of trouble."

Amy suppressed a chuckle and reminded herself that she didn't like this man. This man had dated Lydia. "She's not exactly a looker, is she?"

The dog regarded Amy with an offended expression that was eerily human, as if she understood the insult.

Jeff added his own list of slurs. "She's overweight. Stray or not, she found plenty of food somewhere. Covered with scabs . . . been in a fight or two, apparently. Not surprising, given her temperament. Doesn't relate well to other dogs . . . or to people, for that matter. She had to be muzzled when she first arrived. She was full of lice, ear mites, and even sported a tick or two. All the pests are gone now, of course, but she's still a sight, isn't she?"

"I'll say." Amy gently ran her hands over the dog on the table. Her coat was clean, but it was brittle and scruffy. One ear had a piece taken out of it, and the woeful face had fresh scars that bore witness to a hard, bad-tempered life on the street. The brown eyes that looked at her were both cautious and resentful. Thinking of everything this little corgi must have endured almost made Amy's heart break.

"If you can find a home for this one," the kennel man said, "you'll be a miracle worker."

Amy gave him a sharp look. "It's not her fault she ended up like this. Too many people regard dogs as disposable property, you know. If they become inconvenient, toss them out. If they require a little time and effort, take them to the pound, or leave them somewhere on their own. The Christmas-present puppy grows up to be not so cute, so just put it on a chain in the backyard and throw it a bowl of food every day, if it's not too much trouble."

"Whoa!" Jeff held up his hands in surrender. "I'm on your side."

Amy bit her lip. "Sorry. I get carried away."

"If you end up dealing with many dogs like this one, I can understand why."

"I do," she said grimly. "This girl may settle into being a perfectly lovely little lady once she gets a bit of kind attention."

Jeff snorted skeptically.

"Or not," Amy amended. "In any case, her life is going to get a lot easier from here on out." She addressed the unhappy-looking dog. "You don't know it yet, sweetheart, but your troubles are pretty much over."

She dug into her handbag to retrieve a leash and collar. When Jeff reached down to help her adjust the collar size, their fingers tangled. Embarrassed, Amy drew back, annoyed at her own embarrassment. It wasn't as though she was attracted to this big lummox with his tattered jeans and frayed cuffs.

He had nice, square fingers, though. She couldn't help but notice. And his nails were very clean. Hands were something Amy had always noticed about men. Big, square hands were sexy. Clean nails were sexy. And what the hell was she thinking?

"She'll need to have her stitches out in five or six days."

"What?"

"The stitches. From the spay." He tilted the dog to expose her shaved stomach. The neatly stitched two-inch-long incision looked like a zipper.

"It's fine," Jeff continued. "No sign of infection. But you'll have to keep an eye on it."

"Of course I will." She'd been so distracted by his damned hands that she'd scarcely heard what he said.

"And I'd have your vet do another fecal for worms. And draw blood for a heartworm test."

"My vet just moved to Missouri, but I suppose I can find someone else in the next week or so."

"You can bring her to me, if you like. Considering this is a charity case," he said with a smile, "I'll do the work pro bono."

"What?"

"Pro bono. Legalese for 'scott free.' "

"I know what the term means, but why would I bring her to you?"

"To get her stitches removed. Bring her to my clinic."

"You're a veterinarian?"

"In the flesh."

"Why didn't you tell me you were a vet?"

"It didn't come up until just now. Today I'm filling in as kennel boy. I left my stethoscope at home."

She definitely didn't like the man, Amy decided. She didn't like him because he was pleasant, attractive, smart, and just like 99 percent of the rest of the male population, his taste in women ran to a tall, redheaded, slinky, amoral sexpot whose most interesting aspects were all below her neck. She definitely did not like him.

But the vet who had given her a 50 percent discount on treating rescued dogs had moved to Missouri, and rescue funds were strained at the best of times.

"Where's your clinic?" she asked reluctantly.

"Longmont. Just south of town on highway 287." He dug into his jeans pocket for a crumpled business card and handed it to her. "Bring her by any time Thursday or Friday, and we'll get everything taken care of."

"Thanks. I appreciate it."

"Don't mention it."

Amy felt the chill in the air between them and knew that she had been the one to put it there, not by anything she'd said, but by the look on her face and the tone of her voice. If some New Age guru had tuned in to her aura right then, he would have seen something glacier blue and hung with icicles.

She wanted it that way. She didn't like the guy, so he could take those warm laugh lines around his eyes and those nice, clean square hands and go be charming to someone more his type.

She signed the paperwork taking responsibility for the dog and then lifted her new charge carefully down from the table. "Come on, girl. Move your little brown tush. You're headed for rehab."

"That's right, kid," Jeff commented with a chuckle in his voice. "Mother Nature may have made you a bitch, but it's not really wise to act like one."

Amy got the feeling that he wasn't talking to the dog. She gave him an arch look meant to convey how much she didn't care. "See you Friday, Dr. Berenger."

JEFF BERENGER WATCHED Amy as she walked toward her car with the scruffy little corgi trotting behind her. Now there was a lady with a burr up her butt . . . and a damned attractive butt it was, too. He couldn't blame her for being brittle, however. She'd gotten a raw deal, and the whole world knowing about her personal humiliation couldn't make it go down any easier. If David Cameron hadn't been a Denver city councilman, his murder might have appeared somewhere on page 6 of the local papers, and the television news wouldn't have bothered with the story. But Cameron was a city councilman, so the media blared his death, and the manner of it, all over the morning news and page one, then pried into David's relationship with Lydia, and Lydia's relationship with Amy, and broadcast those details ad nauseam. The public's thirst for scandal made the story last much longer than it should have.

Then, just as the furor had trickled down to nothing, Jeff had read that Amy's Victorian house in northwest Denver had burned to the ground. A photo of a soot-streaked and tear-stained Amy, along with her equally sorry-looking dogs, had shown up on page 3 of the *Rocky Mountain News,* page 2 of the *Denver Post,* and as the second lead story on the evening news. Amy, it seemed, didn't have any kind of luck but bad.

He remembered what Lydia had said about her "best friend" that night after they left Amy's table and sat down at their own: "Amy has a heart of gold, but she's dull as dirt, poor girl. Book smart, but never learned to have fun, you know?"

Jeff didn't think Amy Cameron was dull as dirt. She

had snappy blue eyes and a mop of artlessly curled dark hair that made a man's fingers itch to comb through it. Even in faded jeans and a baggy cotton shirt, she had class. If she ever smiled, Jeff speculated, she just might outdazzle the sun.

Amy Cameron—busy rescuing strays and rehabilitating other people's castoffs. He wondered if anyone had ever given thought to rescuing Amy.

Two

♥

WELL, NOW YOU realize the extent of Stan's twisted sense of humor. Not only did the mean-spirited twerp send me back to Earth as a dog, but as a Welsh corgi, for pity's sake. Do you know what a corgi looks like? Probably not. Corgis aren't exactly a common sight in your average American neighborhood . . . for good reason. Most people want a pretty dog— a dog that friends and neighbors will ooooh and aaaah over. No one, but no one, is going to ooooh or aaaah over a funnylooking bossy little dog that looks like a stumpy-tailed fox on steroids, one that's been cut off at the knees to boot. I kid you not. That's exactly what a corgi looks like.

If Stan had to have his little joke, he could have sent me back to Earth as a dog more in keeping with my nature—an Afghan hound, for example. Amy dragged me to a dog show once, and I have to admit I was impressed by the Afghans. When those dogs move, their hair flows around them like some sort of shimmery gown, and with their long elegant noses in the air, they look as though they don't give a flying fiddle what anyone thinks.

I wouldn't have minded too much coming back as an Afghan. Or an Irish setter. The natural burnished red of the setter coat is a shade I've always craved, but even the most expensive hair coloring doesn't get it quite right. I could have dealt with being a glamorous Irish setter. Maybe.

But a Welsh corgi? I don't think so. I wasn't even a classy corgi. Moth-eaten, pudgy, and lice-bitten, I didn't have a pedigree or fancy kennel club certificate to my name. In fact, I didn't even have a name.

I suppose Stan's excuse was that corgis were Amy's breed of choice. She'd always had one or two of the weasely little dogs living at her place, leaving muddy paw prints on her floors and dog hair on her furniture. And Amy had always been a soft touch for a sob story, especially a doggy sob story.

So, there I was, a walking canine charity case, and of course Amy did what I'm sure Stan counted on her doing and dragged me home with her. Somewhat to my surprise, we didn't arrive at the impressive Victorian she'd shared with David just off Sheridan Boulevard in northwest Denver. What Amy called home these days was a rambling sixties-style brick house on a narrow county road south of Boulder. Now, Boulder, Colorado, is a really classic town, but the countryside around it is strictly dull. Farms, churches, podunk little burgs with podunk little houses. Amy's place looked as dull as the rest. It was a nondescript brown brick house with a few trees shading the front and a big backyard enclosed by Cyclone fencing. Her beat-up motor home took up the entire driveway in front of a big two-story garage. The houses in the neighborhood, if such a place can be called a neighborhood, were at least a quarter mile apart, separated by fields of weeds and scraggly grass. The flat stretch of fields behind the house gave an unobstructed view of the mountains to the west, but that was the only good thing I could say about the place.

I didn't get much of a chance to look around before Amy tugged rudely on the leash and dragged me through the front door. Her living room smelled. Nothing against Amy's housekeeping, though she could use a good cleaning lady. To a dog's nose, everything smells. That was one of the things I'd discovered since Stan dumped me in that alley. The world is a whirlpool of odor. Sound, too. Even the quietest night is alive with noises you wouldn't want to imagine.

The smells that greeted me in Amy's living room were quite informative. She'd had a salami sandwich for lunch, a thought that made my stomach growl. She had two dogs living in the house, and at least one of them had recently rolled in something very interesting. Moreover, in the not too distant past, a cat had lived in the place. The creature wasn't here now but had definitely left its stinky little paw prints.

I had no sooner started to catalog some of the more interesting odors present than the two obnoxious little hairballs who called the place home bounded into the room. I'd met both of them before, but I'd been a lot taller then and in a form that was immeasurably superior to the one I was stuck with now. Molly and Drover. I hadn't liked them when I was human— little short-legged ankle nippers who didn't have a brain cell between them. I liked them even less now.

"Be nice," Amy warned. "All of you."

A frenzy of butt-sniffing followed, with me trying to swing my posterior out of reach and the home team becoming more and more insistent. An urge to join in the disgusting doggy greetings almost overcame me. The furry brown package that Stan had wrapped me in came complete with canine instincts, and my nose itched to goose a couple of dog tushes, but my superior sensibilities triumphed, and I returned the enthusiastic greetings with a curled lip and a throaty rumble. I was instantly rewarded with a jerk on my collar.

"Behave!" Amy chided. "And you two," she commanded the other dogs, "sit!"

Two tailless fuzzy rumps hit the floor, and the dogs smiled up at Amy with lolling tongues and innocent expressions. Butter wouldn't melt in their mouths, the little runts, but I knew from Molly's slightly stiff posture that she wasn't about to let my challenge go unanswered. There's a reason female dogs are called bitches, you know. And Drover . . . he broadcasted a stink that told me his testosterone was in full bloom. Did the moron really think I might find him attractive? The very thought made me want to puke.

"Molly, Drover, this is . . . uh . . . ," Amy gave me a sympathetic smile. "You don't have a name, do you, sweetheart?" She reached down and gave me a patronizing little pat, causing Molly to send me a warning glare. Apparently she thought all the human attention in the house belonged to her.

"Piggy," Amy decided aloud. "Miss Piggy. It suits you."

Piggy? How humiliating. I barked my displeasure, a futile effort, for Amy simply laughed.

"Like it, do you?"

No, I did not like it, and Amy obviously wasn't as good at communicating with dogs as she thought she was. I intercepted an annoyingly superior smirk from Molly and wrinkled my nose to let the bitch know I was on to her.

"None of that!" Amy flipped my snout smartly with her finger. "Clean up your act, Miss Piggy, or you'll have to be on a leash all the time you're here."

Molly's face split in a foxy grin. She understood the tone of the threat and was obviously well pleased. Meanwhile, Drover had rolled over on his back. His rear legs splayed straight out in an immodest display of his assets. The little front legs paddled the air, and he grinned up at Amy with his tongue lolling out the side of his mouth. A disgusting example of practiced cuteness, if you ask me, but it accomplished his purpose.

"Dinnertime, is it?" Amy glanced at her watch. "Okay, troops. Into the kitchen."

With the mention of food, Molly and Drover seemed willing to postpone any confrontation until after their stomachs were full. Corgis have a very strict order of priorities, I've learned, and food is right at the top.

While the home team indulged in a feeding frenzy in the kitchen, I was allowed to eat peacefully in a fiberglass and wire-mesh dog kennel, the sort that the airlines use for their canine cargo. It was roomy and clean, and the food was palatable to my new taste buds, though somewhat lacking in variety and presentation. I was thoroughly enjoying the peace and solitude when who should show up but the twisted being who got me into this fix. He didn't look any more impressive on Earth than he had in the limbo where I'd first met him. Stan still looked like a nitpicking, teetotaling prig of a bureaucrat. The only thing he lacked was horn-rimmed glasses.

"Go away," I told him.

He shook his head. "That's no way to greet someone who's helping you avoid a most unpleasant future."

"The present isn't taking any prizes."

"The present is what you make of it, Lydia. Or should I call you Piggy?" The sadistic bum nearly laughed, then grew serious. "This is your second chance, young lady. Don't squander it."

I munched my kibble and tried to ignore him.

"I see all has happened just as I hoped." He rubbed his hands together in malicious satisfaction. "How are you settling in?"

"How do you expect I'm settling in, Stan? I'm a dog, for pity's sake. I can't talk. I get dragged around on a leash, and I'm expected to go to the bathroom in the open air with the whole world watching."

"And you're in a perfect position to carry out your mission."

"My mission?" At this point, I was getting a bit testy. Not only had the twit intruded upon my solitude, but he'd interrupted my dinner. To a corgi, that's a capital crime. "Who do you think I am?" I demanded sourly. "Jim Phelps on Mission Impossible? Amy doesn't need another husband, if you ask me. And she doesn't want one either. Did you see how she put down that veterinarian who came on to her?"

Not that Jeff Berenger is much of a prize, mind you. I found that out for myself a few years back. But he's studly enough to keep most women from cutting him cold as quickly as Amy did.

"Did you eavesdrop on their conversation, Stan?"

"The name is Stanley, please. And yes, I did happen to listen in on that encounter."

"Did Amy look like a woman craving male company?"

"It hasn't escaped me that Amy has a modicum of bitterness in her heart."

"A mere modicum?" I asked sarcastically.

"I never promised your job would be easy, Lydia. But it is worthwhile. You and David robbed Amy of much of her happiness. I'm giving you the opportunity to give it back to her."

"Just where am I supposed to find Amy another husband? Good men are few and far between. I ought to know. I've dated most of them."

I discounted Stan's twinkle of amusement as my imagination. I've found out since then that old Stan does have a sense of humor . . . of sorts. His jokes are usually at my expense, though.

"Don't give up before you've begun, Lydia. Completing this project successfully would be very much to your benefit. Just open your eyes, and you might learn something that you didn't learn when you were a woman."

By the time I thought up a suitably scathing retort, he'd gone.

AMY WATCHED HER dogs wolf down their food. The kibble lasted about ten seconds, but they kept at it to lick the last crumb, and possibly the finish, from the pans. She felt vaguely guilty about sending Piggy into solitary for her meal, but she didn't want the newcomer to start a fight in defense of her food dish. The dog's girth proved that she was competent at defending her territory, and Amy didn't want to spend the evening cleaning out punctures and doctoring scratches. No indeed. Since she was temporarily without a regular vet, she might have to turn to Jeff Berenger for help in the doctoring, and that would have been awkward, to say the least.

A vision of hazel eyes framed by thick lashes flashed into her mind. Jeff Berenger had nice eyes—kind, intelligent, good-humored eyes, eyes that radiated tiny little laugh lines to crease the suntan of a strong, no-nonsense face. It was criminal that a man with such eyes should seek out someone like Lydia Keane as a companion. Lydia, with her flashy figure and dynamite looks, her do-anything-for-a-good-time attitude, and her utterly narcissistic heart. There wasn't any justice in the world, but then, what else was new?

The dog dishes reflected the kitchen light with mirrorlike cleanliness, and the dogs danced around her feet, letting her know that a spot of dessert would be welcome. Amy ignored their disappointed expressions when she shooed them to the back door and gave them both a gentle push into the yard. Corgi pleas of starvation didn't move her. If she let Molly and Drover eat all they wanted to eat, they would look like furry basketballs with legs—a goal toward which Miss Piggy had a good start.

Piggy greeted her with a similar plea on her face.

"No more, sweetheart. You're on a diet, as of now."

The dog's scowl of disgust was almost human. In fact, Amy reflected as Piggy made a reluctant exit to the yard, the scruffy little stray possessed a repertoire of astoundingly human-looking expressions, and the timing of some of her reactions gave the impression that she understood every word of conversation. She didn't, of course. Amy would be the first to defend canine intelligence and capacity for emotion, and she was often guilty, as were many dog lovers, of treating dogs as little people in fur suits. But dogs were still just dogs. One could love them as children and confide in them as best friends. But they were still just dogs.

Nevertheless, Piggy had an eerie quality that Amy couldn't quite pin down. Her expression. Her sulky attitude. Her uncorgilike haughtiness. All that was strangely familiar. Or possibly Amy was still feeling the effects of too much champagne. She watched as Piggy ambled out into the yard, where the dogs were tending to their after-dinner business. The newcomer stayed well away from the other dogs, her posture clearly conveying her contempt for the resident troops. Molly's stiff demeanor showed her displeasure at the situation, but then Molly always got her matronly little nose out of joint when a rescue dog came in. She generally settled down in a day or so. Drover, on the other hand, was flirting outrageously, racing around the yard, looping around trees and bounding over the flowerbed as if it were an Olympic hurdle. He paused at the end of each lap to observe Piggy's reaction, but her determined scorn didn't discourage him. Drover was usually more discriminating in his attention to females, and spayed females didn't rate so much as a sniff. This little girl, ugly as she appeared to the human eye, must be one hot bitch. It was fortunate for the dog world that Dr. Berenger had spayed her.

Amy grimaced. There he was again—Jeff Berenger, holding Piggy up to expose the zipper on her tummy, his voice reassuring the dog at the same time his damned eyes twinkled at his patient's indignation. He had a nerve, being charming! Not that it was meant personally, Amy was sure. Men seemed to feel a bit of posturing was obligatory when single women were near, just to prove they were men. A man who'd romanced Lydia couldn't find Amy much to his taste. Not that she wanted him to.

Damn! To hell with the man anyway! She was going

to find someone else to take out Piggy's damned stitches!

You'd think that Stan, *being so anxious for me to match up Amy with the Best Possible Husband, would have sent me to Earth as someone who had a bit more freedom of movement. How did he expect me to accomplish anything when I was literally a prisoner in Amy's house and backyard? The other dogs didn't seem to find the situation limiting, but then they were a bit limited themselves. That stupid Drover would have cheerfully stayed tied in the middle of a railroad track—with a train coming—if someone had piled dog cookies on the rails, and Molly wasn't much better. Slavishly eager to please, indecently happy with their dull existence, neither had much brainpower or imagination. I, on the other hand, still possessed my full complement of both, but putting them to use was difficult as long as I was trapped in a dumb dog suit.*

For example, I couldn't use the phone to place an ad in the personals. Have you ever seen a dog use a touch tone phone? I tried. After five frustrating attempts, I was ready to eat the damned thing. Other commonplace conveniences were also denied me: I couldn't fax or e-mail any of my discarded hunks to find out if they might be available. I couldn't cruise the singles' scene to troll for likely men. I couldn't take Amy shopping to buy something other than those dreadful jeans she lives in. Don't get me wrong, here. Jeans are classic. They can make a fashion statement. But Amy's jeans made a fashion statement that wouldn't attract anything but a truck from the Salvation Army.

I could have wasted my energy getting madder and madder at Stan for creating the situation, but I'm too smart for that. I was determined to make short work of this stupid mission, despite the obstacles, then thumb my nose at that officious little twit and demand that he get me out of the dog suit. He could reward my good work with wings and a halo—or whatever it is that angels wear. Anything would be better than big triangular ears and a perpetually wet nose.

So when my chance finally came, two days after Amy had picked me up from that god-awful shelter, I didn't waste any time getting to work.

Fortunately for me, Amy believes that dogs, especially us poor little rescue tykes, benefit from mingling with the public. For my first outing, we drove to a park in Boulder for a stroll. If it was only exercise Amy was after, we could have walked along one of the roads outside Niwot, but social interaction was what she had in mind—not for her, but for me. Little did she know that I had my own agenda as far as social interaction went.

The day was bright and warm, and the path was crowded with cyclists, walkers, and joggers. Boulderites take their exercise very seriously, you know. To be with the truly "in" group there, one must drool over mountain bikes, run in at least three marathons a year, and have a wardrobe consisting mostly of spandex and stinky athletic shoes. Even in the dead of winter, cyclists thumb their noses at motorists on every Boulder street and highway.

I've always cast an admiring eye on guys who are serious cyclists. Have you ever followed one up a hill, watching those buns of steel pumping up the slope? It's a sight that will make you appreciate sports, for sure. But here in the park, I set my sights on slower prey. The bikes whizzed by us too fast for me to evaluate their passengers. And besides, how was I going to get one of those guys down from the bike, what with me being only ten inches tall?

That left the joggers and walkers, and there were plenty of those to choose from. Again, my lowly stature posed some difficulty, but I came up with creative solutions. You can discover a lot about a man from looking at the lowest eighteen inches of him. For example, Best Possible Husbands do not wear dirty sneakers with holes, mismatched socks, or droopy socks with overstretched elastic. Nor do they wear pants that end just above their ankles. Definitely uncool. For those wearing shorts, I immediately eliminated those with toothpick legs, knobby knees, or fish-belly white skin.

Halfway around the park we happened upon a jogger who definitely fit the bill. He wore expensive Nike athletic shoes, color-matched to his socks, shorts, and shirt. His legs were sunbronzed and glorious, with muscles clear up to you know where. Low to the ground as I was, I enjoyed a unique ability to see up to you know where, so I know what I'm talking about.

This guy was obviously well off and knew the value of snappy dressing. Getting him to stop for a more in-depth interview was easy. Amy had me hooked to one of those fancy leashes that go out for twenty feet or so and spool in like a fishing reel. It was a simple matter to catch her off guard, scamper up to the lucky candidate, and bound around him a few times to wind him in the leash. I thought I was very clever to think of this.

The jogger didn't appreciate my cleverness, however. And Amy, instead of taking advantage of this opportunity to flirt with a hunk, makes herself look like an idiot by chasing around the fellow's legs, trying to unwind him as I raced around winding him even more tightly. Then she fell all over herself, tongue-tied and blushing, trying to apologize.

The woman is hopeless, I tell you. Hopeless. And what was she so mad at me about? She got noticed, didn't she?

Amy didn't give up on the idea of socializing me, and I didn't give up either. I counted myself lucky that she didn't catch on to my scheme and lock me in the house for the rest of my days, but Amy sometimes doesn't learn very fast. The very next day, she took me with her on a trip to the Boulder walking mall.

For those of you who've never been to Boulder, Colorado, let me make it clear that the Boulder mall is not just an ordinary shopping mall. No, it's a street in downtown Boulder that's forbidden to cars for several blocks. Quaintly bricked and decorated with planters of trees and shrubs for the enjoyment of pedestrians, the mall is lined with shops that are both trendy and expensive. I was overjoyed at the prospect this presented. Any man strolling the Boulder mall had to have something going for him. I was hoping also that Amy might plan some shopping in some of the better stores. As I've mentioned before, her wardrobe needs a lot of improvement.

Unfortunately, Amy didn't go to the mall to shop. She was composing a photo essay on Boulder for a travel magazine, and insisted on seeing the mall through the viewfinder of a camera, not the eye of a woman who desperately needs clothes. I did manage to pull her over to the window of a dress shop where a totally perfect green outfit was on display—sleek trousers with a darling little short jacket. The ensemble would have hidden so many of Amy's figure faults, like her sad lack of chest and a set of hips that should have belonged to a boy. Through the door of the shop I could also see, not to mention smell, displays of scented soaps, colognes, and sexy lingerie. Just what Amy needed. If the woman would fix herself up a bit, then my job would've been so much easier!

Of course, she didn't buy anything. She didn't even go into the store to take a closer look. The display did provide the necessary distraction for me to slip my collar and trot over to a Brooks Brothers type that I'd spotted sitting on a bench. This candidate I didn't hog-tie as I had the last one. Unlike Amy, I learn my lessons quickly. I was cool, politely sitting in front of him to get his attention, giving him a great big corgi smile, then rolling over on my back and presenting my tummy, complete with its little zipper, for a scratching. He couldn't resist my charm. Corgis can be insufferably cute when they put their minds to it, and I knew how to take advantage of cute. I'd done it successfully all the years I'd walked on two legs instead of four.

I had only a few moments to win this guy over before Amy came rushing over, all in an ugly dither, to scoop me up and shove the collar back on my neck. The fellow merely laughed,

*and he gave Amy a once-over that was more complimentary
than she deserved. But did Amy take advantage of the implied
invitation and strike up a conversation? No! Of course not!
There I was, handing off the ball for a certain touchdown run,
and she fumbled.*

*Foiled again! I just hope old Stan appreciated the amount
of effort and creativity I was putting forth. My assigned task
was going to take longer than I had anticipated, not from lack
of trying on my part, but because of Amy's singular lack of
feminine instinct. How she had won David is beyond me. Stan
might have been right to enlist my help, for Amy certainly
wasn't going to find another man without my assistance.*

DESPITE AMY'S VOW, three days later she stood on the
front stoop of a very modest two-story frame house
fronting highway 287 just south of Longmont. Rusty
metal numbers above the front door proclaimed that this
was the place Jeff Berenger had directed her to, and a
small placard in the window confirmed it. BERENGER ANI-
MAL CLINIC, the sign boasted. LARGE AND SMALL ANIMAL
PRACTICE. WALK–INS WELCOME.

Walk–ins welcome, Amy mused. She walked in,
pulling a reluctant Piggy along behind her. The waiting
room was clean, if a bit shabby. The walls were decorated with the usual photos and drawings of puppies,
kittens, dogs, and cats. Somewhat out of the ordinary
was a photograph of an impressive Brahman bull with a
very pleased Jeff Berenger holding it by the halter.

Only one other person was in the room: a small girl
of about six or seven whose legs didn't reach the floor
from where she sat on a fiberglass-and-metal chair. The
girl stared at Piggy, who gazed back with an expression
of total disinterest.

"Does your dog bite?" the child asked.

"I don't think so," Amy replied.

"Don't you know?"

"I've only had her a few days."

"Oh." The little girl cocked her head at the corgi. "Do you think she likes kids?"

"Most corgis do," Amy told her. Most corgis would have been at the girl's feet by now, gazing up in adoration. The breed as a whole was both fascinated and delighted by children. But with Piggy, one never knew.

The girl got up and approached the dog cautiously. Amy made sure the leash was taut. Her vigilance was unnecessary, however. Piggy's only reaction to the child's gentle pats on the head was a contemptuous roll of the eyes.

"I don't think your dog likes me," the girl observed sagely.

"Don't let that hurt your feelings. I don't think she likes anyone."

The inner door opened, and Jeff Berenger emerged, drying his hands on a towel. He wore faded jeans and a lab coat that probably once had been white. It was clean enough, but gray from too many launderings and decorated with a variety of stains. "Well, hello, Mandy." He smiled irresistibly at the child. "What brings you here today?"

Mandy picked up a small basket from beside her chair. "One of the dogs got my kitten. Look."

The vet peered into the basket, and Amy could tell he had to work to suppress a grimace. "So it did."

"Can you fix her?"

"Well now, we'll try."

"My ma says we don't have any money to spend on a stupid cat. But Flower's my best friend."

"I don't charge much to work on best friends."

"I have fifty cents."

"Well, a quarter ought to just about cover it. Or

maybe you can come in some Saturday and help me throw some sticks for Spot and Darby."

"I would do that."

"Good. Then let's see about this kitty." He winked at Amy in a way that should have infuriated her, but somehow didn't. "Be with you in a few minutes, Amy. Make yourself comfortable."

Amy settled into a chair. Piggy plopped down at her feet on the linoleum floor. The dog surveyed the waiting room with a look of disapproval. Amy chuckled at her expression.

"That little scene was right out of a Norman Rockwell painting, wasn't it?" she commented to the dog. "How do you manage to give a guy like that the cold shoulder?"

Piggy made a sound between a growl and a howl.

"You could find a way, huh?"

For a moment Amy feared she'd crossed the line between imagination and delusion. Talking to dogs was one thing. She did that all the time. But believing the dogs answered back was asking for a one-way ticket to a padded cell.

Twenty minutes passed while she paged through old issues of the *AKC Gazette* and *Cat Fancy*. Various brochures in a rack on the wall pushed heartworm preventatives, canine oral hygiene, and the virtues of spaying or neutering pets.

Amy had just about exhausted the available entertainment and Piggy was sighing in melodramatic boredom when Mandy, minus her kitten, came back into the room. Jeff followed.

"You check back with me tomorrow, Mandy. I think Flower's going to be okay, and she should be able to go home in two or three days. You keep her in the house from now on, where your dad's dogs can't get her."

"Thank you, Dr. B."

"Stay on the path going home. Don't you get close to the highway."

"I promise." The girl waved as she went out the door, looking much happier than when she'd presented the vet with her injured kitten. "I'll come back tomorrow."

Jeff Berenger turned his smile on Amy, who couldn't help but smile back. "What a scene," she said. "If I could have photographed you with that little girl and her kitten, I could have gotten you on the cover of every cat magazine in the country."

"Doesn't that just make my blood race!" One thick brow lifted into a skeptical arch.

"Ah. You don't care about fame or recognition. The classic country vet who patches up kids' pets with no thought of business concerns. You a sucker for kids, Dr. Berenger?"

"Nah!" he denied. "I'm a sucker for kittens." He sent her a telling look. "And speaking of bitches, how's Miss Pudgy, here?"

Amy acknowledged that she deserved that. She was being a bitch—unusual for her, because she generally got along with just about everyone. But she had an overwhelming need to demean the wholesome image Jeff Berenger presented. She wanted him to fit her notion of what he was, what most men were. If he didn't insist on acting so damned decent, she wouldn't need to defend her cynicism by being such a bitch. Her crabbiness was obviously his fault.

And if that didn't take the gold medal for twisted reasoning, Amy didn't know what would.

"Shall we take a look at that incision?"

"What?" Amy pulled her eyes away from the undisciplined wave of hair at his temple. "Oh. Stitches. Sure." She gave a tug on the leash as he led them into a small exam room that had probably once been the front bedroom of the old house. This room was less shabby than the waiting room and spotless. A counter held neatly arranged bottles of disinfectant, soap, jars of cotton swabs, and a very large tin of dog cookies. On one wall hung a framed photo of a magnificent hawk in full flight.

Piggy balked at passing the threshold. Amy tugged gently on the leash. "Come on, Piggy. This way."

"Piggy?"

"I named her Miss Piggy. It seems to fit both her girth and her attitude."

"Well, Miss Piggy," Jeff said, lifting the reluctant corgi to the examination table, "I can help you with your girth, but your new mom's in charge of attitude adjustment."

Piggy regarded him with undisguised dislike.

"You know?" Jeff observed. "Most corgis I've met are sweet little dogs. Devils in their own right, but sweet nonetheless. I'm not sure about this one."

"There's not a sweet bone in this one's body, believe me," Amy confirmed. "In four days she's got my older female sulking in the bedroom and refusing to come out, and Drover, my male, keeps getting a face full of her teeth every time he gets close to her. I've just about decided I'm going to have to keep this one myself. She's cranky enough that I'd be afraid to place her with anyone else."

"Most people would simply have her euthanized."

"I can't do that. She's a sorry excuse for a dog, but there is something about her . . ."

"You a sucker for strays, Amy?"

She recognized her own question as it was tossed back at her with just enough bite to sting.

"I'm not a sucker for anything, Dr. Berenger."

"Call me Jeff."

"Jeff." She pronounced the name as if it were a challenge, but he merely smiled. He smiled too much, Amy decided. It was his way of avoiding a reply.

Piggy put an end to an awkward silence by trying to jump off the examination table.

"Whoa, there, fatso. That floor's hard."

Her escape foiled, the corgi sent the vet a glare that was equivalent to a growl.

"Piggy, behave!" Amy scolded.

Once he got down to work, Jeff Berenger proved to be adept at handling a difficult dog. He turned a squirming Piggy on her back, pronounced the incision healed, and had the stitches removed before the dog had a chance to seriously object.

"Whoever made that incision is certainly a master at his work," Jeff commented.

"You made the incision," Amy reminded him.

He grinned. "So I did."

"I see that modesty is not one of your virtues."

He set a protesting Piggy on her feet. "A man's got to pat himself on the back once in a while. I don't get many compliments from my patients. On the whole, they're an ungrateful lot. Like this little lady, for instance."

"Oh, by the way . . ." Amy held up the bag that contained Piggy's morning offering, smiling as she remembered the dog's obvious embarrassment when she'd collected it.

"Good," Jeff said. "We'll run a fecal and make sure she doesn't have parasites. And now . . ." He deftly wrapped a rubber tourniquet around a stubby front leg and inserted a needle into the raised vein before the dog knew what had happened. As blood flowed into the syringe, he grinned. Piggy rewarded him with a sharp bark.

"I think that was a cuss word," Jeff speculated. "What do you think?"

Amy grimaced. "As far as I can tell, her entire vocabulary consists of cuss words."

Piggy held up her leg in pathetic protest when Jeff released it from the tourniquet.

"Other than being a grouch, she seems fine. I should have the heartworm results from this blood by this afternoon." He scooped Piggy into his arms, stuffed her into a cage, and latched the door in spite of her lunge to escape. "There you go, Pudgy old girl. Why don't you just relax while I show your mom around the place?"

"I really don't have time," Amy protested.

"It's a small place," Jeff assured her. "And I'll just give you the dime tour instead of the two-dollar special."

"Well . . ."

"Besides, you'll want to say hello to my border collies."

"You have border collies?"

"Birds, too. I've got a beautiful red-tailed hawk in back who'd love to meet you. He broke his wing awhile back, and he's almost ready to fly again."

Before Amy could protest further, he wrapped his nice, square fingers around her arm and ushered her through the door to the back. It would have been exceedingly rude to pull away, Amy told herself. Just too rude. She had to go, even though heaven knew she didn't want to spend any more time with Jeff Berenger. She didn't. She really, truly didn't.

THREE

♥

This was a dandy situation! There I was, stuck in a cage like a criminal, while Amy, who was my responsibility, wandered off on the arm of a man who could probably charm her out of her knickers quicker than I charmed David out of his. Amy is bright about some things, but the game of romance isn't one of them. Naive is the nicest word I can think of to describe her lack of savvy with men. In my experience, chumps like Amy don't actually get much smarter about some things. She might boast to herself that she was a sadder but wiser girl, but I figured she was just as much an ignoramus as she always had been. Disaster was about to strike.

Why was I so put out? you ask. I was supposed to find Amy a husband, wasn't I? And here was a fellow presenting himself as a willing victim without my having to do a lick of work. Well, I'll tell you why I was put out! Everything easy in life—and after life as well—has a catch. Stan had made it very clear that my future depended upon finding the Best Possible Husband for Amy. I repeat: Best Possible, with a capital Best. Jeff Berenger was a loser. I dated him once, so I knew. The man was a living example of the maxim that good looks are only skin deep. Beneath that smile and those twinkly eyes, Berenger was a dud—a bomb without a fuse, tequila without the kick, a Jaguar with a Volkswagen engine. You get my drift? He didn't have ambition, style, or the foggiest idea how to have a good time. Dull as yesterday's comic strips. What's worse, he was a terrible businessman with no sense of the value of a dollar, or the greatly increased value of bunches of dollars all sitting in the same bank account.

Okay, I'd had only one date with the guy. But the way he treated me when I got dumped back on Earth in a dog suit only confirmed my first impression.

Sentimental people say one can judge a man by how he treats animals. I used to think that was baloney, but since becoming an animal myself, my point of view has changed. If a man proves his mettle by being kind to furry creatures, Jeff Berenger flunks. Case in point: He's much too quick with a thermometer, let me tell you. How would you like a cold glass tube stuck up your butt without so much as a "pardon me"? Not to mention his sneak attacks with needles. What's more, he insulted me at every turn, manhandled me as though I were a sack of grain, subjected me to indignities that boggle the mind, and, to top it all off, spayed me. If he and Amy thought getting rid of my female organs was going to make me any less of a bitch, then they needed to think again!

But I digress. The point was, Jeff Berenger was not a man any woman in her right mind would consider for the title Best Possible Husband. I was sure that Stan would be only too glad to latch on to that technicality and give me a big fat F on my assignment. I needed to find Amy the perfect mate. Recognizing him wouldn't be a problem. Heaven knew I'd been with enough men to qualify for an advanced degree in the irksome sex.

The only comfort of my predicament was the knowledge that Amy and Jeff couldn't leave me in that stupid cage forever. And when I got out, watch out! I was determined to take charge of the situation.

"HIS NAME IS Jefferson Davis Berenger. Do you believe?"

Selma looked up from the tablecloth she was hemming and made a face. "Does he have a Confederate flag in his office?"

"No. But his mother is from Virginia and she claims to be a cousin umpteen times removed, so she named her only son after the president of the Confederacy."

"I think that's cute." Selma went back to her stitching before throwing out an oh-so-casual question. "Is *he* cute?"

"No, he's not cute." Amy picked up a corner of the partially hemmed tablecloth that was spread across her dining room table. It was more a banner than a true tablecloth, boasting large white letters spelling out PEMBROKE WELSH CORGI on a royal blue background. "That's looking good. I suppose I should finish the table covering for the grooming table, considering the festival starts tomorrow."

"Don't change the subject. Are you sure he's not the least little bit cute? After all, he's single, right? He's a vet. What could be more perfect? And he must be a nice guy if he volunteers time at the shelter."

"I don't know that he's a nice guy, and just because he wasn't wearing a wedding band, that doesn't mean he's single."

"Wasn't wearing a wedding ring, eh? You noticed."

"Jeez!" Amy sighed and collapsed into a chair. Drover, who had been snoozing on the living room couch, immediately jumped off his perch and trotted over to station himself beside her chair, eyes cast upward in supplication. He assumed that anyone seated at the dining room table was eating, and therefore fair game for a bit of mooching.

"Selma," Amy said as she scratched Drover's head, "you're hopeless. Don't you think of anything besides pairing me off with some man?"

Selma gave her an unabashed grin. "It keeps me from thinking about my own sorry situation. So, tell me about this veterinarian. If you're not interested, maybe I am . . . after I get things settled with Gary."

"Considering your experience with Gary, I would think you'd feel just a bit cautious about plunging into another relationship."

"Caution has never been my strong point."

"Neither has good sense."

"Guilty!" Selma admitted unrepentently. "Now, does Dr. Jefferson Davis Berenger have his own practice? Or is he merely a lackey in someone else's?"

"He has his own practice."

"Then he's probably well fixed for money."

"I doubt it. His practice is in an old frame house that looks like it has a date with a wrecking ball, and the only client in the waiting room was a kid with a hurt kitten, which he treated for a quarter. He's got one exam room, a surgery room, and a holding room. The only animals I saw other than the hurt kitty were his two border collies and a couple of hawks he's rehabilitating. He lives on the second floor of the house and looks as if he buys his clothes at the Salvation Army Thrift Store."

"Ooooh. You got a tour?"

"Of the clinic, you dirty-minded wench, not of his living quarters. He insisted I say hello to his dogs and birds."

Selma's eyes twinkled. "Of course."

"All we did was talk animals. One of his hawks is being released in a ceremony at the Scottish festival."

"You don't say! He'll be at the festival then."

"Oh, quit it! Stop with the 'I told you so' tone! The guy dated Lydia, for cripes sake! How on earth could I be interested in a man who once dated Lydia?"

"You think there's any man in the state of Colorado who didn't? I mean, other than boys under twelve and guys over eighty?"

"Good grief!" Amy pushed Drover's front paws

from her lap, got up, and huffed her way into the kitchen, where she poured herself a glass of wine. Selma's voice followed her.

"Come on, Amy. Lydia was a walking testosterone fantasy. The only man who wouldn't have dated her, given half a chance, was the pope, and I'm not too sure he could've resisted if presented with the opportunity. If you eliminate every man who might have found Lydia attractive, you're going to be sitting on your butt, alone and lonely, for the rest of your days. Besides, even though I always thought Lydia was a gold-plated, self-centered, shallow, manipulative bitch, she didn't really steal anything from you that you hadn't already lost, you know?"

"What's that supposed to mean?" Amy demanded from the doorway of the kitchen.

"I mean, how long had it been since you and David had made love?"

Amy's face grew warm.

"Well?" Selma persisted.

"Sex isn't everything."

"Yeah. Maybe. But I've always believed that husbands and wives don't start wandering until the path they're following gets rocky and fades. That goes for my own marriage as well. No sense in denying that I had lots of warning before Gary decided to test the waters elsewhere. The bimbo that he slept with couldn't have snapped him up if he hadn't been available."

Amy sighed and slumped against the kitchen doorframe. Selma's words carried the sting of truth, but it was easier to hate Lydia than to examine her own less-than-perfect marriage. Finally, she surrendered with a rueful smile to Selma's knowing gaze. "I guess I'll have to grant you that." She set down her wine, determined to throw off the depression that had clung to her since the McCoy wedding. "Where's the cover for the grooming table? It's the only thing left to do before we set up the booths tomorrow."

"Don't you touch that cover. I told you I'd finish them both. It's the least I can do, considering you've let me sponge off you for the last month. Besides, you're a disaster with a needle and thread."

"I'm not that bad. Besides—"

Amy's comment was interrupted by a mournful howl. Her brows inched upward.

"Piggy and Molly are in the backyard," Selma explained.

"That was not a corgi howl."

Selma offered a hesitant, guilt-ridden smile. "Wolves?"

"In the garage?"

Amy led the way through the kitchen, out the back door, and across the patio to the stairs leading up to Selma's apartment. The door to the apartment was unlocked. They were greeted in Selma's living room by a beautiful tricolor collie, who let loose one more howl of joyful hello.

"Selma, you didn't!"

"Well, I did," Selma admitted with a grimace. "How do you expect me to have a collie booth in the festival if I don't have a collie to show off? Raven's just sitting around the house . . . Gary's house—" she added bitterly, "doing nothing, going nowhere, getting old before his time because he never gets any exercise. I don't care if Gary's fancy lawyer did get him temporary custody."

"You kidnapped him."

"Kidnapped is such a harsh word. I borrowed him." In response to Amy's accusing glare, Selma's chin thrust forward. "I'm Ray's mother. I picked him from the litter. I raised him, trained him, and I should be able to take him to the Scottish festival."

"You don't think Gary will know who took him?"

"So what if he does? We're going to be gone all weekend, and he doesn't know where in Estes Park we're staying."

"What about the festival?"

"That cheap bastard won't pay fifteen dollars admission to give me a hard time about Raven. And if he does, he wouldn't dare make a scene in front of all those people. He'd look like the jackass that he is." Selma tapped her chest, inviting the big collie to jump up and give her a hug. "You're my boy," she murmured into his lush white ruff. "Aren't you, sweetie."

"I hope you know what you're doing."

"Loosen up, Amy. You worry too much. It's time I showed the creep that he can't walk on me all the time. The lesson will improve his character." Selma smiled at Amy's cynical expression. "Don't give me that 'the only good man is a gelded man' look. The difference between you and me, Amy, is that when my husband made a fool of me, I got mad at him; when your husband made a fool of you, you got mad at the whole male population."

Amy dismissed the accusation with a contemptuous huff.

"Yeah, right," Selma said. "I know your pat answer: You can live without men, and men are welcome to live without you. Just remember," she warned with a grin, "sex may not be everything, but it's a lot."

ESTES PARK, COLORADO, is a colorful little town sitting at the base of some of the most spectacular peaks in the Rocky Mountains. During the summer months, the place is a boom town owing to its strategic location at the entrance to Rocky Mountain National Park. The shops, which sell everything from homemade fudge to fine Native American artwork, seldom see a shortage of customers.

During one special weekend of the summer, however, Estes Park is host to a frenzy of celebration that is matched at no other time. Every year on the weekend following Labor Day, the Long's Peak Scottish Highland Festival brings a thousand Celtic celebrants to town, along with tens of thousands of non-Celtic spectators who come to sample good Scottish whiskey, stuff themselves with homemade scones and shortbread, and watch the clans indulge in Highland antics.

Dogs of Celtic descent join the festivities right alongside kilted caber tossers and Irish dancers. Irish wolfhounds, mastiffs, golden retrievers, collies, shelties, Old English sheepdogs, border collies, Irish setters, English cocker spaniels, cairn terriers, and many more march to the bagpipes, demonstrate their herding and hunting expertise, meet the public, and have an all-around good time. The canine entry this year included four Pembroke Welsh corgis. Three belonged to Amy Cameron, and two were busy winding Amy's legs in a tangle of leashes as she stood in the mass of dogs lined up to join the festival's opening parade down Main Street.

"Drover! Would you leave Piggy alone, please!" Amy fixed Drover with a stern glare as she extricated herself from the latest tangle. Three corgis in the parade were two too many, she admitted, but leaving any two alone together in the limited space of the motor home would be an invitation to a bloody free-for-all. The kennels that would have kept them separated were in her minivan, which, closed and locked, was too hot even on a cloudy day to be safe for a dog.

So she was stuck with a goofy, hormonal Drover, a contrary Piggy, who led the poor boy on just so she could turn her teeth on him when he came within striking range, and a disdainful Molly, who sat as far away as her leash allowed, regarding the chaos with disdainful brown eyes.

Drover whined and prepared for the next round. Piggy curled her lip in anticipation of wreaking mayhem.

"Save your energy, you two! You have over a mile to walk on those short little legs, and you're supposed to show your best face to the public. So behave!"

Drover sat back regretfully. Piggy gave Amy a frosty look, and Molly continued to glare.

At that moment, Selma pushed through the crowd of people and dogs, a perfectly behaved Raven walking sedately at her side. "Hi, you guys. Long wait, huh? It's always this way. They tell you to be here at the park at eight-thirty, but the parade never starts moving until after nine."

The parade had been moving past them on a street beside the park for the last ten minutes, but they had to wait with the dog unit to join the march in their designated place. Selma started to say something else but paused to listen as one of the passing bands, spectacular in dress uniforms, kilts, sporrans, boots, and bagpipes, launched into a loud march. The skirl of bagpipes and heart-pounding cadence of drums echoed off the buildings.

"God, I love this!" Selma declared when conversation was once more possible. "Those pipes give me goosebumps. There's just something about them."

"And the handsome fellows in kilts have nothing to do with those goosebumps?" Amy inquired.

Selma grinned. "They're part of the color, you know? That's the band from Australia. Guys with Aussie accents in kilts! I may have died and gone to heaven! And speaking of handsome guys—that's why I came trekking back. Your vet is here."

"My vet?"

"Jeff Berenger. In the toothsome flesh. I heard someone call him by name. He's in the row right in front of me with two border collies."

"That's nice."

"I thought you said he wasn't cute."

"Cute is not the word I would use to describe him."

"Okay. Split hairs if you want. He's handsome. Nice looking. A hunk."

"I don't know that I'd go that far."

Selma lifted an audacious brow. "I'd go as far as it takes."

Amy rolled her eyes. "Then why don't you?"

"Why don't I what?"

"Go get him, girl. Here's a perfect opportunity to get acquainted with the man. He's right in front of you in the column."

"Uh . . ." For once, Selma was nonplussed.

"It's not like you're really married anymore."

A cloud darkened Selma's face, almost as dark as the clouds that threatened above the mountains. Amy instantly regretted she'd lost her patience.

"I'm sorry, Selma."

"What for?" Selma smiled brightly, but the brightness was forced. "You're right, and maybe I will, since you don't want him. I'd better get back in my place. We'll be leaving right after this clan that's going by. I'll see you at the car after the parade."

"Yeah. See you there." She watched Selma and Raven make their way toward the front of the column, where collies were stationed in the alphabetical lineup. Drover looked up at her in inquiry.

"Open mouth, insert foot," she told him. "I'm getting good at that, aren't I."

Drover gave her a doggy grin of agreement. Molly sighed and settled down for a nap on the cool asphalt, and Piggy sat stiffly with her back to the crowd, a picture of canine contempt.

"Okay! Come on, you three. We're moving."

The column of dogs and handlers filed out onto the street behind the massed representatives of the Douglas clan. The wail of bagpipes and the beat of drums filled the little valley and climbed the heights of the surrounding mountains. The sound and pageantry did give one goosebumps, Amy admitted. She wondered suddenly if Jeff Berenger had any Scottish blood in his veins and what he might look like in a kilt. Drover woofed and glanced up at her, his jaws gaping in a silly grin.

"You're right," Amy laughed. "I've been spending too much time with Selma."

WHERE'S THE SPCA when you need them? I ask you, was this any way to treat man's—or in this case, woman's—best friend? It was cold on that street! And it rained. Okay, it didn't really rain. The clouds descended in a miserable drizzle. And there I was, walking along only two inches from the cold, wet pavement on account of the deformed build of this stupid corgi body. My feet got muddy and my hair was soaked. My ears cringed from those damned wheezing bagpipes, and my nose smarted from an overload of scents from two hundred other dogs and what seemed like a billion people.

Anyone who still believes dogs are smart should take a serious look at the Scottish festival parade in Estes Park. Did those dogs have the basic intelligence to know that they were being abused? No. The Irish setters pranced along with their tails wagging. The collies cavorted, including that stupid Raven. The bearded collies bounced and the West Highland white terriers twinkled through the mud as though their snowy coats were immune to dirt and wet. Not one of them had sense enough to come out of the rain, and the people were as stupid as the dogs.

That's all the people I'm referring to, not just the dog people! The bagpipers went on puffing into their soggy pipes, the clans kept marching, smiling, and waving, and the guy on a horse who looked like he'd ridden right out of the movie Braveheart just wrapped his tartan more tightly about his shoulders and rode on. And unbelievably broad those shoulders were. Just because I'm a dog these days doesn't mean I don't notice such things.

Crowds lined the parade route. From my point of view it looked like a crowd of billions. They smiled, waved, oooohed over this, and aaaahed over that like so many morons. At least they had umbrellas, which is more than I can say for myself. They seemed particularly entranced by the dog unit, which is another point indicating their lack of good sense. We corgis got our share of attention. Exclamations of "How cute!" and "Aren't they adorable!" pelted us as we walked by, along with less complimentary comments on short legs and big ears. Molly and Drover, the stupid twits, strutted on even when people laughed at them. The other member of our corgi row, a husky tricolor boy who, as far as I'm concerned, looked more like a dachshund-collie mix than a proper corgi, stuck to his own side of the street with his master, who wasn't much better looking than his dog. He'd made eyes at Amy when the parade first started—the man, not the dog. That was no surprise. Amy had always been one to attract dorks, even in grade school. In high school, her one and only semiserious boyfriend had been the vice president of the chemistry club. Sheesh!

Speaking of dorks, Jeff Berenger definitely would have been needed in a veterinary capacity if I'd had to walk one more step after that parade ended. Fortunately, my barrage of plaintive looks convinced Amy to carry me to the car, and a short while later I was comfortably situated on a soft rug inside our little portable exercise pen, which was snug and dry at the back of Amy's booth at the festival grounds. A shade covering and side tarps shielded the booth, Amy's exhibits, and most *importantly, me, from the weather, which, with typical Colorado fickleness, had turned sunny as soon as the parade ended.*

Perhaps because the sun was out and the thermometer was climbing, I wasn't too unhappy with my present situation. No one bothered me as I rested on my soft little carpet. Spectators filed past the booth in droves—it's amazing how many people these quaint open-air events attract. I've never understood it, but then, my taste has always run to the more mature forms of entertainment: night clubs, film festivals, and the like. Running about in kilts, tossing telephone poles (I think they call them cabers), and high-stepping in some long-forgotten form of folk dance is rather childish, to my way of thinking. And the fuss the spectators were making over the dogs was just silly.

The dog unit had an area all to itself in one corner of the festival grounds, where Amy and her fellow dog addicts had erected their booths and exhibits to—as they will officiously inform you—educate the public. In the same area, the dogs were given a chance to show off in terrier races, hunting tests, and a herding demonstration.

As I mentioned before, people flocked to see the dogs, and spectators crowded two or three deep around both Amy's exhibit and Selma's collie booth next door. Fortunately, no one bothered me. Drover, who is an exhibitionist if I've ever met one, sat on the grooming table out front accepting attention from all and sundry. Molly did her part by slavishly greeting anyone who ventured close to our little pen, and I lay on my rug glaring at anyone who even thought about coming close. If I wasn't a model representative of the breed, then whose fault was that? I didn't ask to be dragged to that ridiculous festival and exhibited like some sideshow freak.

Once I started recovering from the parade, however, I noticed the abundance of men who were coming by the booth. A number of them were nice looking, even those who were kilted up like some broguish Highlander. I must admit, the full Scottish regalia does something for a man. The kilt even lends a paunchy graybeard a certain manly air. If I could find a fellow here who liked his women sweet but dull, I might be able to accomplish my damned mission and be done with it. After all, how could Amy resist a man who got his kicks from dressing in a plaid skirt and throwing telephone poles? I could. That's for sure. But as I've explained before, the opposite sex is not a subject about which Amy is smart, so one of these guys could be a natural for her.

One problem stumped me for a while, however. I couldn't very well review the likely candidates while sitting in that pen. A bit of a cruise around the festival grounds was called for, and that was going to require an escape.

My opportunity came in the midafternoon, when one of the people wandering the festival grounds in historic costume provided a distraction at Selma's booth and diverted everyone's attention from the corgi prison. Ray was posing on Selma's grooming table, slobbering on passersby, when up walked this rather large woman in an elaborate long gown that looked like something Queen Elizabeth might wear—the first Queen Elizabeth, that is. When I say this woman was large, I don't mean fat. I mean well endowed, a feature that was made even more pronounced by the décolletage of her gown and the corset that nearly pushed her over the edge, if you get my meaning. She came up to Raven spouting exclamations of how beautiful the collie was, and Raven, being a collie, put that long nose of his in the most interesting place he could find. Guess where? Collies are like that. Rude. Those long noses are forever being shoved into unmentionable places.

The lady on the receiving end of Raven's intimate sniff squealed in surprise, then laughed uproariously. "Ooooo! He likes me!"

People can make such idiots of themselves over dogs.

Anyway, the bimbo babbled on endlessly about how handsome Raven was. Selma and Amy were understandably embarrassed by Ray's social blunder, so they gave his victim the honor of their undivided attention. And I got busy digging out of the pen while Molly watched me in horrified disbelief.

The task wasn't difficult once I set my mind to it. Beneath the carpet was damp grass and dirt that were easily removed. Before a minute passed, I had excavated a hole just large enough to let me crawl under the wire barrier. From there it was easy to sneak under the back tarp of the booth to freedom. I could tell from the look on Molly's face that thoughts of alerting the warden were passing her mind, but she kept silent. No doubt she was glad to see me go and hoped my escape would end in an intimate encounter with a corgi-flattening truck.

Freedom at last! I was giddy with it. The sun was pleasant, the smells from the food-vending booths tempted my palate, and the grass beckoned for a session of rolling. I had to sternly remind myself that I had a mission to complete. Never again would I have an opportunity to look over so many suckers who might be maneuvered into falling for Amy. So many men; so little time. I trotted off with hopes high.

"PIGGY'S GONE!" AMY stared unbelieving at the mound of excavated dirt and grass. "That brat! She dug out! I don't believe it."

"At least Molly had sense enough not to follow," Selma said.

"That little stinker is going to be in such trouble when I find her!" Amy lifted Drover from the grooming table and lowered him into the pen beside a smug-looking Molly. "At least she's wearing a collar with ID. I'm going to look for her. Would you move the pen away from that hole so Molly and Drover don't get the same idea?"

"I'll go with you. You can go one direction. I'll go the other."

"We can't both leave. Someone has to watch the booths and the dogs."

"I'll get Joyce from the cairn terrier booth next door."

The search duo canvassed the dog unit, Amy on one side of the grounds, Selma on the other. Piggy wasn't gate-crashing the terrier races or trying to run a rodent to ground in the terrier maze. She wasn't harassing the sheep in the herding arena or standing in line at the portapotties. Amy signaled Selma from across the booth area to extend the search outside the dog unit.

For the first few minutes, they had no luck. No fat corgi waddled through the clan areas, dodged the caber toss, or jigged with the dancers. Approaching the central exhibit field, where a combination of three different bagpipe bands were performing for a packed grandstand, Amy finally spotted a little brown body darting between the legs of a group of kilted clansmen.

"Selma! Over here!" Amy called, then ran toward the spot where the sly furry wench had disappeared among the legs of a band waiting to march onto the field. The dog wasn't visible, but the ripple of reaction to her passing was, and Amy plowed through the kilted ranks close behind her. "Excuse me! Pardon me! I'm so sorry, but my dog . . ."

"Is that your wee dog, lass?" someone asked with a rich Scottish burr. "She's runnin' off that way!"

"Over there!" Selma cried from close behind Amy. "There she—oh no!"

Both women winced as Piggy cut sharply across the path of a fellow strolling from between two sections of the stands. She caught him directly in the shins, toppling him amid a flurry of flying plaid.

Amy was first to reach the hapless victim. "Omigosh! I'm sorry!" She offered him a hand up.

"Stupid damned dog! Haven't you ever heard of a leash?"

"I'm so sorry."

The fellow gave Amy a scowl but accepted the offer of her hand to get up from the ground.

"Are you all right?"

"Of course I'm not all right. My ass is sore, my kilt's near ruined, and all because you can't keep control of your damned dog. If I had my way . . ."

Amy cringed inwardly as Piggy's victim berated her. The stupid dog would choose to trip a fellow who didn't like dogs, didn't like the way the festival was being run, and didn't hesitate to grab an excuse to let everyone know exactly how he felt. Piggy sat and watched as Amy was verbally pilloried, calmly composed as if she hadn't just left British Columbia's finest marching band in disarray, led two very angry and embarrassed women on a foolish chase across the festival grounds, and caused a very cranky clansman to be picking grass and dirt from his bare knees.

Finally, a bystander came to Amy's rescue.

"Enough, Durwood," the man said. "Cut the lady some slack."

Durwood looked ready to give the intruder a taste of his ire as well, but he did a double take and hastily shut his mouth.

"Dinna fash yerself, Durwood," the peacemaker said with a teasing grin. " 'Tis na a good Sco'ish kilt if it canna take a bit of rollin' in the grass."

"Hmmph!" was Durwood's comment. "I guess so. Just keep that ugly beast on a leash from now on."

"Oh, I will," Amy assured him. "She won't cause any more trouble." She clipped the leash to Piggy's collar with a definitive snap, then dug a business card from her jeans pocket. "Just send me the cleaning bill for the kilt."

The surly victim took the card and stomped away, leaving Amy looking up at burnished golden hair glittering in the sunlight. Her rescuer was tall, with strong legs that were positively made to be displayed by a kilt, and broad shoulders that filled out a jacket that was tailored to make the most of an impressive physique.

"Amy Cameron? Is that you?"

"Well . . . yes. Omigod." Suddenly the face looking down at her was more than handsome: It was familiar. "How embarrassing! Tom Gordon. Hi. I haven't seen you since . . . since way before. . . ."

"It has been a long time, hasn't it?" he said, smoothly deflecting the conversation away from his one-time acquaintance and business associate, David Cameron. Amy was grateful for his consideration. Not everyone would have realized that after six months, the pain of David's betrayal had scarcely faded. Not everyone would have realized the mere speaking of his name still caused her to wince.

"I didn't know you came to these things."

He winked and launched into a very good imitation of the Scottish burr. "Well'na, lass, I'm a Gordon, ye see. We Gordons have always held the auld country in our hearts, na matter how far from the lochs and glens and highlands we stray. And we're verra, verra guid at rescuing bonnie lassies from irate ne'er-do-wells."

"Oh! Very good!" Selma applauded.

Amy raised a brow, and Tom grinned. "I got roped into announcing some of the ceremonies here this weekend. I recognized you from across the green and decided you needed a helping hand."

"Well!" Amy said, feeling awkward. "Thank you. It's awfully good to see you again."

"It's great seeing you," he replied. "You're looking wonderful."

Amy bit her lip. Her face was still hot with embarrassment. "I'd better get this girl back to where she can't do any more damage. Thanks again, Tom."

"Don't mention it. We really should get together sometime."

"Right. We should."

"Just lock up that cute wee beastie," he advised, reverting to his Scottish burr, "before she makes the fairgrounds look like Culloden Moor."

Amy gave the obligatory chuckle. "Right. You can be sure of it." She tugged on Piggy's leash and headed back toward the dog unit. The little brown miscreant followed sedately at heel between Amy and Selma.

"You are in such trouble, you little beast!" Amy warned the dog.

"Did you see what she was doing?" Selma asked once they were out of Tom Gordon's earshot. "I swear she was cruising around looking up men's kilts."

"Stop laughing," Amy said, choking back her own laughter. "You're just jealous you don't have her strategic viewpoint."

"She's a trollop."

"She's a menace. And she's spending the rest of the festival in a locked kennel."

Piggy trotted along, tongue lolling in a canine grin. As she glanced back toward Tom Gordon, who was now lost in the crowd, her short-legged gait acquired a satisfied swagger.

FOUR

♥

AMY'S THREAT OF retribution was short lived. Piggy was a master of the plaintive look, and Amy was a sucker for such things. It was a character flaw she admitted to readily and succumbed to just as readily.

Therefore, when Amy left the booth later that afternoon for a photographic cruise around the festival grounds, Piggy, rather than being shut in her escape-proof kennel, walked beside her on a leash.

Their first stop was the Irish setter booth. Amy had made an appointment to photograph one particularly sweet-faced setter female against the background of an Irish coat of arms the booth was displaying. Calendars and dog-fancier magazines were a large market for Amy's photographs, and the Scottish festival always presented abundant photographic opportunities.

The lovely setter girl was a cooperative model. Getting her to pose in a fetching manner took only a few minutes. From there they moved on to several other booths where people were willing to have their dogs pose for the camera. Piggy was a picture of decorum, sitting quietly while Amy worked.

"I can't figure you out," Amy told Piggy after the dog had stayed at her side in a mannerly fashion while she snapped shots of the terrier races. "One moment you're cutting a swath through the festival, raising havoc and hackles; the next moment you're a poster dog for a dog obedience society. I never know what to expect from you."

Piggy accepted Amy's frown with an air of total unconcern.

"You are the strangest dog I've ever met."

"She certainly is the strangest looking."

The voice came from behind them, from the border collie booth. Amy had forgotten that Jeff Berenger's booth was so close to the terrier racing chutes.

"Hello, stranger," Jeff greeted her.

Amy smiled in spite of herself. He was an appealing sight, half sitting on his display table, long legs stretched out in front of him, breeze-ruffled hair shot through with coppery sun-sparks. "Hello, yourself," Amy replied. "Don't be making fun of the royal breed, now. You know the British monarchy favors them."

"British royalty favors a number of things that are worth making fun of. But it wasn't the breed I was insulting. Just that one. I saw some of her earlier antics. Actually, I was about to leap to your aid if Tom Gordon hadn't. I thought that poor fellow Piggy tripped was going to use a certain deserving corgi for his own personal caber toss."

"I know. It was nice of Tom to come to our rescue."

"You know Mr. *Eye on Denver* from somewhere?"

"Why do you say it like that? *Eye on Denver*'s a good show."

Jeff shrugged. "It's not as bad as some of them. I just get tired of the media's emphasis on sensationalism. I think some TV newspeople would incite their own newsworthy mayhem if they had to to get a story."

"Tom's not like that." Amy got to her feet from where she had been sitting cross-legged on the grass.

"He's a nice guy. Used to buy all his cars from my husband. Every year he'd trade in his old BMW and drive out with a brand new one. David ended up sponsoring a race car that Tom used to drive."

"Try convincing Denver's mayor Tom Gordon is a nice guy."

"Yeah. Well, apparently Tom has no patience with politicians, but you can hardly fault him for that. Besides," she informed him with a slight smirk, "he thinks Piggy's cute."

"That just shows what kind of judgment he has."

"Yeah," she agreed with a quiet laugh, then grimaced as she brushed the grass from the seat of her jeans. "The grass is still wet."

"Need any help with that?" Jeff asked with a wicked lift of one brow.

She glared. He grinned unrepentantly. "That's a nice-looking camera you have there."

Amy glanced down at the Nikon. "It's not the best you can buy, but it's not bad. Photography is how I pay the mortgage."

"Is that why you've been taking mug shots of all those dogs?"

"Good dog photos are very salable items."

"In that case, I'm hurt you didn't ask Spot or Darby to model. I realize border collies aren't the Christie Brinkleys of the dog world, but brains should count for something."

Amy held out her hand to Darby, who lay placidly on top of her fiberglass kennel. The black-and-white border collie sniffed her fingers politely. It struck Amy as strange that she was so much more comfortable communicating with the dog than the master. Normally she didn't have this problem with people. She was an outgoing person, seldom at a loss for words. But talking to Jeff

Berenger made her feel as though she was once again a lumpy, awkward teen.

It wasn't that she didn't like Jeff. What was there not to like, after all? He was friendly, intelligent, nice looking, liked dogs, obviously liked her. And if he was a bit flirtatious, that was easy to forgive. She was a bit over-sensitive to such things these days, but looked at objectively, the flirtation was more of a compliment than an annoyance.

Perhaps the problem lay not in her disliking Jeff, but liking him too much when she didn't want to like him at all. He'd gone out with Lydia, but as Selma had pointed out, any man with a complete set of chromosomes would go out with Lydia given the opportunity. That was simply the way men were put together.

"Is this Darby or Spot?" Amy asked. "They look so much alike, it's hard to tell the difference."

"That's Darby. She's big for a seven-month-old pup. She's going to be taller than her mom."

"I would like to photograph these girls, but with some action going on. Action is where border collies shine."

"They do at that. Darby's testing on sheep for the first time this afternoon. Maybe you could get some good shots there."

"What time?"

"Three o'clock, supposedly, but I doubt they're running on time. I hope not, because I have to be at the grandstand at two-thirty to release Fred."

"Fred?"

"The hawk you met last Friday. He's going to be launched back into the wild today to the accompaniment of bagpipes."

"That ought to be something. Do you mind if I photograph the event."

"Be my guest. I'll even buy the photos from you and put them on the clinic wall."

"No need. I'll give you copies."

"It's a deal. Meanwhile, would you like some lunch? They're selling a mean bowl of Irish stew on the other side of the grounds. I could get someone to watch my booth if you'd like to get some."

For a moment Amy was tempted. Something inside her wanted to discover why a man of Jeff Berenger's obvious talents was living in a run-down house and making a halfhearted living from a profession that could have made him a comfortable income. She wanted to talk to him about why he rehabilitated injured hawks, why he took the time to treat hurt kittens for the price of a quarter, and why his two border collies—a breed noted for its restless temperament—were content to lie quietly and watch him as if he were the god of dogs.

But she didn't take the bait. Because she didn't really want to like Jeff Berenger. And discovering anything more than the very shallow acquaintance they shared might make it impossible not to like him . . . like him very, very much. Amy didn't need such a complication to burden a heart still bruised from past mistakes. She didn't want to venture down that road again. Not for a very, very long time, if ever.

"I . . . uh . . . thanks, Jeff, but I have a sandwich back at my booth, and it'll be soggy if I leave it until tomorrow."

He didn't seem surprised at her refusal. Neither did he seem discouraged. "You managed to fight through the crowds of tourists at the grocery store to get sandwich makings? You're tougher than you look."

Amy laughed. "I'm not that tough. I have my motor home parked in a campground just above town. It has enough food in the fridge to feed every bagpiper between here and Scotland." She hesitated, realizing suddenly that after such a statement, not inviting Jeff to share would be the next thing to being rude—especially after he'd been nice enough to treat Piggy for free. "Uh . . . why don't you come to dinner tonight," she offered lamely. "It wouldn't be much more than a frozen pizza and maybe a salad. We have lots of food in the fridge, but it's not necessarily quality food."

He brightened. "Any kind of food sounds good to me."

Amy began to wonder about her sanity. Why on earth had she done that? She just couldn't resist getting herself into trouble.

"Darby and I will see you at the herding test, then."

"Yeah." She gave him a weak smile. "Don't tell Darby I'll be taking pictures. It might give her stage fright."

"I won't. Oops!" Jeff had started to move away from the table, but Piggy stood in front of him, blocking the way. During the conversation, she'd been quiet and well mannered, wandering leisurely to the end of the leash, sniffing the grass, sitting in the shade of the table, and generally behaving with un-Piggy-like courtesy. Now she jumped up to place her front feet on Jeff's knees, which was as high as she could reach.

Jeff laughed at the fresh dog signature on his jeans. "Dirty paws alert. Where'd she pick up that mud?"

"Piggy, get off! You know better than that!"

Amy pulled the corgi back as Jeff stepped around. Suddenly, he froze. "Uh-oh."

They looked down, both grimacing at the freshly deposited mess he'd stepped in. Amy's face flooded with heat. "If I didn't know the limitations of canine intellect, I'd swear that was deliberate."

Piggy's jaw gaped in a toothy grin.

"And here I thought only cats could be diabolical,"

Jeff said ruefully. Then he chuckled. "Thank you, Miss Pudgy."

"I'll get some paper towels."

"Don't bother. I've got some right here."

"Then I'll . . . uh . . . see you later."

"Yeah. Later."

It had to be an accident, Amy told herself as she headed back toward her own booth. It had to be. Dogs did not deliberately plant land mines and then maneuver the intended victim to step in them. They just didn't, no matter how it looked.

Amy's preoccupation with Piggy's Machiavellian talents, along with the crowds blocking the view into the dog booths, kept her from realizing that all was not well at the collie display until she elbowed her way into her own booth. Molly and Drover greeted her with twitching little rumps, but Selma was so busy she didn't even note her return. Gary, the soon-to-be ex-husband and current court-appointed guardian of one tricolor collie named Raven, had come to pay a call, and from the tone of the conversation in progress, Amy gathered he was not happy with Selma.

"I could have you arrested, you lame-brained bimba! You know that?"

"Get real!" Hands on hips, jaw thrust forward in challenge, Selma's pose was a picture of "come get me if you dare." She spit out words like bullets. "You're going to send the cops out to arrest me over a dog? I don't think so."

"Illegal breaking and entering."

"I have a key, Mister Smart-Ass. And until the house is sold it's just as much mine as yours."

"Dognapping."

"My own dog? Raven's registration lists my name as owner."

"The court says he stays with me until the final decree."

"Only because I'd just moved out and didn't have a place to live yet. Now I do, and it's a place where I can keep Ray."

"Over my dead body."

"Don't tempt me." Selma picked up the hammer they had used to pound in tent stakes. "Touch that dog and I'll break your damned arm." An uneasy murmur ran through the crowd, which had swelled to a small mob. Dogs were interesting, but a real live soap opera was even better.

"Okay! That's enough." Amy pointed a finger at Selma. "You! Put down the hammer."

Selma smirked, set the hammer down within easy reach, and gave it a fond pat.

"And you!" The finger swung in Gary's direction. "You are not going to take Raven away from the festival. You know where he is, and you know he's safe. Just let it lie until you two can battle this out in a less public place." Her eyes swept over the growing crowd, and Gary glanced around as if just then realizing how much attention they had attracted.

"I suppose you're the one Selma's living with." Gary's voice crackled with dislike. "I should have known you'd butt in. You're always sticking your nose where it's not wanted."

Selma leaped in. "You're a fine one to talk about sticking your nose where it doesn't belong. If you'd kept your nose where it belonged, along with some other parts of your anatomy, none of this would have happened."

"And if you'd spent more time with me and less with your boss at the store—"

"Oh, don't start that again!"

"I'll—"

The disputed collie sat on the grooming table, watching with worried eyes as his parents traded insults. He barked a sharp rebuke.

Amy lifted her hands in a helpless gesture. "Could you two maybe finish this later?"

Gary had the grace to flush with embarrassment. Selma bit her lip and turned her back. Amy thanked God that the two didn't have any kids of the two-legged variety. If they couldn't be civilized over possession of a dog, she'd hate to witness the mayhem that would have resulted from a custody battle over real children.

For now, though, the battle ended in a draw. Gary gave Ray an affectionate pat and promised Selma, "We'll settle this next week, Selma. Just see if we don't. And don't you forget to give him his rawhide every day."

"Well duh!" Selma made a face as he disappeared into the crowd. "As if I would!"

"I warned you that you were going to get in trouble." Amy stuffed Piggy into her kennel and gave Selma an I-told-you-so look.

"Gary's the one who ought to be in trouble! He's the one who was hopping into every woman's bed but mine."

"Yeah. I know."

"You're just lucky you didn't have to go through a divorce."

Amy's lips tightened, and Selma grimaced.

"I'm sorry, Amy. I didn't mean that the way it sounded. Mad as I am at Gary, I'd be heartsick if anything happened to him. I don't know why. . . . He's such a prick. But I would."

Amy sighed and slumped into her canvas camp chair. "I know how you feel." She stared into space for a moment, then grimaced. "I miss David, Selma. In spite of everything, I miss him. And I miss Lydia, too, damn her treacherous little heart."

"Of course you miss David. But eventually you'll find someone who'll love you like you deserve. Me too," Selma added with a note of bitter determination.

"Sometimes I wonder if love really exists—I mean the kind of forever love between a man and woman that you read about in romance novels."

"Goodness! Aren't you gloomy! You've even got Piggy depressed. I've never seen her look so sad."

Piggy gazed at them mournfully from behind the sturdy wire door of her kennel.

"She just doesn't like being locked up."

"Not so. You've depressed her with all your gloom and doom. I'm the one who should be moaning, seeing that I'm the one who just had the fight."

"You never moan, Selma. You're irrepressible."

Selma smiled blithely. "I know. It's great being shallow. Eat something. You'll feel better. It's nearly one-thirty."

"One-thirty! Oh my gosh! They'll be turning Fred loose!"

"What?"

Amy grabbed her camera and an extra roll of film.

"Jeff Berenger's releasing a rehabilitated hawk in a ceremony at the grandstand. I told him I'd take photos."

Selma's brows rose knowingly. "You don't say?"

"I've got to go. Put a bucket of water in Piggy's kennel, will you?"

"Sure. Here." Selma thrust a half-eaten sandwich at her. "Take this with you. I'll make myself another one."

"Thanks." Amy took the sandwich and ran.

"Go, go, go, girl!" Selma grinned as Amy rounded the terrier chutes at a trot and disappeared behind the herding arena. "You don't want to miss sexy Dr. Berenger and his bird. No indeed."

♥   ♥   ♥

WHEN AMY ARRIVED at the central exhibit grounds, out of breath and breaking a sweat, every seat in the grandstand was taken. The open areas between the sections of the stadium were jammed as well. Stuck at the back of the latecomer crowd, Amy craned to see over the people in front of her. She heard Tom Gordon's golden baritone recounting the story of Jeff's hawk and relating it to efforts of other volunteers all over the country who rehabilitated injured wild birds to be released back into the wild.

"This will never do," Amy complained to herself. A wall of bodies blocked her view—and that of her camera. " 'Scuse me. Pardon me. Official photographer coming through." It wasn't much of a lie, Amy told herself as she elbowed her way through the crowd. She was almost official. After all, Jeff had asked her to take photos, and he was official. "Coming through! Oops! Sorry about those toes."

She reached the front in time to hear Tom's admonition for the audience to be quiet. They didn't want the hawk to be alarmed by so many human voices during this maiden flight, he warned.

Amy chuckled wryly. As if the grandstands holding their collective breath was going to make any difference in the noise level of the festival, not to mention the assembled bagpipe bands who prepared to wail the poor bird on its way to freedom. If Fred was the nervous sort, he was going to soar straight up until he could grab a cloud to hide behind.

Her cynicism left her, however, as the pipes began a stirring rendition of "Amazing Grace." No matter how many times she heard it, "Amazing Grace" played by a bagpipe band never failed to choke her up. She wasn't alone. Several thousand spectators held their breath as the hymn swelled over the field and rose toward the blue Colorado sky.

Amy focused her telephoto on the stage, where Jeff Berenger stood with Tom Gordon. Between the two men was a large cage where Fred the hawk ruffled his feathers and cocked his head as though listening to the music. Jeff looked entirely serious. He was afraid for his bird, Amy realized, much as a father might fear for a son he was sending off into the world. How could one help but like a man who could form such a bond with a wild bird, even if he had once dated a tramp?

She snapped some photos of Tom and Jeff with the cage, then hastily loaded a new roll of film. Jeff opened the cage and stood back. Fred didn't hesitate, but lunged for freedom, taking wing almost before he was clear of his prison. Amy snapped a frame of the bird launching himself from the stage, then almost forgot her camera as the magnificent hawk powered his way into the air. Contrary to Amy's expectation, Fred did not hightail it for the first cloud but rose gradually over the field and swung into a broad, low circuit, as if taunting the crowd with his freedom. For those few moments the hawk, the enthralled audience, and the music all seemed to connect in a powerful explosion of emotion. Amy overpowered her own swelling sentiment, snapped on a wide-angle lens, and aimed the camera at the gliding hawk, the tear-streaked faces of the spectators, and finally, as Fred completed his last victory pass and headed for the blue, she changed back to the telephoto to capture Jeff Berenger. He was probably the only person there whose sentiment didn't run down his cheeks in tears. He looked a bit sad but infinitely proud. The expression on his face as he watched the hawk climb toward the sky made something in Amy's heart move.

The woman sitting beside Amy took out a handkerchief and blew her nose in a loud honk. "God!" she declared. "That was one of the most beautiful things I've ever seen."

"Yes, it was, wasn't it?"

It was beautiful, moving, special, Amy admitted, and she suddenly wanted to tell Jeff Berenger just how special. He was no longer on the platform, however. Amy remembered then that Darby was due at the herding arena. She'd promised to get that on film as well. Come to think of it, Jeff Berenger had managed to tie up a good part of her day.

Jeff and Darby were already in the arena when Amy arrived. Four big ewes were huddled against the fence as far away from dogs and people as they could get. Jeff stood in the middle of the arena with the test examiner, holding Darby on a leash. Amy was acquainted with the examiner from having entered a test the previous year. A pillar of the local Bearded Collie Club, she was at least seventy years old, seemed to have been born with a shepherd's crook in her hand, and could wrestle both the sheep and the dog if she had to. Right at that moment she was pointing an admonitory finger at Jeff, probably warning him to stay out of his dog's way and letting him know that he knew nothing about training a herding dog, no matter what he thought. Amy had been on the receiving end of that lecture herself, but Jeff exhibited much more patience.

Darby, however, did not show a similar restraint. True to her training, the young border collie sat at Jeff's side, but every muscle quivered with anxious anticipation. Her eyes didn't leave the sheep, who returned the pup's stare with stolid indifference. Amy snapped a couple of shots to capture Darby's expression—the intense focus of a creature who has suddenly discovered its place in the universal scheme of things. For a moment Amy wished that human lives could be narrowed to such joyful purpose.

The lecture came to an end, and Jeff approached the

sheep with Darby still on lead. The examiner nodded. Jeff freed the dog.

"Go fetch 'em, Darby," he said.

Darby needed no second command. She bounded forward. The sheep scattered. Barking joyfully, the pup lunged first one way and then the next while the stock milled in confusion.

Jeff shook his head. "No, Darby. Down!"

Panting, Darby immediately dropped. The sheep eyed the pup suspiciously.

Amy grinned. One never knew what to expect from the dog in a situation like this. No training was required to pass the test. The dog merely had to show an instinct to herd. Unfortunately, the only instinct Darby had displayed so far was a talent at creating chaos.

Jeff showed admirable patience with the pup. He took Darby by the collar and moved him close to one indignant ewe.

"Easy now, Darby," he said, releasing the collar. "Move 'em out."

At that point, generations of inbred instinct took over. With the first flush of excitement over, Darby began to listen to her genes and move purposefully toward the sheep. The ewes were experienced old girls, well acquainted with methods of frustrating novice sheepdogs. They bunched together next to the fence in a woolly wall of resistance. It was not for nothing, however, that border collies are renowned as the best working sheepdogs in the world, and Darby was a border collie through and through. She fixed the lead ewe with "the eye"—the instinctive border collie stare that had been known to intimidate people as well as sheep. The ewes crowded more tightly against the fence. Darby crouched and moved slowly forward, never breaking eye contact. The sheep moved.

"Atta girl, Darby. Bring 'em this way," Jeff directed.

By now the sheep had gone from sullen to apprehensive. They were more than willing to move whichever way Darby pushed them, and Darby followed Jeff's commands to take them first in one direction, then another. Finally, the examiner nodded, and Jeff told the dog to lie down.

Darby obeyed with an obvious air of disappointment. Jeff squatted down and fondled the pup's ears.

"That'll do, girl. That'll do," he said in the traditional command of release. When he looked up, his eyes found Amy leaning against the arena fence. "Did you get it?"

"Every bit of it." She went to the gate to meet him when he came out, surprised by the warmth that glowed inside her when he smiled at her.

"You did fine," she told Darby, sitting on her heels to give the youngster a hug. "You were born to work, weren't you?"

"Apparently she thinks so," Jeff said as Amy got up. "Those sheep didn't have a chance."

"Not a chance," Amy agreed with a laugh.

"You ought to run the test with one of the corgis," Jeff suggested as they walked back toward the booth area. "A couple of slots opened up from entries who pulled out at the last minute."

"Both Molly and Drover have already passed a herding instinct test."

"What about Miss Pudgy?"

"You've got to be kidding."

"She's a corgi, isn't she? Corgis are herding dogs, for all that they look like some little kid's pull toy."

"They do not! Corgis are good herding dogs."

"Is that so?"

"It certainly is."

"Then prove it," he taunted. His grin reminded Amy of a "boyfriend" she'd had in second grade. He had also looked like the devil's own imp whenever he'd dared her to race him to the schoolyard fence or climb higher on the jungle gym. She'd never been able to resist that grin, either.

"I suppose it wouldn't hurt anything," she admitted.

"She'd have fun in there. Do her good to learn that a dog's place isn't always on the couch."

"It would take more than a few sheep to convince her of that, I think."

"Tell you what, Amy. Just to make it more interesting, if Miss Pudgy can dredge up enough actual dog sense to pass that test, I'll donate two free spay or neuter surgeries to your rescue group. Now there's an offer you can't refuse."

He was right about that. "Gambling's your game, is it?"

"I figure on this one I can't lose."

"What if Piggy doesn't pass? What do you win?"

"A thick steak, done to perfection in the broiler of your motor home, served with a hot baked potato, sour cream, steamed fresh vegetable, garlic toast, and rocky road ice cream for dessert. And to make sure everything's on the up and up, your friend Selma can even chaperone. I wouldn't want you to think you were bartering away anything more than your culinary talents and the warmth of your company for a couple of hours." He lifted one brow. "Not yet, at least."

Amy laughed, knowing she'd been manipulated but not really caring. "You're on."

FIVE

THE NIGHTMARE GOT worse and worse. Just as I thought I had things well under control, Butthead Berenger goads Amy into this stupid herding business. As far as I'm concerned, sheep are filthy, stinky, boring creatures from which a wise person—or dog—should keep a good distance. But no, corgis are herding dogs. Corgis and sheep go together like Scotch and water—supposedly. That's one good reason, among many, to not be a corgi.

I didn't yet know what was up when Amy tried to entice me from my comfortable kennel, but that scalpel-happy vet was with her, grinning like a jackass, and if he was involved, I wanted no part of whatever they had in mind. Not that Amy gave my wishes any respect. Dogs never get a say in things. Have you noticed? Do this, do that, go here, go there. You can't even take a pee without permission. It's a bum deal, if you ask me, but when you're a dog, no one asks you.

"She's going to walk into that arena and be an embarrassment to her breed," Amy complained.

Arena? Now I knew something was up.

The vet from hell visibly gloated, no doubt thinking he was about to get revenge for the gift I'd left for him beside his display table.

"In that case, I hope you're a good cook."

Amy gave him a puckish face, but her eyes had a sparkle I

didn't like. How could she be paying attention to this bozo when I had just introduced her to one of the most drop-dead gorgeous studs at the festival? Tom Gordon was not only a hunk, he was a celebrity, which meant he was at least well off, if not loaded. Not that being a local TV personality matches, say, being Mel Gibson. But Tom was certainly far superior to any other man who'd ever given Amy the eye.

I didn't have long to fume about Amy's stupidity, however, for when we arrived at the arena, her intent became obvious. The smell of sheep was enough to make me wish I didn't have a nose. I hoped Stanley was perched on a cloud somewhere witnessing the abuse I was forced to endure. Maybe it would convince him that a petty sinner such as myself didn't deserve this kind of punishment. A man standing nearby with a sheltie gave me a disbelieving look as I sat in the shade beneath a table while Amy completed the test entry form. He could tell I was entirely unsuited for this kind of activity. Why couldn't Amy have his good sense?

She didn't, though, and eventually tugged on the leash to bring me from my shady refuge. Like a coach pumping up his football players, she gave me the obligatory pep talk.

"You can do this, Piggy. Make those sheep respect you. Just remember, you're descended from wolves."

If she'd known from where I'd really descended, she'd have turned up her toes in a dead faint. Unfortunately, Amy thought I was a dog and therefore legitimate prey for this kind of nonsense.

"Go get 'em, Piggy!" Selma urged.

Berenger chimed in with a sardonic send-off. "Right, Miss Pudgy. Show 'em what you're made of."

If I'd had time, I would have peed on his boot, but Amy picked me up and carried me toward the gate. I struggled briefly in her arms, but the effort did me no good.

Now, I don't want you to get the idea I was afraid of those silly ewes. Who could be afraid of an animal as stupid as a sheep? Certainly not me. Besides, I planned to stay on whichever side of the arena the sheep weren't, and I was positive the sheep would be happy to ignore me completely.

The examiner strutted up to us, thumping her shepherd's crook on the ground and giving us both a look of strained tolerance. Dogs are good at sensing attitudes; I sensed right away that this old hag was a bitch who made Miss Molly look like a Welcome Wagon hostess.

"Has she seen sheep before?" the old biddy asked Amy.

"I'm not sure. I don't think so."

"Well, set her down. Let's see what she's made of."

I was more than willing to show them what I was made of. As soon as my feet hit the dirt, I headed back toward the gate. The examiner snorted, and the crowd around the arena laughed.

"Look at those short little legs!" someone jeered.

"Is that a dog or a bratwurst?"

"The dog looks stupider than the sheep!"

That got my back up. I might be funny looking, but I was certainly not stupid. I stopped in my tracks and glared at the teenage boy who'd made the last remark. His head was shaved, a nose ring dangled from one nostril, and the crotch of his trousers hung nearly to his knees. If the boy wanted to see something both funny looking and stupid, he should look in a mirror.

The kid seemed to get the meaning behind my glare, because he jumped down from the fence and huffed away indignantly.

Well, I thought. What do you know? This staring bit does work on stupid beasts. I eyed the sheep dubiously, wondering if it wouldn't be just a tiny bit fun to get a similar response from them.

"That's it, Piggy. Go fetch'em," Amy cajoled. As if I would make a fool of myself just because she wanted me to. Still, there was something inside me that really, really wanted to show those sheep who was the superior animal in this arena. It wouldn't hurt just to show them who was boss, I reasoned.

Amy almost turned herself inside out praising my effort when I so much as moved toward the flock. Silly woman. I tuned her out. The sheep had noticed me and were digging in for a stubborn stand, I could tell. They had a nerve. Didn't they know that dogs have had the upper hand in this game for generations?

I would only allow myself one little run at them. Just one. After all, I didn't want anyone to think I was idiotic enough to buy in to this silliness.

I lunged. The huddle of sheep broke, and the biggest of the four took off by herself, a defiant look in her eye. I went after her, nipping at her heels until she turned back and joined her woolly sisters. Amy went into paroxysms of joy at the little exercise, which shows just how little it takes to please the woman. It's no wonder her record with men is so pathetic.

Getting the best of those sheep was surprisingly fun. One more little run wouldn't hurt, I told myself. So I lunged again. This time the girls behaved themselves and moved along the fence in a tight little group. Just for the hell of it I raced around and charged at their heads to make them change direction.

"Here, Piggy! Bring them here, girl."

Amy stood in the center of the arena, where the sheep definitely did not want to go. Such a challenge was hard to resist, so I decided to do this one more thing before calling it quits with the whole senseless business. This time when I charged the sheep, I stayed close to the fence. They scattered in bleating disarray. Three of them regrouped and moved toward the center. One dug in her cloven hooves and stood her ground, the same old spoiler who'd taken off on her own the first time around.

Suddenly it was no longer a game. Something in my corgi brain ignited with purpose. I dove in and nipped at the feet, but the ewe simply lowered her woolly head and fixed me with a petulant stare. The old girl was downright belligerent. She'd drawn a line in the dirt, metaphorically speaking, and she was not going to cross it.

I think I've mentioned before that corgis are bossy little creatures. Even being trapped in a corgi body with a corgi heart and a corgi brain, I hadn't realized before now just how bossy. Whatever instinct had sparked to life at the sight of the sheep now took control. The sane part of me could only watch as I dashed forward under those sharp cloven feet, a fearsome snarl erupting from my little throat, my lips drawn back from my teeth. I drew back short of actually biting the stubborn old thing. I didn't need to bite, really, for that old gal whirled around in a near panic as my teeth snapped within a scarce inch of her heels. Bleating sourly, she took off for the security of the rest of the flock, who were huddled in the center of the arena with a bemused shepherd lady and a delighted Amy. Satisfied, I plopped into the dust and lay there panting. All this running about was hard work for someone not used to operating four legs at the same time.

THE WOMAN WHO opened the door of the motor home was not the woman Jeff expected. His disappointment must have shown on his face, because Selma gave him an understanding grimace. "I'm leaving," she promised. "Right now. You two will have the place all to yourself."

"You don't have to leave. Really you don't."

"Really I do. Someone has to represent collies and corgis at the evening tattoo, you know."

At that moment, Raven pushed past her through the door and nearly knocked Jeff from the lower step.

"Raven! Reallly!" Selma scolded. "I'm sorry," she said to Jeff. "He can be a bulldozer."

"That's all right."

"Molly! Drover! Let's go, kids! Your public's waiting." She scraped shoulder-length brown hair back from her face and fastened it haphazardly with a clip. "The star gets to stay home with you guys. She's tuckered.

Five whole minutes of running, you know. We're lucky she didn't have a heart attack."

"Indeed."

"She's been enthroned on the bed since we got here. Amy!" she called into the back of the motor home. "I'm leaving with the dogs. Back about ten-thirty or eleven. Go on in," she invited Jeff. "Amy's in back, but she'll be out in a minute."

Amid a tangle of corgis and one collie, she hurried to Amy's minivan, pausing at the door with a grin and a wink. "I'll honk when I get back, just to give warning that I'm here."

"Uh . . . thanks."

"Have fun!"

A moment later, the rear wheels of the minivan spurted gravel and sped away with Selma giving him a thumbs-up through the window. Jeff shook his head and ducked through the door of the motor home, coming eye to eye with Amy.

"Oh! H-hi!" she stammered.

"Hi. Selma said to come on in."

"Of course. Have a seat."

In an oversized sweatshirt, jeans, and sneakers, with sunburned nose and cheeks, Amy looked about twelve years old. Her mop of dark curls was in disarray—genuine, not styled, but all the more charming for it. She looked flustered and a bit embarrassed.

All that was an improvement over touchy and stand-offish, Jeff mused. He was definitely making progress here.

"Something smells great," he remarked.

"Garlic bread."

"Garlic bread?"

"Can't have steak without garlic bread."

His face split in grin. "We're grilling steaks?"

She opened the microwave to reveal two thick T-bones placed safely out of the dogs' reach.

"I lost our little wager," he reminded her.

"You bet you did. But this is the least I can do for someone who just donated two free surgeries to the cause of corgi rescue."

"Well, I'm certainly not going to turn down steaks and garlic bread."

"I didn't figure you would." She opened the tiny fridge and took out a big bowl. "Besides that, we've got salad, baked potatoes, and . . ." She grinned.

"And?"

"And rocky road ice cream."

"God bless you!"

As if to ask what all the noise was, an indignant brown face appeared around the partially closed door that divided the bedroom and bathroom from the living area.

"Well! The star appears." Jeff greeted Piggy with a smile. "How does it feel to be a border collie in a corgi suit?"

"Don't insult her." Amy handed him the salad bowl and pointed him in the direction of the table. "She's still recuperating."

Piggy trotted over to Amy, her nails ticking on the linoleum floor, and looked up expectantly. Amy smiled, took a bone-shaped cookie from a jar beside the sink, and tossed it for the dog to snatch from the air. "There's a good girl. Are you a star?"

Piggy gulped down the treat and lay down with a huff of finality—right in the spot where she would be most in the way.

"She's got you pegged as a sucker," Jeff told Amy.

Amy smiled indulgently at the dog. "Only for to-day, because she worked so hard. And speaking of work, why don't you go outside and light the grill?"

"Left any gifts about that I should be wary of?" Jeff inquired of Piggy.

"That couldn't have been deliberate." Amy looked a bit sheepish, in spite of her denial. "Besides, I picked up outside."

Jeff raised a brow at Piggy, and Piggy met his gaze in unmistakable challenge. Jeff had worked with animals all his life, first on the family ranch outside of Montrose, Colorado, and during the last ten years, as a veterinarian. He seldom had difficulty communicating with a four-legged patient, though he sometimes had some trouble with their two-legged friends. Unlike most people, animals were generally straightforward about their needs, feelings, likes, and dislikes. All of them, from aardvarks to zebras, had ways to communicate that were easy to comprehend, if one paid attention. But Piggy was special. Downright uncanny.

Dinner was a welcome treat. Jeff's most nutritious meal since arriving at the festival had been a Big Mac. The steaks were cooked to perfection, mostly because he was the one who grilled them. The baked potatoes had enough sour cream piled on top to disguise the microwave flavor, the garlic bread was only lightly flavored, just as he liked it, and the salad, if plain, was crisp and fresh. Amy claimed to be a mediocre cook. Jeff didn't care. She herself made the meal special.

What was there about Amy Cameron? Jeff wondered, as he cleared the dishes and stacked them in the sink. Amy was warming to him, but it was a slow process. Since they'd met she had spurned his interest by both subtle and not so subtle signals. Over the same short period, he'd been plotting ways to keep her in his life. His latest scheme, he thought, was a stroke of genius. By donating two surgeries to a worthy cause, he'd earned both her gratitude and attention, not to mention a great steak dinner.

Usually he was not so persistent where women were concerned. But there was something about Amy that he didn't want to give up. She was pretty, it was true, but he'd dated women who were so stunning they were a feast for a man's eye, like Lydia Keane, and none of them had caught his attention as Amy had. She had a down-to-earth, unaffected look that he liked, and a very special smile. Often a mere hesitant twitch of the lips, sometimes a wry slant of humor that turned inward on herself as much as outward toward the world, rarely a full-blown beam of delight that lit her face, her eyes, and the atmosphere for a mile around her, Amy's smile was a masterpiece. Every time he saw it, Jeff felt good inside. He wanted to see it more often. He wanted to inspire it.

That was why he had finagled his way into her life, and that was why he was going to stay there for a while.

"You don't have to do the dishes." Amy emerged from the tiny closet, in which she'd been digging for a sweater to combat the cooling temperature.

"No problem," he told her.

She stepped over Piggy, who was still lying in the middle of the way, and brushed past Jeff to get to the table. The passage was narrow, and the brush a firm one. It reminded Jeff there were things that drew him to Amy Cameron that were less high-minded than her smile. As she bent over the table to wipe crumbs from the seat of the booth, he contemplated her trim backside with an acute appreciation for the snug fit of her jeans.

A sharp bark from Piggy made Amy straighten.

"What?" Amy asked the corgi.

Jeff sighed. Piggy's glare couldn't be as knowing as it looked. Dogs weren't that smart.

"I bought a bottle of wine," Amy announced. "We can toast Piggy's unexpected talent."

Jeff sat down on the undersized sofa while Amy

poured two glasses of white zinfandel. "This is quite a setup," he said, looking around the shabby motor home.

"I can tell from the look on your face that comment wasn't intended as a compliment." Amy handed him a glass and sat down beside him, close enough to be friendly, Jeff noticed, but far enough away to let him know that friendliness was all she intended. "Georgette serves her purpose," she said with a smile.

"Georgette?"

"You name hawks; I name motor homes. She has the same lines as my cousin Georgette, and the same lack of get up and go." She patted the wall fondly. "I bought old Georgette from a retired couple who decided that hitting the road wasn't their thing any longer. I even lived in her for a while after my house in Denver burned."

"Yeah," Jeff said, swirling his wine. "I read about that."

Amy was silent for a moment, and Jeff could almost see bitter memories parading through her mind.

"You've had a real run of bad luck lately, haven't you?" he commented softly.

Her head came up abruptly, as if his words had brought her back from some distant place that had nothing to do with Jeff Berenger or a shabby motor home parked in a campground in Estes Park. A ghost of a smile touched her lips, but it held little humor. "You could say so. Life always has its ups and downs, but the last half year or so has dipped lower than I ever want to be again. Things are looking up now, though. For a while, after the house burned, I was so low I got paranoid. I thought someone must be out to get me personally. First my car getting broken into—with poor David and Lydia getting in the way. Then the house burning."

Jeff frowned. "Well, when you put it that way . . ."

"No," Amy assured him hastily. "It was nothing but my imagination. Really. I certainly don't have anything that anyone would want, and there's no reason in the world for anyone to want to hurt me. The whole notion was just silliness on my part."

"I wouldn't call it silly," he said seriously. "I'd call it understandable."

The smile she gave him was a bit strained. The discussion had put a chill in the air that needed to be dispelled, Jeff decided. He indicated the worn motor home with a wave of his arm. "You don't still live in . . . uh . . . Georgette, do you?"

"Of course not." From the eagerness of Amy's answer, he guessed that she was as anxious to change the subject as he was. "Only when I go camping . . . and hit the road with a camera."

"Hit the road?"

"About twice a year I do a road trip to take photos in different parts of the country. Last year I went to New England in October to do the leaves. Before that I drove to Seattle to get some landscape shots around Puget Sound."

"Did you time it to coincide with the big dog shows up there?"

"Of course."

"I should have known." He leaned back on the worn cushions and regarded her assessingly. "You're a total addict, aren't you?"

"What?"

"A dog addict. I've seen the symptoms before. You buy clothes with pockets so you can carry dog treats everywhere you go. When you shop for a car, you consider only vans, and you take a measuring tape along to make sure you can get enough dog kennels into the cargo area. You spend more on vet bills than you do on doctor bills, and you write up a will only to make sure your dogs are cared for if you cash out."

She shrugged an admission. "Guilty on all counts. I'm afraid it's incurable."

"And probably terminal."

"You shouldn't complain. Without people like me, people like you would do a lot less business."

"True enough."

"Besides, you have dogs yourself. Where are they, by the way?"

"In my truck. Now that the sun's down, it's cool enough for them in there."

"You could bring them inside."

"They like the truck. Darby sits behind the steering wheel and pretends she can drive. Spot just sleeps. If they get bored, they each have a couple of rawhides they can chew on."

"And you complain about me."

"At least I'm owned by a reasonable sort of dog." He taunted her with a grin. "Not little couch potatoes whose ears are longer than their legs."

Amy flushed, even though she had to know he was teasing. Living with a woman who was so transparent would be a delight. A man would always know what was running through her mind.

Living with a woman, indeed! Now where, Jeff wondered, did that thought come from?

"Before you insult my dogs further," Amy declared, "you'd better remember that there's still rocky road ice cream to be considered. And I'm the one dishing it out."

He slapped the heel of his hand to his forehead. "I forgot! Bad timing. Still—" he proffered his most charming smile, "you wouldn't deprive the man who's done you so many good turns today."

"What good turns?" she asked suspiciously.

"Without me you wouldn't have that certificate confirming what a talented little dog Miss Pudgy is."

"As I remember it, you conned me into the test in hopes of a steak dinner . . . which you got, even though you lost the bet."

"I gave you at least two great photo ops—one with Fred, and another with Darby."

"Well, that's true." She tried hard to maintain her stern demeanor but failed as a smile broke through. "I forgot to tell you how moving it was when you let Fred fly free. I don't think there was a dry eye in the whole stadium."

"Including mine," he admitted.

"You are . . . an unusual man, Jefferson Davis Berenger."

"Oh yeah. Everybody tells me that."

He could sense her defenses crumbling, as if a wall surrounding her had been breached. It was a pivotal moment, when he could move forward and redefine their relationship or stay put and let that wall rebuild itself, perhaps more strongly than before. Without hesitation, he moved forward.

Jeff could see consent in Amy's eyes. She knew she was going to be kissed, and she wasn't going to put up one bit of resistance. Uncertainty mixed with hesitant desire in her smile. That great smile. God, but he loved her smile. Then her eyes closed. Her head tilted slightly. Jeff felt as if he'd gone to heaven, so sweet was the anticipation. Her mouth was going to be even sweeter. He closed his eyes, inhaled a breath that had just passed from her lips, and—

"Yeechh! Shit!" Jeff pulled back from the sudden hot swipe of a very wet corgi kiss. Amy jumped away as if cold water had poured over her head.

"Piggy!" he accused.

The little brown spoiler still sat where she had

jumped onto the sofa between them. Her jaw gaped in a doggy grin as she breathed dog-food breath into his face.

"Piggy! Get off!" Amy's face was as red as the bright red plaid that upholstered the cushions. Whatever mood had blossomed between them had been effectively squelched. "I'm sorry! The little twerp . . ." She trailed off, then started laughing.

Jeff suspected he might find some humor in the situation once his overheated hormones cooled down, but he couldn't right at the moment. This particular pivotal moment had come and gone, and the damned dog had snatched it away from him like Steve Atwater intercepting a touchdown pass for the Denver Broncos.

"I'd better go." He sighed.

"Don't go." Her laughter calmed to a mere chortle. "There's still ice cream."

The rocky road didn't seem like the height of desire any longer. "That's okay. I . . . uh . . . listen, it was great of you to make dinner. I owe you one."

"No, you don't. You owe me two surgeries, remember?"

"That too. Dinner sometime, though. You pick the place."

"Okay."

"Without the dog."

She chuckled. "My chaperone?"

Jeff just shook his head.

Piggy escorted him to the door, then jumped against his leg, almost pushing him out.

"Watch it, short stuff. If your mom brings you to me for vaccinations, you're going to get the dull needles."

"She looks scared." Amy scoffed.

She stood on tiptoe and gave him a chaste peck on

the cheek—a consolation prize, he reflected ruefully. "Thanks, Jeff," she said softly.

Thanks for what? he wondered. But he didn't ask. With Piggy's weight almost overbalancing him, it was easier just to go out the door.

As he walked to his truck, Jeff set his feet down gingerly. Amy said she'd picked up outside the motor home, but where Piggy was concerned, one never knew.

Six

Next morning, the bright Colorado sun couldn't out-dazzle Tom Gordon's smile as he greeted Amy at her booth. She couldn't help but smile in return. Tom looked as if he'd just stepped out of a poster for Dewars Scotch whiskey. Most men looked good in a kilt, Amy admitted, but some men certainly looked better than others.

"I should have called you after David's funeral," Tom said ruefully. "I always considered you a friend as well as David. But, I didn't know what to say, you know? So I took the coward's way out, and I'm ashamed to admit it. After seeing you yesterday, I knew I had to drop by and apologize."

"There's nothing to apologize for, Tom. To tell the truth, I got so much attention after David was killed that I was praying for anonymity. You did me a favor by leaving me alone."

"Well, I at least should have offered to help after your house burned. God! I'll bet you lost everything."

Amy shrugged. "I lost a lot, but not quite everything. Most of the furniture was unsalvageable, but I managed to save a lot of my work."

"Really?" His brows shot upward in surprise. "That was lucky."

"It was. I lost some prints, but I managed to get most of my negatives out of the house before too much damage was done. They would have been impossible to replace."

"I'll say."

His expression was somber indeed. Amy was taken aback. In her casual acquaintance with Tom Gordon, she would not have judged him to be a man overly troubled about other people's misfortunes. But then, it certainly would not be the first time she'd been wrong about someone. Suddenly, she was uncomfortable with his concern.

"Don't feel bad about not calling, Tom. There was really nothing you could've done. I had plenty of help getting on my feet again."

"I'm glad to hear it." His expression softened to a smile. "You're being nice about me being rude. But then, you always were one of the nicest people I ever knew. What's this?" He leafed through the photo album display of her dog photography—everything from candid action shots to posed portraits. "Are these your work?"

"Yes."

"They're very good."

"Thank you."

While Tom examined the display, Selma feigned a swoon in the next booth, her hands over her apparently overheated heart. Then, with a delighted grin on her face, she motioned desperately for Amy to leap in and take advantage of the opening fate had provided. Amy gestured for her to get lost.

While they were in the middle of this silent conversation, Tom looked up. Both women froze guiltily, like schoolgirls caught passing notes during class. He took in their red faces and smiled. Amy gathered that women making themselves look foolish over him was not a new experience for Tom.

"Hello," he said cordially to Selma.

"Hi. Uh, I'm Selma. This is . . . my collie booth, here, next to Amy's." Selma turned an even brighter red.

"So I see. That's a very handsome collie you have."

Selma melted like wax in a candle flame. Anyone who complimented Raven was all right in her eyes, and Tom Gordon had good looks and celebrity on his side as well.

"That's Raven," she said. "He's one of the nicest collies you'll ever meet."

"Nice as well as handsome. He does look like quite a boy. And who's this pretty little lady?"

Piggy, who had been allowed back into the exercise pen on strict probation, stood with her front feet clawing the side of the pen in a blatant bid for attention. As Tom bent down to scratch her ears, her plush little backside waggled in ecstasy.

"That's Piggy," Amy said. "She's the one who was on the rampage yesterday."

"So you're the culprit, are you?"

Piggy licked his fingers in abject apology.

"She's a real lover, isn't she?" Tom commented with a grin.

"Well, not usually," Amy admitted. "I wouldn't trust her if I were you."

"Don't worry. I like dogs. See—she likes me."

"Looks to me like Piggy's in love," Selma said. "You've made a conquest."

"At least I know she's genuine," Tom said with a self-deprecating grin. "Most girls just want me for the pretty face and the sports car."

"What kind of car?" Selma asked eagerly.

"A red Ferrari."

Amy thought Selma was going to faint—for real this time. "I thought you had one of David's BMWs."

"I do," he said with a half-guilty smile. "I've always driven a BMW, even before I met David. The Ferrari's just a toy."

"Some toy," Amy said.

"It's cute." He gave an ecstatic Piggy a final pat on her head and straightened. "I'll give you a ride in it sometime."

"That would be fun." Amy gave Selma a warning look that she hoped was subtle enough to get past Tom. If the girl wasn't actually drooling, she was doing the next thing to it.

"In fact," Tom said, "we could make it tonight if you'd let me take you out to dinner."

Behind Tom's back, Selma nodded an emphatic yes, but Amy shook her head.

"Selma and I have to get back to Niwot tonight. We've got the booth to dismantle, the van to load, the motor home to pack up. Thanks, but I don't think so."

"Some other time, then," he said with a good-natured smile. "I'm really glad I ran in to you here, Amy. I wouldn't have wanted to lose track of you. I'll take a raincheck on that dinner. I mean it."

"That'd be nice."

"Well." He looked at his watch. "I have to go narrate something or other at the stadium. See you later." He gave Selma a warm smile. "Nice meeting you, Selma. You too, Piggy," he quipped. "But I'm glad you're behind bars this time."

Bemused, Amy watched him as he strode through the crowd. More than one set of feminine eyes widened as he passed. He walked on without breaking his stride or even giving his wistful admirers a smile. Amy wondered if he was so accustomed to his effect on women that he took no notice.

Selma was the most obvious casualty of Tom's charm, or perhaps just the most histrionic. She collapsed into a canvas chair, both hands clasped dramatically to her chest.

"Be still my frantic heart!" she declared. "Amy, you've struck gold! Pure gold! Not only do you have the hunkish Dr. Berenger paying calls on your motor home, but now the famous Tom Gordon is making eyes at you! He's spectacular! Did you get a gander at those legs? And those shoulders! And he has the most beautiful green eyes! Lordy! I think I'm going to overheat and die right here on the spot!"

A worried Raven poked at his mistress with his long collie nose. Amy was less concerned. She'd known Selma longer than Raven had, and she was inured to her friend's penchant for emoting. "Famous?" she queried.

"Yes, he's famous! I watch *Eye on Denver* every day. This is not trash TV we're talking here, Amy! He covers really worthwhile stuff. Don't you ever watch it?"

"I've seen it a few times."

"Remember that series he did about the homeless shelters in downtown Denver? And that story on crooked promotion practices in the police department? Not to mention that he's got the mayor of Denver on the run with that exposé about the construction projects for that big amusement park south of town."

"Goodness! You are a fan, aren't you?"

"Who wouldn't be? Look. Even Piggy likes him."

Indeed, Piggy stood on her hind legs, front feet pressed against the side of the pen as she followed Tom Gordon's departure with a rapt expression.

"She even rolled over and invited Tom to scratch her tummy. I saw her."

"You would trust the judgment of a misanthropic dog?"

Piggy glared at Amy, and Selma sympathized. "I

agree, Piggy. She's not giving credit where credit's due. Besides, what's not to like? Brains and looks in the same package—money too. God! I don't believe he has a Ferrari!"

"Well, go to it, then, girl."

"No, no. He's got eyes for you, not me."

"He was a friend of David's. That's the only reason he stopped by."

"Yeah. Sure."

"Besides, I'm not interested."

"Is that why your eyes were on his tush all the time he was walking away?"

"I was admiring his kilt."

"And the way it set off his tush."

"Don't be ridiculous. Besides, yesterday you were singing Jeff Berenger's praises," Amy said.

"Yeah, well, Jeff's cool, in an unspectacular sort of way, and yesterday he was the only player, you know? But if you've got a choice between hamburger and lobster, I'd take the lobster."

"Only if you're hungry," Amy replied with a wry smile. "It so happens I'm not hungry."

I COULDN'T HAVE agreed more with Selma. One doesn't have to be starving to enjoy a perfectly seasoned lobster tail with drawn butter and a superior vintage white wine. Of course, right then my taste ran more to kibble and Wookie Cookie dog treats, but that was beside the point. Selma's a featherbrain most of the time, but on that day she hit the nail right on the head. Tom Gordon was spectacular. Jeff Berenger was a dud. Lobster versus hamburger. Wild peppered rice compared to a baked potato and margarine—low-fat margarine, at that. Mmmm.

My strategy up to that point had been sheer genius, and I hoped old Stan was taking note of the effort I applied to my mission. It took guts, not to mention smarts, to escape the exercise pen and strike out into the crowd, and finding Tom Gordon was simply inborn talent. A stickler for detail might point out that I didn't find Tom Gordon so much as he found Amy, but he probably wouldn't have recognized her if I hadn't cleverly tripped that fellow Dullwood, or Durwood, or whatever his name was. I fully intended to take credit for the find. I've always had a knack for reeling in the most desirable guy in any crowd, and I still had it. Wreaking mayhem to get attention wasn't necessary in the old days, but then, I was no longer in a position to attract notice with my knock-'em-dead body and trillion kilowatt smile. Mayhem got the job done, didn't it?

Oh yes, I was feeling good as Tom Gordon sauntered away—trying to look like a fish that wasn't hooked—and Selma twigged Amy and Amy tried to deny the light that glowed in her eyes. Things were rolling along quite nicely, thanks to my ingenuity. Stan couldn't possibly fault the perfection of Tom Gordon, and once she'd thought about it, neither could Amy. Tom Gordon was everything any girl could want. My search for the Best Possible Husband was over.

The only sticking point was Amy. She's not exactly centerfold material, and, as I've said before, on a one-to-ten scale of classy, she ranks about a two. If she had done something with that mop of hair—the Shirley Temple look has been out for years—and pay more attention to cosmetics and clothes, she could have been hot. Not nearly as hot as I was, or had been when I still had only two legs, but hot enough to attract Tom Gordon's eye.

Nevertheless, Tom seemed interested, and I wasn't about to question my good luck. Maybe he was one of those guys who didn't want a real head turner on his arm to compete with his own good looks. Or maybe he liked the down-home, natural look. Whatever. He was interested. Amy, even if she wouldn't admit it yet, was interested. I was a genius, and shortly Stan would have to reward me for a job well done.

My morning had been just about flawless up until then,

but things began to go downhill when a certain pair of staring brown eyes broke through my happy reflections and alerted me that my strutting about the exercise pen had irritated the old bitch who was my roommate. Strutting comes naturally to me. It always has. Perhaps as I congratulated myself on my cleverness (certainly no one else appreciated my efforts, so if I was going to reap any kudos at all, they had to come from me), I might have seemed a bit cocky to the old has-been. She's a testy old soul with no tolerance at all. No finesse, either. Old Molly was put out by the arrival of a younger, smarter female in her household, and my little victory dance was the last straw. She jumped me with all the determination of a Steeler lineman tackling a Bronco running back, and the fur began to fly.

To give Molly credit, she was quite a scrapper. I was nearly as eager for a fight as she, but in spite of my obvious advantages, the old gal quickly put me on the defensive. I was younger, bigger, and smarter; but she had battle experience on her side. You'd think I could have outsmarted her. After all, she was only a dog. The truth is, however, that once the blood heats and the teeth are bared, thinking retires and gut instinct takes the driver's seat. Once or twice in my life (at least), someone or other has called me a bitch, but you don't know the meaning of the word until you've met the prototype—a female corgi in a brawl. By the time Amy and Selma waded into the fracas and pulled us apart, I was lucky to have my ears still connected to my head.

No matter what Stan said about my so-called sins, I didn't deserve that kind of treatment. I really didn't.

The worst part of the incident was that it gave that needle-happy vet an excuse to barge into our lives again. This time the needle he wielded was a suture needle, not a hypodermic, and Molly was his victim right along with me. Not that this common ground made us any more fond of each other. It didn't. The old bag's stoic behavior while having her foot stitched and bandaged was pure show, as far as I was concerned. When my turn came, I gave both her and Dr. Ham-handed a piece of my mind. I just know he enjoyed sewing up my ear and cleaning the puncture in my jaw. The sadist!

"They'll live," he told Amy with unprofessional cheerfulness. "But I'd keep them apart until they decide they can behave like ladies."

Behave like ladies indeed! If Jeff Berenger thought the fairer sex was also the gentler sex, he'd never been to a sorority party.

"I don't know what got into them," Amy said.

"Both cranky and tired, maybe. This sort of thing puts a lot of stress on dogs."

He didn't know the half of it! Still, the weekend was almost over, Jeff would have no more excuses to butt in where he wasn't wanted, and I still had a warm glow from my matchmaking success. Tom Gordon wasn't going to be content with a mere hello–good-bye after a chance meeting. I would've wagered a day's ration of kibble that he would call within a week.

Good things were going to happen. I was convinced of it.

Unfortunately, Berenger was determined to make things happen as well—things not so good, from my point of view. With a gleam in his eye, he threw out a lure to Amy.

"Want to do a last tour of the craft tents and maybe watch the caber toss for a while? After all, this is the last day of the festival."

When Amy cast a concerned look at her poor scuffed-up dogs, as she most properly should have, Jeff hastily reminded her that I would benefit from rest and isolation in my kennel while Molly could comfortably recuperate in the pen with Drover to give her sympathy.

Of course Amy fell for his line. No discrimination, that woman. Five minutes later, I watched from my prison while she walked off with the jaunty Dr. Dull. It was a depressing end to an otherwise productive weekend. Trust Amy to complicate matters with her complete lack of taste in men.

It occurred to me then that bringing this mission to a satisfactory end might be harder than I hoped.

♥   ♥   ♥

IT TOOK A full two days for Amy to recover from the festival. After the dogs had been bathed and their paraphernalia cleaned, folded, and stored away, she tackled the motor home. A two-hour cleaning job turned into a good half day because Amy repeatedly allowed herself to drift into contemplation of how strange it had been to have this private refuge invaded by the very masculine presence of Jeff Berenger. He'd had trouble squeezing his shoulders between the stove and the closet—a narrow passageway not designed with a husky six-footer in mind. He'd vainly searched for something to do with his long legs while sitting on the narrow sofa, yet he had seemed amazingly at ease in what could have been a fairly awkward situation. Jeff's attitude was refreshing, in a way. His masculine ego didn't cringe at her rebuffs, nor at being made to look ridiculous by a ten-inch-tall dog.

David would have thrown a hissy fit at being upstaged by a dog. But then, he'd never gotten on very well with the corgis. Selma had told her once, with a wicked gleam in her eye, that the problem between Amy's husband and Amy's dogs was a pack dominance struggle, and the corgis always won. That might have been true. Corgis were very pushy little creatures. The way Piggy treated Jeff Berenger was certainly proof of that.

Amy took a swipe at the scratched table with her sponge and contemplated why she could still see Jeff sitting on the sofa, or standing at the little sink washing dishes, shoulders slightly hunched to keep his head from brushing the ceiling. Why should he seem to be everywhere she looked? Nothing of importance had passed between them in the motor home. A little closer acquaintance. A bit more understanding. A minor flirtation. Nothing heavy or significant.

The problem, Amy finally concluded, was that the motor home was too much like Jeff Berenger. No glossy surfaces. Unstreamlined, scruffy, and a bit dinged. But its engine started every single time she turned the ignition key. It had never left her stranded on the road, and the plain interior was a warm and friendly refuge.

A foolish comparison but fitting in a way. Jeff was not exactly timeworn or dinged up, but his casual scruffiness did fit right in with Georgette's wellworn upholstery and less-than-lustrous surfaces. His manner also was easy and warm in a way that Amy found disconcertingly comfortable. She couldn't help but be curious about how he had survived to the brink of middle age without acquiring a wife. Of course, he might have had a wife somewhere along the way, for all she knew. He might be divorced or a widower. Or, God forbid, he could be married and playing around. He didn't seem the type, but Amy of all people should know better than to dismiss the possibility.

Amy shook her head to free her mind from that train of thought. She almost wished that Jeff would call. Not quite, but almost. She took a last swipe at the table, threw the sponge into the sink, and left before she became even more balmy. When she closed and locked the door behind her, she hoped Jeff Berenger's images were shut away inside.

The rest of the week Amy spent developing the rolls of film she had shot at the Scottish festival. She had converted what had once been a large basement utility room into a photograph lab, and at times like this, when she had numerous rolls of exposed film to process, she spent so many hours in the darkroom that she expected to sprout bat wings at any moment. Her only breaks in the work routine were the dogs' daily walks, usually taken in company with Selma, who usually worked night shift as a cashier at the grocery and had her days free.

One collie and three corgis made quite a sight trotting along the rural roads of Boulder County, so much so that Amy decided the mismatched quartet was a likely subject for her camera. Saturday, with her darkroom work caught up, she and Selma took the four dogs into the fallow fields behind the house and tried to lure them into posing in a manner that producers of dog calendars, magazines, and greeting cards would find irresistible.

Set loose in the field, the dogs bounded about with great enthusiasm, nosing the grass for mice, bugs, and bunnies, and giving futile chase to swooping butterflies. Amy shot off two rolls, catching candid action poses that were sometimes graceful, sometimes goofy. With luck she might get two or three frames out of the roll that were salable.

"It would be nice to get them doing something together," she told Selma. "In some sort of chummy, heartwarming manner."

"Well now, let's see." Selma's mouth twisted into a deep-thought grimace. "Heartwarming, eh? Commercially heartwarming. Maybe if I could get Ray to lie in this little patch of yellow flowers over here, and then the corgis—"

"You expect Ray to stay on command?" Amy chortled.

"Don't laugh. I have him enrolled in obedience class starting next week."

"Obedience class? What do you mean? When are you taking him back to Gary?"

"Not in *my* lifetime."

"Selma!"

"Why should I?"

"The judge—"

"Poop on the judge. Ray's a dog, not a kid. I don't see why the flippin' court should have any say over who gets him."

"Dogs are considered property," Amy reminded her.

"Then he's my property."

"Gary doesn't agree."

"Gary can go stick his head down an outhouse hole."

"Selma . . ."

"Don't worry about Gary, Amy. He's a faithless, lying, woman-chasing dog turd, but it's not like he's going to start stalking me and Ray, or break into my apartment to get him back."

"I don't know," Amy replied. "You broke into his place."

"That was different," Selma said with a superior sniff. "*I* had a key."

Amy laughed. "Your mind works in mysterious ways."

"What? I don't see anything wrong with that logic."

"Just take the dogs out to that patch of flowers and make them look charming."

"Charming or heartwarming? Make up your mind."

"Try for both. Go."

Selma whistled and took a dog treat from her pocket, thus earning the instant attention of all four dogs. "Come on, troops. The slave driver over there says you've got work to do."

The session was not entirely successful. Piggy plopped her tubby little body in the middle of the patch of flowers and managed to look pathetic rather than cute. Molly sulked, refusing to get nearer to Piggy than she absolutely had to. Drover elected to take this opportunity to sniff Piggy in a manner that was neither charming nor heartwarming. Only Ray was well behaved. He sat amiably, gave the camera a silly collie grin, and ignored the canine chaos around him.

At the end of fifteen minutes of futile bribes, pleas, and commands, Amy was ready to start photographing butterflies rather than dogs. Molly and Drover fed upon their own mischievousness, growing more difficult by the minute. Piggy sank into a grade-A sulk, and even Ray became restless. Selma threw up her hands in frustration.

"Give up, Amy! You have shots like this already, you know? Without Piggy, of course, but she's not exactly calendar girl material, is she?"

Piggy rolled her eyes toward Selma in a lethal glare.

"I don't have shots like this," Amy denied.

"Well, you would if you'd bother to develop them."

It was Amy's turn to glare.

"Don't give me that look," Selma said, unimpressed. "It would do you good. And if I have to try to make these creatures look cute for one more minute, I'm going to end up throttling a couple of corgis. Ray's the only dog here who deserves dinner tonight."

Amy snapped the lens cover on her camera and sighed. Selma was a master at poking her nose where Amy didn't want to be poked. Still, Amy knew that sooner or later she needed to come to terms with the little plastic can of film that was safely out of sight—and mostly out of mind—in her office. The thirty-six exposed frames did include some wonderfully heartwarming poses of Ray, Molly, and Drover. It also included some rather artistic shots of Denver's classic architecture from the early twentieth century, shots taken for a photo article she had never finished. She would actually like to see those.

But not at the price of looking at photos from her very last weekend with David. On that clear, beautiful Saturday in March they had driven to a friend's condo at Copper Mountain for a weekend of spring skiing. Still deceiving herself that she was a happily married woman, Amy had taken candid shots of everything from their sleepy-eyed breakfasts to David posing on the slopes in all his sunburned glory. Everything had seemed so perfect, so fairy-tale happily ever after, and it all had been a lie.

Five days later she had come home in the early evening after a hard day's work. As she pulled up to the house, she'd been congratulating herself on taking some very artistic shots of an old post office building in north Denver. The photos were going to be a great addition to the photo article she planned on Denver's historic architecture.

Her own mood had deflated, however, when an angry David met her at the curb in front of their home. She'd forgotten that his car was in the shop and he needed hers to drive to an evening sales meeting at his BMW dealership. David had possessed a biting tongue when he was irritated, and she had reacted with her own little tantrum, storming into the house without giving thought to her precious camera, which was in the back seat of the car. David had driven the car not to his dealership but to a "meeting" with Lydia Keane in the bar of the Wynkoop Brewing Company, where some lowlife had tried to break into the car for the expensive camera, and where David and Lydia were killed interrupting the burglary.

Amy couldn't bring herself to look at those last photos of her marriage. The thought of even touching that film made her cringe. But neither could she throw it away—silly, but there it was. She was a basket case. What else was new?

"Now I've gone and got you depressed, haven't I?" Selma said with a sigh. "Listen, girl, I didn't mean it. Hell! What do I know?"

Amy opened her mouth to apologize for her moodiness when the dogs' frantic barking interrupted her. All four bolted across the field toward the house.

"Someone pulled into your drive," Selma explained, shading her eyes with her hand.

Amy's heart gave an unexpected jump, then fell. She didn't recognize the car that had pulled into the drive. Had she been hoping, somewhere in the buried depths of her mind, that it would be a beat-up truck with muddy border collie prints on the fenders?

"Whoever it is, is going to get mobbed," Selma said. "Hope he likes dogs."

"Damn!" Amy slung the camera strap over her shoulder and trotted after the pack with Selma. "Molly! Drover! Get back here! Piggy! Jeez! You wouldn't know that Molly and Drover both won obedience titles."

Ray was the only one who turned back at her call. The corgis continued on to bounce around the shins of the visitor, who had come into the field to meet them.

"Bingo!" Selma exclaimed in a voice for Amy's ears only. "It's Tom Gordon. You *have* hit the jackpot."

Amy was close enough to recognize him now. Dressed in casual cotton slacks and an expensive-looking tweedy sweater, Tom Gordon didn't seem to mind the horde that greeted him. In fact, he squatted down to scratch corgi ears and accept a deluge of corgi licks.

"Some watchdogs," Amy commented to her visitor when she reached him.

Piggy especially was ecstatic, practically climbing into Tom's lap. Tom accepted the mobbing with good grace, only pushing the dogs away when Piggy got a bit too personal with her nose.

"Piggy!" Amy scolded. "Mind your manners!"

Piggy gave Amy a tolerant look, then gazed up at Tom with obvious admiration.

"That's all right," Tom said. "I like dogs. Remember?"

"And the dogs obviously like you." Selma smiled at him in a way that rivaled the dogs' greeting. Tom smiled back, but his eyes were on Amy.

"You're a hard one to find," he commented. "I should have asked for your address when I saw you at the festival. Niwot's a bigger town than I thought."

"Really?" was the only thing Amy could think to say. The full force of his very masculine good looks, combined with the smile that dazzled thousands of television viewers every weekday afternoon, left her tongue-tied. It wasn't every day that a handsome celebrity came looking for her.

"Really. I finally ran into a fellow at the gas station who knew you."

"That would be Matt."

"He told me where you live. And so"—he spread his arms wide as if presenting himself as a gift—"here I am. You can't hide from a good investigative reporter."

Tom Gordon was every bit as magnetic in plain clothes as in a kilt. If Jeff Berenger could be likened to a well-used motor home, Tom more aptly fit the image of the BMW he had parked in the drive—conservative looking, expensive, every detail in place and polished to perfection. A very quality piece of goods.

"Here you are," Amy echoed lamely. "It's nice to see you again. Uh . . . was there some particular reason . . . ?"

"Why am I here? she asks." Tom addressed the empty field as if the grass, weeds, and butterflies were an audience. "A fair question."

"You did promise her a ride in a Ferrari," Selma reminded him. "But I see you didn't bring it."

He grinned amiably. "Not today. Today I'm here on business."

"Oh." Amy was beginning to become annoyed at the way Selma and the dogs fawned on their visitor. Piggy leaned against Tom's shins as if faint from an excess of adoration. Drover and Molly had been completely won over by a few ear tickles, and Selma looked as though she'd just seen Elvis materialize in a second coming. The dogs, at least, should have known better. Men did not have the market cornered when it came to being suckers for good looks and a sexy smile, Amy decided. Even *she* was bumbling about as if she'd just been broadsided with a bat.

To make up for her own lack of cool, Amy's next words were on the brusque side. "You came here to talk business?"

"In this case, business and pleasure mix." His smile dispelled any coolness she'd injected into the air. "One of the advantages of being a newsman is that I can stick my nose into all sorts of interesting things in pursuit of a story. I'll bet photography is like that too."

"Sometimes," she said cautiously.

They started back toward the house. Molly, Drover, and Ray bounded off toward the back gate. Piggy stayed close to Tom, crowding his every step, just as Selma crowded next to Amy, her ears almost visibly pricked to catch every word.

"Meeting you at the Scottish festival, seeing your dogs firsthand, reading over some of your displays about dog shows and your rescue activities and such . . . it gave me an idea," Tom said.

"Yes?" Amy inquired.

"Well now, this is an idea that requires a bit of help from you, and I'm prepared to marshal all my charm and considerable persuasiveness to get your cooperation."

Amy saw Selma's brows twitch upward. She wished her friend would put her lurid imagination on hold.

"What is this wonderful idea?"

"A proposition involving both you and your little dogs. And you have to allow me to give you the full sales pitch. That gives me the excuse to mix even more pleasure with business, you see."

"Well . . ."

"How about dinner tonight, if you're not busy? I know it's short notice, but it's a cause that will get your interest. I promise."

"All right," Amy consented with a smile. She wasn't sure she wanted to get social with Tom Gordon. He was far too charming, and some silly, schoolgirlish part of her was susceptible to that potent combination of looks, polish, and affability. Yet it would be downright rude to refuse.

What was it lately, anyway? Amy mused wryly. She didn't want a man or need a man. Right now, she wasn't even sure she liked men. And suddenly, for the first time in her life, men were buzzing about her like flies.

A few more minutes of polite chitchat settled the details. Watching Tom Gordon drive off in his sleek BMW—one he'd bought from David—Amy felt as though she'd been blown over by one of Boulder's famous mountain-front windstorms.

"He's a piece of work, isn't he?" she observed to Selma. She didn't know if she meant the comment as a compliment or a cut.

"Yeah. You can say that again." Selma's mouth slanted upward in an impish, naughty smile. "A proposition involving both you and the dogs, eh? Now that, my friend, should be interesting."

Seven

Amy looked around her and reflected that Brittany Hill was not the sort of restaurant that Lydia Keane would have considered a good time. The studied elegance was far too staid, though the prices, which ranged from moderate to astronomical, would have gleaned her date a truckload of brownie points. In Lydia's opinion, anything very, very expensive had to have something good about it.

But that was Lydia. Amy regarded such things in a somewhat different light. She believed that something expensive should deliver quality worth the expense. So far, Brittany Hill appeared to do that. Too quiet and refined for the fast, loud set of young professionals who liked to party after a hard day of climbing the corporate ladder, the restaurant claimed the patronage of the middle-aged to older group who had already achieved success. From atop a little hill just north of Denver, its vast expanse of windows looked out upon the Mile High City and its backdrop of breathtaking mountains. Every table was situated to take advantage of the view. Every detail of the service—the china and cutlery, the quietly efficient servers, the elegant table settings—tastefully reminded the patrons of their elevation above the city, both literally and figuratively. Lydia would have

been impressed by it all, then laughed and called it un-
bearably stuffy.

Why was it that every time Amy met a man, Lydia
seemed to ride along on the coattails of her mind? Her
ghost was a painfully real presence that haunted any interaction with Jeff, for good reason, because Jeff and
Lydia had a history of sorts. But Lydia had no right
invading this very nice restaurant and spoiling Amy's
time with Tom.

Tom Gordon wasn't the sort of man who would
have sought a relationship with Lydia, Amy told herself.
Not that he wouldn't have looked her way. Any man
with eyes would have looked Lydia's way. But Tom
Gordon seemed to appreciate a woman who could carry
on a conversation about something other than last Sunday's Bronco game or the merits of the band in the
hottest new singles' club. Tom Gordon was like Brittany
Hill in a way, and it was no surprise that this was his
favorite dining spot. Like the restaurant, he was elegant,
smooth, sophisticated, and several cuts above the ordinary. A man of intelligence and ambition, he no doubt
preferred women who were just as cosmopolitan as he
was.

Which, Amy acknowledged with a mental smile,
left her even further out of Tom's league than Lydia. But
of course, this little excursion with Tom Gordon wasn't
a date, in spite of the romantic surroundings. This was
business, Tom had assured her.

Nevertheless, when he'd informed her they were
going to Brittany Hill, she had dug through her closet in
despair of finding something suitable to wear. She came
up with a black velvet-looking two-piece with a short,
narrow skirt and a long-sleeved jacket that flared in a soft
drape of material over the hips. Amy hadn't worn the
thing in at least five years. The sharply plunging V neck
of the jacket had always made her feel uncomfortably

exposed. She had tried to close the gap with the discreet placement of a safety pin, but she couldn't manage to make the modification look like anything other than a plunging neckline fastened by a cheap safety pin, so she had decided to be bold and leave it be.

And now here she sat, at a choice window table at Brittany Hill, feeling elegant and a bit exposed, trying to think of how out of place Lydia Keane would have been here and knowing that she herself was even more out of place.

"Is your soup okay?" Tom asked.

"Oh yes. It's delicious."

"You're very quiet."

"Just taking in the view," Amy replied. "It's quite something, isn't it?"

The vista was breathtaking, and not just the sight of the brightly lit suburbs stretching toward the even more brightly lit city. The view across the table was something to look at as well. Tom Gordon was a spectacular hunk of man. Just enough imperfection softened the flawlessness—an ever so slightly crooked nose, a strand or two of golden hair not precisely in place, a small scar that interrupted the pure line of one brow. Without these little flaws, the sheer impact of his looks would be intimidating. As it was, he drew the eyes like a magnet draws iron. The spectacular view out the window was no competition for Tom Gordon.

Amy began to comprehend the spell Lydia Keane had cast on men. Tom Gordon did the same to women, and though she might like to deny it, Amy was as susceptible as the next female. For the first time since David had died, she felt a small bit of sympathy for the weakness that had lured her husband into Lydia's company that fatal night.

As if reading her mind, Tom made the obvious romantic comparison. "The view from here is nice. But the one across the table is just as nice."

Amy chuckled softly. "Only if you're looking in your direction."

He looked surprised. "Don't be coy, Amy. You must know what a stunning woman you are."

"Oh, come now," Amy said with a good-natured smile. "That's stretching it a bit, don't you think, Tom?"

"Not at all," he persisted. "Haven't you seen the heads turning this way? What do you think they're looking at?"

"At you, Tom Gordon. And well you know it."

He declined to make the standard modest disclaimer. "They're looking at us, not just me. There's nothing that sets off my golden good looks like a pretty dark-haired woman." His grin took every bit of arrogance from the statement.

Amy laughed out loud. "How refreshing to find a man who can own up to being beautiful."

"In my line of work, good looks is a business asset—something to be cultivated and worked at, just like a good speaking voice and the ability to face all those hot lights without sweating like a pig. Anyone who says looks and presentation don't count in the television news business has his head so far up his ass he can't see daylight."

"What about a talent for getting the news and the intellect to understand it?"

"Oh well, yeah." His smile became endearingly wry. "If you want to talk about minor details."

She laughed again and suddenly realized she could be attracted to Tom Gordon for reasons quite apart from his physical appeal. "Speaking of minor details," she said as her laughter faded to a mere grin. "What is this proposition you just had to talk to me about?"

"We'll get there, love. Propositions always come at the end of the evening. Don't you know anything?"

"Apparently not."

An unobtrusive waiter cleared away the soup bowls and delivered the salads. When the obligatory ritual of the fresh pepper grinder was accomplished, he left them in peace. For a few moments they concentrated on doing justice to the salad chef's works of art. Usually a victim of her own cooking, Amy was enjoying the gourmet fare enormously when she became aware that Tom's eyes were locked onto her with unnerving intensity.

"What?" she asked uneasily. "Do I have food on my face?"

He gave her what looked like a fond smile. "No. I was just thinking how much I admire you."

Amy lifted one brow.

"It's not a line, Amy. Honest. No ulterior motives. But . . . well . . . I admire strength in a person. It's one of the things I admire most, actually."

"And you think *I'm* strong?" she asked incredulously.

"You wear strength like a cloak that covers you from head to toe." He grinned. "How's that for poetic?"

"It's absurd."

"No, it's not. You should take an honest look at yourself. How long has it been since David was killed?"

"Six months."

"Right. Six months. And how long since your house burned?"

Amy frowned at the unwelcome memories. "Five months. A bit more."

"Five months. Your husband is killed, after betraying you with a good friend, and then your house burns down around your ears, destroying most of what remains of your life. And what? Here you are, carrying

on with life. Not complaining. Running an independent business."

"I complain enough. You just haven't been around
me long enough to hear."

He shook his head, determined. "No, Amy. You
are strong. And smart—as well as beautiful. You see how
much I have to admire?"

Amy flushed. "Is this part of your design to lure me
into a project you haven't yet divulged?"

He blinked, as if he really had forgotten why they
were there, then smiled ruefully. "You're obviously
charm-proof."

"Oh no. Any more of this and you'll convince me
that I can walk on water."

"All honest compliments, I assure you. Ah. Here
comes dinner. One of my rules is that I never proposition a hungry woman. Eat."

The aromas of her salmon steak and his prime rib
made that command impossible to refuse. The food was
delicious, and in order to do the meal justice, they ate in
comfortable silence. Not until the dishes had been
cleared away and the server had poured Tom a brandy
and Amy an amaretto did Tom finally consent to get
down to business.

"Actually . . ." He swirled the brandy in its snifter
and raised a golden brow at her. "What I have in mind
will do us both some good."

"Yes?" Amy invited.

Just as Tom started to expand, a middle-aged couple
hesitantly approached the table.

"Aren't you Tom Gordon?" the man asked in an
embarrassed voice.

"Yes, I am."

"Uh . . . sorry to intrude. I know you must get
people asking for your autograph all the time. But we're
big fans, and if . . . uh . . ."

"I'd be glad to give you an autograph." He grinned engagingly. "As long as it's not on your check."

The woman tittered, and the man laughed. Amy could see the instant change from the private Tom Gordon to the celebrity Tom. Suddenly he was onstage for his public. He signed the cards they handed him—cards taken from the menu explaining the day's specials.

"I did admire that story you did on the mayor," the woman said. "He should have resigned, the crook! Someone should do something about the morals of people holding public office!"

"I totally agree, madam."

"I'll bet you're not too popular with city hall right now," the man added.

"It's a journalist's job to be unpopular with city hall," Tom told them with an indulgent smile.

"Well, keep up the good work," the man concluded. "It's really been a pleasure meeting you."

Amy smiled as the couple left. "You must get that a lot."

"Part of the business. It can be an annoyance, but, well, they and people like them are who I work for, aren't they? Now—" he smiled, "let me show you my ulterior motives."

WHEN THE VALET brought around the Ferrari, Amy watched with a small smile as Tom used his handkerchief to wipe a smudge from the car's shiny hood. The sporty red car was the perfect adjunct to Tom Gordon's racier side, an aspect of his personality that kept breaking through the smooth veneer of sophistication and serious professionalism that he cultured so diligently. It showed up in his wicked smile, in the constant hint of flirtation, in the odd irreverent quip that peppered his conversation. Amy wondered which was the true Tom

Gordon—the sleek sports car or the conservatively up-scale BMW.

As he held the door for her to get in the car, she gave him a smile. "You know, Tom, you didn't have to go to all this trouble to get me to do this. All you had to do was ask."

"Didn't I say I liked to mix business with pleasure? How dull it would have been to simply ring you up on the phone and ask?"

"Well, I've enjoyed myself."

"Then maybe next time I won't need the excuse of business, eh?"

She didn't answer, just broadened her smile.

Sliding into the driver's seat, Tom hesitated. "I suppose I should put the top up, shouldn't I?"

The breeze was sharp with a promise of autumn, but there was a definite thrill in barreling through the night with nothing to block the stars from view. They looked at each other and smiled, saying "Nah!" simultaneously, then laughing like a couple of teenagers.

"There's a scarf in the back if you want it for your hair."

"I'll take you up on that."

She reached into the tiny back seat for the scarf. "You really think your viewing public is interested in purebred dogs and purebred rescue efforts?" she asked as she fastened the scarf over her hair.

"Of course. In the Denver area, dogs get a lot of bad publicity. Every time there's an incident with a dog biting a kid, the media jump in with both feet and blow the incident out of proportion. Every time an official moans about the number of strays picked up by Animal Control, they jump on it again. Ad nauseam. Don't you think it's time the media did a dog story with a positive slant?"

"Of course I think that. But . . . it seems like a

pretty lightweight story for someone who makes a habit of dethroning politicians and exposing unfair practices in police departments."

He started the car, and the engine came to life with a throaty rumble of pure power.

"People enjoy having a bit of lighter material mixed in with the heavy, depressing pieces. Hell! I enjoy doing pieces like this once in a while. Besides, like I said, I like dogs."

From that point on Amy had no breath for conversation. The Ferrari burned rubber as they peeled out of the lot and shot down the hill, and too late Amy remembered that David had helped sponsor Tom in a passion that both men shared—car racing. David had merely watched their car in the races. Tom, however, drove it. And he apparently practiced his racing skills off the track as well as on.

Amy clutched the edge of the leather seat as Tom deftly negotiated the curves that led them down the hill. The narrow, winding road that led from the restaurant limited their speed somewhat, but once they pulled onto the ramp to I-25, the Ferrari surged forward in truly terrifying acceleration.

"Beautiful night, isn't it?" Tom shouted at her over the noise of the wind and scream of the engine.

Amy tried to smile, but an undignified shriek escaped her as they shot onto the freeway in front of a pickup truck three times their size.

"Sorry," Tom apologized with a smile that was more smug than contrite. "Am I scaring you?" He pulled into the middle lane and slowed from ninety-five to a more respectable, but still illegal, eighty-five.

Amy took a deep breath to calm her heart. "I don't remember you driving so fast earlier."

He grinned. "Too much traffic then. We got bottled up. Don't tell me you always do the speed limit."

"Well, no." She began to relax and enjoy the sensation of harnessed power and potential speed. "To tell the truth, my minivan sometimes can't even get up to the speed limit, much less exceed it."

Tom laughed. "Don't worry. This baby's built for speed. She's not happy unless she's doing ninety, at least. It's hard to keep a forty-valve dual overhead cam engine down to the putt-putt speeds of city streets. Wait till we get farther out of town. I'll show you."

"Just keep the speed down to two digits, would you?" Amy shouted back.

"Sure thing!" His twinkling sidelong glance told Amy that he had no such intentions. She clutched the seat in a death grip, but her heart's pounding was not solely from apprehension. Part of her was actually enjoying this insanity as Tom deftly shifted through all six gears and let the Ferrari fly.

Traffic thinned out as they sped north on the freeway. As the glow of city lights fell behind, the stars came into their glory—a million diamonds spangling a black velvet sky. The wind dislodged her scarf and blew her hair into a wild tangle, but instead of annoying, it was exhilarating.

Tom reached over and took her hand. "I know a club in Boulder with a great band. Plays oldies from the sixties and seventies. What do you say?"

Normally, Amy despised bars and nightclubs. She didn't like the inevitable cigarette smoke, the loud music, the subtle—and sometimes not so subtle—competition to be the coolest, sexiest thing in the club. But the idea of dancing in Tom Gordon's arms sounded extremely attractive. For one night, at least, she could afford not to be such a stick-in-the-mud. She didn't have the chance to say yes, however, before the reflection of blinking red and blue lights in the rearview mirror put a sudden damper on the evening.

"Uh-oh!" she said with a grimace.

Tom merely grinned. "Don't worry, love. It's just one of Denver's finest."

Amy wasn't worried. After all, she wasn't driving. Tom had been speeding along well above the limit, however.

As it turned out, the police officer was not one of Denver's finest. They were outside Denver's city limits. The badge of the highway patrol gleamed behind the flashlight beam that stabbed into the car.

"In a hurry, sir?" the officer inquired in an expressionless voice.

Tom was all polite innocence. "Was I speeding, officer?"

"I clocked you at ninety-five."

"That fast?" There was a hint of pride in Tom's voice.

"May I see your driver's license and vehicle registration, sir?"

Tom handed over the required items. His mouth twitched in a smile as the officer's expression softened from officially bland to pleasantly surprised.

"I thought I recognized you, Mr. Gordon." He grinned. "Quite a hot car you have there, sir."

"Yeah. She likes to go."

"I'll bet. I gotta tell you, sir, that I'm a big fan. My wife, she's on the Denver force. Anyway, she said that story you did about the unfair promotion practices was right on. You've got a lot of friends on the Denver force, let me tell you. And a lot of other troopers in the state. That thing with the mayor, too. It's about time someone had the guts to stand up to city hall and let them know they're being watched."

"That's so," Tom replied emphatically. "I'm glad you agree."

"No way am I giving you a ticket. Not Tom

Gordon. Just . . . uh . . . slow it down a bit, okay?"
He grinned. "At least until you get out of my radar
range."

Tom laughed. "I'll do that. Thank you, Officer."

The highway patrolman nodded politely at Amy.
"You two have a good evening, you hear? And keep up
the good work, Mr. Gordon."

"You bet, friend. Thanks again."

They drove off at a conservative pace, and the patrolman gave them a friendly wave.

"Must be nice having an in with the police," she
commented.

"Never hurts," Tom agreed. "You don't encounter
a cop out here this late at night very often. Lucky for me
he was a fan. How about the club, eh? Ready for some
dancing?"

Somehow the incident with the highway patrol had
put a damper on Amy's desire to continue their evening.
"I don't think so, Tom. I appreciate the offer, but I'm a
bit tired."

"We'll just make it some other time," he said cheerfully. Obviously he didn't take the rejection personally.

When they finally pulled into her driveway, Amy
really was tired. Pleasant as their dinner had been, she
was more accustomed to evenings reading a book on
the sofa than stepping out on the town with a man
she scarcely knew. Having a good time involved a certain amount of stress.

When the Ferrari purred to a stop and Tom came
around to open her door, she felt like a teenager on a
first date. Should she ask him in? offer him a drink? Did
he expect a good-night kiss . . . or more?

As it turned out, she didn't need to invite him in,
for Tom smoothly took the key from her hand, opened
the front door, and followed her in as if he belonged.
Molly and Drover launched themselves from the sofa to

greet them, and Tom squatted down to meet the dogs on their level.

"Where's the other one?" he asked.

"Miss Piggy's in her kennel. If I left her loose with these two, I'd come home to a bloodbath. The two girls don't like each other, and the boy hasn't yet learned that Piggy is spayed."

Tom chuckled and scratched Drover behind the ear. "You keep giving her the old college try, do you, guy?"

Drover collapsed onto the floor with his belly topmost, inviting more attention. But at that moment, Piggy, released from her kennel, bounded into the living room and threw herself joyfully at Tom. Wriggling ecstatically, she wedged her pudgy little body between his knees and planted a wet corgi kiss on his chin before he could avoid it.

"Piggy!" Amy rebuked her.

Tom had to stand up to defend himself. All three dogs gave him disgruntled looks. "She's an affectionate sort," he commented.

"Only to you, believe me. I'm sorry. It seems as if I'm forever apologizing for that dog."

"Don't blame her. It's a spell I cast over all females. Can't you tell?"

Amy answered with a smile. "That must be it. Can I . . . uh . . . offer you a drink, Tom? I think I have some wine in the pantry, though it might be the kind in the box."

He laughed. "No thanks, love. I try to avoid wine that's packed in cardboard. But a cup of coffee would be welcome."

"That I can do."

He followed her into the kitchen and leaned with casual grace against the kitchen doorframe while she measured out grounds and water for the coffeemaker.

His eyes traveled to the doorway that led into the room off the kitchen.

"This is a nice place. Is that your office over there?"

"Yes."

"I've always thought it would be nice to run a business from your home."

"It is, except you never escape it. Even when I'm trying to relax, there's a part of me that thinks I should just walk the two or three steps into the office and do some work."

"But at least you could do it in sweats or pajamas," he said with a grin.

Amy had difficulty imagining Tom Gordon in either. If he had anything as casual as sweats in his wardrobe, they were no doubt designer sweats. And she'd be willing to wager he slept in the nude.

"And even better," Tom noted with a grin. "You're only—what?—ten steps away from the refrigerator?"

"A disadvantage that could lead to sweat suits and pajamas being the only clothes one can get into."

He assessed her with an approving eye. "I can't see where that's been a problem."

"Only because I've banned Häagen-Dazs from my freezer."

He accepted a steaming cup of coffee from her and joined her at the kitchen table. Piggy sat attentively at his feet while Molly and Drover stationed themselves beneath the table. Tom didn't seem to mind being followed by the pack. "You have a lab here, too?"

"In the basement. Some of my stuff I send out to a commercial lab. Some I do here."

"Well, I envy your talent, Amy. I wish I had an artistic side."

"Everyone has an artistic side," she told him.

"Nope. Not me. I'm a man of ideas and action,

which brings us back to when we're going to put together this latest idea of mine."

"Well, there's a dog show next weekend at Boulder County Fairgrounds. It might be a good place for you to start."

"Good idea. I'll bring a cameraman with me. Saturday or Sunday?"

"There'll be a bigger entry on Sunday."

"Good enough."

They sipped their coffee while discussing ideas for how Tom should present the different aspects of the dog world. Before Amy knew it, the coffeepot was empty and the hour approached midnight.

"Do you want more coffee?" she asked.

"No. I think I've had enough caffeine for one evening." He stretched and grinned engagingly. "So . . . I guess that's my cue to leave."

"It's been a lovely evening, Tom. Thank you."

"No. Thank *you*, Amy."

The dogs escorted them back to the living room, where Tom retrieved his jacket but didn't put on. He gave her a smile that was almost sheepish. "A kiss for old times' sake?"

Amy didn't know what old times he referred to, but temptation made her walk into his open arms. He gave her a quick hug, then brushed her lips with his.

"You're a special lady, Amy. Don't ever forget that."

Before she could reply, he kissed her again. His mouth moved over hers with gentle exploration, and she could feel a rising excitement in the body that pressed against her. When he released her, his smile was wry.

"I don't suppose . . ."

"No," Amy said firmly. Her senses swam, but she wasn't that confused. "No, Tom. Everything's . . . much too fast."

"Okay." He brushed her lips again. "No pressure. Honest." He gave her a quick grin. "But someday I'll ask again. When things aren't moving so fast. That's a promise."

"Tom—"

He shushed her with a finger across her lips. "See you Sunday. Sweet dreams."

Amy felt slightly dazed as she closed the door behind him. She hadn't been kissed since long before David was killed, except for the aborted attempt by Jeff, and that didn't really count. Suddenly she wondered how a real kiss from Jeff would be. How would it compare to Tom Gordon's. And would he also feel obliged to try for a more intimate conclusion?

Suddenly Amy laughed. Imagine her, Amy Cameron, the world's least likely femme fatale, comparing the attractions of two eligible men like a shopper comparing rutabagas. As if the spectacular Tom Gordon was interested in anything beyond a one-night fling. As if Jeff Berenger thought she was worth dodging around Miss Piggy's pranks and interceptions. And as if, in the final analysis, she really wanted a relationship with either of them.

She didn't, of course. Only six months ago her life had shattered, and she had just begun to heal, to feel a joy in life, in independence, friends, and laughter. A man would only complicate her life and open old wounds. Even tonight, pleasant as the evening had been, just talking about David's murder and the terrifying experience of having her house burn brought back an uneasiness that had haunted Amy long after her life had settled back into a normal routine.

Right on cue, as if choosing the point in her emotional ramblings best suited to giving her a fright, the dogs burst into an explosion of barking and scrambled toward the back door. Amy followed, her heart pounding. A quick movement at the kitchen window caught her eye. Had that been a face she had glimpsed, or was her imagination in overdrive?

When the back door creaked open, she nearly jumped out of her skin.

"Hell-loh-ho!"

"Omigod! Selma! You scared me half to death!" Amy collapsed into a chair at the kitchen table as her friend pushed through the blockade of dogs. "What were you doing peeking in the window like that? That was you, wasn't it?"

"Sorry. I didn't mean to scare you." Selma grimaced guiltily. "I was just checking to make sure your date had left before I came in."

"Just thought you'd drop in, did you?" Amy checked her watch. "At half past midnight?"

"I . . . uh . . . left some ice cream in your freezer. Mine's letting everything thaw."

"Yeah. Right."

"I did! And it is." Selma sat down in the chair opposite Amy, an eager expression brightening her face. "So! How was your date?"

"It wasn't a date."

Selma snorted her disbelief.

"Well, it wasn't supposed to be a date. I guess it kinda ended up that way."

"What's he like? Besides drop-dead gorgeous."

"He's nice."

"And . . . ?"

Amy shrugged. "He's nice."

"There's got to be more than that." Selma got up and took a carton from the freezer, as if to prove the legitimacy of her excuse. "Cookies and cream," she told Amy. "Want some?"

Amy dropped her head into her hands. "Oh jeez."

"Come on. Loosen up. It's easier to talk about men over ice cream."

"I could gain so much weight having you around. There oughta be a law against someone like you who can eat all that junk and still fit into your jeans."

"Your jeans still look great." Selma placed two heaping bowls of ice cream on the table. "Now," she said, settling herself into a chair. "Tell Mother Selma everything there is to tell."

Her reticence eased by ice cream, Amy confessed the entire evening, from Tom's story idea to the good-night kiss.

"You didn't let him spend the night? I don't believe it." Selma sighed disconsolately and appealed to the corgis for sympathy. "What are we going to do with her, kids?"

The dogs gave Selma only a split second's attention before returning to the task of monitoring the ice cream bowls. Selma picked up her nearly empty bowl and tempted them with possibilities.

"Do you think your mother is out of her mind?" She moved the bowl up and down, up and down, and three corgi heads nodded in unison. "See!" she told Amy. "They agree with me."

Amy picked up her own bowl and clucked to the dogs, who scrambled to pay homage to this new ray of hope. "Do you think Selma's an idiot?" she asked them. Their heads bobbed enthusiastically when she moved the bowl. "Good dogs. I knew you were sensible little corgis." As a reward, she set the bowl on the floor and let them have at it.

"How could you turn down a hunk like Tom Gordon?"

"Selma! This was our first date! And it wasn't even supposed to be a date."

"Do you like him?"

"Yes. I like him. What's not to like?"

"You know? I'll just bet this so-called story he wants to do on dogs is a ploy to spend time with you. Whaddya wanna bet?"

"Selma, he doesn't need to employ those kinds of tactics."

"So you really like him."

"Well . . . yes. I like him."

"When are you seeing him again?"

"He's coming to the dog show next Sunday. Don't look like that! He's bringing a cameraman from his show."

"Window dressing. This is great. You have two men after you!"

Amy sighed. "No one is after me." A sudden chill shook her as her brain somehow translated that notion in the worst possible way. After her house had burned so mysteriously so short a time after David's murder, the police had considered the possibility that she was a target, for some reason, that these misfortunes were not merely random acts. She had denied the possibility, both to herself and to the police. There was absolutely no reason for anyone to be after her. None at all.

No one was after her, not in the way Selma imagined, not in the way the police had once feared.

"No one is after me," she repeated, not quite convincingly.

EIGHT

THE GERMAN SHEPHERD was still on a high from his win in the show ring, and he refused to hold a pose long enough for Amy to take his photograph. Some people maintained that dogs didn't know the difference between losing and winning. Amy didn't believe that for a moment. For certain this big guy knew.

"His back leg is out again."

The handler sighed in frustration and reset the shepherd's leg into a show pose. The dog apparently had decided he'd posed enough for one day.

"Now his front leg is out."

The handler muttered a word that could have gotten him ejected from the show if the AKC representative heard it. Amy was getting a bit annoyed herself, as she had three other winners waiting in line.

"Tony, take the dog's teddy bear and try to distract Hans there from being a fidget, will you?"

Amy's assistant had been watching from the sidelines, grinning, while the shepherd made fools of them. Amy had lured him to the show with a promise of time and a half wages. Tony liked dogs, but he hated dog shows. He claimed the cutthroat competition sent out "vibes" that gave him heartburn. He had a point. A show could get a bit intense. But the chili dogs and hamburgers at the food concession were more likely the source of his heartburn.

Reluctantly, Tony picked up the soggy teddy bear that the big dog had been mouthing a few minutes before and gingerly waved it just out of the camera's field of view. "Lookee here, Hans old boy. Want your ted?"

Hans's ears pricked to alertness, and he forgot about the game with his feet long enough for Amy to snap two good photos.

Next up was a pretty Siberian husky female who had been awarded reserve, or runner-up, to the winning female in her ring. The handler was the dog's owner and obviously didn't care that she hadn't won, just as long as she got a ribbon. She grinned from ear to ear for Amy's camera then knelt to give the Siberian a hug once the photo was taken. Amy grinned too. It was good to know that some people still had a good time at these events.

Four dogs later, a familiar voice broke in as Amy congratulated the handler of a golden retriever on a nice win. "Do I have to be towing a dog along with me to get my picture taken?"

Amy's heart flip-flopped unexpectedly as she turned. "Tom! Hi!"

"You look surprised," Tom noted.

"No. Of course not. I guess I expected you a bit earlier." Amy instantly wanted to call the words back. Did she want him to think she'd been anxious for him to get there, constantly looking toward the entrance of the exhibit hall for his arrival, nervous as a teeny bopper expecting her sweetheart's appearance? Well, she wasn't. Not most of the time, at least.

"I didn't want to take up your whole day," he said. "Meet Corky Corchoran, my cameraman."

The cameraman was short, rotund, and red haired.

He carried the big camera on his shoulder as though it had grown there.

"Hi," Amy said. "Nice to meet you."

The cameraman gave her a freckled grin. "Likewise. This is quite a gig." With his free arm he indicated the fairgrounds exhibit hall that was crowded with dogs, handlers, grooming tables, blow-driers, and vendors of canine paraphernalia. The gated-off rings where the dogs strutted their stuff was, areawise, only a small part of the total chaos.

"I had a dog once," the redhead confided. "She was a collie."

"Then you'll want to meet Selma and Raven," Amy said. "If your boss will turn you loose long enough."

"Oh, sure he will." Corky winked at her. "Tom's a good guy. None better."

"See," Tom noted with a grin. "Everyone thinks I'm a nice guy."

" 'Course, he paid me to say that."

"I thought a character reference or two wouldn't hurt," Tom admitted.

Tony had been hovering at the perimeter of the conversation, waiting for his chance to break in. He nudged Amy.

"What? Oh, sorry. Tom, this is Tony Greene, who works for me when the mood strikes him. He's in grad school at CU."

The two men shook hands. "I'm a big fan," Tony told Tom. "I have class when your show's on, but sometimes I tape you."

"I'm flattered." Tom's grin was open and unassuming.

"There should be more go-for-the-jugular journalism like yours. Man, you oughta be in New York or

Washington, D.C., working for a major league network."

Tom shook his head in mock regret. "That's what I keep telling those network boys."

"Guess it's a dog-eat-dog sort of competition, eh?"

"Speaking of dogs. . . ." Amy indicated the borzoi and malemute waiting impatiently for their turns in front of her camera. "Tony, would you take over here while I show Tom around?"

"That's what you're paying me for," he said.

Tom instructed Corky to film some candid footage around the showgrounds while he stayed with Amy to seek out specific items of interest.

"The collies will be in ring twelve in about twenty minutes," she told the cameraman.

He gave her a thumbs-up before wandering off through the crowd.

"I like to get to know my subject a bit before getting down to serious business," Tom told Amy. "I hope it's not too much bother for you to give me a tour."

"That's why I dragged Tony away from Sunday football," she said. "Welcome, sir, to the Wide World of Dog Shows. Don't touch the precious furballs. The dogs seldom bite, but the owners almost always do if you pet the dog and mess up a groom job. And watch where you put your feet."

"Yeah. Good idea."

"Where are your dogs?" he asked as they made their way through the crowded grooming area.

"Drover is kenneled by my friend Selma, so she can keep an eye on him. Molly and Piggy are home."

He took a notebook and pencil from his jacket pocket.

"And why aren't the ladies entered?"

"Well, Molly finished her championship two years ago. She's resting on her laurels. It's what she does best.

And Piggy—" Amy laughed, "Piggy isn't what I would call a beauty queen. Though she was quite indignant to be left at home."

"I'll bet." Tom grinned. "I can imagine she expressed herself quite vocally."

"Quite," Amy said with a laugh.

She gave him the cook's tour of the dog show—the grooming areas, the show rings, the concessions. They paused to watch a seventy-pound standard poodle stand in patient acceptance as its owner teased and sprayed its coat into stiff and stylish perfection. Nearby, an Old English sheepdog sprawled comfortably on its side, its eyes closed in bliss and its wide tongue lolling over the edge of the grooming table while every tangle was brushed from its silvery gray hair. Tom made a note in his book, then asked the owner if he could stop by later for an interview.

When they wandered the concession area, Tom expressed amazement at the variety of goods for sale— everything from original artwork to dog beds.

"I don't believe all this stuff," Tom commented, laughing as he examined a treadmill for dogs.

"It's a huge industry."

"You can say that again."

Amy consulted her watch. "We're due at ring ten."

"We are?"

"Drover will be in the ring."

"Without you?"

"He's going in with a professional handler. I try to stay away from him for a couple of hours before ring time. Otherwise he pays more attention to me standing at ringside than he does to his handler."

"Wouldn't any male?" Tom asked with a twinkle in his eye.

She twinkled back at him. "Wait until you see this professional handler. She's quite an eye-catcher."

"Does that improve Drover's chances?"

"It doesn't hurt."

Tom caught Corky's eye from across the room and gestured the cameraman to follow as they made their way through the crowded aisles to the ring where corgis were now being shown. Selma, watching at ringside, fluttered her hand in a little wave of greeting as they grabbed the two empty chairs beside her.

"How did Raven do?" Amy asked.

"Got dumped. That judge wouldn't recognize a good collie if one walked up and peed on her shoe."

"Ah. Do you have a show catalog?"

"Yeah. Here."

"That looks like a full-length novel," Tom said as Selma handed over the list of entered dogs and scheduled classes.

"More like a script for a soap opera," Selma told him. "Read between the lines in there and you'll see bribery, chicanery, plotting, heartbreak—" She smiled meaningfully, "even some romance."

Amy gave her a quelling glance, but Tom grinned. "Really? Sounds like a newsman's paradise."

Before Selma could drop any more embarrassing hints, corgis started filing into the ring, towing their handlers behind them. Amy explained the competition to Tom, who chuckled as the dogs paraded around the ring on their stubby legs.

"Corky, be sure you get some good footage of these little guys. That should bust the image that all show dogs are dolled up like poodles. But the people—lord! Three-piece suits and uptown dresses?"

"It's considered very tacky to wear jeans into the ring," Amy said.

"I would bet that some of those outfits in there are almost as expensive as the dogs."

Amy's lips twitched in a half smile. "The handlers

try to look the part of a winner, just as you look the part of a successful news personality. Isn't that one of the things you have to do to get ahead in your business?"

He gave her a look she couldn't interpret, and for a moment he seemed someone quite different from the affable celebrity who pursued her with obvious flirtation on his mind. "I do more than buy five-hundred-dollar suits to get ahead in my business."

"Of course you do."

His smile was instantly apologetic. "Sorry. I didn't mean to sound like such a grouch. Why isn't Drover in the ring?"

"Uh . . ." For a moment Amy was nonplussed by the lightning change in his demeanor, then decided she must have touched upon a sensitive topic. Even celebrities were allowed their sore points. "Oh. Uh, Drover's in the best-of-breed class because he's already a champion. This class is for male puppies."

"Ah. Well, I can see this is complicated."

As the corgi classes progressed, Amy explained the order of judging while Tom made notes. Finally, at the very end of the corgi competition, the best-of-breed class strutted in, Drover among them. On the other end of Drover's lead was Amy's friend Melissa Danforth.

"Why aren't you in there?" Tom asked.

"Because Melissa's a better handler than I am, and she offered to take him in today."

Tom grinned. "Do I dare hope that's because you'd rather be out here with me?"

She gave him an arch look. "Just watch the competition."

Drover lost, despite Melissa's best efforts.

"What did he do wrong?" Tom inquired with a frown.

Amy was surprised at how keenly he had followed

the judging. "Drover didn't do anything wrong. The judge simply liked another dog better."

"Drover was better looking than that dog that won."

"Well, of course *I* think so."

"That judge ought to have his glasses checked."

Amy smiled indulgently, and Tom's frown eased. "Sorry. I'm the competitive sort. I like to win."

"I can tell. Don't worry," she said, pushing back her chair and standing, "Drover does his share of winning. Didn't you want to take Corky around to get some footage of that Old English sheepdog?"

Relaxed again, Tom sighed. "Back to work, eh? Has anyone ever noted that you're quite the slave driver?"

Amy replied with the twitch of a smile. "Just ask my dogs."

The better part of an hour's filming gave Tom the footage he wanted. He thanked Corky for a good job and promised Amy he would call her that night to set up the next phase of filming. She was supposed to arrange some interviews, if she could, with people who had adopted rescue dogs from the Corgi Rescue committee and other organizations like it in the Denver area.

As she sat on Drover's grooming table and waved good-bye to Tom and Corky, Amy wondered a bit guiltily at the sense of relief she felt. It wasn't Tom's fault that he was conspicuous, after all. Being recognized by everyone, everywhere, was simply a disadvantage of his profession. He was so accustomed to eyes following him that he didn't even notice it. Amy, on the other hand, did notice. Being stared at made her feel very uncomfortable, and all the time Tom was with her, eyes had turned their way. She wondered what being married to a celebrity would be like. Did one grow accustomed to the attention? Or would it slowly drive a private person crazy.

Amy was willing to bet it would drive her crazy.

"Amy!"

Fingers snapped in front of Amy's face.

"Where are you, girl? And where have you been?"

"What?" Amy blinked. Selma stood in front of her, shifting from foot to foot and beetling her brows. Beside her sat Raven, who looked up at Amy with a tongue-lolling, good-natured grin.

"The herding trial! Raven's in the arena in ten minutes! You promised to give moral support!"

"Oh, sure." Amy glanced at her watch. "I'll meet you there. Just let me check on Tony."

"I was just there, looking for you. Tony's handling everyone like a pro. If you don't watch out he'll be stealing your business from you. Come on! I'm about to pee my pants I'm so nervous."

Amy surrendered as Selma pulled her through the crowd. "I don't know why you're nervous. Raven always screws up."

"What do you expect? He hasn't worked sheep since I left Gary. Besides"—she yanked open the door to the arena building—"I'm not nervous about Raven screwing up. I'm used to that. I'm nervous about Gary being here."

Amy looked about her in surprise. "Gary's here?"

"Well, it's likely, don't you think? He must know that I would enter Ray in the trial, and I can't imagine him passing up a chance to harass me."

Selma searched the half-filled bleachers with anxious eyes, but to Amy, her hunt looked more hopeful than fearful. "If he's here, Selma, I'm sure he'll come talk to you."

"Not if the jerk knows what's good for him, he won't. I've got to go over by the gate. You're going to watch, aren't you?"

"I'll be in the bleachers, right on the fifty-yard line."

Once Amy found a seat, she waved encouragingly to Selma, who stood by the arena gate waiting for a Belgian sheepdog to finish the course. Amy grimaced a bit as she watched the Belgian move the sheep through gates and chutes and between pylons at the behest of its master, who directed the exercise from the gate of the final chute. The dog's performance was confident and polished, and it would make poor Ray's attempt look worse in comparison. Ray was sweet and loyal beyond measure, but working at traditional collie pursuits was not his forte. Selma kept hoping, and Ray kept flunking his tests.

When Ray's turn came, he performed with his usual mediocrity, missing a chute and completely losing track of one ewe, who trotted to the other side of the arena and watched the proceedings with a bored expression. Selma herself seemed as distracted as Ray. Her eyes more than once left the arena to search the crowd in the bleachers. Looking for Gary, Amy mused. She wondered if Selma was relieved or disappointed not to find him.

When the debacle was over, Amy started to leave. She couldn't expect Tony to do the entire day's work. She'd scarcely gotten halfway down the bleachers, however, when she stopped cold and dropped into the nearest empty seat. A border collie had entered the arena, and none other than Jeff Berenger followed.

Of course he would be entered. Why hadn't she realized it? Amy chided herself. Or perhaps she had. Maybe the likelihood of seeing him at the herding trial was the reason she had promised to give Selma moral support during her run.

Spot moved the sheep through the course methodically and efficiently, but Amy appreciated the performance with only a small part of her mind. Most of her attention was claimed by the unexpected knots twisting her gut. She tried to attribute the feeling to the greasy doughnut she had eaten while giving Tom his tour, but after all these years, her stomach was impervious to dog show food. It was not impervious to a sudden appearance by Jeff Berenger.

Over two weeks had passed since she'd seen Jeff. He had called twice, and their conversations had been friendly, but she'd dodged all hints that they get together. Amy didn't like the way she felt short of breath when she talked to him. There was no reason for it. They were not involved, scarcely even friends, really. He had generously volunteered to do some work for Corgi Rescue, and they'd had one friendly dinner together. That was all.

Of course, he had almost kissed her—would have kissed her if it hadn't been for their furry little chaperone. But that was nothing. If he was truly interested, he could have pushed Piggy aside and finished what he'd started. That aborted kiss had simply been a spur-of-the-moment thing, a product of the night, the mood, and the festival. It didn't mean anything. She'd thought about it only once or twice since it happened. Well, Amy admitted, maybe she'd thought about it a few more times than that.

As Spot nonchalantly pushed the sheep into the final pen, making the task look easy, Amy told herself sternly that she needed to get this romantic silliness under control. Over the past several weeks she had lowered her guard to the point where she had not one, but two men on her mind. Honesty required her to confess that she'd given both of them a fair amount of encouragement. One might go so far as to say she had flirted. The reasons were perplexing. Such behavior was very unlike her. She was not a flirt. Lydia Keane had been a flirt, and

Amy was nothing—absolutely nothing!—like her late friend. She was down-to-earth, emotionally independent, and too busy to put up with all this distraction in her life.

Yet there was Tom, who had promised to call that night, and even Amy had to admit by now that he had more than dog research on his mind. And there was Jeff, who hung on Amy's thoughts like a stubbornly attached burr. Worse, the idiotic temptation to greet him when he came out the arena gate was overpowering her good sense. Excuses to talk to him flew unbidden into her mind. Jeff deserved congratulation on Spot's fine performance. She was thinking of training Drover for trials and could solicit his advice. Piggy was in need of a good low-calorie food, and could he suggest one?

All the excuses were bullshit, Amy admitted. She just wanted to talk to him. And why shouldn't she? They were acquaintances, and to ignore him would be just plain rude.

With that thought bolstering her, she got up and headed for the arena floor.

"Hey!" Jeff greeted her when he saw her standing beside the exit gate. "Amy! I saw you in the stands. If you hadn't come to say hello, I was going to hunt you down."

"Well, here I am."

"Here you are."

Somehow, all their conversations seemed to get off on the most awkward footing possible, Amy reflected. She always sounded like an idiot. His eyes distracted her. His smile made her stammer. The baritone of his voice made her stomach flutter like a teenager's. Was all this because of the disconcertingly frank admiration she saw in his eyes, or was it because beneath her facade of capable, independent, modern woman, she really was an idiot?

"So. What did you think of Spot?" he asked.

"Uh . . . beautiful. Nice performance. You've done a good job training her."

"I can't take credit. Spot's a naturally bossy broad. She likes to push the sheep around." His eyes lit with a sudden twinkle. "Speaking of bossy broads, how's Miss Pudgy?"

"Miss Pudgy is a bit disgruntled right now, since she's home in her kennel. But she's lost three pounds and her coat's beginning to shine like it ought to."

"Too bad. Pretty soon I won't be able to tease her about all that fat. I'll have to think up another way to get revenge for the tricks she plays."

Amy smiled. "Piggy believes that she's the one who deserves revenge. I have no doubt about it."

"I believe you're right," he replied, chuckling. "That little girl has an almost human way of holding a grudge. Come on. Let's get out of this dust." He moved toward the exit, bringing her with him by a casual hand at the small of her back. So natural was the gesture that Amy could almost believe his hand belonged on her. Anyone looking at them would assume they were a couple, which of course they weren't, she reminded herself.

Amy waved sheepishly at Selma, who stood at the scoring table watching them with a raised brow and admiring smile. Amy wondered what Selma admired—Jeff's smooth move or her own rapid slide into a very awkward pickle with two men.

"Had lunch?" Jeff asked when they got to the exhibit hall.

"I'm beginning to think that food is all you ever think about."

"It's right up there with breathing," he admitted. "Not eating is unhealthy, you know. Results in crankiness and a lot of other nasty symptoms."

"We can't have that."

"No, we can't. Since you were so kind as to provide me with such a nice meal once upon a time, let me treat you today."

Their choice of places to eat amounted to none at all. The fairgrounds food concession operated a walk-up window that sold hamburgers, fries, and hot dogs. For those with heartier appetites, cheeseburgers, nachos, and chili dogs could also be had.

Even in midafternoon, lines four deep crowded up to the concession window. No tables awaited the customers. Most ate standing up. Amy and Jeff were lucky enough to find two unoccupied folding chairs beside the Pomeranian ring. Spot settled at their feet and hopefully eyed their lunch.

"The prices are outrageous," Jeff commented. "But at least the food is bad."

It wasn't so bad, however, that he didn't happily devour his nachos and double cheeseburger in the time it took Amy to eat half her hot dog.

"How do you eat that stuff and still weigh less than three hundred pounds?" Amy asked incredulously.

"Aerobics," Jeff confided.

"You belong to a gym?"

"Heck no. It's one of the built-in benefits of being a vet. Do you know how high a heart rate I can achieve merely by taking the temperature of a rottweiler? Or giving shots to a German shepherd? Not to mention wrestling Saint Bernards and Great Danes."

Amy laughed. How different this meal was from her dining experience with Tom Gordon. Tom had given her tablecloths and candles, gourmet food served up with a view of city lights against a star-studded sky. Jeff Berenger provided mystery meat on a bun served with a view of Pomeranians prancing around a ring like so many dust bunnies with legs. She recalled Selma's remark about hamburger and lobster. She hadn't known how dead-on, hit-the-nail-on-the-head right she had been.

"Speaking of fat," Jeff said, "why don't you bring Miss Pudgy on our hike tomorrow. Do her good."

"Hike? What hike?"

"Did I forget to ask you?"

"Ask me what?"

"To go with me up Butler Gulch tomorrow. It's a nice trail up to the alpine meadows above Empire. There'll be a little snow, but nothing we can't handle."

Amy was annoyed and amused at the same time. "You know very well you didn't ask me. And I . . . well, I don't think I'm much of a hiker."

"Nothing to it. Just put one foot in front of the other until you get to the top. You'll love it. So will Piggy. There'll be mud to slop through, deer poop to roll in, meadows to run in. All dogs love it."

Amy had her doubts Miss Piggy would like any of those attractions. "Tomorrow's Monday. Aren't you working?"

He shrugged. "Doctors take off Wednesday to play golf. Why shouldn't vets take off Monday to go hiking? The weatherman says tomorrow's going to be a beautiful day, and I don't have anything pressing."

Amy thought of the show photos she should start developing tomorrow. The house needed cleaning, and the pile of laundry was a hazard to navigation in her bedroom.

A host of reasons demanded that she refuse. She had no right to go gallivanting off to the mountains when she should be working. Gallivanting with Jeff Berenger, no less. She should have her nose to the grindstone and her feet firmly on the ground, the ground in Niwot, not some alpine meadow up in the clouds. Just because Jeff was so casual about work and self-discipline didn't mean that she should follow him down the path to irresponsibility.

Amy opened her mouth to refuse when he smiled at her. The man had a million-volt smile. It started on the curve of his lips and grew in wattage until his eyes fairly shimmered with it—mischief, warmth, invitation, challenge, and just a hint of understanding.

Who could resist a smile like that? Amy asked herself. Not her. And after all, how much trouble could she get into on a silly hike?

NINE

I THINK I mentioned already that I wasn't an athletic woman, when I was a woman. It was Amy who played on the softball team in high school, not me. And though I took on the football team whenever I could, our games certainly weren't played out on the gridiron.

In my opinion, exercise is work, not recreation. For years I went faithfully to a fitness club and forced myself to sweat to the accompaniment of really bad music two or three times a week. The effort was a drag, but I was proud of my figure—what woman wouldn't be proud of a figure like the one I had? Age and gravity are every girl's enemies, you know, and I was determined not to let them drag me down without a fight. If I'd known then that middle-age sag wasn't going to be a problem for me, I could have saved myself a lot of money, time, and sweat.

The point here is that exercise has never been my thing, and being stuck with a stuffed-sausage figure and four-inch legs didn't make things any easier. Do you think that Amy took this into consideration when she threw me into the minivan along with Drover and a backpack? Of course not. For a dog lover, Amy is really very inconsiderate of her dogs.

Drover, stupid idiot that he is, wasted energy by dancing about his car kennel, panting, and filling the minivan with his bad breath. He behaves the same whenever he's allowed in the car, whether he's heading to the park or the vet. Shows how smart he is. I, on the other hand, suspected something unpleasant was afoot the moment I spied the backback and hiking boots. When a battered pickup truck pulled into the driveway and Dr. Doom got out, I knew my worst fears had materialized.

During the ride into the mountains, my mood got more and more sour. After only one day apart from me, Amy was already veering off track. What had happened to Tom Gordon? I wondered. Hadn't he shown up at the previous day's dog show? Hadn't he been his irresistibly sexy and charming self? How long did it take a man with money, looks, fame, and a damned hot car to sweep a woman off her feet? What was wrong with Gordon, anyway?

And where the hell had Berenger come from? I had thought after the festival that he was toast, history, a dead issue. Now he shows up with his two annoying border collies and a big smile on his face. I had to admit, for a loser he was showing quite a bit of staying power, more than he showed when he dated me. When I dumped him after one really dull date, he'd bowed out of the picture without so much as a whimper. Obviously, he's not a man who's willing to fight for what he wants. So why was he being such a pest about Amy?

When the minivan finally stopped, I debated whether I should insist on being left behind in my comfortable kennel or sacrifice myself to keep an eye on Amy. When the door opened, a faceful of cold mountain air convinced me that staying put was the wisest course. Isn't there some platitude about picking your fights or saving your energy to fight another day? If there isn't, there ought to be.

As usual, however, my wishes were ignored. Amy opened the door of my kennel and called me out. She was rigged up like some Sierra Club geek with a day pack on her back, a water bottle on each hip, and ten pounds of solid leather hiking boots encasing her feet. I would have laughed, but the closest sound my throat could produce was a shrill yip.

"Don't give me back talk, young lady. You're going to have fun today, whether you want to or not."

I settled onto my blanket like a lump of furry lard and looked down my nose in disdain at the leash that dangled from Amy's hand. Whoever designed corgis had not intended for such ridiculous animals to go trekking through the mountains. I was sure of it.

"Let me have a crack at her," Dr. Dastardly said.

Before I knew it, my kennel was upended and I was unceremoniously dumped out. Before I could scramble back through the door, he snapped on the leash.

"You'll see, Pudgy old girl. Fresh air and exercise are addictive."

Showed how much he knew. Eating is addictive. Soap operas, the Oprah show, cigarettes, and cocaine are addictive. Fresh air and exercise are not.

"You think she's up to this?" Amy asked him.

To answer her question, I tried to jump back into the van.

"She'll be fine," Dr. Dumb assured her. *"We'll take it nice and slow. No problem."*

Easy for him to say. He had long legs and lots of muscle. I, on the other hand, was a little brown bag of furry fat who could get high-centered on a bump in the road.

I thought I had a reprieve when Amy yelped in alarm at something she spied in Berenger's backpack.

"Is that a gun?" she demanded.

"Don't worry. It's not loaded."

"Why on earth are you carrying a gun?"

He shrugged. *"Most country vets carry a pistol. It's still the most humane way to euthanize a large animal, like a horse, or a deer who's suffering on the side of the road after being hit by a car."*

"Are we going to shoot a horse today?" she asked, with the hint of an edge in her voice.

I mentally cheered her on. Amy didn't like guns. I didn't like Dr. Pistol-packing Prick, so for a change Amy and I were of like mind. I prayed for her to set the toad on his ear and climb back into the van.

No such luck. Berenger smiled that boyish smile of his. "I've gotten in the habit of carrying it when I'm in the sticks. It's not necessary, but it never hurts to be prepared."

Amy smiled back at him. "You're right. Sorry. I guess guns just make me a bit jumpy."

I couldn't believe she caved in. She could have made an issue of it, started an argument, and backed out of the hike as any sensible woman would have. I almost wanted to beg Dr. Dud to load that pistol of his and put me out of my misery. Better that than spend a whole day dragging through dirt, mud, pine needles, and grossy unmentionable deposits left behind by wild animals.

We set off up the road, four dogs and two people. Drover bounded through the grass like some kind of oversized weasel. Spot and Darby made like two black-and-white streaks in the woods, dashing here and there, then returning to nag everyone else to move faster. Spot wore a dog pack, a little red number that she obviously thought set her above the rest of the dogs. Just because she carried a couple of bottles of water and a few dog biscuits, she thought that bit of added responsibility made her boss dog. When young Darby got too far away, Spot relentlessly herded her back to the group. When Drover stayed behind to bury his nose in a rabbit hole, Spot pushed him to catch up. But when that self-appointed black-and-white busybody tried to push me around, I gave her a good view of my teeth.

"Piggy! Behave!"

I flashed Amy a scorching look. Not only was I forced to trudge along a steep, rocky, dirty road and watch Amy cozy up to the wrong man, but I had to put up with a bossy, know-it-all border collie who thought she was put on earth to tell everyone else what to do. It was simply too much! To make matters worse, Spot and young Darby groveled and abased themselves for the least little tidbit of attention Jeff or Amy threw their way. Drover wasn't much better, but at least he had no pretensions to be anything but a goofy idiot.

Stupid dogs! They love everyone without regard for what they get in return. Where was their pride? Their independence? Didn't they realize that leaving their hearts out in the open was an invitation to get those hearts stepped on?

We soon turned off the road onto a trail that wound through the pines. If the sun ever broke through the thick cover of trees, it didn't do so with enough energy to dry up the ground, which smelled pungently of wet peat and pine needles. Mud holes abounded, much to the other dogs' delight. They splashed through the slop with great abandon, sending gobs of goo in all directions. I expressed my contempt by hanging as far back on the leash as I possibly could. The hike had scarcely begun, but already I was tired—tired, cold, wet, and freckled with mud from those inconsiderate lummoxes' games. That Jeff Berenger considered this sort of thing fun just proved how much of a loser he really was. The trail he'd dragged us on was littered with rocks and logs, and the farther up the mountain we climbed, the worse the trail got. As far as I was concerned, if the Forest Service knew what they were doing, they would install gutters and culverts so the rainwater wouldn't collect to breed mud puddles. And they would pave the trails and sweep them once or twice a week. Have you ever tried to climb over a log that was bigger than you are? Or find your way through a growth of grass and weeds high enough to block out the sky? Of course, when you're only ten inches high, every patch of weeds is high enough to block out the sky.

Worse than any of this, though, was the irksome rise inside me of an almost irresistible urge to cavort. My nose twitched instinctively with the scents of rabbits and squirrels, and I had to fight down a hideous craving to roll in a pile of dried elk poop. While Drover galumphed about, eating insects and following elusive bunny trails, my feet wanted to run beside him, nose to the ground and ears quivering with the sounds of everything from bugs to mice to porcupines rustling in the brush.

I longed to slop through the mud, inhale the myriad odors of the forest, and bark madly at the squirrels that chattered at us from tree branches.

I fought the madness down, of course. Dragging along the trail, trudging out my legitimate objections to this inconsiderate treatment, was my only way to express disapproval. If I bounded and ran like those other mindless dogs, I would be surrendering to the part of me that was not Lydia Keane, and I refused to do it. If it took every last ounce of my strength, I was going to remain miserable and let Amy suffer pangs of guilt for dragging me up that damned mountain.

Lord, but I hated being a dog.

AMY HAD ALWAYS loved the mountains. Every day from her kitchen window in Niwot she admired the stark outline of peaks thrusting boldly into the sky, and on trips along I-70, she invariably gawked at the spectacular vistas afforded by rocky canyons, tumbling streams, and pine-covered ridges.

Her experience with the Rockies had been buffered by distance or the safe confines of a car, however. Even though she had lived in Colorado all her life, this hike was her first down and dirty, up-close and personal encounter with the high country. A whole new world unfolded before her eyes as they left civilization behind. Here on the trail were no odors of asphalt, garbage, fast food, or gasoline. Here were no sounds of automobiles or human voices, no sirens, no radios or television, no buzz of power from overhead lines.

Freed from the pollution of civilization, her senses reeled from a flood of subtle odors and sounds. The scents of autumn—dying vegetation, damp wood, tangy pine. Wind played through the pines with a muted sigh. Birds whistled, scolded, and trilled comments as they passed, and the squirrels chittered in answer.

Rising above the myriad sounds of nature, however, was a grand and dignified silence. The sound of boots scuffing over rocks and crunching through gravel was an imposition in a private, peaceful world. The dogs, for all their silly running and chasing, didn't bark or whine. They seemed to pay respect to the power of the place, a very tangible power, as if the peaks themselves were alive and brooding over the world below. Those majestic heights were often hidden from view by the thick forest that cast the trail into unending shadow, but Amy felt the constancy of their presence.

She experienced a glow of gratitude for Jeff Berenger. If he hadn't all but twisted her arm, she wouldn't have come on this expedition. In fact, she'd almost backed out the night before when Tom Gordon had called with an invitation to a movie and dinner. The offer had been tempting. But she'd taken a raincheck, regretfully telling Tom she had promised an all-day hike to a friend. Now she was glad she had come. Spending more time with Tom would have been fun, but she would have felt rotten about standing Jeff up, and she would have missed seeing all this magic.

"I'm beginning to see that this is a very special place," she commented.

"That it is," Jeff replied. "Butler Gulch is one of my favorite hikes. No matter what time of year you come up here, it has something special to offer. In July and August the wildflowers will knock your socks off. Clumps of columbine grow in every spot of shade, and paintbrush make the fields look like they're on fire."

Amy envied him having the breath for such a testimonial. She herself was beginning to pant with every step.

"Wait till you see the alpine meadows up above . . . wide open fields of wildflowers stretch right up to the summits. Of course, this late in the year, there'll be more snow than flowers. The snowfields are spectacular in themselves, but you really need to come up here next summer."

"I can see . . . (pant) . . . that I've been missing . . . (pant) . . . something great all . . . (pant) . . . this time."

He stopped and turned to face her. "You mean you've never been hiking before?"

"No. Unless you count a stroll in the shopping mall as a hike."

He laughed. "I'll be. This is a virgin expedition for you, eh?"

Unexpectedly, her face grew warm. "I wouldn't put it quite so colorfully."

"You'll see what I mean when we get on top."

She looked upward. From the little meadow where they stood, the bare rock summit was just visible above the trees. It cut a stark line against an electric-blue sky. Surely one needed a space suit up there. "We're going all the way to the top?"

Jeff followed her gaze, and his expression was reverent as he contemplated the imposing height. When he looked back at Amy, however, his face melted into a smile. "Maybe not the tippy top. There's a great lunch spot in the saddle between the peaks. It's a good place to stop."

"A great lunch place, huh? Do they serve mountain goat stew?"

"No, but they do serve up one of the best views in Colorado."

"I'm not sure I'll be in any shape to appreciate it, even if I do make it that far."

"Sure you will," Jeff assured her. "We'll just take it nice and easy. Trust me, it's worth it."

"Right." Amy wriggled her toes, which were already numb from hiking boots designed for fashion rather than function.

They walked on, or, in Amy's case, trudged on. The trail climbed steeply for a short distance, then leveled off. At the top of the rise, she bent over, hands braced against her thighs, and wheezed. "This would be a lot easier if Miss Reluctant back there would quit relying on me to pull her up the trail."

"Why don't you let her off the leash," Jeff suggested. "Maybe she'll do better on her own."

"I don't trust the little devil."

"I doubt she'll run off. If she does, Spot will bring her back soon enough."

Spot sat to one side of the trail, a model of perfect canine behavior. She looked eager to prove her command of the canine corps by chasing down any dog who would dare to misbehave, especially if the erring one happened to be a corgi.

"Okay." Amy snapped the leash free of Piggy's collar. "I could do without this little sack of lard pulling me downhill while I'm trying to go uphill. Come on, Piggy girl," she called as they resumed the climb. "Let's go."

Spot, Darby, and Drover bounded eagerly ahead. Piggy took an unenthusiastic step forward, looked around her, and plopped down in the middle of the trail.

"Come on, Piggy! Go, go, go! We're headed for fun!"

Piggy didn't budge. Her expression clearly conveyed that she didn't believe a word.

"She has the most human-looking scowl I've ever seen on a dog," Jeff said.

"The little shrew practices that scowl a lot. She ought to have it perfected by now."

Jeff laughed and squatted down to scratch Piggy's ear. "You are a piece of work, aren't you, Pudgy?" He took the leash Amy handed him and snapped it on the collar. "Come with me awhile, my girl. We'll give your mother a rest."

Piggy trotted after him, her legs moving but her heart obviously not in the effort. It was going to take more than a diet to drive the couch potato from her soul.

Amy felt more energetic without Piggy pulling her back, but she did envy the spring of Jeff's step. He moved like an athlete. He looked like an athlete too, with those broad shoulders, slim hips, and long legs. Unruly locks of hair feathered over his collar, but the shaggy mass looked soft, clean, and fragrant enough for a woman to enjoy running her hands through, or putting her cheek against. His hands were square and strong, and his backside . . . Amy's face heated as she remembered something Lydia had once said: "Money, looks, and brains in a man are just dandy, but the coup de grâce is a set of good buns." Amy had laughed, then accused Lydia of looking only at the superficial. Still, walking behind Jeff Berenger, she began to appreciate superficial in a whole new way.

Jeff turned to look back at her. Amy flushed and hastily switched her gaze to a clump of flowers beside the trail.

"Want some sunscreen?" he offered. "The sun up here can be mean, and you're looking a bit red."

"Am I?" she inquired with studied innocence. "My face does feel a bit warm."

Piggy shot her a disgusted look, as if the dog knew exactly what had caught Amy's eye. When Jeff threw her the tube of sunscreen and continued along the trail, Amy wrinkled her nose at the little brown know-it-all. Sometimes dogs were too perceptive.

The trail inclined gently upward for a bit, then turned downhill, curved around a thick stand of pine, and plunged beneath the rushing waters of a mountain stream.

"Oh no," Amy groaned. "Do we have to cross that?"

As if in answer, the border collies splashed across the ten-foot-wide channel with bounding strides, then turned around to look at the humans and short-legged dogs still standing on the other side. When the stragglers didn't immediately follow, Spot gave them a look of strained patience and trotted back across the stream. She stopped in front of them to shake, and humans and corgis alike fled the cold shower that flew from her coat.

"Thank you so much, Spot!" Amy said sarcastically.

"She just wanted us to know that getting wet isn't the end of the world."

Amy wiped droplets from her face. "I'd rather not spend the rest of the day with soaked feet, if you don't mind," she told the dog.

"In that case, you'll want to cross on that log up there."

He pointed toward a tree that had fallen across the stream fifty feet upstream. Splintered limbs stuck up from the log at various angles, and sections of the wood had rotted, leaving powdery pulp behind.

"That log?" Amy asked dubiously.

"It's easy. I've crossed it plenty of times. Even the tubular dogs should be able to do it."

Amy had her doubts as they climbed through the tangled windfall that led to the downed tree. The doubts magnified when she looked out over the steep stream bank and saw the water rushing beneath the log in a foaming torrent. The stream was deeper and swifter here than where the trail crossed. The log provided a bridge about two feet above the flow, but what a bridge! The sloping, half-rotten tree trunk made Olympic balance beam competition look like a cakewalk.

"I don't know. . . ." Amy quavered.

"It's much easier than it looks. Just take your time. Scoot across on your backside if you want. And watch out for that rotten wood on the left side. It won't hold you."

"That's nice to know."

"You go first," Jeff told her.

"First? Me?"

"The corgis will want to follow you, not me. I'll bring up the rear."

Amy mentally retracted every complimentary thing she'd thought about the mountains and her trail guide. If she slipped off this damned log, she was going to be sure that Jeff Berenger got just as wet as she did. She crawled onto the log, which was broken off from the stump about five feet above the ground. Sitting astride, clinging to every branch and handhold within reach, she scooted along the rough surface until she reached a large branch that shot vertically from the trunk. Cautiously she got to her feet. Hugging the branch, she froze.

"You've got plenty of room to get around it," Jeff encouraged.

Easy for him to say. He still had both feet on the ground. The only thing beneath Amy's feet was a damp, slick log, and below that, a dizzying rush of water. Five feet of narrow log, its surface broken by knotholes and pocked with rotten pulp, stretched between Amy and the far bank. With her inadequate boots giving her no traction on the weather-polished wood and her pack making balance precarious, the five-foot stretch seemed longer than the Golden Gate Bridge.

"Okay. Just stay right there," Jeff said. "I'll come out and help."

Amy detected a note of amusement in his voice. He was going to have to do some fancy footwork, she decided sourly, to get back into her good graces.

Jeff took a foothold to climb up the log, but before he could move forward, Drover scrambled up in front of him and shot out along the trunk. Surefooted as an oversize squirrel, he trotted up to where Amy clung to the thick vertical branch. There he paused, plunked down his wide butt, and gazed up at her with an expression that clearly questioned why she was hugging a branch and looking like an idiot.

"Next time you tell me you can't jump into the van, see if I lift you up," Amy grumbled.

Unconcerned, Drover made his way around the branch and walked confidently to the opposite bank, not even glancing at the stream below. The border collies greeted him with congratulatory wags of their tails.

With her would-be rescuer wiping tears of laughter from his eyes and a smug corgi demonstrating just what a wimp she was, Amy decided that if she fell into the stream, the dousing would simply make the humiliation complete. She let go of the branch and teetered her way across to the opposite bank. Surprised to find herself dry and in one piece, she smiled. "Well! That wasn't so bad, after all!"

Jeff lifted Piggy up onto the log and steadied her on feet that seemed rooted to the tree. "Go on, Miss Pudgy. Your mom did it, and if she can do it, anyone can."

Amy made a face at him.

When Piggy showed no inclination to go forward, Jeff climbed onto the log behind her. "There you go, girl. Didn't you watch Drover? Are you going to let him show you up like that?"

Piggy seemed uninterested in living up to Drover's example of canine agility. Jeff sighed, picked up the reluctant dog, and stepped nimbly onto the bridge with Piggy's rump riding his arms and her forepaws digging into his shoulder.

Amy bit her lip. How easy Jeff made it look, balancing on that cursed log with a pack on his back and a squirming, unhappy corgi in his arms. She remembered thinking that he looked awkward in her motor home, his legs too long for the couch, his shoulders too broad for the aisle. Here he fit in, with the mountains, the tall trees, the rumpled, untidy splendor of nature. He was a jigsaw puzzle piece that snapped neatly into place, once the right place was found.

"Hold still, you little devil!" Jeff ordered. "You'll send us both into the drink."

As if she understood his admonition, Piggy ceased her efforts to climb up his chest and simply hid her furry face against his shoulder. Jeff deftly made his way around the large vertical branch and headed for safety. He was only a foot from the bank when disaster struck.

Amy could have sworn she saw the light of malicious calculation in Piggy's eyes as the dog gave Jeff a wet swipe on his ear with her tongue. His hold on her momentarily loosened in surprise, and before he could recover, Piggy pushed off his chest with all the force of her considerable bulk and launched to the nearby bank. Jeff's arms windmilled as he tried to regain his balance, but the weight of his pack acted as an extra pull to tumble him into the stream.

Amy shrieked out Jeff's name, followed by several curses of uncharacteristic potency. With his backside planted six inches under water, Jeff let fly a few colorful words of his own. Spot and Darby joined in the commotion, barking their comments, while Drover peered from behind the refuge of a tree to discover just who was going to die. Piggy sat beside Amy's feet, her tongue lolling in a satisfied corgi smirk.

Amy's mouth began to twitch. She tried to hold back the smile. Finding the scene funny was very rude.

Letting loose the laughter bubbling in her throat would be ruder still.

"I hope you broke a leg, you little fur-bearing imp from hell," Jeff shot at Piggy as he got to his feet and climbed up the stream bank. The seat of his jeans drooped with water weight, and his boots squished loudly with every step. "Then I could set it for you without the benefit of anaesthesia."

Amy lost the battle as a chortle escaped her. "Shame on you, Jefferson Davis Berenger! A veterinarian wishing misery on a helpless little animal!"

"Helpless my moss-covered ass! That dog's as helpless as Jack the Ripper."

Amy grabbed his hand to help him up the bank. Piggy sidled around behind her as he clambered onto the grass.

"Coward," he accused the dog. "Hiding behind your mother so I can't wring your little neck."

Amy tsked. "You are a mess! Are you all right?"

"Do I look all right?"

"Well . . ." She surveyed his dripping, muddy form, biting her lip to keep from smiling. "You look . . . like someone who's just been done in by a ten-inch dog."

He flinched. "Don't rub it in."

"You're going to catch pneumonia, you know. I think we'd better head back."

"Not a chance!" Jeff declared. "That would please Pernicious Piggy very much. No. That diabolical overstuffed sausage is going all the way to the top. I'm going to make sure of it."

Amy shook her head. "You're letting a dumb dog make mincemeat of your common sense."

"There is nothing dumb about that malicious little sack of dog fat. And I am not losing my common sense." His mouth slid sideways into a rueful grimace.

"Most folks who know me contend I didn't have any to start with."

Amy couldn't hold back the laughter any longer, and Jeff chuckled along with her, but not without slipping a sideways glare at Piggy.

"I'll just wring out these clothes. They'll dry soon enough."

"I have a towel in my pack," Amy offered.

"Do you? You do come prepared. Was this little incident a plot hatched between you and your villainous dog?"

"No," Amy said. "Piggy thinks of these things all on her own. She's very creative that way."

"Yeah. A frontal lobotomy would fix that."

"Oh, quit it!" She hit his shoulder playfully, her fist splatting against the wet flannel of his shirt.

"You just watch out, little Miss Smart-Ass." He fixed Piggy with a rancorous glare. "You're messing with the wrong guy."

Amy watched him march into the privacy of a thicket to deal with his wet clothes. He was no doubt trying hard to look incensed and offended, but Amy had seen the spark of laughter in his eyes and the beginnings of a grin on his lips. Making an indignant exit must be very difficult for someone of his natural good humor. Not to mention that water squirting from his boots with every step robbed his departure of any dignity.

Amy sighed. "You are a witch, Piggy. I'd say you're grounded for the rest of your life, but you'd enjoy that too much."

It struck her then how differently this scene would have played had David been the one sitting in the stream instead of Jeff. She would have been wound as tightly as a spring waiting for the icy blast of his displeasure, and his mood the rest of the day would have spoiled whatever fun the hike had to offer. Not that David would have come up here in the first place.

Amy had loved David five years ago when they first married, but camaraderie had never been a part of their relationship. That term, *camaraderie,* was the best word she could think of to describe what she was beginning to feel for Jeff Berenger. Not love. Not romance. She was much too sensible to still have illusions about such things. Yet camaraderie was nice. It might even be addictive if she weren't careful.

Jeff emerged from the thicket still wet, but at least he no longer had a waterfall cascading from his trousers.

"Ready to go?" he asked.

"Sure. Since you're the one who's soaked, I guess I can't complain."

Two hours later they left the forest behind and walked into the alpine meadows that stretched from timberline up to the barren peaks. Amy limped up the trail. Her shoulders ached, her feet hurt, and her stomach rumbled. She had endured two more stream crossings, a set of switchbacks that would have given a mountain goat pause, and the grumblings of a muddy, ill-tempered corgi who balked at every step. But as she stopped to look around her, she had to admit the climb was worth it. She couldn't have imagined anything as beautiful as this top-of-the-world vista. They had emerged into a vast bowl of intersecting valleys bounded on three sides by snowy ridges and the cusps of three separate summits. Behind them lay the forested slopes of Butler Gulch, which descended in pine-carpeted glory until the topography rose once more to meet a seemingly endless array of rugged mountains.

"How're you doing?" Jeff asked.

"Oh, great," Amy panted. Catching one's breath became a chore at an altitude of almost twelve thousand feet.

"Only a couple of miles until lunch."

"A couple of miles . . ." She tried not to grimace as she looked ahead to where the trail climbed through meadow after meadow—an endless expanse of greenish beige and tan decorated here and there with the russet colors of autumn flowers. Dazzling white snowfields encroached upon the meadows from all sides in an omen of approaching winter.

Plopped down on a bed of pine needles, Piggy echoed Amy's tired sigh.

"You and I are going to start an exercise routine," Amy promised her. "Next time we come up here, I don't want to hear any huffing or puffing from either one of us."

Piggy yawned, obviously not interested. She resisted the tug on the leash as Amy got to her feet and started up the trail.

"Watch out," Amy warned her. "I'll give my end of the leash to Jeff."

With a snort of disgust, Piggy followed.

"Don't worry. When we get to this promised lunch spot, you can take a nap." Amy sighed. "So can I."

Jeff's clothing had dried in the arid mountain air, Amy noticed as she followed him up the trail. The jeans that had been baggy with water now seemed shrink-wrapped to his body, giving her cause to wonder if her heart rate had increased due to the altitude or the effect of those tight trousers. She tried to distract herself with the spectacular scenery, but the ploy didn't work. Her eyes kept returning to the scenery directly ahead of her, the male scenery, that is.

Yet another stream blocked their way as the trail curved sharply to head in the direction of a rust-red blemish that scarred a distant slope.

"Old mine diggings," Jeff told Amy. "Nothing up there to see except some old rusted machinery."

"You mean we're stopping here?" Amy asked hopefully.

"Just a little ways further."

Amy groaned.

"You won't be sorry," Jeff assured her. "Hiking is like everything else in life. The more work you put into it, the greater the reward at the end."

Strange remark coming from someone who only dabbled in his profession, Amy mused, whose success seemed represented by the beat-up truck he drove and the frayed cuffs of his sleeves.

They left the trail and followed a snow-choked hollow carved out by one of the many little tributary creeks that drained the meadows. The creek wormed its way in and out of the snow, emerging now and then from intricately sculpted ice caves that echoed the laughter of rippling water. Young Darby, who had never before seen snow, ran wild with delight, stopping periodically to roll onto her back to slide and squirm in the icy crystals. Drover caught Darby's spirit and joined in the game, while Spot stood aside and supervised. Piggy at first cast a woebegone look at Amy, begging to be given a ride over the cold, wet expanse, but Amy answered her plea with a firmly voiced "Fat chance!" and left her to plow her own path through the snow.

They left the hollow to climb a game trail that zigzagged up the side of a ridge. Jeff reached down and grasped Amy's arm to help her the last few feet to the top, and for a moment the hard, pulsing nearness of him kept her from noticing anything but the solid chest confronting her face and the strong hands that held tightly to her arms. Then she looked around, and her breath caught from much more than just the dizzying altitude.

The ridge they had just climbed rose like the crest of a mountainous wave, dropping off in a near-vertical tumble of rocks on one side, and on the other, flowing gently downward into a smooth expanse of meadow and snowfield. They were on top of the world, gazing in every direction at a wild assemblage of mountains and valleys, deep pine green and blinding snow white fading into distant purple and lilac. Above it all arched the glorious Colorado sky, its deep blue punctuated by cottony white clouds.

The dogs had ceased their games and stood poised, looking into the distance. Even Piggy, who had planted her butt firmly on the ground the moment they reached the top, seemed impressed by Nature's show.

"You were right," Amy whispered. "This is truly worth the climb."

"It is, isn't it?"

An enigmatic smile lifted his mouth as Amy looked up at him. She froze, suddenly aware that he was going to kiss her, and recognizing in herself a great need to be kissed. The where and why of that need didn't bear analyzing, but it was there. It was there, and he was there, and this strange, wild universe that stretched around her was a different world, and she a different person from the Amy Cameron who trudged through the workaday world down below, feeling lucky to merely survive from one day to another. Deep, undeniable, normally indecipherable truths seemed suddenly within reach, but she didn't have time to grasp at them, for Jeff's mouth was so close, and hers was so needy.

His lips touched hers, and a delicious thrill set Amy's every nerve alive. The world narrowed to just the two of them, warmth igniting to heat, heat exploding inward and outward at the same time. Amy lost all desire to be strong, and as her heart thundered in her ears, the universe faded to black.

TEN

AMY'S FACE WAS alarmingly pale against the brittle brown alpine grass that pillowed her head. The bright sunlight turned her skin translucent, making her look like a frail waif who might blow away with the next puff of wind. Jeff suffered a moment of panic.

"Amy! Come on! Wake up!"

He tickled her nose with a late-blooming paint-brush blossom. She batted at it with one hand but didn't open her eyes until Drover swiped her cheek with a wet tongue and sent a blast of dog breath into her face.

"Go 'way!"

Amy pushed the dog back and squinted into the sun. Jeff moved so that his body blocked the glare from her face. She touched his cheek and frowned. "Jeff?"

"How do you feel?"

"Huh? Why?" Her gaze left Jeff and traveled around the ring of solemn dogs—two corgis and two border collies—who peered at her with anxious faces. "Why am I on the ground?"

"Altitude. Too little oxygen, too much exertion. You fainted."

A slightly sheepish smile tugged at her lips. "I never faint."

"Well, you did. Right in the middle of a great kiss, I might add."

"Oh." A flood of color warmed her face. "Oh yeah. Now I remember."

He was rather gratified by the reaction. "If you're going to let a man kiss you, Amy, it's rude to leave before the kiss is done. Unconsciousness is no excuse."

"I'm sorry."

"Don't mention it." He grinned. "Come to think of it, not many guys can boast of having a kiss that will literally knock a girl off her feet."

She gave him a horrified look. "You are not going to tell anyone about this! Ooof!" As she sat up, Drover bounded onto her lap to bark his congratulations on her recovery. "Oh jeez! Go breathe on someone else! What have you been eating?"

Drover obligingly bounced away, gave Piggy a fast kiss, then sprinted off in an invitation to play. Piggy curled her lip at his antics, then turned her disapproving attention back to Amy and Jeff.

"Miss Pudgy thinks we're much too close," Jeff conjectured.

"Don't pay her any mind. She's such a prig."

He raised one taunting brow at Amy's furry chaperone. "Take this, Miss Priggy." He leaned forward and touched Amy's lips with his. Her mouth opened in hesitant welcome and irresistible sweetness as they sank together to the grass. Jeff had intended a soft brush of the lips, a quick, affectionate peck that respected Amy's currently delicate condition, but a surge of desire got the best of him. He deepened the kiss, heart pounding as her arms stole around his neck and her legs moved restlessly against his. She was silk against the prickly fall grass—fragrant, pliant, and too tempting to resist. He slipped a hand beneath her flannel shirt, finding the warmth of her breast through the thin cotton of her T-shirt. She arched upward into his caress.

Amy went rigid suddenly as Piggy hit them with both front feet.

"Not again," Jeff groaned.

Piggy yapped into his ear, vibrating his very brain.

"Okay! Okay!" He could have cheerfully strangled the fat little furball. Amy looked charmingly flustered, a temptation in denim, flushed cheeks, and tousled hair. Frustration nearly choked off Jeff's breath.

"The best-laid schemes of mice and men . . ." and corgis, Jeff added to the line from Robert Burns. Not that he had a scheme. On top of a mountain, picturesque as it might be, was neither the time nor the place for this sort of thing. Usually he showed more sense than a junior high jock on a testosterone high, but not today. Amy lit a fire in him that was beyond common sense. Not just today. Always. She did that to him every damned time he saw her.

He took a breath to clear his head, not to mention cool some other parts, then forced a grin. "Couldn't leave that first kiss unfinished. Unfinished kisses can fester into all sorts of afflictions."

"Oh. . . ."

She looked a bit dazed. Did he dare hope it was from his attention rather than the rarified alpine atmosphere?

"You okay?"

"Fine. Great." She took his offered hand and scrambled to her feet. Upright again, she bit her lip as her eyes met his and quickly darted away.

This was an awkward moment, Jeff admitted, and he wasn't adept at handling awkward moments, for all that he was a real crackerjack at creating them. How did a man with amorous intentions impress a woman when he was repeatedly foiled by a stupid dog?

"I . . . uh. . . ."

"Jeff . . ." she said quietly.

He forgot what he had wanted to say. She might be ready to hit him or kiss him again. Her voice gave no clue.

"Jeff . . ." She cleared her throat. "That was . . . that was nice." Her smile began as a tentative lift of her mouth and grew from there. Warm and diffident at the same time, it made Jeff's insides go weak.

"Yes," he agreed, feeling tongue-tied as a boy. "That was nice. Next time I'll manage to catch you alone, without your chaperone."

Amy's mouth pursed and a twinkle lit her eye. "Well now, that's the challenge, isn't it?"

With the sparkle back in Amy's eye and the sass back in her voice, the awkwardness dissolved. They were friends again. Closer friends, Jeff told himself. Progress was being made. Definite progress.

"Just tell me it's all downhill from here." A loud rumble from the vicinity of Amy's stomach made her roll her eyes. "That couldn't have been me."

"Of course not. You're much too polite to make a sound like that. Must have been one of the dogs. I think lunch is in order."

A short distance farther along the ridge was a thicket of stunted cypress. The interior of the thicket was open enough for them to spread the tarp that Jeff had brought. Their packs served as backrests as they dug into their lunch sacks for sandwiches. Here the sunshine could reach them, and the sharp wind was blocked by the walls of the thicket.

Amy held up a deli ham sandwich wrapped in plastic shrink-wrap. "This didn't look very appetizing when I bought it this morning, but it's looked better with every mile we walked."

Jeff eyed her lunch with interest. "I'll trade you my apple for your brownie."

"Not a chance. It's your own fault that you brought only healthy stuff. I, on the other hand, knew I was going to need sugar."

The food tasted as only fresh air and exertion can make food taste. The dogs got their share as Jeff doled out dog biscuits that disappeared at the same instant they were offered. Inevitably, all canine eyes turned to what remained of Amy's and Jeff's lunch. The border collies drooled from a polite distance at the edge of the thicket, while the corgis did a low crawl—hoping, no doubt, to avoid notice—to the border of the tarp and stared intently at Amy's bread crusts and Jeff's apple in turn.

"Okay, okay!" Amy portioned out a tidbit of sandwich to all four waiting dogs. "You guys would take it right out of my mouth if I gave you half a chance."

Half-moon dimples dented Amy's cheeks as she smiled. Was it Jeff's imagination, or were those dimples suddenly more pronounced, her smile deeper and broader than before? The tempting curl at the corner of her lips made his mouth water for much more than the brownie she held in her hand.

Amy unwrapped her dessert and licked chocolate from her fingers with an appreciative sigh. No doubt unaware of the temptation she presented, she regarded him through a thick curtain of eyelashes. "How is it," she asked Jeff, "that a man like you gets to his—what? thirties?—without stumbling into marriage? Not that it's any of my business, you understand, but I thought we women laid out tighter nets than that."

He grinned. "It's thirty-four next March sixteenth. Remember the date. I accept presents, flowers, money, gift certificates—"

"You're avoiding my question."

"What question was that?"

"How you escaped marriage."

"Is it something to escape?"

Her smile faltered, and Jeff immediately regretted his words. "Sorry. That was a stupid thing to say."

"It's okay. Like I said before. I'm over it."

Like hell, he thought.

"Besides, I'm the one being offensively nosy, here."

"Feel free to be nosy. I don't mind."

"Well, all right. Most men at the ripe old age of thirty-four—next March sixteenth," she added with a smile, "are either married or divorced. Or maybe you have a wife or ex-wife somewhere?"

"Not that I remember. I almost did make the leap once, though. Right out of vet school. Didn't work out. She had big ideas about me keeping my nose to the grindstone and earning a partnership in the practice I'd joined in Montrose. Didn't see the use of anything that didn't bring in money."

"Such as damaged hawks and little girls with injured kitties?"

"Or climbing mountains or lazing around throwing a fishing line into a lake. She was a nice lady. Smart. Funny. Had one of the prettiest Maine coon cats I've ever seen."

"Well then, she couldn't have been all that bad."

"She ended up marrying a lawyer from Phoenix."

"And you ended up a free man in Longmont, Colorado."

"Free as a bum." He grinned and shrugged. "The truth is I'm not married because I can't see any woman putting up with me the way I am. And I don't want someone moving in on me, pestering me to change."

She gave him a long, contemplative look. "What's so bad about you that no woman would put up with?"

"Things that are important to me aren't important to most other people. Birds, animals"—he gestured to the windswept ridge and the jumble of mountains stretched out below them—"places like this. And things that are important to most people don't really ring my chimes."

"Like a steady income, matching socks, and haircuts?" Amy supplied.

He grinned guiltily. "You noticed."

"Women do tend to notice such things."

"My point exactly!"

"I'm going to ask a very rude question."

"That sounds interesting."

"And you don't have to answer if you don't want to."

"Okay."

Amy bit her lower lip. She did that, he noticed, when she was uneasy.

"Well?" he prompted. "Now you've got me curious."

"Why on Earth would a man like you go out with someone like Lydia Keane? If you like the wind and the mountains and the fresh air, if you appreciate comfortable sloppiness and natural charm, then what the heck drew you to Lydia?"

"Hm." He could be treading on very thin ice, Jeff realized. "Interesting question."

Amy's mouth flattened to a straight line. Piggy, who had crawled up beside her, shifted her attention from Amy's sandwich crusts to stare at Jeff with uncanny intensity. Strange, Jeff pondered, how dogs could zero in on a bit of tension.

"Lydia Keane," he began with a sigh.

"You don't have to answer. Really. It was rude of me to ask."

"I don't mind answering. I've asked the question a couple of times myself."

"My guess is that men have a totally different set of

expectations for themselves and for women. They don't require themselves to be sexy. But they do expect it of women."

"Well . . ."

"Lydia was very sexy."

"Well, yes. She was. And she was fun, in a frantic sort of way."

"So why didn't you keep dating her? Did she dump you?"

"You might say the dump was mutual. I think the only reason she went out with me was she thought vets make a bundle of money. A common misconception. And I asked her out because . . . well, I guess I'll have to admit I was attracted to her looks." He tried to lighten the tone of conversation with a quick grin. "I can be just as superficial as the next guy, you know?"

Amy lifted a brow in his direction, and Jeff wondered if she knew that in a quieter, more subtle way, she was twice as sexy as her friend Lydia had ever thought to be. He guessed she didn't.

"But once you start to know a person, their looks change. The physical appearance gets colored by what's on the inside. Lydia had some interesting stuff swimming around inside her, characterwise, but she didn't like to let on that she did. She wanted to keep things strictly on the surface. Almost as if she didn't want anyone to look past the surface gloss, for fear they might laugh at what was in her soul."

A loud eruption from Piggy's rear end forestalled any further insight on the subject. Amy fanned the air in front of her face and scrambled away from ground zero. "Jeez, Piggy! What was that?"

"Smells like half-digested rodent."

Piggy sent Jeff a haughty glare of particular aversion.

"Don't look at *me*, you little gas bomb," he said. "I'm not the one stinking up the mountain."

Amy laughed. "So much for lounging around the thicket, breathing in the fresh air and indulging in serious conversation. It's just as well Piggy got me off my duff. I feel better! I feel like doing something." Amy walked to the lip of the ridge, spreading her arms wide to encompass the searing blue sky, the alpine valley below them, and the mountains that marched to the horizon and beyond. Jeff got the message that she didn't want to continue with the subject of Lydia Keane. That was fine by him. The sight of her inhaling deeply of the cold mountain air, small round breasts pressed against the plaid flannel of her shirt, drove all memories of Lydia from his mind. He squirmed uncomfortably. He hadn't thought that any sight could equal the view from this ridge, but Amy Cameron embracing the world certainly did.

"I feel like I'm standing on the edge of the universe!" she exclaimed. "I feel like I could talk to God up here."

"Be careful on that edge," Jeff warned, "or you *will* find yourself talking to God."

She gave him a smile that made his heart stop. "Thank you for bringing me up here, Jeff. I never could have imagined any place as glorious as this. It was definitely worth the hike to get here."

"There's more," he told her.

"More?"

"Come on. I'll show you."

They packed away their garbage, parked their backpacks beside the thicket, and set off with the plastic tarp riding beneath Jeff's arm.

"What's that for?" Amy asked.

"You'll see." He gave her the devil's own grin, feeling like a boy let out of school, young and carefree, ready to burst with energy. The mountains often made him feel that way, but today it was Amy. Amy posing on the very crest of the ridge like a beautiful hawk about to take flight. Amy with the mountain breeze tumbling her hair into a riot of curls. Amy laughing at him from the bank of the stream as he rose dripping from the water. Amy kissing him. Yes indeed. Amy kissing him. Now there was a jolt that would energize a dead man.

The dogs raced ahead of them. That is, Spot, Darby, and Drover raced. Piggy followed at a more sedate pace, eyes fixed stoically on the ground in front of her, ears pinned back in distaste.

"Where are we going?" Amy asked breathlessly.

"There!" He pointed to a steep snowfield that climbed nearly to the summit of the peak that rose above them.

"I'm not climbing that!"

"Nope! We're going to climb just a little ways, then slide down."

Amy gasped—from delight or from consternation, Jeff couldn't tell. But she didn't object when he took her hand and urged her toward their snowslide.

Once on the snowfield, Jeff showed her how to dig in her heels to keep from sliding down the slope. They trudged carefully upward until they had enough elevation for a good ride. Amy giggled like a teenager.

"Are you sure this is safe?"

"I've done it plenty of times."

"Yeah. Right."

He grinned. "Trust me."

"That's what all the guys say."

The dogs capered about in frenzied delight. Spot tunneled into the snow with churning feet and shoveling nose, while Darby chased the snowballs that flew from Spot's excavation. Drover made like a furry bobsled, aiming himself downslope, tucking his little legs beneath him, sliding until he picked up speed, then stopping himself with his front paws. Piggy watched him keenly for a moment, then trotted over to where he had just stopped and set him to sliding once more with a forceful nudge to his rear. He slid out of control, tumbled, and almost had become a one-dog avalanche when he plowed nose-first into the heavy drift at the base of the snowfield. When he picked himself up, he looked more like a snowball than a dog.

"He takes that kind of abuse from her?" Jeff asked, amazed.

Amy shrugged. "He's in love."

"Poor Drover. Fell for the wrong female. I can relate."

She gave him a half smile. "He's a dog. What's your excuse?"

He pondered a moment. "Testosterone poisoning?" he finally offered.

Amy's laugh had a hint of compassion that cleared the air between them once and for all. Her smile suddenly acquired a clarity that made her face glow.

He held up the tarp. "Are you ready for this?"

"Only time will tell."

"Let's do it."

Jeff spread the tarp on the snow, sat down on the rear half with his legs splayed to either side, and instructed Amy to sit in front of him. Piggy watched with interest as Amy settled herself securely between his legs with his arms wrapped tightly around her.

"I'm not trying to get fresh," he assured Amy.

"Like hell." She laughed.

They started off slowly with Jeff pushing them along with his feet. Then their makeshift toboggan picked up speed. The dogs ran alongside, barking frantically. Piggy was in their midst, growling and snapping at Jeff's boot until she could no longer keep up.

Faster and faster they flew. Amy squealed happily and clung to Jeff's arms. He clamped his legs around her as they sailed over bumps and tipped and swayed over hillocks. Finally, just before the snowfield spit them out onto the grass and rocks, he tumbled them off into the snow.

They lay in a tangle of arms and legs, laughing and panting while the dogs barked and charged about with great excitement. Drover plunked his tailless butt down in the snow, raised his head, and aahroooooed his approval to everyone concerned. The only holdout was, of course, Piggy. She sat a safe distance from the commotion, regarding them all with scornful disapproval.

Slowly their laughter died. Jeff saw the dawn of chagrin in Amy's eyes as she became aware of their intimate entanglement. She halfheartedly tried to scramble from beneath him, but he stayed put. He didn't want her to leave yet.

"My clothes are going to be soaked."

He just grinned. In his hand was a dinner-plate-sized mass of packed snow. When she saw it, her mouth made an O of consternation.

"You wouldn't!" she challenged.

"Watch me."

"You'll be sorry!"

He chortled and taunted her by waving the snow in front of her face, but before he could make good his threat, she mounted a preemptive strike. A pile of snow smushed into the side of his face and trickled icewater into his ear.

Amy burst into laughter and slid out of his hold. The dogs trooped after her as she scrambled up the icy slope.

"I'll get you for that!" He let loose a well-aimed snowball that caught her in her tempting little backside.

Their game lasted all of two minutes before they were both panting for breath in the thin air. Amy fell as Jeff tackled her. He had once again gained the superior position, and this time he took advantage of it. The soft kiss he pressed upon her lips was more tender than passionate, though passion was just a whisper away. That was the uniqueness about the nest Amy was building in his heart. It encompassed affection as well as desire, friendship jumbled with lust.

Her lips responded to his. They were icy and warm at the same time, and totally, incredibly sweet. They parted for a deeper caress, and Jeff indulged himself, but only briefly. He didn't quite trust himself to stop at a kiss. Whether it was the altitude that made his head swim or the feel of Amy's tempting body beneath his, he figured his restraint was at low ebb.

Reluctantly, Jeff rolled off her and lay gasping in the snow. "You going to faint again?"

She drew in a deep breath, then exhaled slowly and smiled. "I only faint on the first kiss."

"Ah."

The dogs apparently decided the humans were down for the count, for they closed in, tails wagging—those that had tails—and tongues flapping. Amy laughed and rolled over to Jeff, burying her face in his jacket to fend off a horde of dog kisses.

"Get outta here, you mutts!" Jeff shouted.

Darby and Spot instantly retreated to a polite distance and sat, but Drover persisted. Piggy rushed in to the opening left by the retreating border collies, wedging herself between Amy and Jeff and pushing against Jeff with all four legs while Drover covered the exposed parts of Amy's face and hands with wet swipes of his tongue.

Still laughing, gasping for breath, Amy surrendered and got to her feet. "Well!" she chortled. "The dogs won that one."

She was rumpled and soggy. Damp ringlets of hair stuck out from her head in odd directions, her cheeks were chafed from the wind, and her nose glowed red from the cold. But she was the most beautiful woman Jeff had ever seen.

If anyone had won something, that someone was Amy, not the silly dogs. He wondered if Amy knew his heart—and all the rest of him—was hers for the taking. And if she knew, did she care?

They collected their packs and started down the trail in silence. If Amy limped slightly and moved with a stiffness demanded by sore muscles, there was no mistaking the glow in her eyes as she took one last, lingering look at the meadows.

"I almost hate to leave," she said. "These mountains are seductive. They make you want to not return to the real world."

"I know what you mean," Jeff agreed.

As they headed into the first stand of trees, he glanced back to the snowfield where they had lain and laughed together. Already it was a mere blip of white on the ridge. Back to the real world now, where the shadows of David and Lydia, where past mistakes and present responsibilities, would try to claim them both.

Out of the corner of his eye, Jeff saw the dogs enjoying their last meadow gambol of the day. Spot and Darby chased after some wiley rodent, and Drover—the ever hopeful Drover—bounded circles around Piggy, who sat in the grass and regarded him with utter, contemptuous ennui. Drover wasn't disheartened. The little dog had faith, determination, and a total ignorance of the odds against Piggy ever so much as turning a favorable eyelash in his direction. Stupid Drover. Stupid, ignorant, bumbling, happy Drover.

Sometimes Jeff wished he were a dog.

♥   ♥   ♥

ON THE DRIVE home, Amy couldn't summon the energy for conversation. She pillowed her head against her wadded-up jacket while Jeff drove. In the back of the minivan, all four dogs snoozed in their crates. She was tempted to follow their example, but the certainty that she would do something grossly unattractive such as snore or drool kept her awake.

When she'd first met Jeff, she wouldn't have cared what indelicate habits she revealed. In fact, as she remembered it, that day she'd been hungover, tired, entirely without makeup, and totally unconcerned about how she looked to an assessing masculine eye. Now she worried about offending him with a tiny feminine snore. At least she liked to think it would be tiny and feminine. She herself had never been awake to hear herself snore.

When had her feeling for Jeff done such an about-face? Amy wondered. It might have been at the Scottish festival when he stepped in that pile of Piggy poop and managed to laugh about it. Or perhaps when he released Fred the hawk and sent the bird off with an expression that reminded her of a proud, fond father. His barbecuing skills at the motor home had certainly boosted him a notch or two in her regard. Everyone knew a sure way to her heart was through her stomach. And the sight of him carrying Piggy across the stream on that log made him very nearly irresistible.

She would have been better off, Amy decided, if she had never seen Jeff Berenger in his natural element. Like a jewel that gains brilliance from the right setting, Jeff shone against a backdrop of mountains and forest. After sharing his reverence for such magnificence, one could more easily understand his dismissal of more superficial concerns. The trivial pursuits of the workaday world did seem rather insignificant when compared to what they had seen today.

Then again, she probably wasn't thinking very straight. The altitude may have muddled her brain, and Jeff's kisses certainly had. She had kissed a man or two in her life. After all, she'd gone to college at a notorious party school. She'd married a man who her whole sorority had thought was sexier than Tom Cruise. But she'd never felt a kiss clear down to her toes. She'd never felt her heart pick up speed, her blood heat to the flash point, and her knees start to melt. Never, that is, until Jeff Berenger had kissed her.

Tom Gordon leaped to mind. His kiss had definitely been nice. Nicer than nice. But it hadn't blown her socks off as Jeff's had.

Must be the altitude, she told herself wearily. Or the physical exertion. Jeff wasn't as handsome as Tom, or as smooth, sophisticated, glib, or sexy.

But Jeff certainly could kiss. And he slid down a mountain better than anyone else she knew.

"WAKE UP, AMY. We're home."

"What?"

"We're home."

"I fell asleep."

"Yeah. Out like a light." He grinned. "You have the cutest little snore."

"Oh jeez!" She checked on her jacket for drool and found that she'd been spared that, at least.

"You sound like a cat when you snore. A little cat, curled up in a ball with its nose tucked into its tail."

"You're kidding."

"No. Now me, when I snore, I sound like a hog with a head cold."

"I suppose in your profession, you know what a hog with a head cold sounds like."

"Not like Pavarotti, that's for sure. I've roused myself from a good, deep sleep a time or two."

Amy's mouth twitched in a smile. "You don't have any pretensions at all, do you?"

"Nope. Pretensions don't work unless you're willing to pretend all the time. I figure if you want someone to like you, then you ought to give that someone a chance to like you for the person you really are, not for who you pretend to be."

"I never thought about it that way."

"Maybe because you don't do much pretending, either."

She gave him a wry smile. "Well, I usually don't demonstrate my snore on the first date."

"Second date. You're forgetting the motor home."

"No, I wouldn't forget our evening in Georgette." The smell of pines, the taste of steaks, and the frustration of an aborted kiss rushed through her head. That kiss had been a promise he'd delivered on today.

"Second date, hm? I guess that makes it all right, then." She got out of the car on legs that felt like rubber. Sore rubber. "Why don't you stay for dinner," she suggested.

"Not too much trouble?"

"You get to cook. I've got hamburgers in the freezer. Besides, unless you help me to the door, I'll have to stay right here in the driveway until my legs decide they can move again. That may not be until Christmas."

"We can't have that."

She gratefully stayed put while he got the packs and the dogs from the minivan. Amy wasn't the only one suffering the effects of overexertion. Drover hobbled to the front door looking as though he couldn't decide which leg to limp on. The border collies trotted over to

Jeff's truck at about half their normal pace, and Piggy sat down beside the driveway and refused to budge.

"Stay there," Jeff told Amy. He put her house key in his pocket, stuffed the immobile Piggy beneath one arm and their packs beneath the other, and managed to get the entire burden safely to the front door. Then he came back for Amy.

"What are you doing?" Her little shriek of surprise became laughter as he picked her up in his arms, carried her to the door, and set her on her feet.

"I'd carry you over the threshold, but then you'd really think I was fresh."

"Don't make me laugh any more. Even my ribcage is sore."

"A couple of aspirin and a warm bath in Epsom salts will make you good as new. You can indulge while I'm cooking the hamburgers."

He opened the front door and called his dogs to join them. The corgis dashed inside. Amy limped after them, flipped on the light, and stopped dead in her tracks.

"Omigod!"

"Holy shit!" Jeff said from behind her.

"I don't believe it. I've been robbed."

ELEVEN

AMY'S HOUSE—THE place that had finally begun to feel like home, safe and secure and cozy—had become a jumble of nightmare rooms. Cushions, magazines, books, and newspapers were strewn all over the living room. In the dining room, the drawers of the buffet had been emptied into a heap on the table, and the contents of the antique cabinet in the corner—including a few random pieces of glassware and dog show trophies—were scattered about the floor. The kitchen cupboards had been thoroughly ransacked. Bran flakes, Cheerios, rice, crackers, and oatmeal were a snap, crackle, and popping mess on the floor. Broken dishes lay about in shards. The bottom drawer of the stove hung half off its tracks.

In Amy's office, the file cabinet was ripped apart, the contents spewed across the floor in a riot of bills, receipts, contracts, and bank statements. The drawers of the desk were pulled completely out and ransacked, and the shelves had been swept clear of books and file boxes.

Worst of all was her bedroom, where the clothes from the closet lay heaped on the floor in lifeless piles. Bras, panties, pantyhose, and gym socks were scattered about, and the bedclothes were ripped from the mattress.

Amy felt as though someone had dealt her a physical blow. In every room, everywhere she looked, her personal and professional possessions had been destroyed, abused, defiled. She felt violated and attacked, as if the monster who had done this had treated her with the same violence he had wrought on her house.

"I don't understand," Jeff said. He had tried his best to persuade Amy to stay outside while he made sure there was no danger in the house, and when she had refused, he had preceded her into every room like a guard dog with hackles raised and lips curled. If the situation hadn't been so grim, she would have found his protectiveness amusing. As it was, his strong, concerned presence beside her was a comfort. "You have two TVs in plain sight, along with a CD player, stereo, and tape player, yet all that's still here. All that photo equipment in your lab, too. What was this guy looking for?"

"My camera's missing from the office."

"One camera is all the thief took? It doesn't make sense."

"It was a damned expensive camera."

"It's an expensive TV in there, too."

"Maybe it was just kids . . . vandals out to rip things apart for the hell of it. The camera was the easiest thing to walk away with."

Jeff looked skeptical. "Maybe."

Amy collapsed into a kitchen chair and cleared a space on the table to rest her elbows. Head lowered into her hands, eyes closed, she tried to block out the sight in front of her. "At least Molly is okay. That's the most important thing."

The first place she had run was the extra room where Molly had spent the day sleeping in her kennel. That room, like all the others, was torn apart, but Molly had still been in her kennel—agitated, annoyed, and indignant, but safe. When Amy had shut the other dogs in the room with her, Molly had greeted them with an incensed barrage of barking that clearly implied the whole disaster was their fault for being gone all day.

"Amy, is anything besides your camera missing?"

"How should I know?" she shot back in a flash of annoyance. "Everything is . . . is . . ." Her voice broke with emotion, and tears burned her eyes. It wasn't the mess and destruction that made her feel like a helpless, cringing child, but the invasion of her home space. She wanted to cry, to scream, to throw up.

"Amy . . ." Jeff was suddenly kneeling in front of her chair. He pulled her to him, and she slid off the chair into his arms. Together they sat on the kitchen floor, bran flakes and Cheerios and the rest of the mess crunching beneath them, while he surrounded her with strong arms and tucked her head tenderly beneath his chin. "What an idiot I am to pester you. I'm sorry."

"No," she quavered. "I'm sorry I snapped at you. They're just . . . things, after all."

"It's more than that, kiddo, and you know it. You don't have to be tough with me."

Good thing, Amy thought, because she didn't feel tough. Every time she thought life was getting back to normal, some new disaster came trotting along to knock her on her butt again. Everything around her was in a shambles—her house, her very life. She felt soiled and degraded, as though the vandal had touched her own personal flesh, not just her home and possessions.

More tears came. Amy couldn't stop them. They were as much for the rough understanding of Jeff's embrace as the horror of the vandalism. She'd gotten into the habit of keeping a brave face about everything— small annoyances and disasters alike, because David had never had time to waste on compassion or understanding. He had believed that he was the only one in the world with real problems. Anyone else's complaint was simply a play for sympathy.

Amy allowed herself to wallow in the comfort of Jeff's arms, even though the rational part of her mind warned her that such dependency could become addictive. She had resolved when David died that she would stand on her own two feet and remodel herself into a self-contained, independent woman who had no strings for a man to manipulate, pull, and eventually cut.

Yet here she was, blubbering on Jeff Berenger's broad shoulder, hiding in the circle of his arms, and allowing him to soothe her fears rather than girding herself up with her own strength. This time of irrational emotion was not the time to be changing her game plan.

Reluctantly, she pulled away and wiped ineffectually at her nose. Jeff grabbed a dish towel from the mess around them and offered it with a chivalric flourish.

"I'm afraid I don't keep hankies in my pocket."

Amy blew her nose inelegantly, then sighed. "Why is it when women in the movies cry, their eyes don't swell and their noses don't run?"

He took the towel and dabbed at a tear that trailed from the corner of her eye. "If this were a movie, we would have interrupted the lowlife at his evil work, the villain and I would have had a spectacular battle that broke whatever of your furniture is still in one piece. I would have won, of course, and then I would have forced the jerk to tell us what is going on here."

She gave him a tremulous smile. "Yeah. I guess."

"You are not staying alone tonight."

His authoritative tone should have made her bristle, but it didn't. Perhaps because the prospect of spending the night alone in a house that had just been raped was unthinkable. She would rather spend the night in a roadside ditch.

"I won't stay alone. Selma worked swing shift at the store today. She'll be—oh my God. Selma! Do you think they got to Selma's apartment as well?"

"We'd better find out."

The apartment above the garage had not been taken apart with the viciousness that had ripped through the house. A few drawers were open and disordered in the tiny kitchen. The desk where Selma kept her bills and personal papers looked as though a tornado had hit it. In the bedroom, the bed was torn apart, and clothes draped half out of partially open dresser drawers. Knowing her friend's housekeeping habits, Amy could have almost believed that everything was normal in Selma's apartment, except for the chilling fact that the door had been ajar. Worse, far worse than any other result of this madness, Selma's collie Raven was gone.

"Maybe she took him to work with her," Jeff suggested.

"She works in a grocery store."

"Right. Unlikely."

The sound of footsteps on the garage stairs made Amy jump, but the footsteps belonged to Selma. She came through the door and stopped abruptly. "What the hell?"

Amy confirmed the obvious. "Someone broke in. Both the house and your apartment."

"Jeez!" Selma's expression darkened as she surveyed the mess. "Did they take my laser-disc player? Gary's going to kill me if I let his precious laser-disc player get stolen."

"It's still here," Jeff told her.

"Well, that's a relief. Where's Ray? Did you put him in the house?"

In the silence that answered her question, Selma's face turned pale. "Shit! Ray's gone, isn't he? Some sonuvabitch freakin' slimeball let him out, didn't he?"

The expressions that followed heated up the already warm apartment. Amy hadn't known that Selma possessed such a colorful vocabulary.

"He could've had the damned laser-disc player, or the TV, or the freakin' fifty dollars in the sugar canister, but why did he have to let my dog loose? Or . . ." Selma's eyes narrowed. "Maybe he didn't just let him out the door to wander. Maybe the asshole took him!"

A horrible notion leaped into Amy's mind, and she saw it reflected in Selma's expression.

"The jerk!" Selma wailed. She grabbed a dirty coffee mug from the desk and threw it against the wall to shatter in an angry explosion of ceramic shards. "That asshole! That shit-sucking, belly-crawling moron. I can't believe he would do this!"

Jeff frowned. "What asshole are you talking about?"

"My vile, mean-spirited, round brown hairy one of a husband! Soon to be ex-husband! His name's Gary, but it's going to be Shit when I get through with him."

Amy wasn't sure she could believe it. Gary had always been a bit wild, to her way of thinking. Irresponsible, quick tempered, thoughtless, and oftentimes childish. He'd been possessive of Selma and was unreasonably jealous of the close friendship that had developed between his wife and Amy during the last two years. In addition, the breakup between Gary and Selma was not an amicable one. Both parties had stepped out of line in getting revenge on the other, but something like this . . . ?

Amy tried to picture Gary tearing apart the house and apartment. The motive was there: He didn't like Amy and was angry at his wife's desertion. Not to mention Selma's kidnapping of their disputed canine child, which might have led him to believe he was justified in seeking revenge and taking the dog back.

But what about the fire at her Denver home? The

two incidents might well be linked. Surely bad luck didn't single out an individual for attack after attack without there being some purpose, some reason, for the madness.

Or perhaps it did. Maybe the Denver fire had been an electrical fire, as the police had concluded, and this attack was the vicious prank of Selma's ex. In the face of Selma's seething certainty, Amy couldn't decide. How well did she know Gary, really? She had always thought his temper, though quick to heat, was just as quick to cool, and for all his irresponsibility and wildness, he wasn't vicious. At least, Amy didn't think he was. Yet there was a tempting logic to Selma's reasoning. "I don't know, Selma."

"Oh, it's him!" Selma declared scathingly. "He's got Ray, and he's the one who buzzed through here like a scene from *Twister* come to life. Any other self-respecting thief would've taken the laser-disc player and TV. Was anything missing from the house?"

"My camera. Maybe some other small things. I don't know."

"Well, that's a pit! But he probably took the camera just to make this look like an everyday robbery rather than a freakin' search-and-destroy raid. He's going to pay. First I'm going to call him and tell him that he hasn't fooled us for one minute. And then I'm going to have the police all over him like ants on a rotten banana."

She grabbed the phone and nudged open the refrigerator. "Have a beer, guys. I'll bet you could use one or two."

"No thanks." Amy dropped onto the couch while Selma dialed. "You know, Jeff, you don't have to stay. This isn't really your problem."

He sat down beside her. "You want me out of your hair?"

Just his nearness beside her brought a comforting warmth to the chill that prickled her skin. She wanted to reach out and cling to his arm, curl up and hide her face against his shoulder. His understanding was seductive. His quiet strength and unruffled steadiness were tempting in the face of her floundering emotions. So much for her resolve to be independent and strong, a woman who could take care of herself and depend only upon herself for comfort and happiness.

To hell with independence, she thought. "I don't want you out of my hair," she said so low that her voice was almost a whisper.

"Then I'll stay awhile."

"Thank you."

Selma's foot tapped impatiently as she waited for Gary to pick up. Tapped and tapped and tapped while her mouth drew into a thin line of anger.

"He's not there, the rat. Or he's not answering. I'll try his cell phone."

Another round of foot tapping, and finally Selma's eyes blinked in surprise as a tinny voice answered. In the solemn quiet of the apartment, Amy could hear Gary's inquisitive hello.

Selma launched into a flurry of name-calling, and an audible click sounded as Gary hung up.

"Asshole," Selma muttered as she dialed again. This time when the ringing stopped, Gary beat her out of the gate, for she listened intently with a sour expression.

"Just be quiet a minute, you creep, and listen. Do you have Ray?"

She winced at whatever answer Gary gave her.

"Don't give me that sarcasm, mister. Someone broke in to Amy's place, and Ray's gone. You're top on the list of suspects, and I'm going to call the police unless you bring back my dog and apologize on bended knee to Amy. And a check for the damage damned well better go along with the apology."

Gary's response put a skeptical frown on Selma's face, and as it continued, the frown darkened with anxiety. When she hung up the phone, she sought Amy's eyes. "He said he didn't have anything to do with it. He's coming over to help look for Ray."

Amy's hand tightened on Jeff's. His returned the squeeze. Up until that moment, Amy hadn't realized she was holding on to him.

"Do you think he's telling the truth?" Jeff asked Selma.

"Yeah. Gary can pull some pretty wretched pranks, but he always owns up and apologizes when he's caught. He's perfected the repentant belly crawl, and he's so oblivious, he would think that even something like this could be put right with enough crawling. Oh God," she said in a less confident voice. "Poor Ray's wandering around somewhere in the dark, probably scared as hell. Silly collie. He doesn't have enough brains to keep out of trouble."

"We'll find him," Jeff said.

"We don't even know how long he's been gone," Selma moaned.

"We'll find him."

Jeff's determined tone gave Amy more confidence than she had any right to feel. No one had the heart to state the obvious—that a dog could cover a lot of distance in a very short time, especially if the dog was running scared. They all knew it. Amy felt somehow that Jeff would save the day, though, a symptom of how far she'd fallen.

Stupid Amy, she chided herself. Stupid Amy, stupid Raven, stupid damned world.

♥   ♥   ♥

IT WAS MY luck to be shut away from the action just when things were getting interesting. After a day spent watching Amy and Dr. Dufus cavort in the mountains, I could have used a bit of robbery and mayhem to brighten up my day. I swear, I thought the two of them were going to stand on top of that miserable ridge and warble something from The Sound of Music at any minute. Drover and those goofy border collies would have howled in accompaniment. Major gag! No way is Amy going to get me near a mountain ever again, not without the help of a tractor beam.

Every muscle in my body complained, my feet hurt, my stomach growled, and my fur was littered with grass, twigs, and dirt. All that was bad enough, but while Amy and Berenger viewed the damage in the house, I was stuck in the spare room with no company but the other dogs, who were no company at all. Drover snored, Molly regarded me with a sour glare, and the border collies sacked out on the guest bed. Normally I like my little fiberglass kennel. It's cozy. It's safe. It has a nice, soft pillow for me to lie on. And from behind that sturdy steel mesh door, I can insult Molly to my heart's content without her being able to do a thing about it. Right then, however, my muscles were getting even stiffer from lying in one place. I wanted a big meal, a nice session of brushing, and a massage. I don't think that was too much to ask after what I had endured that day. Do you? I could understand Amy's concern with her house being mugged, but she should have paid some attention to her poor dogs.

The clock in the hall bonged the quarter hour, then the half hour, and I resigned myself to a long wait. Drover, fast asleep and snoring, was oblivious to any problem. Molly looked at me from her kennel. When my eyes met hers, her lip curled in an expression of her esteem. Arrogant bitch. Still, I was generous enough to cut her some slack. She'd had to sit there, frustrated and angry, while some lowlife piece of scuzz invaded her domain. That was enough to make any dog cranky. It was too bad she couldn't talk. A description of the villain would *have been nice. She probably got a good look at him. It was there in her eyes, imprinted somewhere on her little dog brain. If only dogs could communicate by something more than whines, growls, tail wags, and body odor. It seemed unfair, somehow.*

I whined, frustrated and restless. Molly gave me a scathing look before she curled up on her pillow. Ears flat against her head, nose tucked under one paw, the old girl was genuinely upset. Feeling generous, I gave her a little woof of comfort. Like I said before, tonight I had to cut her some slack.

Finally Amy came through the door with five bowls of food. At last! I thought. Release! But my hopes rose too soon. We each got dinner and a cursory pat of affection, but Amy slammed the kennel door as I leaped for freedom. Selma's voice called from the living room, announcing that Gary had arrived. I remembered Gary fondly. He had provided a bit of entertainment during one of the dull stretches of the Scottish festival. From Amy's expression, I guessed she didn't consider that incident in the same favorable light. Gary and Amy had never gotten along all that well. Gary is sort of a twit. But then, in her own way, so is Amy.

We were left to our own doggy devices once again when everyone left the house. I'd heard Raven's name bandied about a good deal among the humans, and I gathered the dimwit was missing. Stupid collie. Some dogs had brains enough to care for themselves on the street, but Ray definitely didn't. Raven is the Forrest Gump of dogs. People dote on him, but he's not too bright. Lord only knew where he'd gone. And the troops who searched for him wouldn't come home to give me some much-deserved attention until they found the big dummy.

I settled in resentfully for a long session of waiting in boredom, hoping that Stanley was feeling guilty for everything I was being forced to endure. To think I once believed this job would be easy.

♥   ♥   ♥

THE HOUR WAS near midnight when the last of the searchers straggled back to Amy's house. They had each taken a different route, with Amy and Gary walking the dark roads close to the house, and Jeff and Selma taking their cars to search farther afield. A cold front had swept through in the midevening, bringing with it a chilly wind and rain. Colorado couldn't have picked a less convenient time to perform one of its famous weather about-faces. Amy was both drenched and cold by the time she finally returned to the house. Even if she caught pneumonia, however, she would count the price well worth it, for she had an equally sodden and dirty Raven with her. After walking the outskirts of Niwot and the margins of farm fields for three hours, after calling until her voice was a hoarse whisper, she had found a very unhappy Ray in a vacant field not a mile from her house.

Selma and Gary were at the house to greet her; Jeff was still out searching.

"Raven!" Selma gave the collie a happy squeeze even before he was through the front door, regardless of the rain and mud that dripped from his coat. "You poor baby! I thought I'd lost you for sure!"

Gary handed Amy a towel, then stood back and watched the reunion with hooded eyes.

"Oh, Amy! Thank you!" Selma gushed. "Where did you find him? What would I have done if we didn't get him back? I wouldn't have slept another night in my life, wondering what had happened to him."

Amy collapsed onto the couch. "I don't suppose the coffee's hot?"

"Yeah," Gary said. "I'll get you a cup."

"Thanks."

Selma's eyes followed Gary as he left the room, then darted guiltily to her dog, as if she were embarrassed to be caught looking at her husband. "Do you think he's okay?"

"Other than being a mess, he seems fine to me."

"Do you suppose when Jeff gets back, he'd take a look at him?"

"I'm sure he would."

Gary returned with three steaming cups of coffee on a tray. At his feet trotted three corgis and two border collies, wet from a short visit to the yard. They gathered around Raven with great interest, sniffing the collie's feet and nether parts. Ray gave them a friendly wave of the tail.

"Can't we just throw all six of these beasts in the dryer and put it on dog cycle?" Amy asked with a sigh.

"Better not," cautioned Jeff's voice from the just opened front door. "You might shrink the normal-sized dogs down to the size of your little beasts. Where did you find him?"

"In a field about a mile off, cowering in a ditch."

"Would you take a look at him?" Selma implored. "He seems fine, but . . ."

To show just how fine he was, now that he was home, Ray indulged in a vigorous shake, sending water and mud in all directions. No doubt thinking it was a grand idea, all the other dogs followed suit.

Jeff wiped mud and water from his face. "Maybe the dryer wasn't such a bad idea after all."

Piggy moved closer to Jeff and shook again, shooting him a smirk of satisfaction along with another spray of cold and wet. Tired as she was, Amy had to laugh as Jeff returned Piggy's smirk and asked the dog dourly: "Why couldn't it have been *you* lost in the cold and dark?"

A cursory examination proved Ray to be none the worse for his adventure. A relieved Selma suggested they call a pizza parlor in Boulder that, for an outrageous price, would deliver a pizza anywhere in the county, any time of the night or day. While the others discussed the alternatives of a pizza supreme versus pepperoni and mushroom, Gary made his excuses.

"I've gotta work tomorrow. It's already after midnight."

Selma bit her lip, then took a deep breath. "Stay, Gary."

He gave her a cautious look. Her eyes slid uneasily away from his. "I'm sorry I accused you of taking Ray and doing all this." She waved her hand toward the mess. "I . . . well, I jumped to conclusions, and I apologize."

Gary stood unmoving in the strained silence. Selma grimaced, then gestured awkwardly. "Just stay and have some pizza."

Amy got the feeling they should leave the two of them alone, but she was too tired to move. Jeff seemed to be of the same mind.

Gary shifted his weight from foot to foot, his eyes fastened on the floor and his mouth pulled down into a frown. For a few moments he didn't say anything. He looked like a little boy who had been unjustly sent to the corner.

"I wouldn't have done any of that," he finally said in a quiet voice. "What do you think I am, Selma? Some kind of friggin' monster?"

"No," Selma answered in a small voice.

"I've screwed up a time or two, and I'm quick to let off steam," he admitted with a wry grimace. "But I wouldn't do something like this."

It was Selma's turn to study the floor. "Yeah. I know. I'm sorry."

The air around the two of them seemed to grow thick enough to cut. Neither would meet the other's eyes. Finally, Jeff dispelled the tension with a firm "Let's order that pizza. If I don't get something to eat, I'm going to start sucking up bran flakes from the kitchen floor."

Piggy woofed in agreement, and Jeff gave her a taunting smile. "Not you, Pudgy. Cheese and pepperoni are definitely not on your diet."

By two A.M., a large empty pizza carton and four paper plates smeared with cheese and pizza sauce added to the mess in the house. Selma and Ray had gone up to the garage apartment, and Gary was on his way back to Boulder.

Amy slumped on the couch. Now that the crisis was over, her muscles were reminding her of the day's abuse. A dozen tiny mallets seemed to be pounding on her brain, right behind her eyes, and the three pieces of pizza in her stomach had turned into concrete. The smell of coffee preceded Jeff into the room. Eyes closed, Amy breathed in the aroma and listened to Jeff's footsteps—the solid thunk of his hiking boots accompanied by five sets of four-footed companions.

"Decaf," he said when she opened her eyes.

Looking up at him from the couch, he seemed impossibly tall. His hair was more rumpled than usual. Several smears of mud still dirtied his face, and his flannel shirt hung half in and half out of the waistband. All in all, he was a sight that made her heart go soft with foolish tenderness. Her resistance was at low ebb at this time of morning and in her state of weariness.

She took a mug from him. "It could have all the caffeine in the world and still not keep me awake."

"It's been quite a day." He folded his long, lean body onto the couch beside her and surveyed the mess in the living room. "Did you believe Gary's protestations of innocence?"

"I'd like to."

"You don't sound confident."

Amy sighed. "Right now I feel as though I don't know up from down, truth from a lie. I'm a notoriously bad judge of character."

"Is that so?"

"Hmm," she confirmed. Look at her deceased husband and best friend, she almost said but didn't. That thorn in her soul was something she didn't want to deal with right then.

Jeff sighed and set his coffee cup aside. "I think I'm too tired to drive home tonight. Would you mind if I slept on your couch for what's left of the night?"

Amy smiled. Jeff wasn't too tired. He knew she didn't want to be alone tonight, in this defiled house, with the shambles of her life scattered about her. She reached out and squeezed his hand. "You're a nice man, Jeff Berenger."

"I've always thought so," he agreed with a grin.

"I'll bring you out a pillow and blankets."

She didn't though. Eyes half closed, she toppled sideways until her head rested upon his shoulder. He took the coffee mug from her hand and rearranged her limp body until she looked up at him from his lap. Her scalp tingled deliciously where his fingers threaded through her hair and massaged away the pounding pain.

"A very nice man," she repeated in a whisper.

He merely smiled.

She closed her eyes, tempted to surrender completely—to need him, trust him, love him. But that would be a mistake. Her faithless husband had been dead but half a year. She'd known Jeff Berenger less than a month. And she no longer believed in trust or love.

Did she?

"I don't need a man in my life." Amy instantly regretted the rude words, but they had escaped her lips before the thought had formed. Jeff's smile didn't falter, however, and his fingers continued their soothing caress.

"You don't need a man in your life," he agreed. "But sometimes the best things in life are what we want, not what we need."

If there was an argument for that, Amy couldn't think of it at the moment, for her lips were too tired to form the words, and her brain was just too weary to think. As her eyes closed in sleep, she could still see the beguiling curve of Jeff's smile imprinted on her mind.

WHAT A WUSS! Honestly! It was no mystery why Jeff Berenger never married. I was beginning to wonder if he'd ever gotten past first base with a woman. Here was Amy, handing him a home run on a silver platter, and what does he do? Sweetly lulls her to sleep with her head on his lap. What a dull duo! Back when I walked on two legs instead of four, you can be sure that when my head was on some lucky man's lap, I wasn't drifting off to sleep, and neither was he!

Not that I wanted their pathetic little flirtation to progress. Amy was already too close to falling for this loser. I was begin-ning to realize, however, that Berenger was too inept a Romeo to pose a real threat. That comforting thought didn't make watching their little romantic scene any easier, however. After what I'd already endured that day, the sight of them together on the sofa threatened to turn my stomach.

So I left them alone and unchaperoned, confident that nothing interesting would happen if I took a few minutes to sniff around the house. Dogs possess tools of investigation that people don't have, you know; it's one of the few advantages of being a dog. The first thing that captured my notice was the spill in the kitchen, which up until now had gone unnoticed due to the prospect of pizza in the living room. I've never been a fan of either bran flakes or Cheerios. Eggs benedict or a nicely done omelet was more my style. Tastes change, however, along with one's situation in life, and corgis are not very discerning when it comes to food. A third of the spilled cereal was in my stomach before the other dogs poked their noses into the kitchen to investigate the sound of munching. From that point on it was a free-for-all. We weren't loud enough to bring Amy and Jeff in to scold us, though. I think the house could have collapsed on those two without waking them.

Tummy full, energy and spirits somewhat restored, I trotted off to do some serious detective work. Somewhere in this chaotic mess must be an answer. Amy had attracted too much of this sort of thing for any of it to be coincidence.

Very little in this world happens at random. Even the most haphazard-seeming incidents somehow fall into a master plan, if one is smart enough to find it. This deep philosophy I had gleaned from a fascination with mystery stories when I was a preteen. After puberty, I preferred reading Danielle Steel and Judith Krantz, but that sort of literature didn't help me in my current situation.

I was convinced that there was a connection between the current vandalism and the "accidental" burning of Amy's house in Denver a few months earlier. Carrying the master plan theory one step further, I figured that my own unfortunate demise—and David's—was also linked with the rest of Amy's bad luck. It didn't take a diploma from detective school to know that something fishy was up, and what better than a dog's smart nose to sniff it out.

So I took my busy nose on a tour of the house. It smelled of dust and dog feet, spilled food and high emotion. Yes, you can smell emotion, if you're a dog. There isn't a deodorant on the market that can hide fear, joy, lust, or hate. Dogs can also pick up individual scent signatures. Every man and woman carries a distinctive odor. Every dog, rat, bird, and beetle as well, but I was assuming the villain was a human being.

Talented as my nose was, I didn't detect anything helpful. The only people scents came from people who had a right to be there. Amy and Selma. Jeff, who didn't have a right to be there, but I hadn't convinced him of that yet. Tom—gorgeous, rich, famous Tom. I sat down in the office mess and wished

Tom were there. He could have comforted Amy far better than Jeff could. What with being an investigative journalist, he could have made suggestions about finding out what was going on. If Amy could only see Jeff and Tom together, so she could really compare the two, she wouldn't give Dr. Dreary another glance.

Finally I gave up. In hindsight, perhaps it's easy to conclude that I wasn't very persistent, that my thinking wasn't as sharp as it should have been. But I was bone weary, after being force-marched up a damned mountain, nearly starved to death, and subjected to frustration and annoyance that would have sent a lesser dog into a fit of howling. I didn't have any more to give right then, so I jumped onto the couch and curled next to Amy's legs. Flopped beside the couch, Molly was too tired to object, and Drover was already asleep. The border collies each opened one watchful eye as I settled in, then returned to their slumber.

We were so like one big happy family that I wanted to puke.

TWELVE

THE INSISTENT RINGING of the phone brought Amy from a comfortably warm slumber. To hell with whoever would call so early in the morning, she thought groggily. The answering machine would pick up soon. She was far too comfortable to move, more relaxed than she had been in months, in years, in spite of her bed having grown hard and lumpy overnight.

The phone continued its shrill insistence, and then the bed itself moved, bringing Amy completely awake. She pushed awkwardly to a sitting position, hampered by legs and arms entangling hers. Her eyes slitted open to spy a man's face entirely too close to hers. Jeff. She closed her eyes and groaned as realization hit her. No wonder the mattress had seemed strangely hard and lumpy. She was not asleep on her king-sized bed with its brass headrail and soft comforter; she was draped atop Jeff Berenger, with his cowlicked hair, sleepy smile, and hard muscle. They had fallen asleep on the couch last night, or had it been early morning? Her brain was too foggy to remember.

"The phone's ringing," he said. His voice was graveled with sleep and just as warm as the rest of him. Amy experienced a flash of fantasy about waking up with this man after a lusty night in a real bed, hearing that husky, early morning voice growling something about whose turn it was in the shower, or making morning coffee, or better yet, seducing her back into bed and into his arms. The flash of fantasy became a flush of heat in her face.

"Amy?"

"Uh . . . what?"

"The phone."

The answering machine was broken, Amy suddenly remembered, along with almost everything else in the house. And whoever was calling was determined to get an answer. "Who would call this early?" she grumbled as she groped for the phone on the end table.

It was Tom. There was no mistaking the rich timbre of his voice.

"Oh good. You *are* home."

"Hi, Tom."

How much more awkward could a moment get? Awakened from a sound sleep on top of one man by a phone call from another man.

"Whoa! Do you sound wrung out! What's the matter? Find out that mountains are easier to look at than climb?"

Amy glanced at Jeff. Studiously examining his square-cut nails, he was trying to look uninterested in the conversation, and not succeeding. She sighed wearily. "Tom, it's early."

"Noon is early?"

"Noon?"

"You *are* out of it. Listen, love. I'm sorry if I got you out of bed. I sympathize entirely. If I'd trudged to the top of some barren rock, I'd be flat on my back too. But I wanted to set up a time for us to talk about the rest of this piece of mine. We got some terrific footage of the dog show, and now I need to go in some other directions. Also—"

"Tom . . . ," she interrupted with a sigh. "Right

now isn't a good time. Could you call back later? Maybe tonight or tomorrow?"

"What's wrong, kid? You're not sick, are you?"

"The . . . uh . . ." Amy found herself reluctant to say the words, as if talking about it would solidify the reality of what she had found when she walked through her front door. She immediately felt silly. Hiding from the truth never accomplished anything. Besides, Tom was a friend. "My house was broken into yesterday while I was gone. Things are smashed and strewn all over the place. And we were up till oh-dark-thirty looking for Selma's collie, who got loose during the robbery."

A stunned silence on the other end of the line concluded with a soft "Shit!"

"Yeah. My feelings exactly."

"Are you all right?"

"Sure. I'm fine."

"Was anything taken?"

"One camera is all."

"Did you call the police?"

"Of course I did. They sent an officer over to take a report. He didn't say it in so many words, but I could tell he wasn't optimistic about finding the culprit."

"Shit, Amy! You're trying to be brave and stoic, aren't you? That's not good for your psyche, you know? I'm coming right over. I can at least offer a shoulder to cry on."

Awkwarder and awkwarder. Jeff gave her a look of inquiry, and she responded with a weak smile.

"Tom . . ." She interrupted his assurances that he would personally use his influence with the police to make sure that a complete investigation was done. "Tom, don't come over."

"You shouldn't be alone."

"I'm not alone. Why don't you call back tonight or tomorrow. I'll be able to think better then. Okay?"

In the silence of his hesitation she could almost hear the wheels of his mind turning, wondering who was with her. She was probably wrong. They'd had only one real date, after all, and even that had been more business than social. Tom Gordon probably wouldn't give two hoots if she was entertaining the entire starting line of the Denver Broncos, as long as she would take time out to help him with his dog story. And wasn't that the way she wanted it? Amy asked herself. No strings for men to pull—not Tom, not Jeff, not the starting lineup of the Broncos, should they happen by.

"Are you sure?" Tom asked gently. "Sure you don't need help?"

"Thanks, Tom. You're a good friend for offering. But I'm fine. Really."

"All right. I'll call back tonight."

Amy released a sigh as she hung up the phone. She could feel Jeff's eyes dissect her expression.

"That was Tom Gordon."

"Ah," he said noncommittally. "The crusader of channel two."

"I'm . . . uh . . . helping him with a story he's doing on purebred dogs."

His lips clamped together tightly, as if holding back words that were better not said. "Great. I hope he's putting a positive slant on it. Dogs have gotten a bum rap in this area."

"He will. Otherwise I wouldn't be helping him." Thinking better of continuing the conversation, she indulged in a huge yawn and stretch, only to be brought up short by a symphony of sore, stiff muscles complaining in painful dissonance. "Yowch! Oooooh! Aaaa!"

"Careful there. You're probably going to need a couple of aspirins."

"Or a whole new body. Yow! I can't move." She tried to get up from the couch, but her legs wouldn't cooperate. A second try launched her into an upright position for only a few seconds before she toppled. She would have landed dead center on Piggy, who still slept, if Jeff hadn't caught her and pulled her back into his arms.

Amy resisted the temptation to cuddle even deeper into his embrace. The feel of his hands on her arms sped her heart and sent a thrill down her spine, both reactions which she tried to ignore. For a moment they were still, eyes locked. Jeff's lips twitched, as if undecided whether to smile or kiss her. Amy was a bit undecided herself. Last night had been strange. This morning was even stranger. Were they friends or budding lovers? Was that gleam in Jeff's eye amusement at her predicament or the beginnings of desire. Which did Amy want it to be?

Piggy spoiled the delicious tension by waking up and announcing the state of her appetite. Amy closed her eyes and grimaced as Molly and Drover, who had been silently flopped beside the couch like two oversized bedroom slippers, joined Piggy's protest. The border collies sat in the middle of the room, politely waiting, but their eyes were bright with the hope of a meal.

Amy clapped her hands to her ears. "All right! All right!"

"You stay here," Jeff said. "I'll feed the brats."

"I'll do it," she protested.

"It'll take you an hour to hobble to the kitchen."

She gave in and watched the corgis mob him as he headed out of the room. He grinned at her over his shoulder. "I want you to notice how polite Spot and Darby are."

The border collies were indeed doing great credit to

their breed. The black-and-white dogs followed at a polite distance while regarding the clamoring corgis with disapproval.

"Not fair," Amy complained from the couch. "They're border collies. Give them a book of manners and they're trained."

Jeff's chuckle warmed her insides as he disappeared into the hall.

The day went downhill from there. While Amy dosed herself with aspirin and soaked in a hot tub of Epsom salts, Jeff managed to prepare a makeshift breakfast of freezer biscuits and salvaged eggs—even the refrigerator had been rifled. After a casual kiss and a promise to call later in the afternoon, he left for appointments at his clinic. Alone with her sore muscles and sunburned nose, which glowed with a wattage to rival Rudolph's, Amy was tempted to go back to sleep, but the chaos in every room beckoned. It amazed her that she was able to sleep the night before. The troubles of the day should have kept her awake, but somehow, cuddled shamelessly against Jeff, she'd been able to put everything aside. That itself was something she didn't want to think about right then. Her resolve to stay away from entanglements seemed to be melting like snow in July. She would never achieve self-reliance if her heart marched into the enemy camp and surrendered every time an amiable fellow smiled at her. Not that all men were the enemy. Amy assured herself that she wasn't one of those embittered women who blamed all men for the betrayal of one. She simply wanted a bit of peace for her tattered emotions. With two men laying siege to the fortress she'd built around herself, it was no wonder she was suffering from shell shock.

She was halfway through the mess in the kitchen when Selma came through the back door.

"Shit." Selma sighed. "It wasn't just a bad dream.

The mess in my place isn't all that different from the usual state of affairs, but this—" she waved a hand at the still chaotic countertops and jumbled drawers, "this is unreal."

"Aren't you due at work?"

"I called in sick. I've been traumatized, you know. Mr. Simon was very sympathetic."

"How's Raven?"

"In the backyard playing with Drover and Molly. Piggy is acting the role of playground monitor. Got any coffee?"

"There's a pot behind that pile of cans on the counter."

Selma poured herself a cup, then strolled into the dining room. She yawned and stretched, trying to disguise her curious look through the hallway to the rooms beyond.

"He's not here," Amy told her with a chuckle.

"He? He who?"

"Jeff. Don't tell me that quick little survey just now was looking for . . . let's see . . . Elvis maybe?"

A quick lift and fall of Selma's brows acknowledged the point, along with a shrug. "Well, I thought maybe, you know, you two seemed to be getting along really well last night."

"Weren't you in Tom Gordon's corner just a day or so ago?"

"I'm in your corner, girl." She scraped back the dangling ends of her rich brown hair and tied it deftly into a ponytail. "Tom's a hunk. No doubt about it. A real winner. But hey, maybe Jeff's the one with the chemistry. Besides, he's got shoulders that don't quit, and that hair of his just begs a woman to run her fingers through it."

"Is that so?"

"That definitely is so."

"Well, I'll thank you to keep your fingers out of Jeff Berenger's hair," Amy said with a little twitch of a smile.

"Ah ha! There *is* something there! Take this." She shoved her untouched coffee toward Amy. "Give me the broom, sit down, and tell me everything."

"There's nothing to tell."

"He spent the night?" Selma asked gleefully.

"We fell asleep on the couch."

"After . . ."

"After nothing. We were tired, Selma."

"I would never be *that* tired."

"You would if you'd spent the day hiking up a mountain and the night sorting through what remains of your home and chasing down a brainless dog."

"Raven is not brainless."

"If you're going to monopolize that broom, will you please sweep?"

"Okay, okay." She took a few swipes at the floor while Amy sipped the coffee. "So, tell me how the hike went . . ." She trailed off suggestively.

Amy fought back a blush. All that had happened after she and Jeff arrived home made the mountain hike seem like a very long time ago. Now she recalled the heady experience in vivid detail.

"You're blushing!" Selma exclaimed. "I don't believe it! Amy Cameron is blushing. What was it? A little afternoon delight in the mountain meadows?"

"Selma, your imagination is entirely too lurid."

Selma grinned. "It is not. It's entertaining. Come on. Give my imagination some fuel. Tell me."

"I don't kiss and tell," Amy said with an impish smile.

"Aaaah! You're blushing again. That good, was it?"

"There was no *it*."

"Uh-huh."

"There wasn't!"

"Well, from the color of your face, I'd say there soon will be."

"Just—just keep sweeping!"

Selma laughed.

Together they bulldozed their way through the kitchen, living room, and dining room before Selma persuaded Amy to drive into Boulder for lunch. When they returned, there were two messages waiting on the answering machine. The first was from Jeff, who had called right after they left. The second was from Tom. Grinning hugely, Selma listened with Amy to the voices on the recorder.

"Well, I'll just leave now and give you some privacy to sort out your boyfriends."

"Don't push it," Amy warned as her friend sashayed out the back door. Before the door slammed shut, all three dogs trooped in from the backyard and circled around her feet, their ears erect with hungry expectation.

"Smell ice cream on my breath, do you?" Amy asked with a smile. "Well, forget it. You're having dog food for dinner."

Feeding the dogs was an excuse to delay returning the phone calls, but it wasn't an excuse that lasted long enough. She wanted to hear Jeff's voice, to endure his teasing, to be reassured by the warmth of his tone, yet she was afraid of her own weakness where he was concerned. And Tom . . . what was she going to say to Tom? She liked him. She even found him attractive, and she truly did want to help him with this report he was doing on purebred dogs. But he wanted more from her, and while Tom Gordon had to be high on the list of Denver's most sought-after bachelors, he inspired more uneasiness in her heart than romance. How did one tell a man to back off and still keep him as a friend? Amy wondered. It wasn't a problem she'd ever encountered.

She wasn't the sort of woman, like Lydia, that men compete for and pursue, at least she hadn't been, up until the past few weeks.

She sighed and picked up the phone. When Jeff answered, her heart jumped.

"Hi. It's Amy."

"Amy! How're you doing over there?"

"Still sore," she said, steering away from the personal. "And Piggy can scarcely be persuaded to get off her little duff even to go into the backyard and pee."

"And that's not normal?" Jeff asked with a chuckle.

A few seconds of silence nurtured a growing awkwardness. Amy could almost see Jeff's smile fade.

"I'm sorry I had to run off this morning—or I guess it was afternoon, wasn't it? But I hate to stand up clients. I have so few," he admitted with a quiet laugh.

It hadn't occurred to Amy that he should have stayed. "Jeff, you're not obligated to hold my hand. You went above and beyond the call of duty last night. After all, this isn't really your problem."

"It is my problem. You're my problem."

Amy wasn't sure she liked the possessiveness she heard in his tone—possessive of her problems, possessive of her. At the same time it made her want to smile. Damned confusing.

Once again she tried to head for safer ground. "Anything interesting in your appointments?"

"Nah. One respiratory infection, one case of overeating, and one pregnancy."

"Oh. Well, I hope the pregnancy was a blessed event rather than an accident."

"Nope. Roaming canine Romeo got in with a virginal poodle. The poodle's mother is talking paternity suit."

"Oh, dear."

"The poodle seems quite happy about it, though."

Amy laughed. How did one stay serious with this man?

"Why don't I come over?" Jeff suggested. "You've got to have enough mess left to need some help."

Amy wanted to see him more than she wanted to breathe, and that was why she hesitated. The racing of her heart frightened her, as did the intensity of her longing. She needed to settle down. Time and distance would give her time to cool off and knock her thinking back into line, not to mention other less cerebral parts.

She searched for an excuse, then discarded the notion. She hated lying. If she had to lie to preserve a relationship, then perhaps it wasn't worth preserving.

"Not tonight, Jeff." She heard the regret in her own voice and wondered if Jeff heard it too. What would he make of it? Was she a coward? Was she running from him? Or was she just a dunderheaded nincompoop who couldn't make up her own mind? All of those things were true in a way. "I—I need some distance. Things . . . everything has been happening too fast."

A momentary silence on the other end of the line was followed by a very neutral "Okay."

"Jeff, this is not a brush-off. Really. It's just that I'm not a person who rushes into things." Her heart was rushing, though, dragging the rest of her along with it. That was why she needed time to bridle it.

"I know it's not a brush-off, kiddo. I have a lot of confidence in how irresistible I am."

Amy laughed, a sound that noticeably lightened the weight that had settled on their lines of communication. "Irresistible, are you? Someone should take that over-confidence of yours and whittle it down to size."

"I can't think of a better woman for the job than you."

"Me and my sharp tongue?"

"Made to order for whittling male egos."

"Well, I haven't used it on you much lately."

"For which I am truly grateful."

Another silence recharged the awkwardness. "Uh . . . listen, Jeff, when I get things cleaned up here and get back to work, I'll give you a call. If you're still up for the punishment of my company, we can do something."

"My choice of what we do?" he asked with a wicked chuckle.

"Lady's choice. Always."

"Lady's choice. Rats. Just bear in mind that I can be very persuasive when I put my mind to it."

"I'll just bet you can."

"Just give me a chance. And Amy"—his voice became serious—"you be careful. Something about this whole business makes me damned uneasy. Promise you'll call me if you hear anything go thump in the night. In the day as well."

His uneasiness reinforced Amy's own growing fearfulness, something she had told herself over and over again was akin to a child being afraid of nameless monsters lurking in the dark. Hearing him echo her foreboding made it sharper and more real.

"I promise I'll call if anything comes up."

"I mean it, Amy. Don't try to play the stalwart and go it alone. Call me at home, or on my cell phone. You've got the numbers?"

"I've got the numbers."

"And you'll call?"

"I'll call. Promise." Amy shook her head and smiled as she hung up the phone. Damn the man for being such a charmer. If Jeff had come over, she knew very well what would have happened. It had been rushing at them since that dinner in Georgette. It had crackled in every word since then, trailing them up the mountain and shouting for attention at every touch, smile, laugh, and look. Even the night before, with her home in chaos all around her, it had intruded on her anguish. His protectiveness had warmed more than her heart. His understanding melted more than the last shards of her reserve toward him. If they hadn't been so wrung out and exhausted, the night would have ended with them together in her bed. And if Jeff had come over tonight, they would have been sucked into that bedroom just as surely as thunder follows lightning. And she would wake up the next morning, probably smiling, happy, and feeling full of herself. But how long would that feeling last? she asked herself mercilessly. She had been smiling, happy, and full of herself the day she married David. How long had that lasted?

On the other hand, Jeff had not even hinted at anything as serious and binding as marriage, and Jeff was not David. Not even close. Maybe she needed some thunder and lightning in her life again. It had been only months since David's death, but it had been years since she really felt cared about.

As if she didn't have enough in her life to be confused about.

"Well, what would you do?" she asked the three corgis who had gathered at her feet to listen in on the conversation. Drover rumbled low in his throat, his wide butt wriggling with pleasure at her notice.

"I know what you would do, you walking hormone. How about the girls?"

Molly whined, and Piggy, never one to miss an opportunity, got up and trotted toward the kitchen and pantry, where the dog food was securely stored in corgi-proof plastic garbage cans.

"You've been fed, Pudgy old girl, and you don't get any more until tomorrow morning."

Miss Pudgy—Jeff's less than affectionate name for Piggy. The man had her borrowing his silly nicknames, among the other inroads he was making into her life. She leaned back on the couch and tapped one fingernail on the plastic casing of the phone.

"He is a very nice guy," she told the gathered corgis. "A bit rough around the edges here and there, but a very nice guy all the same. But every time I let a man into my life, things start to get complicated. I don't deal well with complication."

Molly lay down and rested her chin on Amy's foot, looking up at her with liquid brown eyes that clearly said males were not worth the trouble.

"It might be a physical thing," Amy speculated. "You know, something that bursts into flame, then burns itself out. No complications there."

She ran a finger back and forth along the phone, which had so recently held Jeff's voice within its electronics and wires.

"No, it's more than that," she admitted finally. "Jeff makes me feel alive. His smile makes me want to smile. And his kiss makes me want to . . ." She surveyed her audience, the lolling tongues, the corgi grins, the avid gazes. "Well, never mind what his kiss makes me want to do. That's private."

Piggy rumbled out a growl.

"Yes, Piggy, I know you don't like him, but you don't like much of anyone except Tom Gordon." Amy grimaced as Tom's name reminded her that she had yet another man to deal with. "One more phone call," she told the corgis. "Then we get down to some more serious cleaning."

The call to Tom turned out to be little easier than the conversation with Jeff. He was eager to help, concerned by the housebreaking, anxious for her welfare.

"I'm fine," she assured him. "A little mess never killed anyone, and the camera was insured for a whopping amount of money. After the house fire and now this, my insurance agent is going to have a cow."

"You're a wonder, you know that?"

"No doubt about it."

"Positive you don't need help?"

"Positive. I have more offers of help than I can handle."

"Well, all right. We got some great footage at the dog show, thanks to you. I'd like to show it to you before it goes through editing. And we need to talk about some other aspects of the dog world for this show. When do you have time?"

"In the next few days I have a wedding to photograph, two portrait sittings, one dog portrait, and a senior class picture for the daughter of a friend. And I need to replace my camera. But Friday looks open."

"I have a better idea. I have tickets to the symphony Thursday night. Why don't we go together? We could do a late dinner afterwards and strategize about the show."

"You do like to combine business with pleasure, don't you?"

"Always. Life's more fun that way."

Amy wished she had time to think of an excuse. She wanted to keep Tom as a friend. She wanted to help him with this show. But given the state of her feelings for Jeff Berenger, doing the symphony and dinner with Tom seemed wrong. It was too much like a date. Tom's interest was veering toward personal rather than professional.

"I . . . uh . . . I'm not sure I have time, Tom."

"It's Beethoven night at the Colorado Symphony," he tempted. "Beethoven's Fifth. The *Emperor* Concerto."

Amy bit her lip.

"Friday I'm tied up, and this weekend is looking

rough. Time's getting short, and I'd like to get things set before next week."

She supposed she owed him an explanation in person. Wasn't that the upstanding and civilized way to tell a man you weren't interested? It was the only decent thing to do.

Amy gave her own weak rationalization a wry smile.

"Thursday night. All right, but no speeding along I-25 at a hundred miles per hour."

She could hear the grin in the devil's voice. "I promise."

She hung up the phone and met three toothy corgi grins, all of which seemed entirely too knowing.

"It's not a date," she told them. "I'm helping him put together a show about dogs."

The grins got wider.

"Besides, I love Beethoven, and how many chances do I get to enjoy the symphony with some amiable male company? Jeff's idea of a concert is a Beatles revival." She sighed. "Isn't it a shame you can't cut and paste in men the way you can on a computer? Take one man's humor, another's consideration, another's taste in music, and another's body. Press F6 for merge, and presto, you've got the perfect lover."

Molly and Drover settled to the floor and yawned. Only Piggy was bright-eyed and encouraging.

"But I do kinda like Jeff just the way he is."

Piggy growled, and Amy gave her an arch smile.

"Just live with it, Miss Pudgy."

DOGS HAVE AN infinite capacity for sleep. Next time you're in some household owned by a dog or dogs, look around you. What are the dogs doing? Most likely they're sleeping, unless, of course, your invasion into their house woke them from a foot-jerking, nose-twitching slumber to bark their fool heads off at you. Dogs are like that. They're either going full tilt at being obnoxious or they're snoring beneath the kitchen table. It doesn't matter how much sleep they get; they can always settle down for another nap.

I was much more than a dog, as you know, and in my waking hours I was charming rather than obnoxious. After all, a certain amount of my human personality shone through that little brown fur coat. My liking for sleep, however, was the same as any other dog's, and lately, what with climbing mountains, getting robbed, and worrying about Amy's disastrous taste in men, I hadn't gotten nearly enough downtime.

This evening was going to be different, though. Amy had given up the cleaning and gone to bed early. No men lurked about. She'd put Jeff Berenger in his place, not as firmly or permanently as I might have hoped, but at least he wasn't around to worry me. And Tom wouldn't make an appearance until Thursday evening. Selma was at a movie, so she wouldn't be barging in. For once in my life—if my present existence could be called a life—I was looking forward to a pleasant, quiet sleep alone. Even Drover's snoring couldn't keep me awake. I really wanted nothing more than a good ten or twelve hours of solid unconsciousness.

So, of course, this was the night that Stanley decided to visit. I'm sure his timing was deliberate. He's like that. Always trying to keep me off balance. Always butting in when I least wanted him around.

He appeared sitting on the foot of Amy's bed, his ankles primly crossed, a satisfied and superior smile on his face. Amy didn't wake at the intrusion. Neither did Molly or Drover. So much for the theory that dogs can see ghosts and angels, or whatever label Stanley goes by.

I regarded him balefully from my pillow beside Amy's bed.

"Good evening, Lydia. I see there's been a bit of trouble here. Glad to see you're weathering the storm."

"I suppose you sat up there on some cloud, watching all this happen," I said.

"The common image of heavenly beings lounging about on clouds is entirely false, young lady. In fact, we do very little lounging at all. There's too much work to be done."

"If you work so hard, why weren't you around to keep Amy's house from being torn apart, and poor, stupid Raven from getting scared out of his silly mind?"

"We usually don't take a direct hand in that sort of thing," Stan said primly.

"Well, maybe you ought to. You know, Stan, Amy's on the dull side, but she's a sweetheart of a friend and an all-around good person. She's the kind of Sunday-school, honor-society type that should be on your A list, and she doesn't deserve what she's getting down here. I don't understand how you can just sit on some cloud and casually crack your knuckles while she's getting the shaft she doesn't deserve."

"As I said before, Lydia, I don't sit on clouds, and I certainly don't crack my knuckles."

"I was making a point with the image," I told him. Sometimes Stan is a bit slow on the uptake. "You know what I mean."

"You mean I should intervene to make sure Amy is protected from bad things happening to her."

"Right."

"Like perhaps her husband being stolen away from her by her best friend."

That was a low blow. After living day in and day out with Amy, seeing how unguarded she left her heart and witnessing the hurt she still felt at David's and my affair, I was beginning to feel just the slightest bit guilty about my behavior. Guilt was a sensation I wasn't familiar with, and I found the best way to deal with it was simply to ignore the uncomfortable twinges of conscience. But of course, Stanley delighted in bringing to the fore anything that would make me squirm.

I came back at him with a good defense. At least I thought it was good.

"No, Stan, that's not what I mean. I mean things like

having her damned house burn down in Denver, and now having her new house torn apart like it was in some sort of friggin' tornado.''

"Lydia, cursing never adds to the effectiveness of a statement."

"That shows how much you know. I mean it, Stan. Amy deserves heavenly protection just about as much as anyone could. Can't you send some sort of guardian angel to help her out with some of these problems?''

"Guardian angel?"

"Yes, guardian angel! Don't you ever watch TV or go to the movies? They're supposed to be all over the place."

"Ah. You mean like Angels in the Outfield."

"Your video releases up there must be really dated, but that'll do. Only this angel's going to have to be a dog-showing angel, not a baseball-playing angel."

Stanley smiled. The expression was rare in itself, but the touch of amusement and tenderness in the smile was even more rare.

"Lydia, dear. Or perhaps I should call you Piggy. What do you think I sent you here for?''

"Me?"

"You."

I snorted indignantly. "What kind of guardian angel suit is this?"

"For your information, guardian angels come in all shapes and sizes. And all temperaments, unfortunately."

"The only job you gave me was matchmaking. You didn't say anything about all this other crap."

"Watch your language, dear." This time his smile was wicked. "You'll give angels a bad name."

"Shit! Like I care. Stanley, this isn't fair! None of this is fair!"

He began to fade, his favorite trick in sticky situations. "Life's not fair, Lydia. Sometimes the afterlife isn't fair either."

He was gone, but a last comment drifted back from what-
ever limbo he'd retreated to. "Use your head, young lady. And
all its attachments."

Easy for him to say. His head didn't sprout two big
pointy ears and a wet nose. Attachments. Ears. Nose. Nose!
An attachment to the head. Was that what the double-talk
meant? I wondered. I'd thought a scent in the house would clue
me to the villain, but I'd searched every room and come up with
only scents that should have been there. People I knew. People
Amy knew.

Hell! Who did Stanley think I was? A frigging Sherlock
Holmes?

Disgusted, I finally drifted off to sleep. Somewhere in the
oblivion of slumber, my mind integrated everything I knew—a
conversation here, a scent there—and put it together in an
answer. I had it!

THIRTEEN

"HELLO, LOVELY LADY." Tom flashed Amy a smile full of charm, along with a neatly wrapped package, as she opened the front door.

"What's this?"

"A package."

Amy rolled her eyes. "I know it's a package, Tom. It's for me?"

"Well, it's not for your dogs."

"You didn't need to—"

"I know I didn't." His eyes appreciatively took in the sight of her stretch tights and tunic tee. "I apologize for being early, but"—he grinned, and Amy contemplated the cost of the dazzling white caps that gave him that perfect smile—"I left time to have my usual conversation with the police on I-25. They all know me, and I think they pull me over just to talk, but tonight they must be off somewhere eating doughnuts."

"How fast were you going?"

"Only ninety-five."

"Tom, you promised."

"I promised not to speed while you were in the car."

Amy shook her head. "You're hopeless."

He was also hopelessly handsome this evening, Amy

noted. A weeknight symphony at Denver's Performing Arts Complex was not a formal affair, but Tom was dressed to kill. The suit must have been tailored for him. No jacket off the store rack would fit so well. And he had the build to complement a tailor's efforts.

"Not hopeless," he denied. "Conscientious. I have a race to drive next month. So you see, I was just practicing."

"That hobby of yours is going to kill you someday."

"Would you mourn?"

"Yes." Her answer was a dark rejoinder to his flippant words. "I've already lost too many people to foolish escapades."

Tom was immediately chagrined. "Just smack me, Amy. For a man who makes his living talking, it's amazing how often I stick my foot in my mouth."

"I'm sorry." Amy made a face. "I'm too sensitive. And with all this . . ." She waved an arm to the rooms beyond the living room.

He took in the clutter with a long, dark look. "I'd like to get my hands on the asshole who did this."

"Me too, as long as I had gloves on. You should have seen it before I started picking up. And my office . . . hell! I just started sorting through that mess today."

He tore his eyes away from the chaos and brightened his expression with visible effort. "Enough depressing conversation. Open the package."

"Tom, this isn't—"

"Just open it."

The box was about the size of a deck of cards. It was wrapped in paper decorated with cartoon drawings of dogs. The paper itself was so cute Amy hated to tear it. Trust Tom Gordon to package a gift in something that would appeal so especially to her. Packaging, she reflected, was very important to the man. Just look at how he packaged himself.

Inside the box was a folded piece of stationery bearing Tom's letterhead in fancy gold script. Below the letterhead was a handwritten note: "Look in the BMW's trunk."

"The BMW? You were going ninety-five in the BMW?"

"It's not as speedy as the Ferrari, but it gives the old college try." He gestured expansively toward the front door.

"Tom! I don't have time for this. If I don't get dressed we're going to be late."

"Then let's hurry and get whatever's in the trunk."

What was in the trunk was a very large box, and what came out of the box, when Amy finally was able to cut open the industrial strength packaging tape and dig through the Styrofoam peanuts, was a camera. A very sophisticated, very expensive camera. Amy knew exactly how much it cost, because it was a step higher than the camera she'd been using for the past two years, and she had often looked longingly at it in catalogs of photographic equipment.

"Tom! This is . . . this is . . ."

"A camera."

"What . . . why . . . ?"

"Consider it a thank-you for helping me with the show."

"Tom! This is much too generous! I can't accept this!"

"Of course you can. Yours just got stolen—"

"It was insured."

"Well, now the insurance company won't have a cow, as you put it. No strings. Honest. This isn't a come-on. I want you to have it, as a friend. I'll be very hurt if you say no."

Amy wondered if she could, in all her life, get herself into a more awkward situation. She ran appreciative fingers over the camera's casing. She would give her right arm—almost—for one of these.

"Tom, you are such a sweetheart."

"Aren't I though?"

"But . . ."

"But what?"

"But I can't accept the camera."

"Why not?"

"Even if we were really involved, I couldn't accept such an expensive gift."

He grinned, undiscouraged. "Well, since I know you want the camera, I guess we need to become really, really involved."

Amy suspected he was only half-joking. Lord, but she hated these social games that men and women played. She made a face. "I think I should tell you that I'm already involved, sort of. With—with someone else."

His smile stayed in place, but it was frozen in place. For just a moment Amy thought she saw a spark of anger in his eyes. "Lucky man. Who is he?"

"A veterinarian."

"How appropriate."

"You remember the guy at the festival with the hawk?"

"Yeah. Tall, rumpled looking. Talks to birds as if they were people."

Amy smiled at the description. "That's the one."

"Oh."

"We're not into anything serious, or committed, or anything like that. But right now, I wouldn't feel right leading you on about any relationship between us. Not that you've really asked. I know you're just joking. But, I just thought I should tell you."

His smile regained its warmth. "Amy, you are one of the few good-hearted, straightforward women left in the world. I always envied David his wife, and I still do. I want you to have that camera. Call it your fee for helping me out with this show."

"It's a rather hefty fee."

"I'm fortunate enough to be a highly overpaid media star. Take advantage of it. And speaking of stars, where are your little corgis who generally come running to say hello?"

"They're shut in the kitchen. I didn't want them to get hair all over your suit."

"It'll brush off. I'd feel deprived if I didn't greet your kids. And besides, I'm a very determined man, and I know the way to your heart is through your dogs."

Amy laughed, glad that he was such a good sport. "You do have my number, don't you?"

"Not, of course, that I could compete with a veterinarian. Rooting evil out of city government and molding public opinion will never be as glamorous as cleaning dog ears and looking through a microscope at cat turds."

"You're going to carry on like this all evening, aren't you."

"You bet."

Amy gave him a wicked grin. "Well, since you expressed the desire, why don't you visit with the dogs while I make myself presentable." She let the thundering corgi herd out of the kitchen. Drover led the pack, charging out to greet the visitor. Molly trotted along behind, uncharacteristically reserved, and Piggy stood in the kitchen doorway, looking at Tom with an unsettled expression on her furry face.

"What's wrong with Miss Piggy?" Tom asked. "I always thought I was her favorite."

"Who can guess what goes through her mind?" By

now Amy had given up trying to understand the little foundling. "One never knows which way the wind blows with that little girl."

STANDING IN THE kitchen doorway while Tom accepted greetings from the other two dogs, I myself wasn't certain which way the wind blew, but I knew it carried a rotten stench. I wasn't in the friendliest state of mind right then. To be honest, my mood made PMS look jolly. My temper was on edge and my mind in a whirl, trying to find sense in the conclusions that had come to me the night before. The puzzle of it had robbed me of sleep for the balance of the night and made me too restless to grab my usual naps during the day. I was tired, cranky, and confused. Nothing made sense. In the middle of the night, the answer to all the questions seemed so clear, my conclusions as bright as a hundred-watt bulb. Now they seemed insane. Yet what other explanation was there?

Here is my brilliant logic, in a nutshell. Tom Gordon's scent was all over Amy's house, yet the evening he had brought Amy home from their first date, his travels were limited to the living room, hall, and kitchen. I'll admit, I didn't have my eyes on him the whole time, but I heard his footsteps, and with my current set of extra large radar-quality ears, I knew exactly where he was at all times. He hadn't been anywhere near the office or bedrooms, yet now his scent was everywhere in the house. A dog's nose doesn't lie.

Needless to say, this wasn't an idea that made me happy. I had failed to put two and two together when I first nosed around the house because Tom's scent was such a comfort to me. I was preoccupied with wishing Tom was there to comfort Amy, Tom instead of the ever present (whether you want him to be present or not) Dr. Dreary. I still had trouble accepting that Tom Gordon—handsome, sophisticated, charming, loaded, and moderately famous—would have broken into Amy's house and trashed it like a hog rooting through some-

body's garden. He drives a Ferrari, for heaven's sake! He has his own TV show! How could any guy so cool be a villain? I ask you, was it any wonder my brain was a bit slow on the uptake?

The idea was even harder to accept now that Tom was standing there in the house, looking wonderfully sexy and totally desirable. Giving Amy that camera was a stroke of genius. I could tell that she was very impressed at his thoughtfulness. If this little scene had happened before the revelations of last night, I would have watched and patted myself on the back for finding the perfect man. As it was, however, I ground my teeth and wondered how the world came to be so insane. If Tom had been the one who robbed Amy's house, it was only logical to suspect he had something to do with the other attacks on her property as well, including her car, her husband, and just incidentally, me, Lydia Keane, a beautiful, fun-loving, sophisticated woman near and dear to my heart, someone who didn't deserve to die, and certainly didn't deserve to die as a footnote to someone else's plot.

The longer I sat in that doorway looking at Tom, thinking about that awful night when I met my end, the potential and beauty that had gone down the drain, the good times that had probably been in my future, the madder I got. I hadn't seen my attacker's face, and my human nose had been useless for gathering information, but the more I thought about it, the more certain I was that for some reason, Tom Gordon had been the man after Amy's camera that night. Tom Gordon had been the lowlife who torched her house, even though the police had blamed it on faulty wiring. And Tom Gordon was the creep who'd staged this latest break-in.

And then the villain started toward me.

"Hi there, Miss Piggy." Mr. Innocent, with a smile that gleamed like white diamonds. The jerk. Drover trotted slavishly at his heels. Stupid mutt. But Molly hung back with a touch of disdain. Her reserve convinced me past a doubt that I was right. What would cause Molly, who sucks up to anything *human, to give Tom the brush-off? If Tom had been our home wrecker, the answer was obvious.*

He squatted down for a bit of man-to-corgi camaraderie. It didn't work. I gave him the same eye that I'd used on those dumb sheep at the Scottish festival.

"Feeling a bit out of sorts, are we?"

If he'd touched me, I would have shown him out of sorts. But he wasn't quite that dumb. Leaving me to my pique, he wandered into the kitchen, looked around briefly, then had the nerve to slip into Amy's office. As if he hadn't seen enough already! What in hell was the jerk looking for? Obviously, Amy had something he wanted, and it had something to do with her camera. He'd tried to steal it once, and committed murder instead. He'd succeeded in stealing it in the robbery, and then had given Amy one much more expensive. And now his eyes were methodically exploring the mess that still ruled Amy's office. The expression on his face as he perused the scene of his crime, or at least, one of his crimes, was neither remorseful nor embarrassed. If anything, he looked frustrated. Almost desperate. Hunted.

As a matter of fact, he was hunted—by a corgi who had been pushed beyond restraint. I was furious. My two ex-husbands and many ex-boyfriends can tell you about Lydia Keane's temper, and that temper hadn't lost anything in translation to dog. A volcanic eruption had been building all day inside my head, and seeing Tom Two-Face tiptoe into Amy's office as if he had every right to be there set me off. I couldn't stop myself. I didn't want to stop myself.

He looked up in alarm as I launched myself toward him, and well he might have been alarmed. You might think that a corgi is too squatty and cute to scare so much as a fly, but I had a full set of teeth, and I knew how to use them. Right then, my teeth literally itched to sink into Tom Gordon.

The screech he let out was soul satisfying, rather like the squeak of a chew toy, only much louder. He ran. I pursued, nipping angrily at his heels. The other dogs took off in consternation, and Amy emerged from her bedroom wearing slippers and half a head of curled hair.

Panting and wide-eyed, Tom skidded to a halt behind Amy. The coward. I stopped with all the dignity I could, eyeing him with a royal contempt worthy of one of the queen's own corgis.

"What happened?" Amy demanded.

"That little monster bit me!"

"Omigod! Where?"

Keeping a wary eye on me, he pulled up one pant leg to display a lovely set of teeth marks in his ankle. His socks—the silky, really expensive kind—sported ugly runs spreading out from each hole. How sad.

Amy regarded me with an expression best left undescribed. Suffice it to say, she was not pleased with my efforts on her behalf.

"We'd better get that cleaned up," she told Tom solicitously. "It doesn't look bad, but a bit of antiseptic would be a good idea."

"Try garlic and a cross," Tom suggested sourly. "She was after my blood."

"I'm really sorry, Tom. And totally embarrassed. I can't imagine what got into her."

And that was that. So much for Amy's date with Beethoven.

"I DON'T KNOW what the hell got into her." Amy sat cross-legged on Selma's thrift store couch and rested her head on her hands. Raven lay beside her, looking up at her with sympathetic brown eyes. "Tom said he didn't do anything—didn't frighten her, didn't tease her, didn't try to take anything away from her. She's never shown any signs of aggression before this."

Selma raised a brow.

"Well, she hasn't! She can be cranky and cantankerous, and she's one of the strangest little dogs I've ever met, but she's never offered to bite anyone. At least not anyone human."

"Is he going to report it?"

"No." Amy wove her fingers through Raven's ruff, her lips pressed into an unhappy line. "He was a really good sport about it. Said it wasn't that bad. She ruined his sock and the leg of his trousers, though. God! I was so embarrassed."

"And you didn't go to the symphony?"

"No. We would have been way late. And neither of us felt like talking about his dog program right then, for obvious reasons."

"So that's that? No more Tom?"

Amy sat up straighter and brushed her hair back from her face. "No more dates. If he wants to continue that dog thing for his show, I'll help him with it, but no more dates. He asked me to some kind of annual beer drinking affair at his house a week from Saturday—said it was his version of Oktoberfest—but I said no."

Selma huffed disconsolately. "There goes my vicarious romance with a TV star."

"Yeah, well, Tom's nice. But all that perfection can be hard to take. I felt strange going out with a guy who's prettier than I am." She watched inquisitively as Selma shimmied into a pair of tailored slacks and a silk knit top.

"You look nice. Are you going out tonight?"

"Uh . . . yeah."

The hesitant tone instantly made Amy suspicious. "Who with?"

"Uh . . ."

"Not that it's any of my business." Her raised brow conveyed just the opposite.

"Nosy wench," Selma chided. Then she sighed. "I'm going out with Gary."

"Gary!"

"Yeah . . . well, we're thinking about giving it another try. Gary can be a jerk, but then, so can I, sometimes. Overall he's a good guy. He did help find Ray."

"Well, yes."

"And Ray adores him. Dogs always know when a man has a good heart, you know? I never argue with a dog's instincts."

Amy wasn't going to argue either. She wasn't terribly surprised. Angry as Selma had been with Gary, her leaving him had always seemed more like an ultimatum to her husband than a final breakup. They had found too many reasons to seek each other out, if only to shout each other down. Amy wished she didn't still have doubts about Gary's role in the attack on her home.

Selma looked at her, clearly craving approval for her plans. Amy didn't know what to say, so she changed the subject.

"What am I going to do about Piggy, Selma?"

Selma chose a pair of shoes from her closet, grimaced, then tossed them on the bed and got out another pair. "Compliment her on her taste in men. I wouldn't mind taking a bite or two out of Tom Gordon." Her eyes danced. "In a very friendly way, of course."

"This is not a joke. I can't have a dog that bites."

"Maybe she just doesn't like the media. A lot of people would agree with her."

"Very funny! The one she doesn't like is Jeff, but she's never tried to bite him. Well, only once, when he was giving her a shot, but Jeff was too fast for her. Piggy's always seemed to adore Tom. Every time she's seen him she's thrown herself at him like he was made of chopped liver."

"Corgis are fickle beasts. You can't trust them."

"You just said you never argue with a dog's instincts," Amy reminded her.

"Oh." Selma slanted an impish smile toward Amy. "Well, then obviously, my opinion can't be trusted either. Look at the turnabout I just did on Gary." The smile faded to uncertainty as she examined herself critically in the mirror. "Do you think my tan blouse would look better than this knit?"

"No. Go with what you have on."

"Thanks. What about my hair? Should I wear it back in this new clip I bought?"

Amy threw up her hands. "Selma, you're going out with Gary. He's seen you with your hair in curlers and a toothbrush sticking out of your mouth. Why all the worry about looking glamorous?"

"This is a date. We're starting from the beginning. You know, like we're not married, so we have to look good and be nice to each other."

Amy sniffed. "Seems to me the sniping you've done lately is a more realistic rehearsal for marriage."

"Don't be cynical. And don't look at me like that. I miss Gary, and I miss being married. I miss waking up each morning to the sound of him gargling. I miss spending Sunday mornings lounging around the house in Gary's pajama tops, laughing with him at the comics and eating sweet rolls. I miss knowing that at least one person in this world cares whether I live or die—not because he's expected to, like family, but because he chooses to." She sighed disconsolately. "I miss all that."

"I guess I can understand that."

Selma sat down on the coffee table, knee to knee with Amy as she sat on the couch. Raven welcomed his mistress with a poke of his long nose, and Selma absently scratched his ear.

"You never had any of that stuff with David, did you?"

"We didn't have that kind of marriage."

"You've never said much about your marriage."

Amy shrugged. "There was never much to say, nothing out of the ordinary except the way it ended. I think now that even though we were married five years, I never knew David very well, and he never knew me. When he proposed, I thought I was incredibly lucky. I never dated much, and it seemed absolutely unbelievable that someone who was sexy and popular would want to marry me. Now—" she hesitated; it still hurt to think it, and was even more painful to put the thought into words, "now I think maybe he was more interested in my father's money than he was in me. My parents were crazy about David. Dad gave him the funds to start the BMW dealership. When my folks came up from Florida for David's funeral, they still could scarcely believe their perfect son-in-law had been playing house with Lydia."

"What a jerk he was. I always thought David was a cold fish."

Amy shook her head. "He wasn't really a jerk. I just think we were roommates rather than lovers, and I'd hoped for more."

"When Gary and I were first married, we were best friends as well as lovers. It was great. We didn't work at it, though, after the first flush of passion wore off." She smiled wistfully. "But there were still some awfully good times. Enough to make it worth putting back together if we can. Being alone for a while made me realize that, if nothing else."

Amy couldn't help but feel a flash of envy.

"You don't miss being married at all, do you?" Selma commented.

Amy shook her head.

"Then Lydia didn't really take anything from you that mattered all that much, did she?"

"Maybe she didn't." Amy sighed. "They shouldn't have sneaked around, though. And they really shouldn't

have gotten themselves killed in a stupid stunt like running after some thief."

"Yeah. And I'll bet wherever David and Lydia are,
they're wishing the same thing."

*IF I COULD live the last year of my life over again, you can bet I
would make some changes! I would turn up my nose when
David first starts to strut around spreading his tail feathers like
a peacock with the hots. Or, if I couldn't bring myself to be
that virtuous, I would at least stay home and watch TV on
that cold March night when he asks me to meet him at the
Wynkoop. Or if I just have to give into temptation, I certainly
would run the other way when David takes after that thief,
instead of following like a fool without half a brain. You bet. If
I got a second chance, I'd make damned sure I didn't end up in
a dog suit, locked in the slammer in a dark, lonely room while
the villain of the story prances off free as a bird.*

*There's no justice in the world, and don't I know it! Amy
should have treated me like a heroine for driving off the bad
guy, but what did she do? She looked at me as though I'd
grown horns in place of my ears and shoved me into my kennel
with some very sharp words about my ancestry and IQ. Right
then I had a few thoughts about her IQ as well. After all, she
was the lamebrain who was dating the very fellow who'd
trashed her house and, I suspect, burned another, and snuffed
out the promising life of yours truly, not to mention poor
David.*

*All right, all right! I'll admit I didn't have much room to
blame Amy for being fooled. I myself—a much more astute
judge of men—was taken in by Terrible Tom. It was embarrassing, and the humiliation of being made a fool soured my
mood even more. I should have seen through that sly, charming
smile, the dazzling capped teeth, the tailored clothes, and the
damned Ferrari. That syrupy mellow voice of his should have
given me a clue. Any guy who works that hard to sound good*

couldn't be on the up and up. And his clothes . . . I'll bet if he hadn't had a wardrobe coordinator for his TV show, he would have looked every bit as sloppy as Jeff Berenger. Maybe not as frayed, because he did have money, after all, but just as sloppy.

Where did Tom get off, anyway, thinking that he could make Amy's life miserable and get away with it, just because he was rich and famous and had the local airwaves in his pocket? He wasn't that great, you know. Too short, for one thing. His tan looked like it came from a salon, and I was willing to bet his eyes wouldn't have been nearly so green without tinted contacts.

I sat there for quite a while chewing on Tom Gordon's faults, and though mentally taking him apart limb from limb gave me a bit of sour satisfaction, it didn't bring me any closer to answering the puzzle of what was happening—or finding a solution. Why was Tom Gordon harrassing Amy? Obviously he was looking for something, but what? My area of expertise is men, not crime, and I didn't have a clue. Not only did I not know the answer, I couldn't even warn Amy that she had befriended a creep. What I would have given for the gift of speech right then. You never appreciate something until you lose it, I've learned. Sitting there in my kennel, frustrated enough to start chewing the metal bars, I would have given a week's worth of kibble to be able to talk for just a few precious moments. Well, maybe not quite a week's worth.

Things seemed pretty black to me right then, but nothing is so bad that it can't get worse, which is something I learned when Stanley made his appearance in the dark spare bedroom, where my kennel was isolated in solitary disgrace. Stanley is seldom amusing company, but his mood on that night was more officious and self-righteous than ever. Just what I needed!

He folded his arms across his skinny chest and regarded me with a look that could have singed any angel's wings, if that angel was lucky enough to have wings instead of paws.

"I suppose you saw," I said. There's very little use in

lying to someone like Stanley. You might as well come clean and admit your sins, because he knows about them anyway.

"I did indeed. And I'm amazed at how little you have learned."

"I've learned a hell of a lot more than you saw fit to tell me!" I snapped.

Stanley doesn't much like cussing. Even mild cussing. His spine got even stiffer, if that were possible.

"You could have told me Tom Gordon is a creep!"

"Lessons are more effective when learned through investigation and struggle."

"Nice work, Stan. While you're letting me 'investigate and struggle,' Amy gets her house looted and pals around with a guy who should be warming a cot on death row!"

Stanley wasn't a bit contrite. "And you propose to deal with the misguided Mr. Gordon by attacking his ankle? Nice work, Lydia."

I hadn't thought Stanley capable of sarcasm. But he was.

"How else was I going to get him out of Amy's office?"

"Did you think he was going to do any more harm there, or did you simply go into a rage to get revenge against a man who hurt you?"

"Now, why would I do that?" I sneered.

"Lydia, violence is never a solution. That is one of the immutable laws of the universe."

"Bullshit! It felt good."

"But did it do any good?"

"It kept Amy from going out with the prick."

Stanley's frown was thunderous.

"Well, it did."

"And where did it get you?"

I laid my head between my paws and sighed. "Locked in the slammer."

"Do you know what generally happens to dogs who attack people in such an unprovoked manner?" *he asked in a gentler tone.*

The consequences of my little tantrum hadn't occurred to me before then. The question brought me up short, because I was afraid that I knew the answer, and it wasn't a pleasant one.

"You may have rung the curtain down on your mission prematurely, young lady. If Amy decides to dispose of you, I can't do anything about it."

His choice of words made a lump form in my throat. "Dispose of . . . me?"

"Indeed. Thousands of sweet, innocent, perfectly well-behaved pets are euthanized every day, simply because they have no one to care for them. With all that happening, do you imagine that anyone would give a second thought to ending the life of a dog who attacks a human being? I know that death isn't the dreadful experience that most fear it is, but my dear young lady, do you really want to repeat the experience so soon after your last demise?"

I hoped he was joking. He could have been. Stan had a rather twisted sense of humor. But his expression was dead serious.

"Amy wouldn't do that," *I whined.* "She can't step on a spider without apologizing to the bug."

"We shall see," *Stanley pronounced.*

"And you've got to do something about Tom Gordon." *My indignation was beginning to revive. Stan didn't have any call to use these scare tactics on me. This mess wasn't really my fault. If Tom Gordon weren't such an asshole, none of this would have happened. If not for Gordon, in fact, David and I would still be alive, and Amy wouldn't have need of a matchmaking guardian angel. Or if she did, it wouldn't be me.*

Stanley milked my humiliation for all it was worth. "It's not my place to take care of Mr. Gordon, Lydia. I only take care of you, and you take care of the rest. If you're around long enough. I recommend you contemplate the lessons learned here and garner a bit of wisdom from them."

He began to disappear, and I growled after him as he left. "Go sit on your halo, Mr. Smart-Ass."

His smile only grew more superior as he faded from view.

I had little time to recover before Amy came to visit the prisoner. Switching on the light, she sat on the guest bed and regarded me with a puzzled frown. I looked back at her, tilting my head and perking up my big ears in an appearance of charming innocence—a corgi trick as old as the breed. No one with a heart as soft as Amy's could have resisted. She got up and opened my kennel door.

"Come on out, you little grinch."

Sprung at last. I began to hope that Stanley's dire prediction was so much bullshit. Amy didn't look happy, but she wasn't exactly lusting for my blood either.

She sat back on the bed and patted the mattress beside her. Obligingly, I jumped up and looked at her with soulful eyes.

"I wish you could tell me what's going on inside that little brain of yours." Amy sighed. "That's assuming you have a brain, you nitwit."

Strangely enough, Amy had made the same disparaging comment about my brain, or lack of one, when I was human. Some things never change.

"What did Tom do to set you off?" she asked.

Murder, for one thing. And that was just a start. How I wished I could talk!

Amy scratched my chin, an intimacy I accepted only because I was still in deep shit.

"What am I going to do with you?" she lamented quietly. "You've become a friend, little girl. You're odd. You're cranky. You're a pain in the butt. But you're still a friend. You're full of vinegar, but you're not vicious. I just wish I knew what's going on."

I would have told her if I could have. You have no idea how frustrating it is not to be able to do more than growl, bark, and whine.

Amy released me on parole. Stan's doom and gloom was

just so much noise. I didn't feel as relieved as I might have, however. Things were getting very serious, and I was beginning to realize that more than my matchmaking efforts were in peril. Maybe it was her understanding that brought home to me how good a friend I had in Amy—had always had in Amy. She'd been a better friend to me than I'd been to her, and I vowed that she would not suffer a fate similar to mine. Amy deserved better.

Yeah, I know. Such nobility of purpose is a bit out of character for both Lydia Keane and Piggy the wonder dog. Concern over someone else's welfare was a strange feeling. I had to let it roll around my brain awhile before I could decide whether I liked all this loftiness. The sensation wasn't all that bad, I concluded. I could handle it.

But in limited quantities only.

FOURTEEN

THE FOLLOWING EVENING, Piggy stood on a grooming table in Amy's kitchen, head drooping and ears at half-mast. Jeff extracted a thermometer from her nether parts and shook his head. "I don't see anything obvious wrong with her."

Molly and Drover sat at attention at Jeff's feet, watching with eyes that were hopeful of getting their fair share of attention, even if it did involve the indignity of a thermometer.

"Temperature's normal. Eyes are clear. Gums are nice and pink. Nose is cold."

"Nose is cold?" Amy gave him a look from where she nursed a cup of coffee at the kitchen table. "Temperature's normal? Geez, Jeff. For that kind of diagnosis you went to veterinary college? *I* could have told you that."

"True. But *you* don't get paid the big bucks."

"You mean you're going to charge me more than a quarter?"

"Oh yeah." He massaged Piggy's neck and chest, feeling for swellings. "A quarter is the charge for broken kittens. This dog's going to cost you at least another cup of coffee."

"I'm not sure she's worth it."

"Sure she is. Aren't you, Pudgy?"

Piggy turned with only a mild glare when Jeff gave her a pat on her well-padded rump. "She's a sorry excuse for a dog, but you can't deny she's a real individual."

"A little too individual." Amy sighed unhappily. "She seems depressed to me. Haven't you noticed that she hasn't played any of her usual tricks on you tonight."

"Maybe her bag of tricks is empty." He gave the dog a rueful half grin as he lifted her down from the table. "I *hope* her bag of tricks is empty."

Piggy trotted over to the dog bed in the kitchen's corner. Drover happily followed, his nose stretching toward her rear end until his lady love rounded on him with a snarl. Molly sat at Amy's feet and watched the action with serene disdain. Amy's eyes were on Jeff instead of the dogs. He propped himself on the edge of the kitchen table, one side of his mouth slanted upward as Drover suffered yet another rejection. In spite of his casual attitude, Jeff Berenger was a good vet, Amy knew. He didn't miss much about an animal's well-being or behavior. He didn't miss much about people either.

"Piggy looks like her normal disagreeable self, if you ask me, Amy."

"You don't think there's something wrong that might explain why she bit Tom Gordon last night?"

"I'd say she just wanted to make an editorial comment."

Amy exhaled in a huff. "You're no better than Selma. You both think this is a big joke."

"No, I don't. I just think you're taking it too seriously." He folded his long body into a kitchen chair. "Piggy is not a danger to the public at large. Tom Gordon obviously did something to frighten or annoy her. It's not difficult to get on Piggy's bad side, you know."

Amy scowled and contemplated the swirling rise of steam from her coffee.

"I think," Jeff said gently, "that you're on edge. You have every right to be on edge. And I think your nerves are magnifying a molehill into a mountain bigger than the one we climbed Monday."

As she had reflected just a moment earlier, Jeff Berenger didn't miss much about people. "You think?" she asked with a sigh.

"That's my diagnosis."

She was on edge, Amy admitted to herself. Not only because she seemed to be crime's favorite target in the Denver area, but because she was losing a battle with herself. Only three days ago she had told Jeff she needed space and time. She'd planned to give herself a month, or at least two weeks, before subjecting her susceptible heart to seeing him again. During that period her life would calm down. The emotional crisis of the break-in would pass. Her senses would regain their normal balance.

And here the man sat in her kitchen, at her invitation, only three days after her great resolution. She had latched on to the first excuse to call him, had actually caught herself primping in anticipation of seeing him. Amy could have taken Piggy's temperature and felt her nose, and well Jeff must have known it. He was probably laughing to himself right then at her transparent maneuvering to see him again.

Jeff didn't look like he was laughing at her, though. His hazel eyes were dark with concern, and his caring made her go warm inside. When he got up, she searched her mind for an excuse why he should stay just a bit longer.

"My coffee so bad you're going to run off?"

He picked up his cup and grinned. "Not hardly. You don't expect me to leave before I get paid, do you?" As he poured them both another cup, he gave her a keen-eyed glance. "What was Gordon doing over here, anyway? Are you still helping him with that dog story?"

"Yes." Amy could have left it at that. The rest wasn't really Jeff Berenger's business. But his eyes questioned. He didn't even attempt to look politely uninterested.

"Tom offered to take me to the Beethoven symphony, then to dinner where we could talk about where he could go with the show."

Jeff sat back down and glumly stirred a small mountain of sugar into his coffee.

"Don't look like that, Jeff. Tom and I aren't dating. David sponsored Tom's race car, and they were buddies. We're just friends."

He regarded her from beneath thick brows that had drawn together into a solid, disapproving line. "Quite a guy, Tom Gordon. TV celeb, race car jockey, and culture lover."

She smiled and shrugged. "I can't resist Beethoven."

"I'll have to remember that."

He was jealous, Amy realized, and wondered if she was to be treated to a cold shoulder or a fit of pique similar to what she had sometimes gotten from David. Perhaps she should have made up some more innocent explanation for Tom's visit.

The thought struck a painful chord in Amy's memory. She closed her eyes and remembered how much she had always hated tiptoeing around David's feelings. Her husband had possessed an unpredictable temper, and she'd gone out of her way to avoid talking to him about things that might upset him. She'd even told a few white lies to maintain peace in the household. How she had hated that. Did all relationships get so tangled and twisted that deception was necessary to keep them going? she wondered. Or did people simply allow them to get that way?

She opened her eyes and caught Jeff looking at her with eyes that penetrated with unnerving clarity. "Shall I be perfectly honest?" Amy asked.

"About what?"

"About anything and everything."

He shrugged. "Go ahead."

"Tom was more than an old acquaintance. He's been pushing for a closer relationship. But I told him that I'm seeing someone else." She smiled wryly. "He gave me this incredible camera to replace the one that got stolen. Said it was a thank-you gift for helping him with the show, but I really think it was more than that. Too bad I'll have to give it back."

"You're seeing someone else." Jeff was still back on that one sentence. A dimple appeared as a precursor to a smile. "And who might that be?"

"Who do you think, dim-bulb?"

"I think he's one very lucky man."

"Well . . ." She tried to sound stern, but in the glow of his smile, it was difficult. "He's not going to get lucky yet. I meant what I said the other day. My life needs to settle down to where I can make rational, sensible decisions."

Jeff shook his head, but he was still smiling. "Amy, my love. Haven't you learned yet that life rarely settles down. There is no such thing as normal. Things always intrude, good and bad, to get our minds in a whirl when we least want them to be in a whirl."

She looked at him dubiously.

"When something good comes along, kiddo, you've got to grab it while you can."

"And you're that something good?"

"You bet I am. You can't hide yourself away because you discovered the hard way that life—and love—sometimes isn't what it's cracked up to be. And I'm just the guy with the persistence and the brass to yank you out of hiding."

Amy arched a cautious brow. "Do tell."

"I will tell, thank you very much. I'll tell you that you're the best thing that's walked into my life since I sprouted my first growth of whiskers. I'll tell you that the thought of seeing you makes me glad to get out of bed in the morning. Being with you makes the things I love more beautiful, more wondrous, and makes the ordinary parts of my life take on a new gleam. Before I met you, I never realized what I was missing by going through life alone."

A glow started inside Amy. Her heart picked up its pace, and she couldn't keep a smile from her lips. She tried to caution herself that this was just talk. A line. A come-on. But Jeff didn't look as though he were spouting a line. The words resounded from his heart, and they surrounded her with a warmth that was impossible to ignore.

"Jeff . . ." She briefly brought her hands to her face, as if she could hide behind them, but then dropped them back to the table to grip her coffee cup with white-knuckled intensity. "I've told myself since David died . . . I don't need a man. I don't need anyone."

"That's bullshit. Everyone needs someone. If we don't have someone, we just plaster over the hole in our lives and hope to fool ourselves along with everybody else. I don't want to chain you, Amy. I don't want to change you, or limit you, or make you pretend to be someone you're not. But as long as we're being honest with each other here, I'll confess that I am plotting to become an important part of your life."

As if they sensed the gravity of the conversation, the corgis had gathered in a trio beside the kitchen table and hung upon Jeff's every word. When he paused and fastened his gaze on Amy, they turned their heads to her in unison, expressions expectant.

Suddenly, she wanted to laugh—at all four of them, man and dogs, so still and intent, riveted upon her as if the world depended upon her next words. She was obviously too tired to think straight, Amy decided, for the dogs' expressions seem to say, "Go for it, you chicken-hearted stick-in-the-mud." Except for Piggy. Her keen-eyed look was sharp and troubled, with the furry brow between her ears puckered in an almost-human wrinkle of anxiety.

How ironic that her own vacillating emotions were so accurately reflected in her little pack, Amy noted. Half of her longed to throw herself into Jeff Berenger's arms and bury her face in the warm flannel of his shirt. The other half quibbled that it was too soon, and she was diving into the emotional deep end without so much as a pair of water wings.

"I am—I am . . ." she stuttered. She was what? In love? In lust? Incapable of asking him to stay at the same time she was unwilling to ask him to leave?

All of that, she concluded.

"You are . . . ?" he prompted. A twinkle lit his eyes, and the grave set of his face started to relax.

She should insist that he go, even though a few minutes before she'd been groping for an excuse to have him stay. But she did need time, not to mention the safety of distance, to relieve her of the mix of adolescent excitement and womanly longing his presence created. She couldn't let him know how just a look from him, or a smile, or a word, could thaw her resolve.

Amy opened her mouth on an excuse—any excuse—when once again the need for honesty tweaked her. She didn't want games, and she didn't want to dance about trying to save face.

Biting her lip, she met his eyes openly. "I'm confused, Jeff. You muddle my senses."

He grinned. "Glad to hear it."

"I don't know whether I'm in love with you or simply longing for a strong anchor in a stormy sea."

"There's nothing wrong with a strong anchor. It's a good beginning."

"You sound as though you want more than a beginning."

"Everything starts with a beginning. Beginnings don't bother me. What I want is something that doesn't have an end."

Amy grew cold with a moment of absolute panic. Jeff's eyes flicked over her face, and he smiled ruefully.

"If the idea of endless love scares you, I'd settle for being really, really good friends. Intimately good friends. Endlessly, of course."

Amy smiled. "You know me too well, Jeff."

He got up and came over to where she sat. The dogs trotted at his heels, then arranged themselves in a supporting phalanx as he sat on his heels in front of her chair. She didn't resist when he reached out and took both her hands in his.

"I'm going to stay here tonight, Amy."

Her heart thumped erratically.

"All other considerations aside, you shouldn't be staying here alone until the police find whoever's got you in his sights."

"No, Jeff. You can't. Don't take advantage of what I just told you."

"I'm not going to take advantage of anything. I'll stay in the guest room if you want."

Like hell, Amy thought. She would cave like a house of straw in a tornado. And well he knew it.

"I'm not alone," she objected. "Selma's just over the garage."

"Selma works most nights."

And when she wasn't working, Selma was "dating" Gary. Giddy as a teen going steady, she'd become oblivious to everything else.

"I've got the dogs to protect me."

"Oh, yeah." Jeff glanced at the tongue-lolling, grinning corgis. "They're going to scare off the bad guys, all right."

"There's Raven."

"Who's already proved himself a sentry dog supreme."

Amy sighed and extracted her hands from his hold, despite the warm comfort of them being there. "Jeff, I appreciate the thought, but there's really no need—"

"*I* need," he told her emphatically. "I can't sleep at night wondering who's sneaking up on your house or planting a bomb in your car."

"You've been watching too many TV thrillers."

"Just indulge me, here, Amy. Think of me as a cheap bodyguard. I'll even buy my own groceries. You wanted time to get to know me better. This is it. When all this is settled, I'll move out. And you can have your independence back, if you want it."

But what about her heart? Amy thought desperately. Could she have her heart back as well? Or perhaps her heart had already defected to his camp, because through the sense of panic and indignation, a peculiar glee was rising to the surface of her soul.

She got up and started pacing, driven by a need to put a bit of distance between them. The dogs followed her every move, their heads swinging back and forth with her like spectators in a tennis game. "You can't make me let you stay."

"Sure I can. You're too softhearted to make me camp out in my truck in front of your house."

"I don't like this macho shit," she warned.

"You like wimps? You're going to love it when I start whining out there in the cold."

Amy paced, keeping her eyes on the floor in front of her. Looking at Jeff would do her in for sure. When she turned and bumped up against him, she was unprepared for the shock of their sudden contact. She jumped backward and found the refrigerator at her back. Jeff took instant advantage, making his body into a barrier and caging her with a hand on either side of her head.

"Is it a deal?" he demanded.

Amy could scarcely breathe. Up close and personal, he was impressively broad and intimidatingly tall. The heat from his body was rapidly melting what little reserve was left to her, and suddenly she wondered why she was fighting so hard against something that might be so very good. Had five years of a mediocre marriage scared her that badly? Was she so easily chased onto the sidelines to watch the rest of the world compete in games she was afraid to play?

"You're making it very hard to say no," she whispered up into his smile.

"Aren't I, though?"

She gave in to the need to slip her arms around his waist. He was firm muscle, a pillar of physical strength, very much like that solid anchor she'd mentioned earlier. He leaned into her, and she closed her eyes, surrendering to bliss. Touching him felt so right. Holding him seemed to loosen all the knots that had kinked her stomach over the past days.

"Jeff, you know if you stay here, it won't be in the guest room."

"I know."

"You know entirely too much—about me, about all the holes in my defenses."

"I do," he whispered, his mouth so close that his lips brushed her ear. "Because I love you, Amy. How's that for letting down defenses?"

Before she could answer, he slipped an arm behind her knees and lifted her into his arms.

"What are you doing?"

"Giving you a ride into the bedroom."

"You know I don't go in—"

"For this macho shit," he finished. "But this seemed the surest way to get you there."

Once in the bedroom, he swung her easily to her feet and kicked the door shut with his foot, narrowly missing the three inquisitive noses that followed behind them.

"Now." He took her hands and placed them in their former position on his waist. "Where were we?"

Amy surrendered to a smile, exasperated, aroused, and amused at the same time. She didn't know whether to rip into him for his high-handedness or to kiss him for the endearingly boyish hint of mischief in his voice.

"Do you always get your way?"

"Nearly always." He fingered aside a tumble of curls and kissed the tip of her ear. "I'm a persistent cuss."

A current that was both icy and hot shivered through Amy's nerves as his mouth traveled the column of her neck and thence downward. The breath she'd been unconsciously holding seemed to shudder when she finally exhaled.

"Someone should—" She gasped as the snaps on her shirt popped open. "Someone should put you in your place."

"Someone should," he agreed. His big, blunt-fingered hands were warm against her cold flesh as he carefully peeled away the shirt and pushed it off her shoulders. A swift spasm of desire arrowed from her heart to her groin when he splayed his fingers over her bare ribs and ran his thumbs beneath the elastic of her bra. His eyes captured hers. "Do you know where my place is, Amy?"

"W-where?"

"Right here with you. Better yet," he said in a voice growing husky. "Inside of you."

He brought her close, and Amy could feel the extent of his arousal as she pressed against him. With unhurried deliberation, he lowered his mouth to hers and kissed her. First a soft brush of the lips—toying, tasting, inviting. Slowly evolving to a kiss that was more than a kiss. It surrounded her, consumed her blossoming passion, and stole the very breath of her desire.

Amy's insides turned to liquid, and her mind melted to mush. When Jeff guided her to the bed, she sank down onto the mattress with him, past resistance, past regret, caution, or modesty. Their clothes came off in a hurry, but the rest of the encounter was slow and deliberate. They explored and caressed, toyed with each other's urgency, tempting, teasing, feeding a desire that devoured them both. When they could take no more, they came together in a joining that sent them beyond need and desire, to a place where physical boundaries dissolved, leaving them with one soul, one joy, and one beating heart.

WOULDN'T YOU KNOW that Dr. Dud would be such a prude, shutting us out of the bedroom so that no little dog eyes could watch his manly endeavors? So rude, slamming the door in our faces like that! Not that I cared. Berenger couldn't have any tricks I hadn't seen—and tried—a zillion times. Besides, when you've done the dirty as much as I have, second-hand excitement becomes less than thrilling. Encounters in the flesh sometimes aren't bell ringers either. Of course, in my current situation, that particular problem had been removed from my list of things to worry about.

Another worry I no longer had to bother about—the possibility of Amy falling for a total loser. It was fait accompli, getting more "accompli," if you get my meaning, every minute I stood glaring at the bedroom door. Stanley was going to pin this on me. I just knew it. That celestial nerd had specified the Best Possible Husband when he charged me with finding Amy a new spouse. Obviously he didn't mean a man whose idea of ambition was climbing a mountain every weekend and whose "dress clothes" were clean hiking boots and a shirt without elbow patches. Oh yes, Stan was going to use this loophole to keep me from getting a just reward for all my hard work on this mission. Just my luck!

I didn't panic, though. After Tom Gordon's villainy, Jeff Berenger didn't look quite as bad to me as he'd looked before. Yes, he was dull. Yes, he was annoying and far from perfect. But he wasn't as awful as I'd once thought. Besides, Jeff may have won a battle or two, but the war was far from over. Passion can be a very temporary thing. No one knows that better than I, who spent my adult life discarding husbands and lovers as readily as chucking out last year's wardrobe. There was another man out there for Amy—a Perfect Man. And I would find him. It just might take a bit longer than I'd planned.

I'll admit my spirits were a bit low at this point. My blunder with Tom left me feeling less confident about my judgment. It occurred to me that my standards for the Perfect Husband might be a bit off the mark. I didn't dwell on it, though. Years of cruising singles' bars, dating services, and the personals had given me a good education in the ABCs of men, and I wasn't going to lose faith in myself because of one little stumble.

Besides, I had more important things to worry about than Amy's juvenile little affair. Tom Gordon was up to no good. I was determined to find out why and to shut him down before he hurt Amy any more than he had already. After all, how could I find Amy the Perfect Husband if she was six feet under? Not that I knew for sure that Tom had murder on his mind. I didn't even know for sure that Tom was the villain who had broken into Amy's car and just happened to kill two innocent people in the process. Or if he was the one who had torched her Denver house.

I did know that he'd trashed her current house, however, and it seemed reasonable to assume that he hadn't done that just for the joy of going through a lady's drawers. He had to have had a powerful reason. And if Tom Gordon had a reason to turn Amy's Niwot house inside out and upside down, that same reason probably had driven him to the other mischief as well. I intended to find out what that reason was . . . with the help of a couple of acquaintances.

I'm sure you've guessed by now that corgis are natural busybodies. They don't like their curious little noses kept out of any goings-on, especially goings-on involving their own people in their own house. Accordingly, Molly and Drover were less than happy about the closed door to Amy's bedroom. Their big corgi ears picked up evidence that things were happening in that room, things that they should be supervising, or at least participating in. They weren't often deprived of Amy's company when she was home, and they didn't like it one bit.

Corgis are also vengeful little creatures, so it was easy for me to enlist the resident troops in my plot. They followed me to Amy's office readily enough, and when I tipped over the wastebasket and dove into a stack of loose files beside the desk, they got the general idea. It doesn't take much to persuade a corgi to indulge in general mayhem, and that's exactly what all three of us did.

Poor Amy. She'd just gotten the office tidy again. Fortu-

nately for me, it wasn't too tidy. She'd sorted the files, but she hadn't yet put them back in the cabinet, and the trash was still piled in plastic garbage bags beside the door. There's no garbage bag made that can withstand an onslaught of just one corgi, much less three.

What was the purpose of this? you ask. What did I expect to find? I'll admit it: I didn't know. I simply hoped that once the innards of the office were laid bare by the three of us, something would jump out at me to connect Tom Gordon with Amy, or David, or someone else linked with Amy. Tom Gordon wanted something Amy had, and most probably that something was here. Unless it was in the lab downstairs, or the kitchen, or the living room bookcases, or the hall closet. Unless he had found it during the robbery and taken it with him.

No, I told myself. If he had found it, why would he have snooped around the office while Amy was dressing for the symphony? He sought something that should be in the office, and that made my task less hopeless.

The upshot of it was, I didn't find what I looked for. We had a good time, at least. Creating chaos is a corgi specialty, and Molly and Drover were masters at it. They dove into stacks of files, dug through the trash bag, and frapped around the room, chasing each other, rolling and wriggling in piles of paper, chewing on pencils, eating erasers, and being idiots in every possible way. While they had fun, I went from pile to pile, sniffing, reading, thinking. All I found were bills, dull correspondence, contracts, check stubs, a ream of stationery, a few catalogs, a box of file folders, mailing labels, and files spilling out photo proofs of dogs, kids, weddings, a fall landscape, more dogs, and someone's cat.

Tom's scent was still pervasive in the office, but it was fading. He'd touched much of the stuff I sniffed, though not all. He probably hadn't been quite as efficient at going through the office as my little helpers were. It's hard to match a corgi's talent at tearing things apart.

But there was nothing there that anyone in their right

mind would have found interesting. My head pounded with the frustration of it all, and just for good measure, I ripped apart a few old bank statements to relieve the pressure, wishing all the time they were Tom Gordon's leg.

TOM GORDON'S LEG throbbed. It had throbbed all day and evening, and it still throbbed. The tooth holes that miserable half-assed excuse for a dog had inflicted were in his ankle, but his calf and knee complained in sympathy. The pain wasn't bad, but it was just one more irritant added to an already irritating Friday.

He'd started the morning by oversleeping, probably because he'd slept very little the night before. Why did worries always magnify at night? he wondered. Concerns that were bearable during the day became stalking predators the moment a man sought sleep. He'd finally gotten up and poured himself enough straight Scotch to put away an elephant. The liquor had knocked him out in the small hours of the morning but had extracted a stiff price for that sweet oblivion—the mother of all hangovers.

Tom had scarcely put himself together in time to meet Dick Stafford for lunch at Duffy's Bar in downtown Denver. Dulled senses and a queasy stomach had dimmed the professional charm he'd cultivated for ten years. His mind had not been sharp, and what wit he had left was more acid than clever, following the example of his stomach. His lunch partner had given him more than one quizzical look. It was the wrong time to screw up. Stafford was recruiting for NBC, and it was an open secret the network was looking to add Tom to its stable of journalistic stars. It was Tom's chance to play with the big boys, and he had no intention of letting fate, bad luck, or his own stupidity take that chance away from him.

The afternoon had gone downhill from there. A sick headache had kept him from focusing on work, and thoughts of Amy Cameron had taken advantage of his faltering concentration to prey on his mind. Amy was a problem for which he had no solution. He was beginning to think he'd been incredibly stupid from the beginning of the situation, and now his options were damned near gone. The irony was that he wasn't even sure that there was a problem. He didn't like leaving uncertainties unresolved, however. That was why he was a great investigative reporter. He anticipated problems before they appeared, the same as he had anticipated a danger to his career before it came to light.

His plan had been so simple to begin with—a simple, quick, clean solution to an unexpected problem. But then, like a single thread that manages to get tangled in a huge snarl, his simple solution careened out of control. There was no end to it. He either had to trust to luck and let it go, or wade even deeper into waters that were already over his head.

At a soft knock on his office door, he swung his feet off his desk and sat up straight in his chair. "Come in."

Marla Spitler came through the door, and Tom mustered a smile.

"Hard at work?" One artistically sculpted brow lifted in inquiry. "Or taking a nap?"

"Marla, love, you know me too well."

"How's the ankle?"

"Hurts like hell. The little bugger probably had rabies."

Marla was the assistant producer of *Eye on Denver*, and she had her eye on the producer's job. She also had her eye on Tom, partly because he was the show's star, Tom knew. And partly because he was one of Denver's top bachelor hunks. He respected her ambition, and her taste in men. In fact, her do-anything-to-get-ahead attitude reminded him of himself. What's more, if he were a woman, which thank heaven he wasn't, he would probably slink around just as she did, full of seductive invitation and sensual promise. He was well aware of what his combination of looks, charm, and celebrity did to women, and he enjoyed every minute of the attention.

Still, tonight he wasn't in the mood for playing innuendo games, or any other games, with Marla. It was nine in the evening, and the only reason she was still at the studio was that Tom was working late. She talked a good story about having to finish some work, but Tom knew better.

He yawned and stretched, but she didn't take the hint. Perching on the corner of his desk, she peered down at the scribbled copy he worked on.

"Still doing the dog piece, are you?"

"It'll fly."

"A bit of a departure from your usual stuff, isn't it, Tom? Randy and I were talking the other day, and we both have some doubts."

Randy Teller was *Eye on Denver*'s producer. He and Marla both liked to pretend they had a say about what Tom did on the show. That would be a cold day in hell, Tom mused. If Randy had had his way, Tom would have killed his piece about the mayor's construction kickbacks. The producer had been afraid of political risks, afraid of the big players and high stakes involved. Tom had been a bit afraid himself, but he'd insisted, and on Tom Gordon's show, Tom got what he wanted. As always, Tom's instincts had been right. The story he had literally sold his soul to get had brought him to the big networks' attention. The final bricks in his road out of this nowhere local broadcast had been laid.

"Don't worry about it," Tom told Marla. "People like this light crap now and then. They'll eat it up."

"Like that mutt ate up your ankle?"

Tom gave her a frosty smile. "Hazards of being a journalist. Sometimes sources bite."

She shrugged one shoulder and sauntered toward the door, presenting him with an inviting view of her miniskirt-clad backside. Sometimes her mixture of tart challenge and come-hither body language turned him on. Not tonight. Tonight he wasn't in the mood.

"Go home, Marla. I'll see you Monday."

Her lips thinned to a disgruntled line.

"Go home," he repeated.

He sighed when she closed the door behind her, leaving him in peace. He would be glad to get out of this rathole and away from bit players like Marla and Randy. Not for him the small time, the small pond where life's guppies played their games and pretended they were Jaws. A framed photo on the wall caught his eye as he stuffed papers into his briefcase and picked up his coat. The photo was of Denver's chief of police shaking Tom's hand in a ceremony where he'd been presented a commendation for his work exposing a group of crooked insiders in the Denver PD. The chief hadn't liked giving him that commendation. Damn but he hadn't liked it. Still, he'd had to swallow his resentment and kiss up to Tom Gordon. It had felt good standing behind the podium, seeing the chief try to smile until his face damn near cracked, and knowing the man didn't dare cross him. No one in power dared cross him for fear their own little peccadillos and nest-padding habits might become public knowledge.

Lord, but Tom loved this profession! He loved the power. He loved the excuse for being in your face and nasty to every fat cat who thought he or she was too high and mighty to be touched. A network job meant more power, not to mention more money, attention, and the lifestyle that went with stardom.

He'd sell his soul to get to the big time. In fact, he already had.

FIFTEEN

♥

THE SKY OUTSIDE the bedroom window was gray with dawn when Amy turned over and opened her eyes. Images from sleep still filled her mind. A muzzy contentment weighed her down, inspiring her to snuggle more deeply into the bed and let the erotic trance of her dreams capture her again.

Next to her, something stirred, shifting the bedclothes and admitting cold air to her cocoon. Amy murmured a sleepy protest and pulled at the blanket.

"Cold?" a husky voice asked.

Her eyes flew open as a large, warm hand slipped over her naked waist. "Omigod!" she croaked.

"Good morning to you, also."

Even with her back to him, Amy could hear the smile in Jeff's voice. It soothed her momentary panic. The night before flashed through her mind—the mutual explosion of their first coming together, the quieter but just as passionate scenes that had followed. Somewhere in the night she had lost track of their encounters—laughter, teasing, exploration, ecstasy, and a driving fever that never lost its heat. She hadn't known passion could be so sharp, nor desire so daunting. Before last night, she had not known what all the hoopla about sexual fulfillment was about.

"Good morning," Amy murmured, unsure of how a woman should behave after such a wanton night.

"How are you this morning?"

She took a deep breath and closed her eyes. "I'm good. I'm great. I'm . . . uh . . ."

"Go on," he urged. His lips were close, so close. The caress of his breath brought a warm flush to her skin—her very naked, exposed, vulnerable skin.

"Uh . . . I'm a bit embarrassed?"

"Embarrassed. Hmmm." He mulled over the word as his hand drifted over her hip and thigh. "Embarrassed about this?" His caress traveled up the back of her thigh and curved over her buttocks.

"No . . ."

"Or this?" His fingers played a tune on her ribs.

"Of course not, you goon."

"Then it must be this." He pressed his lips to her shoulder, then her throat, while turning her onto her back and letting his hand capture a breast.

"Don't be silly!"

"This is nowhere close to being silly," he assured her warmly.

Suddenly she was trapped beneath him with his elbows resting on either side of her shoulders and his knees firmly between hers. He looked down at her with a triumphant grin. "I've heard that familiarity with something eliminates embarrassment. And the more you do something, the more familiar it becomes."

"A likely excuse, Lothario."

"I don't need an excuse. I love you."

The words rang chimes in Amy's heart. Looking up into clear hazel eyes dark with intensity, she was possessed by an impulse to say she loved him, too, but caution won out. Some people said the word *love* more easily than others, some were more careless with it than others, less awed by its power to hurt. Even though she lay in his arms, did she know Jeff Berenger well enough to be certain of him? Was she certain of herself?

"Jeff . . . you are one hell of a guy."

He grinned wickedly. "I am, aren't I?"

"One of a kind," she assured him. "The best friend a person could have."

"And . . . ," he prompted.

"And I feel very, very friendly toward you this morning."

His eyes flickered for an instant, but the sparkle quickly recovered. He lowered himself slowly until his mouth almost touched hers.

"How friendly?" he whispered.

"Very friendly," she whispered back. And proceeded to prove it.

Jeff was right. Embarrassment did disappear with familiarity. But passion didn't.

BREAKFAST WAS LATE. Very late. In fact, it could have qualified as lunch. Nevertheless, they cooked pancakes, eggs, and bacon.

"A meal that will stick to your ribs!" Jeff declared as he crisped a skilletful of bacon to just the right amount of doneness.

"That's not the only place it will stick," Amy predicted.

"Don't worry. I'll still love you if you outgrow those size six jeans."

She blinked, then blushed. Jeff wouldn't have guessed that any woman anywhere in the country could still color up from embarrassment the way Amy did. But Amy was not the usual sort of woman—the sort who made him feel like a square peg in a round hole, the sort who was all too ready with a file to smooth off his rough edges. Just the opposite. Being with Amy made him feel more comfortable with himself, odd as that seemed. He felt more complete, more relaxed, and more satisfied with the world when she was within reach of his hand or the sound of his voice.

Jeff had no illusions that Amy felt the same. Still full of doubts and barriers, just barely peeking over those walls she'd built around her heart, Amy was still on the battlefield of her uncertainties. He knew his straightforward declarations disconcerted her, but he'd never learned the civilized art of tiptoeing around a hot subject without sticking his foot squarely on it. He didn't even try. Amy deserved his honesty. In a world of half-truths and shades of gray, it was the brightest gift he could give her. When she learned he wasn't like David, that he wasn't going to take any cheap shots at her heart, then she would recognize that she loved him. Jeff knew Amy loved him. She had touched his soul, and only a woman who loved him could have done that.

"These are not size six jeans," Amy told him as she measured out oil for the pancake batter.

He studied her backside appreciatively. "They look like size six."

"They're not, Dr. Know-It-All."

"What size are they?"

"None of your business," she said archly.

"Maybe I'm going to buy you jeans for your birthday."

"My birthday was last month."

"For Christmas, then." Lord how he loved the stuttery little smile that played with her lips when she was teased. "Take 'em off so I can see the size."

"In your dreams."

He flipped the last of the bacon strips onto a paper towel. "I could take them off for you, if it's too much trouble."

"Whoa there!" Amy warned as he advanced with a

leer. "I've got batter in this bowl. It could be all over your head."

He took the bowl from her and set it on the counter. Then he hooked his thumbs in the waistband of her disputed jeans and pulled her toward him. "Or we could forget breakfast and just go back to bed."

His hands made themselves at home in her back pockets and pressed her hips forward to nestle against his. Jeff felt her melt against him. The face turned up to his was full of tenderness and laughter. Her smile was a soft invitation that he couldn't resist. He kissed her, feeling rightness and warmth suffuse his every fiber. Such rightness couldn't be a lie. They belonged together.

Her lips softened beneath his, lingering in delicious contact. Finally, she sighed against his mouth. He could feel the yearning in her, and also the resistance.

"We already spent half the day in bed," she reminded him.

"We'd still be there if not for . . ." He shot a disgusted look at the troop of dogs beneath the kitchen table.

Somewhat apologetically, Amy gave him a half smile. "They consider my bed their own."

"I'll remember that."

Unlikely that he could forget, since it had been impressed upon him with the subtlety of a cannon. Jeff had been pleasantly dozing when Amy slid out of bed to let her dogs into the yard. At the first crack of the bedroom door, the dogs had charged into the room and onto the bed, indignant at being kept out of their bedroom and away from their bed all night. They exacted retribution upon Jeff with a barrage of cold noses, sloppy tongues, and feet placed in the most anatomically sensitive regions.

The corgi invasion had put an end to further romantic lingering in bed. Jeff had pushed Drover's butt end out of his face and greeted the morning spitting dog hair, to the accompaniment of Amy's laughter.

Jeff would gladly endure Piggy's paw in his mouth and Drover's nose in his ear to hear the music of Amy's laughter every morning for the rest of his life.

Breakfast was an unqualified success. They easily slipped into a routine of domesticity, almost as if they'd awakened together and fixed breakfast as a team every morning for the past year. The bacon was done to a turn. Amy's pancakes were as light and fluffy as the box promised. The coffee was strong enough to clear out the last cobwebs of sleep. And the dogs volunteered their services to prewash every dirty plate and bowl before it went to the sink, making cleanup easy.

After breakfast, they took turns in the shower, even though Jeff suggested that showering as a duo would save wear and tear on the hot water tank. He accepted with good grace that Amy wasn't ready to open all the doors of her life to him . . . yet. He would grant her time to realize she couldn't live without him. No one had more patience than a loner who had decided he no longer wanted to be alone.

"I meant what I said about moving in here," he told her when she emerged from the shower. Wrapped in a plush white towel, black ringlets springing about her face in a shining wet mass, eyes glowing with life, Amy looked good enough to give a man a heart attack. When her face fell, Jeff wished he hadn't reminded her of the less-than-romantic situation that prompted his stay.

"I'll find the spare key for you." Her smile picked up again, and his heart skipped a beat.

"So, I'll just go pack a few things and pick up the dogs. You don't mind if they come too, right?"

"The more, the merrier."

On his way out, Jeff stopped by the kitchen for a cup of coffee to go. He was looking through the cupboard for a plastic cup when he noticed something not quite right about Amy's office. She'd told him it was almost back in order, yet the slice of office he could see through the slightly ajar door looked anything but orderly. The door, he noted suspiciously, was open just about the width of a corgi's little sausage body.

When Amy came into the kitchen, he hated to break the bad news to her.

"They what?" She looked into the office and groaned. "I don't believe it. When did the little morons do this?"

"Last night?"

"Then why didn't we notice it when we were in here fixing breakfast?" Her gaze slid away from his as the obvious answer came to her. "Well, I guess we were a bit distracted."

From Amy, that was at least as good as her earlier admission that she was feeling very, very friendly toward him. Jeff grinned.

"You think it's funny? I spent days cleaning up that office."

"Next time we'll let them in the bedroom."

Her eyes glinted at his assumption that there would be a next time, that he was a fixture in her bedroom, and that the problems of her house were suddenly a matter for "we" instead of "she." He waited for the rebuke, for the reminder that she was an independent woman with her own space who didn't need a man butting into her life. It didn't come. She flashed him a look, but it was a mere caution delivered with a faint smile.

"They'll be lucky if they're not banished to their kennels after this. You notice they've made themselves scarce?"

"I have a feeling I should do the same."

She grimaced and motioned to the office. "I've got

work to do. More than I thought, thanks to some corgis who are in deep, deep trouble. Go get your stuff and your dogs. Maybe Spot and Darby can teach my herd some manners."

"I'll be back tonight," he told her. "I've got some appointments this afternoon, then I need to run by the shelter and do a couple of spays."

He could feel her eyes follow him as he shrugged on his jacket and grabbed his coffee.

"Wait," she ordered before he was halfway to the door.

He turned, and she was there, her lips curving in a half-reluctant smile. She stood on tiptoe to kiss him, then pushed him toward the door.

"See you tonight."

He left the house on a cushion of air. Brick by lousy brick, Amy's wall was crumbling.

"WELL, THIS IS just fine! Thank you, kids." Amy stood surveying the mess, arms akimbo, corgis crowding around her feet. "I think the furry-coated creatures in this house need a reminder of who's boss here."

All three dogs gazed up at her with expressions that said they knew very well who was boss, and that boss didn't walk on two legs.

Amy snorted in disbelief and waded into the mess. The office was carpeted with a jumble of paper. Pink and yellow credit card receipts provided a dash of color among black and white correspondence, contracts, and tax forms. Computer floppy disks were scattered here and there. Photo albums had been pulled from the bookcase, along with a number of books, and lay open on the floor. The wastebasket lay on its side, the desk chair had somehow been pushed into a corner, and file folders were strewn chaotically about the room.

"You kids did a more thorough job than the vandal. You've missed your calling."

While Drover and Molly watched uncertainly, and a bit guiltily, from the doorway, Amy sorted through the clutter. Piggy helped by sticking her nose into every piece of paper, every album, every book that Amy picked up. When Amy found a glossy of a best-in-show corgi that she had photographed two years previously, she held it up for Piggy's inspection.

"This is what a proper corgi is supposed to look like, Miss Piggy. Buttercup's her name, and she's not only beautiful, but she has obedience titles, tracking titles, and is a therapy dog at a veterans' hospital. What do you think of that?"

Piggy chose that moment to sneeze, spraying the photo with moisture. Obviously she thought that the illustrious Buttercup ruined the grading curve for corgis in general, and her in particular. Amy carefully wiped the picture with a tissue and sent Piggy a chilly look.

"You could learn a thing or two from her, believe me!"

This time around, Amy vowed to herself, she would make sure the office was corgi-proof. There would be no halfway measures of stacking files on the floor or the chair. Every bill, receipt, letter, and photo would go into the proper file, and the file would be locked away in the proper drawer. Organization and tidyness had never been one of Amy's strong points, especially in her office, but the little brown demons who lived with her were forcing her to mend her ways.

The sun was setting by the time the job was done. Amy was wondering what she could fix for dinner as she placed the last file in the bottom drawer of the filing cabinet. Jeff would be home soon. The thought made her stomach flutter with something other than hunger. Knowing that he would be coming through the front door because he lived there, at least temporarily, was such a strange notion. It inspired a mixture of heart-thumping giddiness and tormenting doubt. This home was her own personal haven, the place where she could escape the world and discard the need to be anyone but her very basic, unpretentious self. In the months she had lived there, she had never shared it with anyone. Even Selma lived in her own space over the garage.

Privacy and independence—did she really want to relinquish either one? The attacks against her weren't the only reason Jeff wanted to move in. He'd made no bones about what he wanted from her. Part of her wanted to do a little jig in celebration of the way he made her feel—wanted, womanly, special. Yet another part remembered all too clearly that romance was quite different from a day-in, day-out long-term relationship.

Smart people, she reminded herself, didn't go charging into the fire again once they'd been burned. How big a fool was she to let Jeff Berenger move into her house and into her heart?

The drift of Amy's thoughts didn't put her in a mood to deal with an uncooperative drawer when the bottom set of files refused to close. She muttered in frustration while carefully pulling the drawer all the way out and trying once again to push it shut.

"Damn it to hell!" she muttered. The dogs came over to investigate the game she played, and she warned them back with a glare. "Watch out that I don't lock you kids in here after the way you behaved."

Once again the drawer refused to close, and no amount of jiggling would make it cooperate. Finally Amy yanked it off the tracks and stuck her head into the opening to investigate, muttering curses that made the dogs' ears flatten.

"All right. Here's the problem."

She emerged with a plastic film case in her hand.

Somehow it had gotten wedged behind the drawer. The little container was labeled with subject and date, as was all Amy's exposed film. It had been shot the previous winter. And the subject scrawled on the label simply read David.

"Shit!" Amy sat back abruptly, her backside landing on the floor with a painful thump. More painful still was the name that jumped out at her from the film case. She knew exactly what was on this undeveloped roll. Months ago she had tossed it into the back of the filing cabinet like a hot coal, unwilling to develop the film and watch as the last images of her marriage to David take substance before her eyes. Most had been shot during a ski trip at a friend's Copper Mountain condominium. The roll had a few other subjects as well, but nothing important enough to make her face the false, lying images of a world that had shattered so soon after they were imprinted on the film. The day of David's funeral, she had taken the roll from the camera, shut it tightly in its little plastic case, and put it out of sight, trying to put it out of mind as well.

Yet somehow that tiny roll of 35-millimeter film had a life of its own. It had survived the fire in Amy's Denver home, along with the rest of the contents of the file cabinet, and even though exiled from Amy's sight, it had lingered these months in the back of her mind as a symbol of disappointments she couldn't face and lies that still hurt too much to confront. Amy had vowed several times to throw the film into the fireplace and be done with it, but she had never quite mustered the courage. So it had stayed in the back of the file drawer, a kernel of her failed life hidden away, contaminating her new beginnings, until the manhandling of the cabinet during the break-in had made the film fall behind the drawers and wedge itself against the back.

"Damn!" Amy muttered, looking at the film case.

She felt as though her hand burned, even though the plastic nestled in her palm was cool. It was identical to a thousand other film cans she'd handled during her years as a photographer. Black case. Gray snap-on lid. Innocent and ordinary. Yet this one was like a black hole, sucking in the grief, humiliation, heartbreak, self-doubts, and anger that had come with David's betrayal and death. All the failure, false hopes, and smashed dreams swirled within the case in a nasty mire she wanted to discard. But she couldn't.

Clenching the case, she bit her lip and looked at the dogs. "I should develop this."

Piggy answered with a soft woof. Drover and Molly both cocked their head in interest.

"I'm acting like an idiot. It's just a roll of film. It's not as though I don't know what's on it."

"Woof!" Piggy agreed.

"And this was in the camera the night someone tried to steal it, and killed David and Lydia instead."

She should have examined the film long ago. But it was the last remnant of her marriage. She had avoided it long and desperately, giving it a power far beyond its intrinsic importance. She should develop the shots and face them, or she should throw the film away and dismiss it from her mind. Maybe then she would be free to give her heart again, if that was what she wanted to do.

Piggy woofed once more and nudged the hand that held the plastic can. Her dark eyes were bright with curiosity.

"You think this is something to eat, Miss Pudgy?"

Piggy rumbled indignantly, then whined.

"Okay. You win. Let's go down to the lab."

A strange mixture of dread and buoyancy carried her down to her basement darkroom.

Not until Selma came home from work, well after ten P.M., did Amy actually look at what had come to life in her darkroom solutions. The prints hung on the drying line, long since dry, waiting for Amy to find the courage to take them down. But she couldn't face them alone.

Jeff had not yet returned. He had called earlier from the TLC shelter to tell her one of his spay patients—a stray cat—was not recovering well from anaesthetic, and he would stay until the animal was fully awake. He had wanted to make sure that Amy had his cell phone number so she could reach him.

"Some bodyguard you are," she'd teased him.

He had laughed. "Let anyone touch your body but me and you'll see how much of a guard I can be."

Sweet, silly man, Amy had thought. But his concern, the warmth of his voice, and the electricity that flowed between them even through the phone had made her smile. That warmth had lightened the load of hours spent alone with the photographs taunting her from the basement. She had almost gathered the courage to view them by herself when Selma floated through the back door and into the kitchen, an empty coffee cup in her hand and bliss beaming from her face.

"Well, don't you look like a cat with canary feathers between its teeth!" Amy commented.

Selma gave her a beatific smile.

"Do I need to ask how the date with Gary went night before last?"

"You can ask." Selma grinned and gave her head a little toss that made her brown ponytail bounce.

"I certainly haven't seen much of you since then."

Selma's eyes slid sideways to meet hers as she poured coffee into her cup and got another cup for Amy. "That's because I haven't been here," she cheerfully admitted.

"I figured. I fed Ray."

"I knew you would."

Selma waltzed to the table, sat down, and stared dreamily into her cup. "Gary came by the store tonight during my dinner break. We ate in the deli next door. He bought me a meatball sandwich with the works. You know, that's always been my favorite, and I thought he never noticed, but he just walked up to the counter and ordered it without my having to ask. Isn't he sweet?"

Amy rolled her eyes. "Absolutely."

"We had only one eensy-weensy disagreement."

"What was that?"

"I want us to go to a counselor, and he thinks it's a silly idea."

"Sheesh! Of all the—!" Amy bit down on her opinion of Gary as Selma shot her a swift look.

"He'll come around," Selma assured her with a smile. "You'll see."

Amy thought it wise to change the subject. "I developed that roll of film today."

Selma gave her a blank look.

"The roll you've been bugging me about for the last six months."

Her eyes grew wide. "Oh. *That* film. You're kidding! You really scraped up the guts to develop it? Good girl! What was on the roll? Anything worth sealing into a brick wall for all eternity? Isn't that what you wanted to do?"

"The prints are still hanging in the basement."

"You haven't looked at them?"

"No," Amy admitted shamefacedly. "You don't need to really, really look at them just to put them through the solutions."

"I take back what I said. You're not a good girl."

Five minutes later, Selma returned with a stack of prints and waved them in front of Amy's nose. "Sit!" she ordered, as if commanding a recalcitrant dog. "Stay! And look."

"Hey. Don't be so pushy."

"Isn't that why you told me? You knew I'd make you look at them?"

Yes, Amy admitted silently.

"Let's see what we have here." Selma switched on the light fixture directly over the table. "This won't hurt a bit," she assured a dubious Amy. "And you'll feel so much better when it's over. Did I ever tell you that I was minoring in psychology when I dropped out of college to marry Gary?"

"A little bit of knowledge is a dangerous thing." Amy sighed.

The prints showed exactly what Amy thought they would. Most of them were shot during the ski weekend at Copper Mountain with Faith and Donald Sevier. Donald was a member of the Denver city council, along with David. His wife, Faith, had made a bundle of money as a real estate agent. They were nice people, but they lived high and loved to party. David had been far more comfortable in their company than Amy had. She hadn't wanted to spend the weekend skiing. Drover had been entered in a show that Sunday, and though Melissa was going to handle him, Amy had wanted to be there as well.

David had blown a fuse when she suggested he go without her. In retrospect, Amy didn't blame him. He had a right to expect his wife to occasionally do the things that he wanted to do. Not that he had ever been with her at a dog show or obedience trial, or gone with her on one of her photography treks.

"You look as if you had a good time," Selma said quietly, sifting through the pictures. "Who took this one?"

"Donald took that."

The photo showed David sitting on a chair in the condo with a laughing Amy on his lap. Faith sat on the arm of the chair, and David's arm was casually draped around her waist. In his other hand he held a beer.

Amy looked at the little slice of her past. The smile on her face looked false, she thought. She had really tried to have a good time, and she had still believed that she had a fine marriage and a fine husband. How easily the human mind gulled itself into believing what it wanted to believe.

She wondered if she and David could have made their relationship work had David not been murdered. Probably not, Amy admitted. They had so little in common. David hadn't done anything unforgiveable. He hadn't done anything that a million husbands and wives hadn't done before him. But he and Amy had lost whatever connection they'd had, if they'd ever had one.

"This is nice," Selma said of another shot. It showed David posing beside his upright skis. In the background was Copper Mountain's main lodge. "He was a handsome cuss. A mover and a shaker."

"That he was."

Amy had been so giddy when they first dated. David had been all charm and wit, handsome enough to make a woman dizzy with his looks, his smile, the roguish twinkle in his eye. They'd scarcely known each other when they married, she realized. After the glow of the honeymoon had worn off, Amy had suspected that her husband had been more attracted to her father's money than to Amy herself, but if that was true, at least he had tried to make the marriage work, in his own way. He hadn't deliberately hurt her, just as she hadn't grown away from him on purpose, finding a life of her own that excluded her husband.

Amy touched the print with her finger, as if she could bring the man in the photo back to life. For the first time, she felt more sorrow than anger at what had happened. Poor David certainly hadn't deserved what he got. And Lydia hadn't really stolen anything from Amy that wasn't already lost, just as Selma had said. Looking at these photos of the last "good times" of her marriage, she realized what a lie these happy images told. The handsome man that stared at her from the pictures hadn't held her heart, even then. The Amy captured in a few of the frames wore a smiling mask, but that wasn't her. She'd been sticking it out, fooling herself, desperate to believe she was happy. But if her world hadn't flown apart just days after this weekend jaunt, it would have disintegrated in a very short time. Not because David had betrayed her, but because they lived in separate worlds.

"This is pretty." Selma held up a photo with a totally different subject. "What is it?"

"That's the old post office building in north Denver. I'd almost forgotten that I'd taken it. There should be a couple of others like that in there."

"Yeah. Here's one. Geez! Look at those turrets!"

"I was working on a photo essay—Denver's historic architecture—but I dropped the idea after David died." Amy picked up the photo of the old post office. How could she have forgotten it? She had taken that shot in the early evening, just before rushing home to give David the car for his "sales meeting"—the meeting that had turned out to be a date with Lydia. His car had been in the shop, and he'd been really angry with her for being late. A familiar twist of anger knotted her stomach, and she tried to banish it. She'd been ready to let the resentment go and didn't want to step in that mire again.

"Who is that coming out of the building?" Selma asked. She pointed to a lonely figure huddled against the wind. Amy had wanted to catch the post office empty. A rush of people would only have distracted from its aged dignity. She'd scarcely noticed the one customer coming from the lobby. She had shot four frames of the building, but he was in only one.

"He's just someone walking out of the building. The post office was closed, but the lobby with the boxes would have still been open."

A quizzical smile spread slowly across Selma's face. "You know who that looks like?"

"No, who?"

"Tom Gordon."

Amy looked closely. "I can't tell."

"Sure it is. I recognize the sweater. It's the same one he was wearing when he first came to the house. Don't you remember?"

"I didn't notice."

"Well, I noticed everything about him."

A feeling of unease grew upon Amy as she studied the photo. She couldn't put her finger on why. The figure in the photo was probably not Tom Gordon, and even if it was, so what?

Yet this film had been in the camera that night, the camera that had, indirectly, caused David's and Lydia's deaths. And since that night, someone had stalked her with mayhem on their minds. In the last incident, the target still seemed to be a camera.

She flipped through the photos again. Skiing; skiing; partying in the Seviers' condominium; two photos of Raven, Molly, and Drover in Selma's rose garden; more skiing; a turreted building by moonlight; and a relic of a post office with a lonely looking figure coming out the door, looking straight toward the camera, which had been mounted on a tripod, standing on the other side of the parking lot.

The only suspicious photo, the only one with anything questionable, was the one of the old post office.

And the only suspicious thing about it was the unidentified figure.

Even while thinking this was nonsense, Amy felt a chill go down her spine as she held the print up to the light. "Tom Gordon, huh? Wouldn't *that* be a coincidence."

Sixteen

"Tom Gordon," Amy muttered to Piggy. "It *is* him."

Molly and Drover were asleep under the desk, but Piggy stared at Amy's computer monitor as intensely as Amy. What stared back at them was undoubtedly an image of Tom Gordon, staring straight into the camera with an expression of surprise on his face, coat blowing open to reveal the sweater Selma had recognized.

After Selma left, Amy had gone to bed, but curiosity had refused to let her sleep. At two A.M. she had stumbled wearily to her office, determined to solve the puzzle. She had scanned the questionable photo into her computer, which miraculously had survived the break-in, then enlarged the small area that included the figure. Her software cleaned up the graininess and clarified the details, and the result left no question in her mind. Either the man in the photo was Tom Gordon, or Tom had a twin running about wearing his clothes. The expression of surprised dismay on his face made Amy wonder why he hadn't wanted to be seen. She hadn't been using a flash that might have startled him. And if he had recognized her, then wouldn't he have looked pleased instead of alarmed? She tried to remember if he had come toward her after she took the shot, but she couldn't even remember him being in the frame. She had taken several frames of the same view. The camera had been on a tripod, angled exactly the way she wanted, and she hadn't even looked into the viewfinder for the last two shots, just pressed the shutter release when the shadows had reached just the right length. Afterward, anxiety about getting home late had made her hurry away.

Piggy growled softly at the monitor, and Amy instinctively jumped. "Quit it, you silly dog. So what if Tom was at the post office that day? So what if he doesn't like having his picture taken?"

Tom could have been startled for many reasons. High-profile celebrity that he was, he was no doubt leery of overenthusiastic fans and stalkers . . . or worse. He had offended some powerful people lately, not least of whom was Denver's mayor, and the fellows who had been fired when his exposé revealed the corrupt promotion scam in the Denver police department. Tom would be a fool if he wasn't cautious. Something pointed in his direction, whether it be a gun or a camera, might well make him nervous.

She printed the enlarged computer image, then stretched and yawned. Mystery solved, she could now get some much needed sleep. She switched off the computer equipment, set the print on top of the file cabinet, and dragged herself to bed. Molly and Drover followed sleepily, but Piggy sat firmly in the middle of Amy's office, staring at the top of the cabinet.

"Come on, Pudgy girl," Amy called. "If you think I'm leaving you here for an encore performance, think again."

Piggy rumbled out a final growl, then reluctantly followed. But before she trotted out the door, she glanced suspiciously over her shoulder, as if Tom Gordon's image might come to life and pounce upon her from atop the file cabinet.

When Amy awoke the next morning, she wasn't alone in her bed. Jeff had tiptoed in without waking her. His big body stretched out on top of the covers, warming the bed next to her. Presumptuous man, Amy thought sleepily, but it was a delicious feeling to wake up next to him. She could get accustomed to such a thing very easily, if she let herself, but she would need a bigger bed. With Molly and Drover sleeping at her feet and a six-foot two-hundred-pounder taking up more than his share, Amy found herself bent into a pretzel shape among man and dogs. Worse, Spot and Darby eyed the bed from where they lay beneath the window. They obviously considered the possibilities that they might be welcome on the mattress. Piggy curled in a corner, balefully eyeing Amy's sleeping arrangements.

She ought to get up, Amy told herself. Feed the dogs. Fix breakfast. Get cracking. Even though it was Sunday, she had a portrait appointment that afternoon, which meant she had to get her gear together and take it up to the studio in Boulder that she rented for such things.

The bed was warm and cozy, however, and Jeff made it even cozier. His breath feathered through her hair. One of his hands rested warmly in the indentation of her waist. When she moved, his fingers tightened as if to hold her where she was.

"Don't go," he murmured sleepily.

"Don't you want breakfast?"

"No."

"Well, they do."

There was no question about who "they" was. Five sets of hungry eyes fastened upon Amy and Jeff with the force of a tractor beam.

Jeff muttered an unintelligible word into his pillow. "Do you think children are this demanding?" he groaned.

A sudden vision popped into Amy's head—a tribe of wild little scamps bouncing on and off their bed, the boys with Jeff's square chin and the girls with her unruly curls. The notion took her by surprise, making her let out a gust of laughter at her own foolishness.

"Not that funny," Jeff mumbled.

"Not funny at all," Amy agreed, controlling her chortles. "Go back to sleep."

His grip on her waist tightened, and he placed a random kiss on the back of her neck. Amy got the idea that the first place his mouth landed was the place that got kissed. Finally, his breath against her slowed and steadied. He had taken her suggestion to go back to sleep.

Jeff slept through the racket of the dogs greeting their breakfast, through the smell of brewing coffee and sizzling bacon and the clatter of the dishwasher being unloaded. Amy wasn't left alone to eat, however. Selma danced in just as the eggs plopped into the skillet. Amy automatically got out another place setting and broke two more eggs to fry beside the others.

"Good morning!" Selma practically sang.

Amy did little more than grunt. The sound of a car door slamming and an engine starting made her look out the side window. Gary's old Volvo station wagon was backing out of the drive. She raised a brow.

"Guess what!" Selma caroled.

"Gary slept over last night."

"Well, don't make it sound like a crime!"

"Sorry. I'm still tired. I was up half the night working on that photo."

Selma was not about to be distracted by talk of photos, however, when she was almost bouncing with her own news. She sat down at the kitchen table, curled her feet around the chair legs like a little girl, and grinned ecstatically. "Gary and I are getting married."

Amy paused while reaching for the coffee carafe. "You're already married."

"Well, yeah. We're still married. Technically. The divorce isn't final. But so much baggage goes with the old marriage that we thought that we'd start over. We're going to renew our vows and start from scratch. Isn't that romantic?"

"That's great, Selma."

"And Gary's agreed to go to counseling with me. Is he a dear or what?"

"A real prince." She flipped the eggs, then put the bacon and a jar of salsa on the table.

"*Huevos rancheros,*" Selma said happily. "My favorite. Oh, Amy! You've been such a friend. I wish you could be as happy as I am."

"I'm great. When are you going to do the vows?"

"Wednesday. It's our sixth wedding anniversary."

"That makes sense, I guess. If you're going to get married, you might as well do it on your wedding anniversary."

Selma frowned for a moment, then laughed. "Right! This is so perfect! And we want you to take photos. For money, even!"

"For you it's free."

"No! Seriously. Gary wants to pay you." She lowered her voice, as if her husband might hear. "He thinks you don't like him."

"I don't dislike him."

"You don't still think he's the one who broke into the house, do you? I was just shooting off at the mouth, you know. I do that too often."

"You know Gary a lot better than I do. If you say he wouldn't have done such a thing, then I'll believe you."

"He wouldn't. Gary can be a shit, but he never would have turned Ray loose." Selma's eyes brightened with sly mischief. "Speaking of Ray, I put him out with the other dogs. I noticed some border collies among the corgis."

"Yes?"

"So . . . is *he* here as well?"

Amy tilted her head in the direction of the bedroom. "Still sleeping. He came in late after sitting up with a patient."

Selma closed her eyes and clasped her hands in triumph. "Yes!"

"Don't jump to conclusions."

"Jump to conclusions? Hah! That nonchalant act of yours doesn't fool me, Amy Cameron. I've known you too long."

Amy shoved a plate of eggs across the table toward Selma and took one for herself. "It's not what you think."

"Jeff Berenger's in your bed, you're talking about him like he lives here, and it's not what I think?"

"Jeff moved in for a while because he's concerned about me getting robbed or burned out every time I turn around. He's a worrier."

"Of course he is." Selma smiled shrewdly.

"Well, he is."

"And of course he couldn't sleep in the guest room. If he's going to play the part of bodyguard, how better to guard your body than as close as humanly possible? And I do mean close."

Amy threw a napkin at her. "Oh, be quiet! You're blowing the whole thing out of proportion."

"No, I'm not. I know you, Amy. You're not a bed hopper. You wouldn't sleep with a guy unless you loved him. Really loved him."

Amy was silent.

"Can't deny it, can you?"

"I haven't thought about it."

"Yeah, right. Haven't admitted it to yourself is more likely."

Amy gave her a look.

"Don't make such a face!" Selma advised. "What's wrong with letting yourself fall in love? I think it's way cool. Jeff Berenger's a hunk, in his own way, and it's about time you had someone around who appreciates you for the fine catch that you are."

"Selma! I am not a catch, and Jeff is not—as you put it—a hunk."

A voice from the kitchen doorway startled them both. "You don't think I'm a hunk?"

Amy's heart somersaulted as Jeff smiled at her. He leaned against the doorframe, filling it almost as effectively as a door. Exercise shorts and a T-shirt did absolutely nothing to hide his "hunkiness"—long, muscular legs, lean waist, and shoulders that would make any woman look twice. Selma was right, Amy admitted. Jeff Berenger was a hunk.

"My sainted grandma always said," Selma smirked, "that he who eavesdrops seldom hears good about himself." She took her plate to the sink, refilled her coffee cup, and headed out the back door. As a parting shot she ventured: "I'm sure you can convince Amy what a stud you are, Jeff. Just keep trying."

Amy's face heated so fast that even her vision turned a fiery, embarrassed pink. When Jeff leaned down to kiss her cheek, she was sure his lips would come away blistered.

"Selma always says what she thinks, doesn't she?" he commented.

Amy nodded. She didn't trust herself to speak.

"I like that." He tilted her face upward with one finger under her chin and grinned. "All that color in your face goes well with that red sweatshirt you have on."

"You're as bad as Selma," Amy muttered.

"Probably worse, if the truth be known. I may not be a hunk, but you are definitely a catch."

"You also say exactly what you think, don't you?"

"It's one of my better qualities."

"And you have so many," Amy observed with an impish smile. She slipped out of her chair to take her dishes to the sink. She wondered if she should talk to Jeff about the photo of Tom Gordon. Something about that shot nibbled bothersomely at the edge of her mind, just beyond consciousness. Perhaps Jeff could help her pin it down. Then again, perhaps not. Jeff wasn't exactly neutral when it came to Tom Gordon.

"Do I get eggs?" Jeff asked somewhat wistfully.

Amy laughed. "Is that what you want?"

"Not really." He came up behind her and trapped her against the counter with an arm on either side of her. Her backside was tucked into the hard curve of his groin, and the position left very little doubt about what Jeff really wanted.

Amy's body responded instinctively, sending a flash of fire through every vein and a hot flush to her skin that had nothing to do with embarrassment.

"You're supposed to be tired," she said a bit breathlessly.

"I'm not that tired."

"So I see."

"Did I forget to tell you I'm not into one-night stands? I'm not that kinda guy."

She turned around so that they stood front to front, breast to chest, belly to groin.

"What are you into, Jeff Berenger?"

He grinned down at her, but declined to voice the obvious pun. "I'm into commitment."

"And if I'm not?"

"I'll just have to take the risk that the better you

know me, the more of my wonderful qualities you'll see. Eventually, I'll be irresistible."

He was nearly irresistible right then, Amy admitted. She merely laughed when he reached down quickly and scooped her off her feet. His mouth came down on hers for a slow, tantalizing kiss.

"To hell with the eggs," he murmured against her lips. "I've got a hunger that has nothing to do with my stomach."

As she was carried toward the bedroom, any thought of Tom Gordon showing up inside her camera fled Amy's mind.

SELMA'S WEDDING. OR should I say rewedding. It was so disgustingly cute that I wanted to throw up. Actually, I did throw up—the result of too many liver snaps filched from the buffet table. The reception boasted as many goodies for the dogs as the people. Lucky for Selma she had the reception in the backyard of her Boulder house, not her newly carpeted parlor.

But back to this silly wedding. It's true I'm not crazy about dogs, but even people who melt at the sight of a wagging tail should have enough sense to realize that a collie is not a suitable best man. With his shiny black coat and white chest, Raven might look like he's wearing a shaggy tuxedo, but the best man drooling all over the groom's trousers really detracts from the ceremony.

Worse still, the rest of us four-legged fur bags were expected to be bridesmaids. I've never been so embarrassed. Selma managed to find tiny little headbands with sprays of white netting to make the corgis look even more ridiculous than they normally do. Even poor Drover was dolled up like a bridal Barbie doll. I couldn't help but pity the poor fellow, obnoxious as he is. I had noticed earlier, with mixed feelings, the new sympathetic turn of my temperament. My mellow attitude seemed to include the other dogs as well as Amy. With that silly little veil sprouting from between his big ears, Drover was really ripe for the kind of royal put-down that I delivered so well, but I just couldn't bring myself to do it. The poor boy must have felt like a cross-dressing disaster.

Needless to say, the brownnosing border collies played their parts like the suck-up artists they are. Spot and Darby really needed more pride. They seemed to think their mission in life was working hard at anything they were asked to do, whether the task was bossing around sheep or looking like morons with wedding veils on their silly heads. Even dogs should be allowed some dignity, after all.

I, of course, refused any part in the farce. A fierce ripple of my lips got me a sharp rebuke when Selma tried to treat me to the same torture she visited upon the other dogs. I responded with a sullen pout, which cast such a pall on the affair (I really have sullen down to an art) that Amy relieved me of my costume and allowed me to retreat under the picnic table. It was a strategic position from which I could emerge now and then for snacks of liver snaps, which resulted in the slight upset I noted earlier.

Silly as it was, the rewedding seemed to be a smash hit with the onlookers. Maybe it was appropriate that this bride and groom were attended by a drooling collie and a mismatched quartet of embarrassed corgis and tongue-lolling border collies. I'd always thought Selma was an airhead, and now I knew it for sure. And Gary, well, Gary probably deserved Selma. That's all I'll say about him.

For me, this was not a day to celebrate. Dr. Dufus had been living in Amy's house for five days. Five long days. His scuffed boots sat next to Amy's shoes in the closet. His socks and underwear filled one drawer of Amy's dresser. His BVDs were as frayed as the cuffs of his shirts. I swear, the man has no sense of how to dress! And his stupid dogs paraded about the house and yard as if they owned the place.

Hard as it was to swallow, the situation suited me fine for the moment. As I explained earlier, more than Amy's pathetic little affair was at stake here, and having Jeff in the house made Amy a little safer. Not a lot. Just a little. After all, I put my safety in the hands of a big strong man once, and look what happened to me.

Still, having Dr. Dimwit and his toady dogs constantly underfoot strained my temper. And my mood wasn't improved by Amy's dull-witted dawdling in the matter of Tom Gordon. I had brilliantly provided her with evidence of his villainy, as well as a clue to discovering what was behind all this mayhem. After all, if I hadn't trashed the office, she wouldn't have had to clean it up, and she never would have developed that roll of film. But does she pursue the matter? No. She puts the evidence on top of the file cabinet and goes off to play house with you know who. I had seen her glance at the enlarged print a time or two with a wrinkle of worry in her brow. And once she studied it for a good long time. But she put it back on the cabinet to gather dust. Amy would never make it as a heroine in a detective novel, that's for sure.

Not that I knew what the blasted photo meant. It had to mean something, though. Too many coincidences involved Tom, and as I said before, I don't believe in coincidence.

The wedding ceremony was mercifully brief. The minister, a dumpy little woman with a ready laugh, barely held it together while she said her piece. It's not every reverend who's asked to officiate at a wedding where half the bridal party has four legs. She can hardly be blamed for chuckling halfway through the Lord's Prayer when the best man, or should I say best collie, decided to lift a leg on one of the border collie bridesmaids. We were fortunate that the wedding wasn't reduced to a canine rumble.

The tense moment passed, however. The reverend finished her prayer, Selma and Gary said their I do's, and the party got down to serious celebration. The day was bright with Colorado sunshine, the air balmy with just a hint of autumn, and the twenty or so guests soaked up the good weather along with Gary's champagne. Selma uncovered the reception spread that she and Amy had laid out earlier—an assortment of not-so-gourmet selections from the deli at Selma's place of employment. Talk about tacky. The liver snaps were good, though. I can attest to that. And everyone seemed to have a good time stuffing their faces and dancing to the horrible music of a band organized by one of Gary's friends.

To give Gary and Selma some credit, they only had a few days to put this affair together, and I suppose they did the best they could. But there I go being sympathetic again. If I didn't watch myself, this experience as a corgi was going to change me beyond recognition.

Things were going moderately well. Selma was keeping the bowl of liver snaps full. Drover was sufficiently embarrassed by his costume that he left me alone. Molly was occupied with trying to get her silly headband off. Ray busied himself courting Darby under Spot's suspicious eye. And I, left peacefully to my own devices, found plenty of entertainment in people watching.

It's amazing the perspective one gets from a mere ten inches off the ground. Selma's mother, I noted, really needed help with those varicose veins. And Gary's brother wore mismatched socks. Amy's photo assistant, Tony, had a nervous twitch in his big toe whenever he talked to a woman. Really. I saw it right through the leather of his shoe.

Get the idea of how interesting this wedding crowd was? I'd had more fun watching Drover do somersaults to get at a tick on his rear end. The party livened up for all of us about halfway through the reception, though. That was when Tom Gordon arrived.

Now that was entertaining. Selma's eyes widened as she dramatically rolled her eyeballs in Amy's direction. The soul of subtlety, that girl. Amy was taking a candid photo of three guests trying to get their mouths around mountainous sandwiches, as if that was something that needed to be preserved for posterity. At Tom's entrance, she froze momentarily. I could literally smell the bolt of panic that shot through her. Dogs can smell emotion, you know. Fear smells sour. And panic can burn your nose quicker than a hefty dose of ammonia.

But Amy's panic only lasted a second or so. It settled down to a steady current of anxiety/curiosity/exasperation that was much easier on my senses. She managed to wave a friendly hello to the villain when he sent a blazing smile her way, but she watched him suspiciously as he paid his regards to Selma and Gary.

The reception came to life at Tom's appearance. Heads turned. Eyes widened. Conversations dropped to a hush. There's nothing like a celebrity to turn a dud affair to dynamite. Everyone was instantly under Tom's spell. Even Selma, who had shared Amy's speculation about the photo. Tom smiled at the bride with a flash of perfectly capped teeth and a twinkle of gorgeous green eyes, and Selma was gone. If she'd melted any faster, she would have ended as a steaming puddle beneath that silly bridal gown she wore.

Most everyone else reacted the same way. Astounding how fast fame and looks throw sand into the eyes of good judgment. Consider what it did to me. I, too, once thought Tom Gordon was the next best thing to liver snaps. As a pro at using beauty to get what I wanted, I should have been immune. But I wasn't. And if Gordon affected me, these drab little people didn't have a chance when he walked into their midst, even though he was a stinking bag of slime.

So it was up to me, I decided, to protect Amy. Besides, one taste of Tom Gordon's ankle had given me a yen for more.

"WHY ON EARTH did you invite Tom Gordon?" Amy demanded of Selma in an intense whisper.

"I didn't think he'd come!" Selma whispered back, just as intense. "You'd been dating him, and, you know, I thought . . ." At Amy's narrow look she grimaced. "Well, it was sort of a connection! I thought if he did show up, he might slip and give us a clue about why he's in that mysterious photo."

"It's not a mysterious photo. It's nothing."

"Then why are you upset?"

"I'm not upset!" Amy growled.

"Then stop looking as if you swallowed a mothball. Geez! This is great. My mother is *so* impressed. Everyone is impressed! Just look at them."

Not everyone, Amy thought. Gary's smile showed more teeth than sincerity as he chatted with Tom. Selma's husband had never liked being upstaged as the center of attention. Then of course there was Jeff, who had just walked out of the house with a fresh pitcher of iced tea. The bland expression on his face told Amy volumes. Jeff was never bland. He was mocking, teasing, intense, puckish, taunting, loving, laughing, or fervent. He was not bland. He was probably as glad to see Tom Gordon as Sitting Bull was to see Custer.

"Uh-oh!" Selma said.

"What?"

"Isn't that Miss Piggy who just came out from beneath the buffet table? She's headed straight for Tom with something on her mind. I can tell."

"Oh shit!" Disaster was just a moment away as Piggy aimed for Tom like a loaded torpedo. Amy managed to catch her by the scruff before she connected. Piggy voiced her frustration in a yelp that was almost human.

Tom took the near miss in stride. He turned a thousand-watt smile on Amy.

"Still harboring attack corgis, I see."

"I don't know what her problem is, Tom. I'm sorry."

His laugh eased what could have been a sticky moment. "Don't apologize, Amy. I've always wanted my

very own stalker. It proves you're really a celebrity, you
know. I'd just hoped for something classier than a dog."

Piggy rumbled her displeasure, and Amy tucked the
squirming dog firmly under her arm. "Into a cage with
you, young lady. You're wearing my patience really
thin."

Piggy wasn't the only thing that had Amy's patience
stretched to the limit. As she carried the cantankerous
corgi into the house, she wished she could do the same
to Tom—into the house and out the front door with
him. What in blazes was he doing there, anyway? She
wasn't surprised that Selma had invited him. Selma did
crazy things like that. But he couldn't be here to see
Selma, whom he scarcely knew. Tom was here because
Amy was here.

The thought made her uneasy, though Amy wasn't
sure why. The photo was just a coincidence. There was
nothing sinister about it, or about Tom. He had warned
her that he was determined. Tom Gordon probably
wasn't accustomed to being turned down by women.

Yet his proclaimed interest had seemed strange from
the first, considering he was a jet-set kind of guy with
big ambitions, and she was a jeans-and-sweat-suit kind
of woman whose idea of a good time was reading a good
book in a steaming hot bath. Surely Amy Cameron was
the girl least likely to inspire Tom Gordon's amorous
determination. What could she say to make him go
away?

"I could send you out as a one-corgi hit squad," she
told Piggy. "What do you think of that?"

Not much, apparently. Piggy rumbled in displeasure
when Amy stuffed her into Raven's kennel.

"Don't you be mouthing off at me, young lady.
You'll find yourself grounded for the next ten years or so
if you don't start behaving yourself." Amy shut the crate

door and locked the latch firmly in place. Piggy shot her a look of martyred indignation.

"Is the little demon locked up?"

Tom's voice nearly made Amy jump out of her skin. She turned to find him behind her, grinning with his usual charm.

"Sheesh! Where did you learn to sneak up on a person like that?"

"No sneaking involved. You were involved in your conversation with the dog."

Amy smiled halfheartedly. "Bad habit of mine. I talk to dogs as if they're going to answer me."

"I wouldn't be surprised if that one did."

"Piggy needs a few good sessions of obedience training."

Tom chuckled. "Piggy needs a few good sessions with an exorcist, if you ask me. That dog's not natural."

"Well, she won't wreak any more havoc this afternoon, at least."

Piggy glared at them both. The light in her eyes almost made Tom's assertion believable. Feeling the hairs prickle on the back of her neck, Amy urged Tom toward the back door. "It was nice of you to drop by the reception. Selma's thrilled."

"Actually, I came by to boast to you about getting a job offer from NBC."

"That's wonderful, Tom. Though I can't say I'm surprised. You've made a name for yourself in the news game."

"That's what I set out to do."

"Something tells me you're a man who generally accomplishes what he sets out to do."

"You could say that. Except in affairs of the heart."

Amy threw him a cautious look as they walked out into the backyard. He held up his hands.

"Just kidding." He nodded toward her assistant,

Tony, who was busy reloading her camera. "I see you're using the camera I gave you. Do you like it?"

"It's great, Tom. Really great." Amy had salved her conscience with a promise that she would pay Tom back for the Nikon. "I can't believe you went out and got me the exact camera I would have gotten for myself. I didn't know you knew that much about cameras."

"I can't take credit. I told Corky Corchoran what camera you were using, and he told me the one you'd probably rather have. You remember Corky, my cameraman at the station?"

"Sure I remember him. He knows his cameras, sounds like."

"He knows a lot more about it than I do. Hand me a camera and I need a half hour to find the clicker button."

"You mean the shutter release."

"Yeah. Shutter release. Even on a simple one."

"Well, Tom. This is one great camera you got me. But I'm going to pay you back for it."

"You don't have to, Amy. It was a gift."

"Just your thinking to do such a nice thing was a gift. But I'm still going to pay you back."

"I'd settle for a kiss as full payment."

Amy opened her mouth to deliver a rebuke, but he beat her to the punch with a devilish grin.

"Or you could change your mind and come to my party on Saturday. I have a great view from my bedroom window, but the view would be better with you in it."

"Uh . . ."

"I know, I know. The dog doctor. Is he watching?"

"Tom . . ."

"Just teasing. I have to go, anyway. He's that tall fellow over there who looks like a hillbilly with a bad tailor, right?"

"Oh, he does not!"

"Don't hit me. I'm leaving."

"I'll show you to the door," Amy offered in an exasperated voice.

"I can find my way out. As long as the demon dog is still in her slammer."

"Behave, or I'll let her loose."

"I'm going. I'm going."

Amy's smile slowly faded after Tom disappeared through the back door. Since discovering that cursed photo, she'd used every excuse not to think about the expression on Tom's face as he had looked into the lens of her camera. She wanted to forget her uneasiness and leave the enlarged print in her office to gather dust. She really wanted to.

But if Tom knew so little about cameras, how had he told Corky Corchoran what model camera she used? Unless he had a good deal more interest in that camera than he let on. And as long as she was admitting her silly suspicions, why did Piggy turn into an attack corgi whenever Tom was around? And what had Tom Gordon been doing in the lobby of a post office building so out-of-the-way that scarcely anyone but its neighbors knew it existed? Why would he have a box in such an un-likely, inconvenient location?

Unless, for some reason, he didn't want anyone to know he had a box there. If he didn't want anyone to know, that would explain the look of surprise and alarm when he was caught by her camera. And if for some reason he didn't want anyone to know, would he stoop to robbery and mayhem to make sure that photo was never developed?

SEVENTEEN

♥

"STOP LOOKING AT me that way!"

Amy struggled to unhook the fastening at the top back of her dress. This was the third outfit she'd tried on and discarded. Her stomach roiled. Her mouth was dry. And the daggers shooting from Piggy's eyes weren't helping her mood.

In her impatience, Amy tore the stubborn hook and eye when it refused to give. The curse she mumbled as she stepped out of the dress was about as close as she ever came to being truly foulmouthed.

"Take that!" She tossed the wool sheath so that it landed on Piggy's head. The corgi yipped in annoyance as her head popped through a sleeve opening. One big triangular ear sprang free of the dress. The other bent at an odd angle under a fold of the wool.

"Now go lie down and quit giving me the evil eye."

While Amy dove back into her closet to search for the perfect ensemble, Piggy rumbled out a disgruntled growl, shook herself free of the dress, and plunked down on top of it.

"What do you think of this?" Amy asked as she emerged with a soft rayon dress cut in a free-flowing, southwestern style. "Not slinky, not sexy—we wouldn't want him to get the wrong idea. But not all that casual, either."

Piggy continued to glare.

"Sheesh!" Amy swept past the dog and held the dress up in front of a full-length mirror. "I'll need another slip."

Piggy yipped.

"I have to go," Amy insisted as she dug through her underwear drawer. "It's the only way. This thing has been eating at me all week long. These suspicions are the stupidest flights of fancy I've ever had. I'm probably losing my mind, but I'm going to lose it for sure if I don't prove Tom Gordon is totally innocent of any involvement in stealing my camera, trashing my house, gutting another house with fire, and murdering two innocent people. Have you ever heard of a more ridiculous idea? Do you believe I would even think such a thing?"

Piggy cocked her head alertly, and if Amy hadn't known better, she would have thought the dog understood every word she spoke, understood and itched to make a few comments of her own.

"So what if he showed up in a photo that was in the camera the night someone tried to steal it from the car? That doesn't mean anything. So what if he had that peculiar expression on his face? Maybe he doesn't like having his picture taken unless the makeup men have taken the shine off his nose. How should I know?"

The rude sound that came from Piggy's mouth was remarkably human and unmistakably skeptical.

"I would like to know why you decided to dislike Tom almost immediately after the house break-in, though."

"Rrrrr . . . woof!"

"And why he knew so much about my camera when he doesn't even know what a shutter release is.

And why an uptown guy like Tom Gordon is sniffing around a country-livin', RV-drivin', don't-give-a-damn-about-image kinda girl like me. I'll tell you one thing, Piggy. If Lydia Keane were alive, I wouldn't stand a chance with a guy like Tom Gordon."

Piggy yipped.

"He never would have looked my way. Not, that is, unless he had some ulterior motive."

Amy felt silly uttering such nonsense, but the suspicions were there, lodged inside her mind, and they were going to stay there, bugging her, until she satisfied herself that there was absolutely nothing to them. Up until a few hours ago, she had been at a loss for some way to lay the silly notions to rest, other than asking Tom outright, which didn't seem like a good idea at all. Then she had remembered a detail about the police investigation of David's and Lydia's murder. It had seemed insignificant at the time, but she still recalled it vividly, as if the memory had been filed away with some eerie foreknowledge that someday she would need it. Preserved in the wet sand and gravel of the alley behind the Wynkoop were footprints, remnants of the scuffle between David and the murderer. The police had made a cast of two distinct shoe treads. Amy remembered vividly when a detective had shown her a cast of the tread that had not matched David's shoes, which were still hidden away in some evidence box in police custody. The tread had been very distinct, and the detective had mentioned it wasn't a pattern one would find on an everyday pair of Reeboks or Nikes or a pair of loafers bought from Sears. Amy would recognize it if she ever saw it again.

If Tom Gordon owned a pair of shoes with that tread, she would call the cops. Even his popularity with the local police wouldn't protect him from such damning evidence. On the other hand, if Tom didn't own a pair of shoes that matched the tread, Amy would slap her own hand for being a paranoid idiot, discount every slimy suspicion, and try to forget that she had ever been so stupid.

That was the reason she had decided to go to Tom's beerfest, even though she had earlier declined. What better way to sneak through a man's closet than to come in by invitation?

Piggy didn't seem to agree, however. But then, Piggy was just a dog. She probably had her nose out of joint because Amy hadn't let her steal Drover's dinner an hour earlier. Jeff probably wouldn't think much of her scheme either. But Jeff was paying a call on a horse who'd decided to kick down its stall, gashing its leg in the process. Besides, Jeff didn't need Amy to bother him with such offbeat suspicions as these. She hadn't said anything to him about the photo. All week she had been torn between wanting to confide in him and wanting to elude the trap of becoming dependent upon a man once again. Not financially dependent, but emotionally and intellectually. Such a tie ran far deeper than mere money and hurt far worse when it was severed. How well she knew that. How very well.

Amy was recovering from David. Looking at those last snapshots had helped immensely. The load of bitterness was dissipating, leaving a glimmer of willingness to try again. But the idea of commitment was scary, especially commitment to someone like Jeff. He could be a danger to a girl's very soul. Attractive, kind, understanding, smart, sexy, and loving. Just looking at him could give her a high. Loving him, really loving him, might catapult her higher than that mountain they'd climbed together.

The higher the climb, the farther the fall, she reminded herself.

"It's not as though I'm being unfaithful to Jeff by going to this party," Amy explained to Piggy. She belted the dress around her waist and adjusted the scoop neckline. "I'm going there for one reason, and one reason only. After tonight, I'll help Tom finish that piece for his show, if"—she arched Piggy a telling look—"he still likes dogs enough to do it. After that, I don't care if I see him ever again. Jeff doesn't need to know that I went there tonight, or that I ever had such a stupid idea that Tom Gordon could be leading a double life as a murderer."

So why did she feel so guilty? Amy asked herself. Perhaps because, in spite of her own reservations, she felt committed to Jeff Berenger? Or because she hated to introduce any kind of deception into a refreshingly honest relationship?

"He wouldn't care," she told her image in the mirror. "Why should he mind if I want to spend an hour or so at a friend's party?"

She lied to herself, and well she knew it. Amy grimaced at her image, then glanced toward the door. She would go. There was nothing wrong in her going. What was she supposed to do? Wait around until Jeff told her what she should do about the problem? Not a chance.

She put the dogs in their kennels, got her coat and handbag, and, at the last minute, scrawled a note to Jeff: *Gone to talk to T. Gordon. Business. Back soon.*

That lightened her conscience. After all, this was business. Of a sort.

TOM GORDON'S HOUSE in Evergreen perched on the side of a mountain overlooking the whole Denver basin. With soaring expanses of glass and smooth, sculpted curves of wood, it was an architectural testament to Tom's success—and his personality. Showy but private. Conservative in its way, yet ambitious in design and flawless in its good taste.

As she drove her minivan up the circular drive, Amy was impressed, and not a little daunted. How could a man who lived in such a place have something shadowy about his existence? She was being a nincompoop. She didn't deserve Tom's friendship, and if Jeff ever found out about this escapade, he would laugh and say she was as silly as her corgis.

The front entrance of the house was a sweeping atrium of glass that rose from the ground to the second story. Amy stopped the car, stared at the door, and almost lost courage. In fact, she did lose courage, but before she could drive away, a college-aged valet opened the car door.

"Good evening, ma'am."

"Good evening," Amy replied with a sigh.

The valet didn't even lift a brow at the dog hair and portable dog kennels that filled the minivan. He drove it away with a dignity befitting a Mercedes. Amy vowed to give him a big tip.

The man who greeted her at the front door wore a suit, but he looked as though in real life he wore a football uniform. A tree-sized neck merged into a stalwart jaw, which framed a much broken nose.

"Good evening. May I see your invitation?"

Security. Of course. People, especially high-profile people, had to worry about stalkers and all kinds of unpleasant weirdos these days. She ought to know. "Well . . ." she hesitated, and the linebacker frowned. "I'm not sure that I—"

"That's all right, Mr. Colton." Tom was suddenly beside the well-dressed bouncer, smiling his surprise. "Mrs. Cameron is a very special guest."

Tom plucked her away from the guard and threaded her arm through his. "Amy. What a pleasant surprise."

"I decided I could make it after all."

"I'm glad." He arched one brow in wicked glee. "I

don't suppose this means that you and the dog doctor—"

"Jeff is on a call."

"Really . . ." His voice trailed off suggestively.

"Now, Tom. Don't get the wrong idea. Jeff and I aren't married, engaged, or even pinned, as my sorority sisters used to say in college. There's no reason I can't go to a friend's party and enjoy myself."

"No reason at all, Amy. I just wouldn't have guessed you had it in you to be so . . . flexible. I'm delighted."

"Besides," she said with a grin, "I wanted to see your house." That was close to the truth, Amy comforted herself. What she actually wanted to see was his clothes closet. That was part of a house, wasn't it?

"Well, let me give you a tour, then."

They stopped by the bar first, where Tom got a pale wheat beer and Amy ordered a Bloody Mary.

"Bloody Mary?" Tom scoffed. "This is a beerfest, woman."

"Beer and I have never gotten along," Amy confessed.

Amy seldom drank. Not since her college days. But a Bloody Mary seemed the appropriate thing to order, somehow. Lydia had loved Bloody Marys. She had insisted the drink could count as a vegetable serving in any diet regime. Amy hoped wherever she was, Lydia could eat as much as she wanted without worrying about damaging her eye-catching figure.

She missed her friend, Amy realized. She missed her with an ache that no longer included bitterness and anger. They had been about as opposite as two women could be, she and Lydia, but their bond had gone past all that and straight to the heart. Amy glanced at Tom and tried to imagine him breaking poor Lydia's neck—all that charm and polish melting into grotesque, killing viciousness. She couldn't imagine it. Her suspicions seemed as far off base as a foul ball popping into the stands at Coors Field.

"Tom, this is absolutely beautiful!" They strolled from the spacious great room, where most of the guests were gathered, into a formal dining area. "Did you decorate it yourself?"

Tom laughed. "Absolutely not! No one, even me, would want to live with my ragbag taste."

"I don't believe you have ragbag taste."

"Believe it." He spread his arms. "All this splendor you see before you, including me, is the product of someone else's careful design. An interior decorator for the house, a publicist for me. Unfortunately, when journalism became part of the entertainment industry, image became a newsman's best friend. Not talent, truth, hard work, or an instinct for a story, but Image with a capital *I*."

"That's a very cynical viewpoint."

"No. That's truth. But I'll tell you something, Amy. What I do is important. Investigative journalists like me are what make politicians and bureaucrats at least pay lip service to honesty. Anything I need to do to perform that job is worth it." His somewhat grim expression softened into a sudden smile. "Even if it means dolling myself up like a walking Ken doll."

Amy refused to buy it. "Poor Tom! Such a sacrifice. Putting up with that big paycheck, wearing designer clothes, driving designer cars, and living in a shack like this. And now you're headed for even better and bigger things with NBC. How will you stand it?"

Tom laughed. "That's one of the things I like about you, Amy. You're not impressed, and you keep me humble."

"Something tells me that's an impossible task."

"Oh, woman! You wound me!"

They peered into the kitchen, where a catering staff was hard at work. The facilities would make a professional chef drool. Even Amy, who spent as little time cooking as she possibly could, admitted that such a kitchen might inspire her to something more than dry cereal and frozen dinners.

The house was huge, and Tom took his time giving Amy the tour. They chatted and teased, and the longer she was with him, the more certain Amy became that Tom Gordon had no shadowy mysteries to hide. If she wanted to uncover her nemesis, she would have to look beneath another rock to find the slime.

A stroll around the second floor ended in the master suite. A king-sized bed faced a bank of floor-to-ceiling windows that stretched from wall to wall. The distant lights of the city twinkled like stars that had fallen to Earth. Their intensity turned the surrounding night into a golden glow.

Amy sighed when she imagined waking up to such a view each morning. "Yes, indeed. You have certainly made the tough sacrifices, Tom Gordon."

His chuckle warmed her ear, and Amy suddenly became aware that he was very close behind her, looking over the top of her head at the view beyond. Before she could ease away, he put his hands on her shoulders. His fingers squeezed in gentle caress.

"You're a corker, Amy Cameron."

"Tom, don't."

He nuzzled her ear, and before she could protest, turned her and brushed her lips with his.

"Don't."

"Mmmm. You taste good." He helped himself to a deeper taste. Amy stood unmoving, rigid. One kiss was no big deal, she told herself, but the clamor of conscience rang loudly in her head. Perhaps that was why Tom's kiss didn't move her. That in itself disturbed her.

His breath was sweet. His technique was as polished as the rest of him. He was charming from the top of his perfectly groomed head to the toes of his designer shoes.

At the thought of shoes, Amy pulled sharply away. She didn't really want to make a scene, but playing kissy-face with Tom Gordon wasn't the reason she'd come.

"Why did you do that?" she snapped.

He gave her a lazy, confident smile. "Why do you think?"

"Because you're a tomcat." Her glower softened a bit. "And you kiss every woman who comes into your bedroom, simply out of habit."

"I certainly don't kiss my cleaning lady. She's fifty-five and chews tobacco." He reached out and touched Amy's cheek. "Did I get the wrong message about your coming here?"

He didn't know the half of it, Amy thought. "I'm sorry if I gave you the wrong impression. I only . . . I only sleep with one guy at a time."

"That's good news."

"And right now I'm involved with Jeff."

"That's bad news."

"I really just want to be friends, Tom. Is that beyond your comprehension?"

"Not at all." He took her arm and ushered her out of the bedroom. "I can be very friendly."

She did want to be friends with Tom Gordon, Amy told herself. She wasn't lying . . . much. For his sake as much as anything else, she had to prove that her suspicions were out of line. She was more sure than ever that Tom Gordon was innocent as a lamb. Well, maybe not innocent as a lamb. No man who kissed like that, whose eyes turned to liquid fire the minute he walked into his bedroom, could truly be called innocent.

Once back with the party, though, Amy put off her

task. Searching through someone's personal shoe rack might not be in the same league with the murder and arson, but it was still a distasteful prospect. She found plenty of distractions among the guests. Though she'd gotten the impression from Tom that this gathering was an informal "sit around, drink good beer, and crack bad jokes" sort of party, it was certainly the most stylish affair Amy had been to. The bar was stocked with every liquor one could want, and every label was an expensive one. Three huge kegs from a local microbrewery rounded out the liquor menu. The eats were catered, of course, and the hors d'oeuvres, canapés, and assortment of crackers, breads, and spreads, including caviar, truly made Amy's mouth water, just as the guest list made her want to gape. All the regulars on the *Denver Post*'s society page were there, along with local political bigwigs and media stars. The notable exception was Denver's mayor, who was understandably put out by Tom's exposé of his construction kickbacks.

Tom introduced Amy around, and she tried hard not to feel like Cinderella crashing a ball. Much to her surprise, when Tom explained that she was helping him with a project about dogs, quite a few of the high and the mighty pricked their ears with interest and regaled her with stories about their own pets. Dogs and cats were great equalizers, Amy reflected. Nobody really cared where she bought her clothes if she laughed at the cute antics of Buffy the Cat or sympathized with the news anchor whose Great Dane had just passed away.

Tom stayed close to Amy's side while she mingled, which gave her an excuse to put off her detective work. In spite of their conversation in his bedroom, he didn't seem convinced that she wasn't simply being coy. Finally, with the party in full stride and the hour getting late, Amy realized she had to do what she had come to do or let the opportunity pass. Jeff would have arrived home by then, and her note about Tom was certain to raise his hackles. He didn't like Tom Gordon. Not that he'd said anything outright, but his humor sharpened to a cutting edge and his voice dropped to the dark registers every time Tom was mentioned.

Jealousy, Amy thought. Or maybe instinct, a still suspicious part of her countered. In any case, if she wasn't home soon, Jeff would worry.

She was running out of both time and excuses. It was now or never. With a reluctant sigh, Amy put her half-empty Bloody Mary on a tray and touched Tom's sleeve. "Where is the powder room? That's one little necessity you didn't show me on our tour."

"Down the hall and around the corner to the left. If that one's occupied, there's another upstairs."

How convenient, Amy thought. *So is the master bedroom.*

She tried to look nonchalant as she left the room, but the moment she was out of sight, her pace quickened. Her heart pounded so loudly that she was sure Tom could hear it even half a house away.

"This is so, so stupid! Stupid, stupid, stupid!" She muttered the litany to herself as she ran lightly up the spiral staircase and hurried down the upstairs hall. She wasn't cut out for this sort of thing. Intrigue was beyond her. Underhandedness made her stomach churn.

Between the master suite's dressing room and bath, Amy found a walk-in closet. Closet, though, was hardly an appropriate description. She had seen whole houses that were smaller. Shirts, trousers, suit jackets, sport jackets, and a Scottish kilt hung in neatly regimented organization. On one side, built-in drawers of clear plastic housed sweaters, T-shirts, undershirts, and shorts. On the other side, a shoe rack held at least twenty pairs of shoes—everything from dress shoes to loafers to athletic shoes.

Heart pounding, Amy started at the athletic shoes and worked toward the dressier models, confident she was on a fool's errand. She'd scarcely begun when a pair of walkers grabbed her eyes, expensive walkers, designed for the ultimate in comfort, and having a tread design that perfectly matched the one stored in her memory.

Amy was scarcely aware of the minutes ticking by as she knelt in the closet and stared at the shoe in her hand.

"Hello, Amy."

Amy dropped the shoe and turned so fast she landed on her backside in the plush carpet. Tom Gordon looked down at her, and he definitely wasn't smiling.

STUPID, IDIOTIC, IMBECILIC, half-witted fool of a woman! I used to believe that Amy had brains. I mean, she whizzed through high school and college, and her parents spent one whole summer bragging about her SAT scores. I think my parents burned mine. I guess this goes to show you that real life can spring pop quizzes that require some real smarts to survive. And Amy had just earned a big, fat F. Can anyone out there really believe she waltzed right into Gordon's arms like that? She might as well have painted a target on her chest.

When Amy took off for Tom Gordon's lair, I realized there were some frayed wires in the common sense area of her head, and it would be up to me to save her. The Bumbling Bodyguard wasn't around, of course. Though I hate to give him credit, Jeff probably would have had the wit to stop her. He was off somewhere sewing up a horse, however. By the time he got home, Tom Gordon would probably have poor Amy tied to the railroad tracks and a locomotive would be coming around the bend, so to speak.

I was more than willing to charge to the rescue, but being a dog made matters complicated. For one thing, I was locked in my kennel. For another, I couldn't do all the other things necessary for a rescue of this sort—dial the phone, open the front door, drive a car. I was frantic. Amy was about to get herself in deep, deep trouble. Maybe six feet under. I couldn't ride to the rescue, and Stan, the officious jackass, was going to pin the blame on me. I just knew he was. Amy would go to heaven wearing angel wings and a halo, while I would probably get reassigned somewhere as a worm.

Not that I was thinking only of myself at that point. The pesky sense of responsibility that had been growing on me was still in full bloom. I whined, yipped, and dug at my kennel floor, which was fiberglass and impervious to corgi toenails. Then I threw myself at the kennel door, which accomplished nothing except to imprint the pattern of the metal grate on the side of my head. The goody-two-shoes border collies, who were lounging nearby on their dog beds, regarded my efforts with mystification. Molly and Drover, content and ignorant in their own kennels, clearly thought I'd gone insane. I barked at them in frenzied frustration, though they were unlikely to be of help. After all, they were mere dogs.

Then the thought struck me. That was the problem. I was behaving like a stupid dog instead of the higher being I truly was. I had to use my brains and ingenuity if I wanted to solve this dilemma. From that point on, I used my head for something other than a pointy-eared battering ram. Before long I figured out a way to release the latch, and after a mere hour's work with teeth and toes, the door to my crate swung open and I was free.

Free to do what? you ask. I asked myself the same question. For a few minutes I trotted about the house whining, half hoping that Stanley would appear and tell me what to do. That didn't happen, of course. Stan never shows up when you need him. Then my brain kicked in again. With a bit more ingenuity and a little luck, I could call in the cavalry.

I looked at the phone, which was within easy reach of the couch, and wondered if it was possible to push the buttons with corgi toes instead of fingers.

♥   ♥   ♥

JEFF BERENGER LAY on his side in the straw. From shoulder to fingernails, his arm was coated with blood and mucus.

"That was a job, Doc." Ted Gottlieb shook his head at the foal that had just struggled from its mother's womb. "Glad you happened to be here."

"Yeah. Me, too."

"Chessie's never had trouble delivering before this. Three prime foals she's given me, and not a hitch in one of the birthings."

Heedless of the mess, Ted extended a hand to help Jeff to his feet. Jeff struggled to an upright position, wincing as cramped muscles objected. He'd come to the Gottlieb stable to treat a simple leg gash, and he'd ended up spending three hours squatting, sitting, and lying in the straw, helping a prize mare deliver a foal that had gotten tangled up in the birth canal. He was dead tired, filthy, and just about ready to limit his already limited practice to animals weighing less than a hundred pounds. "I wouldn't worry too much. Probably Chessie's next will go as easy as pie. These things happen sometimes."

"Yeah. I guess that'll be the way. In spite of it all, that's a fine-looking little stud colt she just popped out. Every foal she's given us up to now has been a filly."

The newcomer, still wet from birth, tried diligently to get up on his spindly legs, those same long legs that had been so awkwardly tangled a few minutes before. His mother nudged him helpfully with her nose.

"He's a fine one, all right," Jeff agreed.

"Come on. You can wash up in the house, and Cathy'll have a pot of coffee hot. In fact, you can spend the night on the sofabed, if you like. You look done in, and it's almost eleven."

"Thanks. But I need to get home."

"You sure? Cathy made a lemon pie this afternoon. It's mighty good."

Jeff was tempted by the offer, but the thought of Amy waiting at home made him turn down not only a bed, but pie and coffee as well. Strange how Amy's house in Niwot had become "home" in just a few days. Or perhaps Amy had become home. After years of being a loner, a confirmed bachelor who played the field with only casual interest, suddenly this woman pops up, prickly as a porcupine and tempting as an unscaled summit. Except that he'd scaled the summit, metaphorically speaking, and discovered that the attraction was more than just the challenge. In fact, it was more than just attraction. Much more.

Damned if he wasn't going to cling to his foothold on Amy's mountain and stay there until she realized that she couldn't live without him. It was the truth, Jeff told himself. Amy just hadn't grasped it yet.

"You okay?" Ted asked.

"Huh?"

"You were staring off into space like some sleep-walker."

"Oh. No, I'm just—" The ring of his cellular phone cut him off. His heart jumped. The first thought that leaped to mind was that something was amiss at home. He fished it from his pocket, flipped it open, and jerked up the antenna.

"Yes? Amy?"

A barrage of barking made him wince.

"What the hell?"

More barking. Loud. Demanding. Frantic. The beginnings of fear began to coil tightly in Jeff's belly. He didn't have a good feeling about this. Not good at all.

EIGHTEEN

IF JEFF HAD ever deserved a speeding ticket, he deserved one while driving the fifteen miles between the Gottlieb ranch and Niwot. The speedometer crept up a notch each time he tried to dial Amy's house on his cell phone and got a busy signal. Calling her cell phone number only got him a terse announcement by the operator that the party was not answering or the phone was switched off. He prayed that Amy was safe at home and had simply knocked her phone off the hook.

When he burst into the house, however, the only ones who greeted him were the dogs. Spot and Darby met him at the door with worried expressions and apologetically wagging tails. What they apologized for became obvious when Jeff spied Piggy. She glowered at him from the living room couch, half sitting on the phone receiver. The indicator light on the receiver glowed a steady red. In the guest room were the remnants of her kennel and two indignant corgis whom the escape artist hadn't bothered to spring.

Other than Piggy's pranks, all seemed to be normal. No mayhem or mischief other than one contrary corgi.

"Not your fault," Jeff told the border collies. Naturally they believed it was their job to keep order in the house. "You girls just aren't a match for Miss Pudgy."

Piggy barked a staccato command at Jeff. It was simply amazing how much authority the little fur ball could put in her tone.

"That couldn't have been you on my phone." He pushed Piggy aside and put the receiver back on the cradle. A slip of paper lay on the end table by the couch, the paper on which he'd scrawled his cell phone number for Amy. He looked from the paper to Piggy, who smirked in a way that only a corgi can smirk. "It couldn't have been you. That's impossible."

She replied with another imperious bark and took off at full speed toward the kitchen. Jeff let her go. Scowling, he called for Amy, even though he didn't really expect her to be there.

"It couldn't have been that damned dog," he kept telling himself as he walked through the house. "Amy's got to be here, playing a joke." Either that, or he had just crossed the line into the Twilight Zone.

As he went into the bedroom, Piggy caught up with him. She grabbed his trouser leg and yanked hard.

"Stop it, you four-legged featherbrain! Goddammit! Let go!"

Piggy yipped, dashed toward the kitchen, looked back at him, and yipped again.

"Didn't Amy feed you?"

She bounced up and down on stubby legs. Jeff was reminded of a pig on a pogo stick.

"All right. All right. I'm coming."

Piggy dashed to the kitchen and slid to a halt beside the table, where a note in Amy's handwriting waited for him: *Gone to talk to T. Gordon. Business.* Jeff grunted skeptically. Business. Amy might honestly think it was business. But if Tom Gordon had business on his mind, it wasn't the kind that Amy was counting on. The sonuvabitch just couldn't believe that Amy hadn't fallen for his smooth line.

Piggy didn't give Jeff time to sink into a jealous funk. She shot off with uncharacteristic energy and clawed at the closed door to Amy's office.

"Feel like eating some more files, do you?"

Jeff had become accustomed to Piggy's repertoire of eerily human expressions. They ranged through disgust, contempt, impatience, vexation, and boredom. But the look on her face as she threw herself against the office door communicated something he didn't expect. Desperation. Pleading. Fear. Not knowing quite why he did so, Jeff opened the door. Piggy hurtled in, ran to the filing cabinet and clawed at the side with her front paws. The photo on top of the cabinet immediately caught Jeff's eye. He stared, then scowled with a ferocity that matched the expression of the man in the photograph— Tom Gordon, of all people, looking extremely surprised and unhappy to have been caught in the eye of a camera. When Jeff turned the image over, the date scrawled on the back made his heart plunge. It was the very date that David Cameron and Lydia Keane had been killed by a burglar who had broken into Amy's minivan. The minivan with the camera lying on the back seat. The camera that apparently had this photo inside it.

"Shit!" he groaned. "Shit, shit, and more shit!"

A SLOW SMILE spread across Tom Gordon's face, but any semblance of geniality was superficial. Actually, the expression was more a grimace than a smile, and it transformed his face from handsome to feral.

"I don't suppose you came back here because you wanted to relive our latest kiss," he said quietly.

Amy thought fast, but her mind seemed bogged in a mire. Several desperate explanations flashed into her mind, none of which he would buy. "I . . . uh . . ."

"No need to explain. You're a smart lady, Amy. It's

one of the things I like about you. But being smart can sometimes get a person into trouble."

Amy didn't feel smart. Not at all.

Gentlemanly as ever, he offered a hand up. Not knowing what else to do, Amy accepted his help. "Well!" She took a steadying breath. "Now you know. I'm a pathological snoop. I'm always sneaking about and pawing through people's personal things. Selma says I need a shrink, but—"

A sad shake of Tom's head stopped her mid-lie. "Not good enough." He picked up the shoe she had dropped and examined it minutely. "What were you looking at?"

"Nothing."

He gave her a glare.

"I . . . just . . . like to nose around in people's things."

He frowned at her, and then the shoe. Understanding dawned on his face. "A shoeprint. Of course. I didn't think of that. Stupid of me. But then, I've done more than one stupid thing lately."

Amy's heart plunged.

"You must have found the photo and put two and two together." The regret in his expression was more chilling than a fit of rage.

"I have to go now," Amy said. "I really do need to get home."

"No. Sit down, please." He motioned her to a footstool in the corner of the huge closet. "I need to think."

"And I need to go. Really." She tried to push past him, but he effortlessly blocked her way. Gently he took her by the shoulders and pointed her toward the stool. "Sit down, Amy."

"Tom, I really don't understand any of this."

"You're lying. Of course you understand, or you

wouldn't be here. Maybe you've known from the first."
He sighed. "It just goes on and on."

"What does?"

"Believe me, Amy. There's no such thing as a tiny
bargain with the devil. Once you've got one lousy toe in
hell, Old Nick grabs you by the ankle and yanks you the
rest of the way in. I'm not a criminal. I'm not a murderer. Shit, I was Phi Beta Kappa at CU and voted
newsman of the year by the . . ." He trailed off into a
sigh. "But I guess that doesn't matter."

Amy wondered when the anger would start. Unbelievable as it seemed, Tom Gordon had killed David and
Lydia. If the incriminating shoe wasn't evidence
enough, Tom's strange chatter put the damning cap on
the case. She had come here to prove Tom innocent and
ended up stumbling onto his guilt.

What she didn't understand was why? No doubt
that stupid photo was tangled in the plot somewhere,
but the whole thing seemed surreal to Amy—a nightmare from which she would soon wake in a cold sweat.
She felt more numb than angry, more confused than
afraid.

Tom regarded her with sympathetic regret. No
longer did he look threatening or feral. "Amy, where is
the photo?"

She pondered the merits of lying and decided the
time for that was past. "On top of my filing cabinet."

He looked at her in amazement. "On top of . . .
shit! How long has it been there?"

"A few days."

"Where was it?"

"I didn't develop the roll until a few days ago. It got
stuck behind a file drawer."

He closed his eyes as if in pain.

"Tom, you can have the photo, if you want. I'll just
go get it, and—"

He laughed, and for a moment the sound was manic and bitter. Then he clamped his jaw with icy control. "I'm not stupid, Amy."

"Okay," she said cautiously. "You're not stupid."

"You don't really know what this is about, do you?"

"No."

He gestured to the shoe. "You just know I was in that alley with David and Lydia."

She was silent. Tom squeezed the bridge of his nose between his fingers. "I wish to hell you didn't know that. But since you do, I guess I owe you the whole story."

A stab of alarm penetrated Amy's numbed feelings. If Tom was willing to provide her with the whole story, did that mean she wasn't going to get a chance to tell it to anyone?

"You don't have to tell me," she offered.

He gave her a sad smile. "And I suppose next you'll tell me that you won't ever tell anyone about that shoe you just found."

Amy bit her lip.

"Amy, Amy, Amy. I wish to hell you weren't mixed up in this."

So did she.

"But you are. I'm sorry, love. I never dreamed in a million years that things would get this out of hand. I was just doing my job, and if there weren't so many people in the world who can't see the forest for the trees, none of this would have happened."

"What do you mean?"

"I mean sometimes the end does justify the means. I told you before, my job is important. That exposé I did on the mayor's construction kickbacks needed to be done. If he's not recalled, at least he won't be reelected, I'll guarantee that. He should have been impeached, the crook. He abused the people's trust, took money under the table, probably misused taxpayers' money for his own personal projects, and on and on. I never would have tripped him up if I hadn't stretched the rules a bit. A good reporter sometimes has to do that, no matter what the stupid bureaucrats think."

"Stretched the rules?"

"Yeah." He grimaced. "Stretched them quite a bit, really. A lot of the evidence I compiled against the mayor came from his own post office box. The one he keeps under another name at that out-of-the-way post office I was coming out of when you shot that photo. That's where he got mail from his friends at A and D Construction."

"You broke into his box?"

"I didn't have to break in. I had a key."

"I don't suppose the mayor gave you that key," Amy said wryly.

"Hardly. But we investigative reporters are good at getting things like that."

"Tampering with the mail's a federal offense."

"Exactly, my love. It's an investigative method not too popular with the big boys at the networks either. A fellow convicted of such a thing could kiss a journalism career good-bye, not to mention pull a jail sentence."

"Then why did you do it?"

"Because it needed to be done, Amy! Don't you understand what I've been saying? It was the only way I could get the goods on the mayor. I knew I wouldn't get caught. That wasn't the only time I've broken a law or two to get information. No big deal. Until you showed up with that damned camera."

Amy shook her head. "I wouldn't have known what you were doing."

"Probably not. I'll admit after so many months of stalking the mayor, I was spooked, thinking he might be stalking me as well. If he'd been able to start a scandal about my methods, nothing I could have said would have stuck to him. I thought maybe he'd put a photographer on my tail, hoping to trip me up. I couldn't let that photo be developed."

"So you tried to break into my car."

"I followed you to your house. By that time I'd recognized you. I didn't know exactly what was going on, but I did know if you published that photo and the mayor happened to see it, the shit was going to hit the fan. My shit, to be exact. When David took your car before you took the camera out, I followed him. It was supposed to be a simple car break-in. It happens every day downtown, and no one would have thought twice about some thief seeing an expensive camera on the backseat of a car and breaking in to get it. Insurance would've replaced the damned camera and repaired the damage to your car. Nobody would've been hurt if David hadn't come along and tried to play hero."

Amy could scarcely believe what she was hearing. "So you killed him over a stupid photo in my stupid camera?"

"No. Well, yes. But I didn't mean to. He followed me into the alley and got a look at my face, dammit! We fought. I was scared. I knew he'd blow the whistle on me and I'd be royally screwed."

"And what about Lydia?"

"That stupid bitch. She followed us into the alley, screamed her silly head off when David went down, and then ran for help. I just meant to stop her and shut her up, but when I grabbed her from behind, she slipped. I felt her neck snap, actually felt it. It's the most horrible feeling in the world. I wasn't trying to kill her. It was a freak accident."

Amy looked at him incredulously.

"It was supposed to be a simple robbery, goddammit, and look what happened! It wasn't my fault!"

"It wasn't your fault," Amy repeated skeptically. "You killed two people, but you didn't mean it."

"I was scared, goddammit! I wasn't thinking, just reacting. All I wanted was to get out of there without getting caught."

"But you didn't take the camera."

"There's no way I would have gone back into that street after what had just happened. Lydia could have brought the whole city out with those screams. That bitch had a set of lungs on her, and I don't just mean what filled out her bra."

Amy couldn't find it in her heart to feel much sympathy for him.

"Later I calmed down a bit and realized I absolutely had to get that photo. After what had happened, it was even more important. I'd figured your being there had probably been an accident, but when you developed the film and saw me coming out of that post office, or if you published it in some photo essay like the one you did for the *Denver Post* last year—Christ! There's no telling who would have seen it and what conclusions they would have drawn."

Probably no one would have concluded anything, Amy thought. But if one earned a living exposing other people's dirty secrets, perhaps paranoia about your own secrets was a natural consequence.

"So my house getting torched, and the burglary in Niwot . . . it was you looking for the photo?"

He sighed. "When I couldn't find it in Denver, I figured a fire would be a good way to destroy it. I assumed it was gone, until I saw you at the Scottish festival and you made that comment about having been able to save so much."

"So you wormed your way into my life to find out where it was. Don't you think I would have said something if I'd seen it?"

"I concluded you hadn't seen it. Either it was destroyed or you hadn't developed the roll for some reason. I wanted to find out for sure."

"Why did you take my camera? You must have known that by then the roll of film wouldn't be in it any longer."

He sighed. "Frustration, maybe. It sat on your desk leering at me, as if it knew what a screw-up I had made of this whole thing. I took it to the nearest Dumpster and smashed it into a thousand pieces. Serves it right."

She shook her head in disbelief. "You got revenge on a camera?"

"I gave you another one to make up for it. I didn't want to hurt you." Tom rubbed the back of his neck. Amy hoped he had one hell of a headache.

"The show about dogs, the romantic dinner—all that was for that stupid photo."

"I'll admit it was mostly an excuse to get close to you. But once we got together . . . well, I remembered why I'd always envied David his wife. I really do like you, Amy. I'd hoped I could settle the matter without you ever suspecting, and then maybe we could go on from there. If you hadn't taken up with the dog doctor . . ."

Who was a hundred times the man that Tom Gordon could ever hope to be, Amy thought as Tom let his words trail off into possibilities.

"I'm not a criminal, Amy. I'm not a bad person. I'm not a killer. The situation got out of my control. It started out simple and snowballed into a nightmare. You've got to understand. All the choices were taken away from me. The damned thing just gets bigger and bigger."

He paused, his eyes sliding away from hers. Not until then was Amy sure that Tom meant to kill her. When he started explaining the twisted coil of his actions, the prospect of her staying alive had looked dim. But now she was sure. He wouldn't meet her eyes, and his expression was set in grim finality.

A sudden, overwhelming regret washed through her. How quickly priorities rearranged themselves when death showed its ugly face. A clutter of pride, apprehension, hopes, prejudices, and past hurts fell away to reveal what was truly important in her life, and through her own stupidity, she was going to die before she could act upon the revelation.

She regretted letting fear rule her life. Fear of being lonely had led her to marry David; fear of upsetting the status quo had kept her in a mediocre marriage; fear of sustaining another blow to her pride—and it had been her pride, not her heart, that David and Lydia had hurt—had driven her behind a wall of prickly words and vaunted self-reliance. Her "self-reliance" hadn't been a true wish for independence, but an excuse to isolate herself from anyone who might hurt her again.

What a stupid way to live. She regretted the cowardice, the excuses, the lies she had told herself; but most of all she regretted not telling Jeff Berenger that she loved him. She'd thought she had all the time in the world to shilly-shally and vacillate behind the wall of her hurt pride, all the time in the world to let poor Jeff convince her past a doubt that he would treat her heart with eggshell tenderness. And she had never had the courage to tell him she loved him.

Jeff was what was important in her life. He was the opportunity for real love that many never find. But she had been too much of a coward to reach out and take that opportunity. Now Jeff would never know. Not unless she managed to get herself out of this predicament.

Well, she had wanted to be a self-reliant woman.

"What are you going to do, Tom?"

He gave her a bleak look.

"Be careful," she warned, trying to stay calm, to think. "A good attorney could probably get you off the hook for David and Lydia by reducing the charges to manslaughter, or maybe pleading temporary insanity. It was an accident, as you say. But you'd get nothing less than first-degree murder for getting rid of me."

Amy had no idea if what she said was true. She knew nothing about the law. She knew only that she wanted out of that closet in one piece.

Tom's eyes lifted to hers and held there. They held a wealth of sadness. "I'm sorry, Amy. Please believe me."

"You won't get away with it, Tom. It would be better just to give yourself up and explain it just as you explained it to me."

"I can't do that, Amy. I've worked too hard to get where I am. NBC's offered me a place on the evening news team, and I'm going to take that job. If this comes to light, I won't see the outside of prison walls for the rest of my life."

"How are you going to explain my disappearance?"

"No one will link me to your death. Your body will be found in Chatfield Reservoir, no doubt dumped there by whatever twisted stalker has been harassing you for the better part of a year. Or maybe we'll make it look like suicide—sliced wrists or something equally dramatic. You've had enough go wrong with your life to make that believable."

"Thanks to you," Amy said tartly.

"Now, don't get bitchy on me. That's not you."

"You're going to get caught, Tom. People saw me at your party."

"And saw you leave early. The police would never think of me as a suspect. I'm their crusading champion, remember? And don't worry about the photo. I'll get rid of that, now that I know where it is. No one will be the wiser."

"You can't do this, Tom. It's not fair. I've never done anything to you."

"I know. Neither had David. He was my friend, and I grieved for him just as I'll grieve for you."

Amy closed her eyes. "I don't believe this."

"I'm sorry, Amy. A few years from now, my name is going to be a household word, and even the big guns in Washington are going to take note when Tom Gordon turns a sharp eye their way. I'm going to be an important man on the national scene, and I'm going to do some good up there. That's worth the price I have to pay."

Only he wasn't the one paying the price. It was on the tip of Amy's tongue to tell him that Selma and Jeff would both guess his involvement, but she stopped before endangering their lives as well.

"Don't worry. I guarantee you won't feel a thing. I wish it had worked out some other way. You're a damned tempting woman, Amy, if that's any comfort to you."

She considered her chances of making it to the closet door as he pulled a couple of ties and some handkerchiefs from a drawer. Before she could act, however, he grabbed her arm and pulled her up from the footstool.

"For right now, I'm going to tie you up in the closet. And gag you, of course. I wouldn't want you to disturb the guests downstairs. And when the party's over, you and I will take a ride. Don't fret about it, though. As I said, you won't even know what hit you. Promise."

Amy tried to jerk away, but her strength was no match for his. He yanked her back, then when she opened her mouth to scream, he slammed her against the drawers behind her and drove the breath from her lungs. Before she knew it, he stuffed a handkerchief in her mouth and secured it with one of his expensive ties.

"Don't make me get rough, Amy. And don't make me get to the unpleasant part any sooner than I have to."

He took both of her wrists in one hand and reached for another tie with his other. She kicked at his shins, tried to butt him with her head, and did succeed in stomping on his toes, but that just made him chuckle.

"You do have guts," he observed calmly. "I've always liked that about you."

He tied her, hand and foot, pushed her down onto the stool again, and stood back to survey his handiwork. "That should keep you quiet and out of trouble for a while. Comfortable?"

Amy glared at him, and he gave her a measuring look.

"I wonder if I should trust you, even bound up like a mummy." He took a putter from the golf bag in the corner and hefted it meaningfully. "If I hear any noise up here, any thumping or bumping, then we'll have to change the plan from poor Amy commiting suicide to poor Amy being battered to death by some miscreant. It wouldn't be nearly as nice for you. It's your choice, my love."

Amy looked at the putter and felt her chances for escape sifting away like sand through an hourglass. Then a little brown torpedo dashed through the door, teeth foremost.

I NEVER THOUGHT to see the day when Dr. Deadbeat would save the day, but I have to give the guy credit. Once I cleverly maneuvered him into seeing the problem, there was no holding him back. He practically ripped Amy's address book apart looking for Tom Gordon's house number, and then ran out to his truck in such a state that he didn't even notice I'd slipped out the front door and jumped into the cab with him. Inept as he was, he was going to need my help, I figured. The curses that came out of his mouth when he noticed me proved he didn't share my opinion, but he wasn't about to waste time dragging me back into the house.

Good thing, too. He was so anxious to rip apart Gordon's house in search of Amy, he would have left his gun behind in the truck, where it was stashed under the seat, if I hadn't practically dropped the thing in his lap. If you think that was an easy task, try picking up a .38 with your teeth.

I give Jeff credit for his courage—dashing into Gordon's house like some kind of John Wayne, pushing his way past that beefy security fellow and alarming the gathered politicos and society celebs. Did I mention he still had horse blood, horse slime, and other horse unmentionables on his clothing?

It was actually me who led the charge, however, so I should get a lot of the credit. Jeff never would have found our Amy if not for my nose. A dog's nose is not a pretty thing. It's cold, often slimy, and almost always pushing into places where you don't want it. But you can't beat a canine nose for finding something that needs to be found, whether it be a buried bone, a stray crumb that's fallen to the floor, or a person near and dear to the heart who is about to get snuffed.

I knew exactly where Amy was from the moment I got in the house. Straight up the stairs I went, Jeff hard on my heels. When I flew into that closet and sank my teeth into Tom Gordon's leg, I'd never tasted anything quite so satisfying. I was so mad that I scarcely noticed Gordon's putter batter viciously at my ribs. Until Jeff pushed his .38 in Tom's face and tore the putter from his hand, I heroically refused to let go.

Poor, poor Tom. The entire party followed Jeff up those stairs. Half of them were thoroughly swacked, but even drunk, they couldn't deny that Tom Gordon was up to his neck in nastiness. I, of course, was hailed as heroine of the day, and I even made the morning news. Unfortunately, the picture they used was not very flattering.

But back to the scene of my heroism—Tom was handcuffed and marched out of his house by the cops he thought would never believe ill of him. In the great room, among the refuse of the last party Gordon would ever throw, Amy indulged in a bout of tears in Jeff's arms after enduring an endless round of questions from an endless parade of police and detectives. Her crying jag came from more than being scared out of her pantyhose. Somewhere in those tears I heard grieving for a wasted marriage, for David, who shouldn't have died, and even for me, the best friend who had betrayed her.

Yeah, yeah. By this time I had gotten Stan's point: I should have kept a tighter rein on my libido back in those wonderful days when I looked like an hourglass rather than a sausage, and maybe I should have thought of someone other than myself once in a while. But we don't need to dwell on that. I was in a good mood, for a change. The villain who had killed me was headed for the slammer, unless he could afford a lawyer good enough to turn the truth inside out. Amy was being cared for by a man who, I had finally come to admit, was the best possible husband for her, even if he wasn't my idea of a hot date. And I had come out of the whole mess smelling like a rose. Actually, I smelled like dog, but no one there seemed to mind. I'd gotten enough petting and tummy scratches to satisfy even a corgi, and one of the cops had even snuck me two leftover canapés that had been sitting on the bar. Heaven!

I waited around with admirable patience while Amy used Jeff's shirtfront as a crying towel, but finally I pushed my nose in to remind them who was the real hero—or should I say heroine—of the day. Amy half laughed and half sobbed while she scratched my ears. And Jeff finally admitted that I deserved a lot more respect than he'd given me.

"I still can't believe how smart that little gal is. She as

*good as told me in plain English what was going on. I really
think she had the whole thing figured out.''*

''You don't give yourself enough credit,'' Amy told him.

*Love is blind I guess. Even a dog addict like Amy couldn't
admit she'd been saved by a dog. Jeff knew, though, because he
gave me a wink. After all is said and done, he's really not that
bad of a guy.*

*Amy got to her feet, though from my angle I could see that
her knees still shook. ''Not that I needed to be saved, you
understand. I would have figured out something.''*

*Her attempt to give Jeff a saucy, teasing smile made me
glad she was getting her liveliness back, but I wasn't going to
put up with any of this ''I don't need a man in my life''
bullshit. Not after I'd served her Jeff Berenger on a silver platter.*

*''Not that it wasn't very convenient that you came along
when you did.''*

*''Why, thank you, ma'am. Maybe I should apply for a
position as permanent bodyguard.''*

*Amy laughed, and I couldn't tell from that shaky little
laugh whether she didn't know how to answer the veiled proposition—or was it a proposal?—or was still quivery from a very
tough evening. Just to make sure she wasn't about to back out
of a happy ending, I used the old trip-over-the-corgi trick. As
she took a step toward the couch where Jeff still sat, I strategi-
cally tangled myself in her feet. Down she went, straight into
Jeff's lap. After a few exclamations and some laughter, they got
themselves sorted out, but Jeff didn't let her up.*

''I think Piggy wants you to say yes,'' he told her.

''Yes?''

*''Marry me, Amy. I can't promise you a perfect life, but
you'll never have any doubt you're loved.''*

*She pulled his head down and kissed him. And what a
kiss it was. If Amy had kissed David like that, he never would
have cast an eye in my direction, I never would have met him*

for drinks, dinner, and diddling on that Friday night, and we wouldn't have followed Tom Gordon into that dark alley.

So you see, what I said at the beginning of this tale is true. What happened that night in the alley behind the Wynkoop Brewing Company was not my fault.

It was Amy's.

EPILOGUE

FOR THE NEXT month I rested upon my well-deserved laurels, amusing myself with thoughts of the rewards I might receive for my splendid work. You have to admit I rated something really nice. After all, I not only found Amy a man eminently suited to her dull nature, but I saved her life and helped put a murderer behind bars. Not a bad list of accomplishments for someone working around the disadvantages Stan piled on me— namely, that I was a dog.

For once I was anxious for Stanley to make an appearance. He owed me big time, and I was anxious to watch him eat crow. He took his time working up the nerve to acknowledge my triumph, though. While he procrastinated, I was forced to live through another hike up a damned mountain and the start of obedience school (can you imagine me in obedience school?). I must admit, however, that things could have been worse. Being a dog isn't half bad when you're a heroine. Everywhere I looked—at home, on walks, even at that stupid obedience class—my fans offered cookies, toys, tummy rubs, ear scratches, pillows for me to lie upon, and rawhides for me to chew. Even Dr. Dullard showed me more respect. As well he should, after what I did for him!

Dr. Dufus did manage to get Amy to the altar without any further intervention on my part. I'm glad to report that the wedding was much less silly than Selma's. The best man was not a dog, thank goodness. He was Jeff's brother from Grand Junction. Of course Selma was Amy's matron of honor. Dogs made up a large portion of the audience, but that's to be expected, considering the two who were getting married. And dogs accompanied the bride and groom on the honeymoon, if a photo-taking trip in that rattletrap motor home of Amy's could be called a honeymoon. It certainly wasn't my idea of a romantic getaway.

It was during the honeymoon that Stan finally made an appearance. In the wee hours, I was curled upon my soft little dog bed in the "kitchen" of the motor home, and the other dogs clumped together in a snoring pile on the couch. Stan materialized sitting atop the stove—the proverbial hot seat, I noted, but I tactfully refrained from commenting.

"Well, well, Miss Piggy. It seems several rounds of congratulations are in order."

"You bet they are, Stan. What took you so long?"

"Yours is not the only case in my workload, young lady. There are other concerns in the universe besides your problems."

"No problems here, my good man. I solved them all."

Stan gave me a smile that can only be described as tolerant. "You're a great success as a dog," he admitted.

"I am, aren't I? With very little help from you, I might point out."

"Did you learn anything more as a dog than you did as a woman?"

I rolled my eyes. The question deserved it.

"Well, Lydia?"

"Yes, Stan, I did. I learned to never trust a TV reporter."

"Anything else."

"If you have short legs, don't squat in tall grass to pee."

Stan tilted his head in patient expectation, and I gave in. "Okay. I learned that caring about others can feel good. That *there's more to a man—and a woman—than clothes and a hairstyle."*

"That's a good start."

"I could have learned all that without being a dog."

"Perhaps, but in my job I have to find entertainment wherever I can. I thought this persona was quite appropriate to your basic nature."

"Do tell." I growled. "Just couldn't resist handing out a last insult, could you, Stan? I'm waiting for my reward. And don't try to find any loopholes, you self-righteous bean counter. I did everything you told me to do, and then some!"

"Yes, Lydia, you did. You did very well."

"So? Do I get wings and a halo?"

"Lydia, you should know by now that angels don't have wings, and halos are merely an artist's rendition of inner beauty."

Stan always insisted on being picky about such things. It was enough to grate on a saint's nerves.

"Furthermore," he went on, "angels do not lie about indulging in sloth. Every angel has fulfilling work to do, caring for people, promoting the universal good . . ."

Stan likes to prattle about such things. Let him get going, and you invite a terminal case of the yawns. I cut him short.

"Okay, okay! I get the point, Stan. No wings, no halo. But I do get a promotion, right?"

"Well, you've certainly risen in the estimation of several very important beings."

This sounded better. "And . . . ?"

"And, because of your excellent work, we're giving you a choice."

This sounded very good!

"You may progress to the next level of being, where you would have higher status, more power, and, of course, greater responsibilities."

"Responsibilities?" I wasn't sure I liked the sound of that. "You make it sound like a lot of work, Stan."

"As I said, Lydia—"

"Yeah, yeah. What are the bennies?"

"The what?"

"The benefits!"

"Oh. Well, you would be a formless being with considerable power, no discomforts, no hunger, no anger, and endless affection for those in your care."

"Affection for those in my care, not from?"

"They wouldn't know you exist, Lydia."

That hardly sounded like fun!

"The upside is, you won't be a dog. No fleas. No collar. No leash. No yearly shots. No obedience school."

No cookies. No tummy rubs. No endless affection from those who cared for me. Suddenly, hikes in the Colorado mountains didn't seem so bad, and obedience school looked better and better.

"Uh . . . that sounds great, Stan. It really does. But I do feel a responsibility to Amy and Jeff." I tried to make myself sound like the caring and selfless being I was now supposed to be. *"I think I owe it to them to stick around for a while and make sure they don't get into trouble. Don't you?"*

"Well, I don't know. . . ."

The satisfied slant of his smile told me Stan had an agenda here, but I didn't care. Now that the moment of parting had come, the reality of leaving my dog bed behind, of never again seeing Molly, Drover, or those obnoxious suck-up border collies, made my heart grow sad. Not to mention Amy and Jeff. Inept and dull as they were, they really did need me to brighten up their lives.

"Come on, Stanley. It's not as if dogs live that long, you know. In the eternal scheme of things, I'll be laboring that new job in the blink of an eye."

"That's true," he agreed with a nod. *"And I suppose you could still be of use down here. All right, Lydia. I'm glad to see you taking your responsibilities to heart."*

I gave him a big corgi smile. The prospect of a few years as a dog was taking on the luster of a vacation.

"Just remember, I'll still be watching." I could have sworn he winked, and his impish smile was very unlike the stern Stanley I knew. "Be a good dog, my girl."

As he faded into the night, I pondered what I had done. There are many advantages to doghood—free meals, a constant supply of kind words and treats, no bills, no income taxes, no worries about keeping my wardrobe in fashion. Oh, sure, there are disadvantages, too. I've howled about them often enough. But now that all the excitement was over and my mission complete, I planned a good long time of doing nothing but lying about and letting Amy and Jeff show their gratitude. I might put up with obedience class and a hike or two. Maybe. And I'll definitely let Amy drag me to the Scottish festival again. A few more peeks at those breezy kilts and gorgeous hairy legs wouldn't bore me at all. No indeed.

Well, what did you expect? I'm an angel, not a saint. Take heed, you people out there. Next time a pooch comes into your life, treat it well. I might not be the only angel taking R and R in a dog suit.

ABOUT THE AUTHOR

EMILY'S FORMAL EDUCATION is in geology, and she spent 12 years working in that field. After her first historical romance was published by Warner in 1987, her primary profession became writing. She has published nine historical romances under the name Emily Carmichael and six writing as Emily Bradshaw. A 1996 Rita finalist, her awards include three Reviewer's Choice awards from *Romantic Times* and several nominations, as well as three Golden certificates and three Reviewer's Choice awards from *Affaire de Coeur*.

Emily lives in Illinois with five sheep, five dogs, and a husband. Her hobbies include showing dogs and flying small planes, useless activities that bring her great personal joy.

Read on for a preview of Emily
Carmichael's next romance,
the hilarious and romantic story
of a young woman who finds herself
the owner of a haunted
bawdy house out west. . . .

**Look for it in the
summer of 1999**

PROLOGUE

BEING DEAD AIN'T all it's cracked up to be. Take my word for it. The afterlife is about as dull as one of Sadie Johnson's tea parties. Not that I was ever invited to one of Sadie's stupid parties. Sadie would have turned up her toes in a dead swoon if I'd come within fifty feet of her house, especially when she had her lady friends visiting. Still, it's reasonable to figure those parties were about as dull as kicking dirt—all those stiff-necked, dried-up hens cackling about the weather, their lumbago, and whose cross-stitch wasn't quite up to par. You can't get much duller than that.

Or maybe you can. Like I said, the afterlife is pretty damned dull. At least mine has been so far. You've heard them preachers shouting that you've got to be good? That the folks who pray in church every Sunday are getting a harp when they cash in, and the folks who have a bit too much fun are getting a pitchfork? Horseshit! All of it. I'm here to tell you it's a lie. If anyone should have been pitching brimstone when she checked out, it would have been me, because I'm about as wicked as you can get. Or at least I was a hundred years ago, before Jackass Jake shot me dead. Being wicked ain't as easy once you're planted six feet under.

Let me introduce myself, folks. Robin Rowe's the name. Red Robin, the fellows call me, and the name brings a smile to their faces. It surely does. With my red hair, sultry smile, and the curviest shape God ever gave a woman, I'm the hottest thing in Jerome, Arizona. Hell, I'm the hottest thing in the whole wild west. I can knock a man off his feet with a twitch of my hips and send him to heaven with a smile. I can make a man forget his troubles with a touch of my lips and a soft whisper in his ear. As I said, I'm wicked. And I'm very, very good at being wicked. My girls are good, too. They're not in the same class as me, of course. But damned close. I don't hire no cheap strumpets to work in my house. Only the classiest ladies, ladies who know how to please a man and send him away smiling. Fellas always got their money's worth at Robin's Nest.

But that was a hundred years ago. Things are different now. Jerome's mines aren't cranking out copper, silver, and gold no more. The shafts and tunnels are boarded up tight. The miners who flocked to Robin's Nest are long gone, replaced by busloads of gray-headed folks from New Jersey and curious sorts who're looking for a hint of the Old West. And the kind of places that get flocked to are the T-shirt shops and ice cream joints, the store that sell jewelry, artwork, and those pitiful dresses that pass for fashion these days. I could give these modern gals a hint or two about looking good, I tell you. And that advice would include not showing off every lump and bump under tight stretch pants or sauntering along the street in denim trousers that look as if they've been dragged behind a horse. But then, nobody cares what I think anymore.

That's what I get for being a ghost. It took a good while for me to get used to that. I wasn't happy about getting shot, as I'd been counting on a lot longer life than a measly thirty-eight years. It don't seem fair somehow. I worked hard all my life—and if you don't think we sporting ladies work, why don't you try it for a while? Lying down on the job don't always mean you're slacking off. I started out as a lumberman's daughter with only two dresses to my name: my workaday dress and my Sunday-go-to-meeting dress. But when Jake Schmidt shot me, I had a mansion in Jerome, a closet full of fancy gowns, two dresser drawers full of jewelry, and a pile of money that made the bankers my very good friends.

Oh yeah—I also had a seventeen-year-old daughter in school in South Carolina. She was one of the reasons I really wasn't ready to make an exit. How could I go when Laura still needed me? Seventeen is such a fragile age, and she was so sheltered. Too sheltered. My fault, I reckon, but what was I supposed to do? Let her lead the same hardscrabble life I'd put up with? She didn't even know how her mother made a living. I told her I owned a hotel. Hey! I told you I was wicked. One lie more or less was not going to tip the scales for me in the hereafter.

Understandably, little Laura was a tad put out when she learned the truth. Embarrassed, too. I can't blame her. Still, she carried resentment too far when she erased my name from the family Bible and vowed not to speak it ever agian. Disrespectful, that's what that was. Fancy woman or not, I was still the mother who birthed her. And her marrying that Homer Pilford was just plain stupid. He just wanted her money—my money it was really. I would have told her that if I'd been alive at the time. But I was new at being a ghost, and I hadn't gotten the knack of getting people to listen to me. Now it ain't a problem. If I say hi, you'll hear me—if I want you to. I guarantee it. But that was a hundred years ago, and even ghosts need to learn their trade.

Well, Laura was unhappy with that gold digger Homer, as I could have told her she would be. I watched it all, just as I watched Laura's two daughters screw up their love lives and their daughters get dumped on in turn. And so on, till I was sick and tired of the sorry lot of them. Maybe this was hell for me, seeing all this. Maybe my wicked ways had cursed the women of my line to deadly stupidity in matters of the heart. Whatever! But sure as the twentieth century was about to bite the dust, my family was too. There was only one little gal left who carried my blood, and she was so busy muddling up her life that she'd be eighty before she figured out the basic birds and bees. Not that she was so pure and virginal. Not hardly.

Her natural urges weren't the problem. Her heart was the problem. She was headed for spinsterhood, sure as hell. And there went the glorious legacy of Robin Rowe. Not only did the family pedigree lack my name in its proper place, thanks to Laura, but the whole family was about to peter out like dust blown away by the wind.

Then something happened, something that let me know that somewhere in Heaven, someone had taken up my case. Someone up there understood, at least a little, and gave me a shot at fixing things. I don't know who was looking out for me: a saint, or an angel, or some little cherub just playing a trick. But whoever it was did a helluva good deed by dumping my great-great granddaughter Maggie Potter, right smack on my doorstep. It was spring of the year 1999, a day of blue skies and blazing sunshine, and she stood like a lost child in the middle of the lane in front of Robin's Nest. I recognized her right off. Blood calls to blood, you know, even when you no longer have any. I'd kept track of all my relations through the generations, even when they left Jerome. A sorry lot they were, my descendants, but that's not my fault.

So anyway. There she stands. Pretty as a picture, she was—or at least she could have been, with her flyaway reddish hair (a little gift from me), her long legs (another gift), and curvy form. Too bad she didn't have a lick of sense between her ears. Not that I didn't have sympathy for her plight. I knew what was troubling that gal, what made her soul cower like a skinny stray kitten covered with dog spit. Not pretty, what had happened to her. But then, life ain't pretty usually. Most of us get over it.

What really wasn't pretty, to my way of thinking, was that this little gal was last on earth to carry anything from Robin Rowe, and she seemed determined to keep it that way. Depressing. Still, I didn't give in to gloom. She was here. I was here. How hard could it be to bump Maggie on to the right path? A push here, a shove there, a hint or two or three.

I was confident. I had all the cards in my hand, you see, and the deck was stacked.

♥   ♥   ♥

Maggie Potter had never before heard a house call to her, but she heard this one. It stood in the warm April sunshine, two stories of gleaming stucco and red Spanish tile, and called out her name. The house not only called out her name, it winked at her. Her mouth open in amazement, Maggie stood in the middle of High Street and stared.

"Oh my! Isn't this just quaint?" Maggie's step-mother Virginia wasn't looking at the house. She was looking at the little cafe across the street, aptly named the Haunted Hamburger. "Do you suppose it's really haunted?"

"I'll bet it is!" Catherine, like her mother Virginia, was blond, blue-eyed, and plumpish. Her eyes twinkled and her smile was as infectious as the cheerful sunshine. "I'll bet they have ghosts frying the hamburgers. Cheap labor, you know."

"You're making fun. It's a sin to make fun of your mother."

Catherine laughed.

"It's not so ridiculous. Jerome is a ghost town, you know. Something should be haunted."

"Ghost towns don't have ghosts," Catherine told her. "It means the town is a ghost. You know, deserted. Once alive but now a mere husk. Ghost. Get the connection?"

"I get the connection. And don't use that school-teacherly voice on me. It's a cute name, all the same. I like the idea of ghosts flipping the hamburgers."

Only half tuned to their conversation, Maggie muttered. "There's no such thing as ghosts, Virginia."

"Don't be a spoilsport, Maggie. We're having fun." Virginia raised her sunglasses and peered at her step-daughter. "What're you looking at so intently, dear? You look a bit ghostly yourself."

"That house. That wonderful house."

"What house?" Catherine asked dubiously. "That house?"

"Yes."

"Well, I suppose it was wonderful at one time. Maybe."

"It looks as if no one's lived there in a while," Virginia noted.

The boarded-up windows and weedy yard hadn't escaped Maggie's eyes. They simply hadn't mattered. The house had something. It called with a siren's song, promising comfort, refuge, security. It promised home.

"Let's take a closer look." Maggie climbed the cracked and crumbling concrete stairs that led from the street. The wrought-iron gate creaked when she opened it, and weeds batted at her ankles as she traversed the brick walkway to the front porch.

"Be careful, dear!" Virginia called. "It looks as if you could fall through to one of the mine tunnels underneath the town."

A big front window had somehow escaped the damage of time. It afforded a view into a large, airy room with a huge fireplace and beautifully carved crown molding.

"Wonderful," Maggie sighed. She turned, and her face lit up at the sight that met her eyes. This house, like every other building in the old mining town of Jerome, Arizona, clung precariously to the side of Cleopatra Hill. The arrangement made for some exciting times, for buildings had been known to slide down the mountain, but it also ensured that every place in town had sweeping views of the valley below, and beyond that, the Mogollon Plateau country and the towering red buttes of the Sedona area.

An idea nibbled at her mind. A ridiculous idea. Ludicrous, farfetched, impractical.

But it was an appealing idea. Compelling even.

Why hadn't she thought of it before? It was just what she needed.

Virginia didn't think much of the idea when Maggie brought it up over a haunted hamburger, but Catherine's eyes lit up.

"What fun! And when school let's out next month, I'll have the whole summer to help you."

"That's what I thought. Look at the number of tourists up here. And how many rooms are available to accommodate them? Twenty? Twenty-five?"

"You're both nuts!" Virginia chimed in. "There's a bunch of motels just down the road in Cottonwood. Who'd want to stay in an expensive bed-and-breakfast that's about to roll down the mountain when they could get a nice, safe motel room for thirty bucks?"

"The view!" Maggie enthused. "The ambience! The history!"

"That old jail building we saw has slid a half mile from where it was built!"

"It hasn't slid a half mile," Catherine corrected succinctly. "Only a couple of hundred feet."

"Always the schoolmistress. The point is, it's not where they put it."

"This house is fine," Maggie insisted.

"You don't know the house is fine."

"The house is fine. I know."

"That's silly. How could you know? Are you an engineer? Are you a contractor?"

Maggie shrugged, and Virginia gave her a suspicious look. "That's an odd smile on your face. Are you all right?"

"You're imagining things. And the house is fine."

"It's probably not for sale."

"It is."

"There was no 'for sale' sign."

"It's for sale."

"Something else you just know?"

"I . . . well, yes."

"I kept telling you, ever since you came home, that you should see that shrink. Someone who's been through what you've been through . . . well, you should see the shrink. It's no disgrace to need a little help. A shrink would help you more than a falling down house that's sliding down a mountain."

"Virginia . . ."

"Well, I think Maggie's idea is just wonderful!" Catherine interjected diplomatically. "Just think! Maggie and I running an inn in picturesque Jerome. Fresh air. Interesting people. It's ideal. Sedona's just down the road—big draw, there. And the Grand Canyon's an easy drive away. Tourists will be flocking to our front door. It's almost destiny, isn't it? We come up for a day's outing, and Maggie finds her life's mission. I think it's terrific!"

"Terrific, schmerific. It's insanity. That's what it is. Insanity."

Maggie tuned them both out. She was busy looking out the cafe window at The House. That was how she thought about it, in capital letters. She knew in her mind that the windows were boarded, the stucco dirty, the yard overgrown, the tile roof in need of repair. But in her heart was a different picture: the windows gleamed, the stucco blazed a new, clean white in the sunshine. And was that a carriage in front of the old carriage house?

Beautiful. Glorious. Maggie smiled and somehow didn't think it odd that the house seemed to smile back.